BEL

0583-MILL

BELIZE

Carlos Ledson Miller

0583-MILL

CONTENTS

AUTHOR'S NOTE

English loggers and African slaves settled the desolate southeast coast of the Yucatan Peninsula in the 17th Century. This region came to be known as British Honduras. In 1981, after four centuries of colonialism, England decided to rid itself of this far-flung piece of its empire. Today the independent new nation, now known as Belize, fights for survival.

This book is a work of fiction. Although it is set during actual periods in Belizean history, the characters are fictional, except for cameo appearances by a few historical figures. The dialogues and the specific incidents involving all characters—fictional and historical—are products of the author's imagination or are used fictitiously.

There's a Belizean proverb: "If you drink our water, you will always return." This novel is dedicated to the people of Belize who, when the author was a youth, extended their hospitality, and shared their water.

MEXICO

COROZAL

AMBERGRIS CAYE

SAN PEDRO

NORTHERN HIGHWAY

GALLON JUG

BELIZE CITY
(Belize)

GUATEMALA

BELMOPAN

WESTERN HIGHWAY

SAN IGNACIO
(El Cayo)

HUMMINGBIRD HIGHWAY

DANGRIGA
(Stann Creek)

CARIBBEAN SEA

BELIZE
(formerly British Honduras)

RIO SARSTOON

BELIZE

If the world had any ends, British Honduras would certainly be one of them. It is not on the way from anywhere to anywhere else. It has no strategic value. It is all but uninhabited.

—*Aldous Huxley*

Bullshit, Aldous.

—*Carlos Ledson Miller*

PART I: THE COLONY

Man di walk; death di watch.

—Belizean Proverb

1. STORM WARNINGS

October 29, 1961

Ramón and Kay Kelley waited in the Pickwick Club, along with most of the other white residents of Belize City. Ramón checked his watch; it was almost eleven. Usually on a weeknight, most club members would already have left for home. Tonight, however, word had spread that a hurricane was forming in the Caribbean, and the venerable clubhouse was still full and buzzed with uncertainty.

Ramón slumped in his chair, making no effort to mask his fatigue. He had spent the past week at his jungle logging camp. Dried sweat lined his khaki shirt and trousers, and mud from the interior clung to his boots. As he looked at his alert young wife, it occurred to him that, at forty, life in the Tropics might finally be catching up with him.

Ramón shifted his gaze across the room. At the bar, a dozen or so community leaders huddled around a Mestizo bartender. The local radio station was off the air, and the swarthy youth was trying to tune to a broadcast coming from somewhere in Mexico's Quintana Roo Province.

"Ramón," Kay said, "you look awful. Should we go?"

He shook his head. "I need to find out what's going on."

Their exchange was interrupted by Sir Peter Stallard, the graying Briton who served as the colonial governor of British Honduras. He stood near the bar, arms raised. "Ladies and gentlemen . . . could we have quiet, please?"

The conversations died down, and the excited voice of a Mexican announcer rose over a background of electrical static. Most of the people in the room couldn't speak Spanish and looked around for someone to translate for them. A khaki-uniformed British colonel, standing near a snooker table, shouted, "What's he saying, Adolfo?"

"He says bad storm coming this way, *sah!*" the bartender said.

"A hurricane?" demanded a stocky German, pushing his way toward the bar.

"He don't say, sah. But it sound like one to me!"

A murmur of concern passed through the room. "Please, ladies and gentlemen . . ." called the governor, again raising his arms for quiet.

The room hushed. "Where is it, Adolfo?" the governor said. "Did he say where it's located?"

"Out with it, man!" the British colonel said impatiently. "Give us the bloody facts!"

"He says storm has been moving north toward Cuba, sah," the bartender said, "but now it changing direction." He paused, again listening to the radio transmission. "Say storm 250 miles from Chetumal . . . winds blowing seventy-five miles per hour . . . storm moving fifteen miles per hour . . . coming southwest, sah!"

The room exploded, as the club members all began talking at once.

Ramón, who spoke Spanish and had not needed the translation, pulled his wife's chair close to his and said into her ear, "Kay, if a hurricane hits here, I could lose everything I've got. I need to get hold of my office manager right away. You'll have to wait here for me while I track him down."

"Wait here?" Kay said anxiously. "You're not leaving me with a hurricane coming!"

"I won't be gone long," Ramón said, heaving himself out of his chair. "I'd take you with me, but God knows where I'll have to look for Michael at this time of night."

Kay remained seated, looking helpless and out of place.

Ramón extended his hand. "Come on, Kay. You can wait over there with Karl Schrader." She reluctantly got to her feet, and he guided her over to the bar. "Karl," he said to the German bush pilot, "I need to go find Michael Flowers. Will you look after Kay until I get back?"

"I can't stay too late tonight," Schrader said, warily eyeing the frail American woman. "I have to be up at first light to move my airplanes inland."

"I'll be back within an hour," Ramón said. Schrader nodded, and Ramón quickly threaded his way through the crowded room and down the exterior stairway that led to the street below.

At the foot of the stairs, he opened the white wooden gate and stepped onto Front Street. He paused, testing the humid Caribbean night air. It felt like rain was on the way. He grunted as he swung his tall heavy frame into his battered Land Rover.

Although the shops were closed, the narrow street was congested with people, out for nightly promenades. Ramón pulled away from the Pickwick Club and cautiously weaved through the stream of dark faces, occasionally tapping his horn. The indolent response of the bicyclists and pedestrians brought to mind the frustration of the past week. Of the ten workers he had trucked out to the logging camp, three had quit the first day, and five more had failed to last the week. He shook his head. Damn these churches and their schools! Everybody wants to be a clerk.

Ramón turned onto Queen Street. He was well-known in this ramshackle city of 30,000, and several people called to him as he drove by. He gave quick waves in the general directions of the voices, but kept his eyes straight ahead and both hands on the steering wheel, as he navigated the twisting littered streets.

A few minutes later, he had left the city behind and was heading north on Barracks Road, which ran along the edge of the sea. On the horizon, he saw the occasional flicker of far-off lightning. Fatigue made it difficult to think, but he forced himself to begin making a mental list of things he needed to do before the storm. He hit a pothole in the rough road and cursed as his head struck the metal roof.

He rounded a bend in front of the city's dilapidated soccer stadium and saw the lights of the Belize Club up ahead. The Belize

Club was the gathering place for the nonwhite community leaders. Although it was late, two players still occupied a lighted tennis court.

He turned into the muddy driveway and pulled up in front of the two-story wooden building. Through the open windows above, he heard the sounds of voices and calypso music, punctuated by occasional bursts of laughter. News of the approaching storm apparently had not yet reached the Belize Club.

Ramón climbed out of the Land Rover and took the exterior stairs two at a time.

"*Mistah* Kelley, sah!" cried the bartender as he entered the club room. "We don't see you for such a long time!"

Most of the people in the room turned in his direction. Ramón forced a smile and nodded to several men and women he recognized. He knew he was welcome here. Although he was a white American by nationality, he was a Central American by birth, and a Belizean by choice.

He didn't see his office manager, but at the bar he spotted his old friend, Elijah Ruiz, president of the Bank of the Caribbean and a leader in the People's United Party. The black Carib stood out among the various shades of brown.

Elijah motioned for Ramón to join him and met him with a friendly handshake. "You look very serious, my friend," Elijah said with a resonant chuckle. "Let me buy you something to drink."

Ramón shook his head. "Have you heard about the storm?"

"No," Elijah said, his smile fading, "but the air does feel like we might be in for a squall."

"It could be a hell of a lot worse than that. Over at the Pickwick, we picked up a Mexican radio station. It said a storm out in the Caribbean is gaining intensity and is heading this way. It's supposed to be about 250 miles offshore, but as bad as Mexican communications are, it might be closer. They're guessing landfall sometime tomorrow on the Yucatan Peninsula, but it could hit here."

"Damn! Did they say how powerful?"

"Supposedly, the winds are only about seventy-five miles an

hour. But it wouldn't take much more than that to level this place."

"You don't have to remind me," Elijah said softly. "I was a young *bwy* here when the big one came in 1931." Then he added with a sigh, "Yet here we are, thirty years later, still sitting on the God-damned coast, waiting for a next one."

"I need to get hold of Michael Flowers so we can start preparing for the storm. Have you seen him?"

"He left about an hour ago," Elijah said, "probably headed for the Blue Angel." Then he frowned thoughtfully. "Is the governor at the Pickwick?"

"He was there when I left, but he probably won't be for long." Ramón sensed that Elijah was assessing both his business and political responsibilities. The storm might provide opportunities for an ambitious man.

Elijah extended his hand. "All right, my friend. I'll be at the bank first thing in the morning. Hail me when you can."

As Ramón started down the outside stairway, he heard the music abruptly stop and Elijah's resonate voice boom out, "May I have your attention, please . . ."

Ramón reentered the city and drove to a row of shabby bars on Water Lane Street. Although the sea was only two blocks away, the fresh Caribbean breeze couldn't dilute the stench from a nearby open canal, gray and thick with raw sewage.

The Blue Angel Club was an unpainted shack, perched precariously on the edge of Haulover Creek. Ramón's Land Rover was the only vehicle on the street. He parked directly in front of the club. Through an open window, he heard an American rhythm-and-blues song playing on the jukebox.

He climbed out of his vehicle, stepped across an overflowing gutter, and entered the rundown bar. Several dark faces turned his way, some showing open hostility. Ramón peered through the smoky haze and finally spotted his office manager, playing cards with three other Creoles in a far corner.

"Mistah Kelley, sah," Michael said with a look of surprise.

Ramón gave a quick nod to the others at the table, then said to Michael, "There's a hurricane out in the Gulf. We need to get ready in case it hits here."

A young Creole, seated across the table, looked up from his cards and said with a sneer, "*Chuh!*"

Ramón recognized him; he was one of the three men who had left the logging camp the first day. Ramón gestured for Michael to follow him out of the bar.

Outside, Ramón said, "I didn't want to get into an argument, or start a panic in there, but this could be damned serious. I want you to get hold of Robby and have him move the tugboat upriver to Burrel Boom. Tell him to take his family with him. Then track down Hilbert and Emilio, and you three start loading our operating equipment and supplies onto the lorries."

Michael nodded uncertainly.

"I want to get started, right away," Ramón said. "Understand?"

"Yes, sah," Michael said with a worried frown.

"Have your wife pack up the baby and be ready to leave," Ramón continued. "If the storm comes close to here, we'll take our families inland to El Cayo. Now, I've got to get back to the Pickwick and get Kay. Any questions?"

"No, sah. I understand."

"Okay, I'll meet you at the office in a couple of hours." Ramón climbed into his Land Rover.

"Sah," Michael said, coming around to the driver's side. "Maybe the hurricane just pass us by?"

"Maybe, Michael," Ramón said, as he started the engine. "But they've hit here before, and sooner or later, one's going to hit here again."

It was after midnight when Ramón arrived back at the now nearly deserted Pickwick Club. Only a few heavy drinkers remained, seated around a snooker table and watching a final game in progress.

Kay was the only woman in the room. She sat at a table with Karl Schrader and stared vacantly past the players. Her head jerked up as Ramón approached. "Where have you been?" she said, tears forming.

"I had trouble tracking down Michael," Ramón said, helping her to her feet. He turned to Schrader. "Sorry it took so long, Karl, but thanks for staying. Can we drop you?"

Schrader shook his head and shuffled off to pay his bar tab.

A few minutes later, as they drove up Front Street, Kay blurted out, "Ramón, please, let's get out of here!"

"What?" he said, preoccupied with hurricane plans. "Oh, yeah. Tomorrow morning, if it looks like the storm's going to hit here, we'll go inland to El Cayo."

"Not just because of the storm. I mean leave for good. I hate this God-forsaken place!"

He didn't respond, wanting to avoid a pointless rehash of the hardships of life in the colony.

"Ramón," she pressed, "why do you insist on staying down here, where everything is such a struggle? Won't you at least consider going up to the States and trying to find work?"

Ramón didn't reply; he was unaccustomed to sharing his uncertainties with others, even his wife. Her recurring plea that he leave British Honduras frustrated him. It wasn't that he was insensitive to the hardships; it was simply that he had no choice but to stay and to overcome them.

Kay acted as if he were an expatriate American, capable of returning home. But he wasn't; he had never lived in the United States. Born of an American father and a Panamanian mother, he had spent his entire life in the Tropics. It was too damned late for him to become an American!

They approached Haulover Creek, which cut through the center of the city. The rusty, one-lane swing bridge was in place. They bounced across it and down onto the other side. On the left stood the dilapidated open market, deserted at this time of night. Ramón heard Kay emit a soft gasp and turned in time to see her shudder. She recently had tried to shop at the market and, for reasons he didn't understand, had been upset for days.

Reaching for her hand in the dark, he tried to reassure her. "I've told you, Kay, it takes time for American women to get used to life down here." She pushed his hand away, and he remembered too late that she felt patronized whenever he used the term, "American women". They drove on in silence for several blocks.

Ramón pulled up to the white frame house he had rented for Kay on Southern Foreshore Drive. Like most in the city, it had been built on tall pilings to catch the cooling sea breeze and to protect against possible rising water.

As Ramón followed Kay up the exterior stairway, he gazed across the street. Night waves lapped at the low concrete wall that kept the sea out of the city.

Later that night, Ramón stretched out on top of his bed, naked and alone. He perspired slightly; the heavy mosquito netting, which hung from the ceiling and encircled the bed, blocked most of the breeze from the open window.

Kay switched off the bathroom light and entered the dark bedroom. Ramón expected her to climb into her own bed, and started when she lifted the netting and joined him in his. She stretched out beside him and rested her head on his chest.

"What are you going to do about the hurricane?" she said.

"We're getting ready in case we have to evacuate. Michael's at the office, getting started, but I need to get a couple of hours sleep before I go in and take charge."

Kay held him tightly. "Ramón, I'm so frightened here. Not just tonight, but all the time."

He stroked her back. Despite the tropical heat, she continued to wear a nightgown to bed. "You need to get out on your own more," he said. "You'll never get used to this country if you stay cooped up in the house, lost in a book and letting the maid take care of everything."

"Ramón, I'm not used to these kinds of people."

"What 'kinds of people'?"

"You know what I mean. Colored people. In Louisiana we

don't socialize with them. Here, that's all there is. I don't know what to say to them. And when they talk to each other in that Creole patois, I don't understand what they're saying. But I know they're talking about me and laughing behind my back."

"Kay, they're not talking about you," Ramón said, trying to reassure her. "Creole is just their own language."

"I can't help it," she said, digging her nails into his shoulder. "I . . . hate it here!"

Ramón softly kissed her forehead and resumed stroking her through the nightgown. She raised her head and hesitantly kissed his lips. He passionately returned her kiss.

"Please, care for me," she implored.

Ramón gently eased her onto her back. Kay put her forearm across her eyes, and he hesitated. After a moment, she lowered her arm and gazed up at him, with an all too familiar look of mute resignation. He sighed and started to draw away.

She reached up and locked her arms around his neck. "Please . . . don't leave."

A short while later, with Kay sleeping in his arms, Ramón reflected on their troubled marriage. Her current attempt to live in the colony wasn't going any better than her earlier one, and he foresaw the possibility that soon she would want to return home to the States again.

She stirred fretfully, and he gently patted her shoulder. She quieted. It was unusual to have her sleeping in his arms. Their love making was infrequent and, like tonight, usually awkward. Tonight was the first time she had not insisted that he use a contraceptive.

A gust from the open window stirred the mosquito netting, and his thoughts returned to the impending storm.

2. GOVERNMENT HOUSE

The sound of someone hammering on the front door startled Ramón out of a deep sleep.

Kay pushed away from him and said groggily, "What is it?"

Without answering, Ramón fought his way through the tangled mosquito netting, yanked on his trousers, and raced for the stairway. Downstairs, he fumbled open the lock. A gust of wind blew the door back at him.

An exhausted Michael confronted him. "We have loaded the lorries, sah," he said, gesturing over his shoulder to two ancient British Leyland trucks parked in the street. Their tattered canvas covers flapped in the stiff breeze. And behind the trucks, a red sun rose from the Caribbean.

"God damn it, Michael! I overslept! Why the hell didn't you call me?"

"Telephones broke down, sah. I think you come later, so we just keep loading."

"I'm sorry, Michael. I was exhausted last night and forgot to set my alarm clock. What's the latest on the storm?"

"I don't know, sah. Radio station broke down too."

"You say we're all loaded?"

"Yes, sah. The chain is in one lorry; the file cabinets and office things are in the other."

"What about the storeroom?"

Michael frowned uncertainly.

"The tools?" Ramón pressed. "The boat parts?"

Michael shook his head.

"Damn it, man! You mean you loaded logging chain, and left the tools and parts?"

Michael looked crestfallen. "I am sorry, sah, but we don't load the things from the storeroom."

Ramón shifted his gaze past Michael. Usually the morning sea was placid. Today, small whitecaps slapped against the seawall and sprayed onto the cobblestone street. Several wooden sloops, tied offshore, pitched at anchor. The crew of one prepared to get underway.

Ramón turned back to Michael. "I should have been there to help you," he said, forcing a smile.

"I let you down, sah," Michael said.

"Chuh! You were working, while I was sleeping."

"Sah!" Michael said, pointing past Ramón. "They raising hurricane flags at Government House!"

Ramón turned toward the stately wooden mansion, a half-block away. A British soldier hoisted two red flags with square black centers to the top of a thirty-foot pole. Until that moment, Ramón's plan had been simply to look after his wife and his business. But the flags triggered a sense of foreboding. The friends he had made over the past five years were in extreme jeopardy, and they weren't prepared to handle it.

He turned back to Michael. "Kay will need about an hour to get ready. How about your wife and baby? Are they ready for the trip to the interior?"

"No, sah. Bernice say she no go to the bush."

"Won't go?" Ramón exclaimed. "Doesn't she understand there's a hurricane coming?"

"She more afraid of the bush, sah."

"Why?"

"Sisimitos," Michael said, looking down.

"Sisimitos!" Ramón said in disbelief. Local folklore credited these legendary, hairy denizens of the jungle with tearing men to pieces and carrying off their women.

"When Bernice a young *gyal*," Michael said, "she hear the stories. Then her auntie, who raise her, go to the bush. Her auntie disappear. They never find her."

"For Christ's sake, Michael! Surely you don't believe that superstitious shit!"

"Bernice believes it," Michael replied noncommittally.

"Michael, that house of yours won't last five minutes in a hurricane."

"I know, sah. If it is possible . . . we would like to stay here in your house."

Ramón sighed. "Take the lorry with the chain back to the office and replace the chain with the stuff from the storeroom. Then go by and pick up Bernice and the baby. Bring them over here, and I'll try to talk some sense into her."

Michael left, and Ramón hurried back upstairs.

When he reentered the bedroom, Kay was still in her nightgown, staring out the front window at the churning sea. Preoccupied, Ramón hurriedly finished dressing without speaking. As he headed back down the stairs, he shouted over his shoulder, "Get dressed and get packed! I'm going over to Government House. I'll be back in a few minutes."

"Ramón!" Kay cried, but he was already hurrying toward the front door.

Southern Foreshore dead-ended at a low wooden fence that enclosed the backyard of Government House. An elderly Creole servant in a starched white uniform stood on the wide veranda, looking out to sea. He was the respected head of the governor's household staff. Ramón crawled over the fence and jogged across the manicured lawn.

"Mistah Kelley, sah! We got a blow coming!"

Ramón bounded up the stairs. "That's what I hear, Wilford. Is Sir Peter awake?"

"Yes, sah. He has been up since five o'clock." With a wry smile, Wilford added, "And George Price is here too, sah."

Ramón shook his head. George Price was the leader of the People's United Party, which advocated independence from Great Britain. He used any event out of the ordinary as a forum for nationalism to confront colonialism.

"Come this way, sah," Wilford said, opening the door.

Ramón entered the familiar polished hallway. On his right, the kitchen bustled with excitement, as the household staff prepared an unplanned, early breakfast. At the end of the hallway, he arrived at the governor's study. The door was open and four men were in conference. George Price, an ascetic Mestizo-Creole, stood with his back to a window and was in full oratorical stride. The British governor, unshaven and obviously ill at ease, stood behind his desk, politely trying to interrupt. The governor's chief administrator, a pale Englishman, sat in a straight-backed chair. The superintendent of police, a light-skinned Creole, stood near the doorway.

The governor saw Ramón. With visible relief he interrupted Price and walked around his desk with his hand extended. "Ramón, old fellow, please come in!"

Price gave Ramón a quick nod, then continued where he had left off. "If we had been granted independence, or at least fair representation in the Legislative Assembly in 1954, we would now have an inland capital and this city would return to the mangrove swamp it wants to be!"

"George," the governor said, "you can't seriously believe that self-determination will overcome the economic limitations that—"

"Gentlemen!" Ramón interrupted. "You've got the hurricane flags flying. What's the latest?"

For a moment, no one responded. Finally the superintendent said, "The storm in the Caribbean has gained strength and is now a hurricane. Unless it changes direction, it will probably hit here sometime tonight."

The two leaders were about to resume their debate, when Ramón interrupted again. "What preparations have you made?"

Everyone looked toward the governor. "Well . . . you see . . . actually . . ."

"'Actually'," Price interjected, "there is no plan! The Crown has had thirty years since the last hurricane, and still there is no plan!"

"There's little we can do," the governor said lamely.

The young British administrator spoke up for the first time. "Most of the families are planning to evacuate, sir."

"The *bakras* can evacuate!" Price responded vehemently, using the derisive Creole term for foreign whites. "The Belizean people have no way to leave and no place to go!"

"I'm afraid he's right, sir," the young man acknowledged. "I was referring to the European and American families."

"What's the matter with the damned telephones and radio station?" Ramón said.

"They're working now, sir," the administrator said. "One of the workers at the power station accidentally tripped a circuit breaker last night."

"Sir Peter, George," Ramón said levelly, "everyone's got to pull together on this."

After an awkward pause, the governor responded, "Ah, yes." Then he turned to his administrator. "Roger, collect all the information we have and get it over to the radio station—severity, probable time of arrival . . . and the like."

The young man began jotting notes.

"Tell the Belizean people they must move inland," Price conceded, "if it is at all possible for them."

"Tell them they must board up their houses," said the superintendent.

"And they'll need to store water," muttered the administrator, as he scribbled furiously.

"Sydney," Price said to the superintendent, "many of the people don't have radios. You can use the PUP sound truck. I'll have one of my men bring it around."

Ramón saw they temporarily had set partisanship aside. "Unless you need me right now," he said, "I've got to get back home."

"We'll call on you if we need you, Ramón," the governor said.

"Unless you too are evacuating," Price said, challenging Ramón with a tight smile.

Ramón hesitated, then said, "I'm sending my wife to El Cayo. I'll be staying."

Ramón reentered his house and found Kay standing in the center of the living room, arms folded. "Get your stuff together," he said. "You're going to El Cayo in that truck out front."

"*I'm* going?" she said angrily. "What about you?"

"I've got to stay here. I'll come for you after the storm."

"You're staying here! Why?"

"I've got responsibilities."

"What about your responsibility to me?"

"Kay, we don't have time for this." He grasped her shoulders. "You've got to get moving!"

She glared up at him. For the first time in their marriage, he saw hatred in her eyes. "You bastard!" she exploded. "You think these . . . *niggers* . . . are your family . . . and that your only responsibility is to them and to this . . . *hellhole!*"

Ramón firmly turned her, and pushed her toward the stairway.

"God damn you, Ramón!" she cried as she started up the stairs. At the top landing, she shouted down, "And don't bother coming to El Cayo, because I won't be there. I'm going home!"

3. HURRICANE HATTI

A little after midnight, Ramón and Michael stood at a front window, peering through the shutter slats. Wind-driven rain, sounding like gravel, pelted the wood-frame house. Lightning jagged between towering dark thunderheads, illuminating the harbor. Lower clouds raced across the horizon from left to right.

The trucks had left for El Cayo twelve hours earlier. Ramón was relieved that Kay was safe in the interior, but regretted how he had handled her departure. She was probably gone for good this time. She was as out of place down here, as he would be in the States.

A blast of wind struck the house, followed by a deluge of rain. Ramón glanced back at Bernice. Michael's sturdy Creole wife rocked contentedly on the couch, breast-feeding her infant son. She had stubbornly resisted Ramón's attempt to send her to the interior.

A blinding flash, followed by a thunderous boom, plunged the room into darkness. The baby responded with a terrified, hacking cry. Continuous lightning flashes illuminated the room like a strobe light.

"Look there, sah," Michael said, pointing toward the northern end of the harbor.

A procession of waves swept into the normally placid harbor at an unusually oblique angle. Several sailboats, staked offshore, pitched wildly in the building seas. Two disappeared under the incoming rollers, leaving only their masts exposed.

A powerful blast of wind slammed the front of the house. The concussion drove both men to their knees. Michael scrambled over to his wife and baby, and took them in his arms.

Ramón edged back to the window sill and looked through the

shutters. "The waves are over the seawall! There was a thirty-foot sailboat out there—" He halted in mid-sentence and reflexively threw up his arms. An instant later, a shadowy object crashed through the window, driving glass and wood at his face and knocking him to the floor.

Stunned, he sat up amid the debris. A deafening roar filled the room. Salt-laden rain drove through the empty window frame, burning his eyes. He frantically wiped his face and discovered he was bleeding from the forehead. He pressed his handkerchief against the laceration and turned back to the others.

The corpse of a king vulture lay at Michael's feet. Bernice and the baby screamed hysterically. Michael stared at the dead bird, transfixed.

Ramón scrambled back to the couch. "Get to the rear of the house!" he shouted.

Michael remained motionless. His lips moved. Ramón leaned forward, straining to hear.

"Carrion crow pick who is to die."

"Forget that superstitious shit!" Ramón shouted into his ear. "We've got to move to the rear of the house!"

Michael reluctantly got to his feet. He and Ramón put their arms around Bernice and the baby, and shepherded them toward the kitchen. However the next concussion sent them sprawling across the floor. The front of the house reared up from its pilings, then shuddered back into place, as the raging wind ripped away the roof and the bedrooms above. Rain and debris pelted them as they crawled across the floor.

They struggled through the kitchen door and found the walls intact, but the roof gone. The refrigerator lay face down. Utensils and broken dishes littered the floor. Another blast of wind slammed the crippled building. They took refuge in the far corner, huddling together as rain and debris poured down on them. The house shuddered from a succession of waves crashing against the pilings below. Something lodged between the pilings, slammed against the floor, and then broke loose—probably the Land Rover.

"Oh, please, Jesus, don't take my little one," Bernice prayed. "Please, don't take little Allan."

The storm buffeted them unceasingly. Even the infant's shrill screams couldn't pierce the storm's ceaseless roar. Ramón lost track of time.

Finally the wind and rain died down. Ramón stood up, wiping the blood and salt water from his face. "Stay here," he told the others. He edged over to the doorway. The living room was gone. Only the pilings and a few patches of flooring remained. Continual lightning flashes illuminated the turbulent sea. Oh, God, no! A massive hump of water raced across the harbor toward the coast.

Ramón rushed back to the others. "Stay down!"

A moment later, the storm surge hit the remains of the house. The front pilings crumpled, but those beneath the kitchen withstood its force. A series of waves, riding atop the surge pushed against the floor beneath them. White foam flew through the open doorway, stinging like blown sand.

Then abruptly there was an eerie calm. They sat up and gazed through the open ceiling at a clearing in the night sky. The baby held its ears and screamed at the change in atmospheric pressure.

"Storm has passed," Bernice said with relief. "Thank you, Jesus!"

Ramón shook his head.

Bernice frowned and turned to her husband.

"There be one next half," Michael said softly.

"No!" Bernice cried, clutching her baby to her breast. "We had enough!"

Michael took the baby from her. "Tend Mr. Kelley, gyal."

Bernice crawled over and knelt in front of Ramón. "The bleeding almost stop, sah." She tore a strip of cloth from her skirt and tied his blood-soaked handkerchief in place.

Ramón nodded his thanks, then got to his feet and looked out the rear window. "Oh, no!" he gasped. His next-door neighbors' ground-level shack was submerged. It was the home of a washwoman and her two teenage boys. Had they tried to ride out the storm there?

He scanned the other nearby houses. Most, like his own, had been built on pilings. All had sustained severe damage. Slow-moving figures emerged from the doorways, assessing their own losses and calling for their neighbors.

The sky darkened again. Ramón looked for a sturdier structure in which to ride out the second half of the storm. A sheet of heavy rain inundated the neighborhood before he saw a safer place.

The pounding wind and rain resumed. Bernice clutched her baby, and Michael and Ramón protectively huddled around them. The waves now hammered them from the opposite direction. Ramón looked in vain for something that would float. Suddenly the floor beneath them emitted a groan, then bent at a sharp angle, sliding them feetfirst into the churning chest-deep water. Ramón and Michael grabbed Bernice, who struggled to hold her baby above her head. Ramón frantically pointed to a small kitchen corner that was still intact. He positioned himself with his stomach against the bent flooring and gestured for Michael to use him for a ladder.

Michael scrambled over Ramón, placed his feet on his shoulders, and reached back. Bernice handed up the screaming infant, then climbed over the two men until she was able to stand on Michael's shoulders. She took the baby from Michael and pushed it into the corner. Then she managed to pull herself up on one knee and grasp a window sill. She extended back her other leg. Michael grabbed her ankle with both hands.

A wave crashed over Ramón. He struggled out from under Michael's feet and surfaced, gasping. Michael still clung to Bernice's ankle. Ramón grasped the back of Michael's shirt and pulled himself out of the torrent. "Hold on!" Ramón shouted in Michael's ear as he crawled over him. "Hold on!"

Bernice screamed; she was losing her grasp on the window sill. Ramón had a foot on Michael's shoulder. He saw the terrified baby crawl out of the corner and move dangerously close to the edge, reaching out for his mother's contorted face. They were going to lose the baby! Ramón instinctively lunged, knocking the infant back into the corner. When he looked back for Michael, all he saw was the churning water below.

"Michael!" Bernice screamed.

Ramón grabbed her around the waist and held on tightly. She fought to free herself and plunge after her husband. "Stop it, Bernice!" Ramón screamed in her ear. "He's gone!"

"Oh, Jesus, no! Oh, please, no!"

Ramón forced her onto her side, and pinned her and the baby between himself and the remains of the wall. Finally she stopped struggling. There was barely enough room for the three of them. She clutched her terrified infant and sobbed inconsolably. Ramón shielded them with his body, as the storm raged on.

4. AFTERMATH

Ramón awoke in the predawn light. Bernice lay with her back to him, her body contoured to his, her head resting heavily on his extended arm. She too apparently had lost consciousness sometime during the night. The baby! Ramón frantically reached across the sleeping woman and accidentally struck the infant in the face. It responded with a rasping cry. Bernice awoke with a start.

"Don't move!" Ramón said. "I'm right on the edge." He painfully withdrew his arm from under her and eased himself into a sitting position. His muscles and joints ached; his eyes burned.

Dark thunderheads still loomed above the silvery-gray horizon. He looked about at the rubble that had been his home. Except for the corner where they had taken refuge, only broken and twisted pilings remained. The water, now placid, extended over the low seawall and across his yard. Debris, sucked from the town, jammed the pilings and covered the street. There was no sign of his Land Rover.

Bernice sat up, clutching her baby. "Michael?" she said apprehensively.

Ramón shook his head. Remembering Michael's anguished cry, he gazed out at the sea, overwhelmed with a sense of total loss.

The baby began to fret, and Bernice pulled it to an exposed breast. "We must get help, sah. We must find Michael."

Ramón stood up. Muffled shouts echoed throughout the neighborhood—calls for the missing and cries of despair. The shack next-door had withstood the surge, but a woman's body hung grotesquely from a side window.

Ramón lowered himself into the waist-deep water, and reluctantly waded over to the shack. The corpse in the window was the washwoman. He forced himself to look past her twisted form and into the room. The bodies of her two sons floated near the rear wall. Ramón looked away, stunned by the deaths of his neighbors and filled with foreboding that Michael and many others in the city had drowned during the night.

Voices from the nearby alley drew his attention. Two men appeared, paddling a dory hewn from a mahogany log. Ramón called out hoarsely, "Over here!"

They stopped paddling at the sound of his voice. The man in the bow was Mestizo; the other was Creole. They studied Ramón for a moment. Then the Mestizo gave a quick nod, and they paddled over to where Ramón stood. He had to grab the bow of the boat to keep from being rammed.

"Yes, sah!" the Mestizo said sarcastically, glaring down at Ramón. The man had the face of a fighter—flattened nose, distended lips, and scarred eyebrows. He gave the washwoman's corpse an unconcerned glance, then eyed Ramón with open hostility. "Yes, sah!"

Ramón pointed toward the ruins of his home, where Bernice stood at an empty window frame, clutching her baby. "We need help."

"White *mon's* woman," the Mestizo said with a sneer.

"That's Bernice Flowers. Her husband, Michael, works for me."

"What you got, mon?" the Mestizo said.

"I've got a woman and a baby that I need to get to shelter."

"No, mon," the Mestizo said, menacingly shifting the paddle in his hands. "I mean, what you got for we?"

Ramón looked into the boat and saw two bulging burlap bags. "Not a God-damned thing!"

"What you think, bakra?" the Mestizo snarled. "You think you in the States?" He threateningly lifted his paddle from the water.

Ramón, still holding the bow of the boat, braced himself to capsize it.

"No, mon!" the Creole shouted from the stern. "Left him. Make we go."

The Mestizo slowly lowered his paddle back into the water, and Ramón pushed the boat away. They circled him, then disappeared up the alley. Shaken, Ramón waded back to Bernice.

"Those men in the dory, sah," she called down, "have they seen Michael?"

"They were looters. Hand down the baby. We've got to get out of here."

"Shouldn't we wait for a next dory, sah? I can't swim."

"The water's shallow. We can wade."

Bernice lowered the infant, then awkwardly climbed down herself.

Ramón carried the baby, as he and Bernice started up the alley. The filthy water was waist deep, and they repeatedly stumbled into unseen potholes. All the homes in the neighborhood had sustained severe damage—roofs blown away, walls caved in, and fences and trees knocked down. Many, like his own, had been destroyed. Looking at the clusters of bare pilings, he was unable to remember what the structures had looked like, although he had driven down this alley countless times.

As they arrived at Regent Street, a British Army truck plowed by. Its muddy wake rolled up to Ramón's armpits. He had to hold the baby over his head. "Stop, God damn it!" he shouted. "Stop!"

The driver glanced back, but continued on in the direction of Government House.

Bernice recovered from the wake and waded toward a wood-frame house on the corner, where several people congregated on the second-floor veranda. "Do you know my husband, Michael Flowers?" she called up. "Have you seen him?"

An elderly Creole woman leaned over the railing and said sympathetically, "No, gyal, we don't know your husband. Come up here out of the water."

Bernice shook her head. "I must find my husband."

Ramón put an arm around her shoulder. "Wait up there with the baby, Bernice. I'll find Michael."

She reluctantly let him lead her up the wooden stairway.

A pretty Creole waited for them at the top of the stairs, holding another infant in her arms. "I'll take the baby, mistah Kelley."

It took Ramón a moment to recognize the young woman. She was the clerk from the tiny newsstand on the next street. "We were stranded all night," he said, handing her the baby. "They need to rest."

"We'll look after them," she said, now with a struggling infant in each arm.

"Thanks," Ramón said gratefully. "I'll be back for them as soon as I can." He gave Bernice a reassuring nod, then headed back down the stairs.

He waded south on Regent Street. In the neighborhood shops, he saw proprietors salvaging stock and standing guard against looters. Most of the houses along this street had withstood the storm, and the residents crowded the verandas. Behind the buildings, he caught glimpses of furtive men paddling dories. Once he thought he saw the two who had confronted him earlier.

He arrived at the Government House gate and looked across the street to St. John's Cathedral. The small 150-year-old Anglican church had withstood yet another hurricane. There was no apparent damage to the brick exterior, but water still lapped against the window sills. The rector and several parishioners passed furniture through the open doorway.

On the other side of the church lay a cemetery. Only the taller grave markers could be seen. Something caught his eye: the corner of a casket bobbed in the water. A short distance away, he saw another. The storm had unearthed the city's dead from their shallow graves.

Ramón turned and waded up the circular drive to Government House. Usually, a guard was stationed at the gate, but this morning he waited on the raised porch. Ramón climbed the slippery wooden stairs.

"Can I help you, sah?" the guard said.

"I need to see the governor," Ramón said. He started past the young Creole.

The guard stepped in front of him. "The governor has retired, sah."

"He's what?" Ramón said in fatigued confusion. "Retired?"

"Yes, sah. The governor—" the guard began.

"Mistah Kelley, sah," interrupted a familiar voice. Wilford, the aging head of the household staff, eased past the guard. "The bwy means the governor is sleeping, sah. He was awake all night and went to bed less than an hour ago."

Another figure emerged—a young British army officer. "I'm Lieutenant Faulkson. May I help you?" Then he flushed, apparently recognizing Ramón as the white man, who a few minutes earlier had been holding a black child over his head.

Ramón disliked these pale centurions almost as much as the Belizeans did. Ignoring the officer, as he had been ignored in the street, he continued with Wilford, "My house was destroyed last night. Michael Flowers was staying with me and got swept away."

"Oh, no!" Wilford said.

"I need to get downtown," Ramón said. "Do you have a dory or a skiff I can use?"

"Ah, sir," Faulkson interjected, "I'll be returning to camp shortly. I'll be glad to drop you in town."

Ramón gave the lieutenant a curt nod.

"Sah," Wilford said, "we have no water for washing, but before you leave, let me get you something to eat and a clean bandage for your head."

"Thanks, Wilford. I'd appreciate that."

"Come this way, sah."

Government House was a shambles. Gray silt covered the wood floor and extended three feet up the paneled walls. Antique furnishings lay piled in corners, mixed with rubbish that had been sucked from the surrounding neighborhood by the receding tide.

They entered the kitchen. A corporal and two privates sat at a table. The household staff members, usually ensconced in the kitchen, were missing. Apparently Wilford was the only servant on the premises.

Ramón sat down at the table. The soldiers looked at him with mild curiosity, but didn't speak.

Wilford brought Ramón a sandwich and a cup of water. "I'll just be a moment, sah," he said, then left the room.

Ramón wasn't hungry, but managed to down a few mouthfuls of the processed meat and dry bread. He turned to the lieutenant. "What's the latest report?"

"The damage apparently is quite extensive. There are reports that the winds reached 200 miles per hour."

"Is a relief effort being organized? All I've seen patrolling the streets are looters."

"Ah . . . I really don't have the details," Faulkson said uneasily. "My men and I were inland at our camp during the storm. We just came in this morning to see if we could assist the governor."

Wilford reappeared with bandages and a pan of water. "Mistah Kelley will be ready to travel directly, sah," he said to Faulkson. He removed the rag from Ramón's head and carefully dabbed around the laceration. "The bleeding has stopped, sah." He applied a clean dressing.

"We'll wait for you outside," Faulkson said. He and his three men filed out of the room.

Ramón rose to leave.

"Sah," Wilford said, "is there any chance Michael is alive?"

Ramón sighed. "Possibly . . . I hope so . . . but the waves were awfully strong."

They walked down the hallway and out onto the front porch.

"Thanks for the food and bandage, Wilford," Ramón said. "When Sir Peter wakes up, tell him I'll be in touch with him later today."

"I will, sah. Good luck!"

Ramón waded out to the truck and pulled himself over the tailgate. Neither of the soldiers in back moved to assist him. As soon as he was in, the engine started and the truck lurched forward.

They plowed up Regent Street, propagating a muddy wake.

They passed an elderly man and woman, floating their few remaining possessions down the street in a skiff. The couple glared back at Ramón, as they struggled to keep their boat from capsizing.

Ramón moved across the bed of the truck and pounded on the back of the cab. "Slow down, God damn it! Watch out for these people, and slow down!"

One of the soldiers in the back of the truck shook his head; the other stared impassively. The driver slowed. The lieutenant kept his gaze fixed straight ahead.

When they arrived in the middle of town, Ramón shouted for the driver to stop at the Court House. The truck bounced over a submerged curb and pulled up close to the wide stairway in front of the white stucco building. Flood waters lapped at the lower panes of the first-floor windows. Grasping the ornate wrought-iron railing, Ramón precariously swung his bulky frame over the water and onto the stairs. The lieutenant gave a halfhearted wave as the truck bounced back onto the street and sped off toward the swing bridge.

The stairway and the second-floor veranda overflowed with people, talking among themselves as they watched the activity below. Ramón paused on the lower landing and surveyed the scene. Scores of displaced residents waded up and down the streets in the waist-deep water; others paddled dories.

"Mistah Kelley!" someone cried. Ramón turned and saw his tugboat captain, Robby, paddling a dory down Regent Street. The wiry Creole secured the boat to the Court House handrail, then climbed the stairs. "I see you make it all right, sah!" Robby said as they shook hands.

Ramón nodded. "How about you, Robby? Is your family okay?"

"Yes, sah. We get a big blow at Burrel Boom and the river rise five feet. But me family is fine, and the boat is riding high."

"Good. How'd you get back here?"

"In me dory, sah. I want to make sure everything all right before I bring back the boat."

"Thanks, Robby," Ramón said. His conscientious captain had paddled fifteen miles down the swollen Belize River. "Michael was swept away in the storm last night. Have you heard anything about him?"

"No, sah," Robby said, frowning and obviously troubled. "But when I come through town . . . I see many dead people in the water."

"Let's go inside," Ramón said. "Maybe somebody in here can tell us what's going on."

"Sah, storm headquarters are not here. They are at the police station."

Ramón followed Robby down the stairs. As Robby untied the dory, Ramón looked across the water-covered plaza. On the other side of Battlefield Park stood the Bank of the Caribbean. A crowd of perhaps two dozen people congregated around the front door. Ramón climbed into the dory. "Before we go to the police station, take me over to the bank."

Robby paddled across the plaza, skillfully weaving between the waders and the other boats. On the other side, a Creole policeman stood guard in knee-deep water at the top of the bank stairs.

Robby back-paddled to a stop. Ramón grasped the side of the dory and draped one leg into the water. The dugout rocked erratically.

"Mind, sah!" Robby said. "The dory is cranky."

The policeman grabbed the bow and steadied it. Ramón eased into the water. "Is Elijah Ruiz in there?"

"Yes, sah, mistah Kelley," the policeman said.

"I need to see him."

The policeman rapped on the glass, and another policeman on the inside unlocked and opened the door. "Mistah Kelley wishes to see mistah Ruiz."

The guard on the inside nodded. Suddenly the crowd, standing in the water, grew vocal. "I want me money!" cried an angry Creole. Another man echoed his demand. "Why do the bakra get they money, and we don't?" shouted a woman.

The guard stepped forward, pulled Ramón inside, and quickly locked the door behind them. The din outside continued as Ramón sloshed across the bank lobby.

Kerosene lanterns flickered behind the tellers cages. The guard ushered Ramón over to the staircase that led to the second floor. He gestured for Ramón to continue, then returned to his post at the front door.

At the top of the stairs, Ramón found the hallway floor lined with papers laid out to dry. In the offices along the hall, bank officers and clerks were busy trying to salvage documents.

Ramón continued toward the front of the building. The door marked "Bank President" was open. Across the dimly-lit office, Elijah Ruiz stood with his back to a window. At another window stood a light-skinned Creole in a tan uniform, Assistant Police Inspector Albert Bradley.

Elijah frowned at the dressing on Ramón's head. "Are you all right, mon?"

"I'm okay," Ramón said as they shook hands. "What about you and your families?"

"Everyone is safe," Elijah said. "Albert and I got them off to El Cayo last night. And Kay?"

"El Cayo," Ramón said with a nod. "But Michael Flowers was lost in the storm. He and his family were staying with me last night, and he got swept away."

"Oh, no! What about Bernice and the baby?"

"They're okay. I left them at a house down on Regent Street. But I need to find out what happened to Michael."

"Any reports, Albert?" Elijah asked the inspector.

Bradley shook his head. "It will be days, perhaps weeks, before we'll be able to account for all the missing. Coming over this morning, I saw at least thirty bodies floating near Cinderella Town."

"Three people drowned in the house next to mine," Ramón said grimly.

"I have to get back to the police station," Bradley told Elijah.

Then he turned to Ramón. "I'll let you know if I hear anything about Michael. Don't give up hope; maybe he was lucky."

"I'll come by the station in a few minutes," Ramón said. "Maybe they've heard something since you've been gone."

Bradley nodded and left the office.

Elijah walked over to the door and closed it. "Ramón," he said, "I'm afraid there's nothing you can do out there, until the water goes down."

Ramón nodded, but couldn't accept the thought of idly waiting.

Elijah walked back to the window and motioned for Ramón to join him. The unruly crowd below had doubled. Their shouts grew louder as Bradley emerged. He raised his arms for quiet, then spoke to them briefly in Creole patois. Ramón understood little of what he said, but the crowd remained quiet as he climbed into his dory and paddled away.

Elijah turned to Ramón. "This is a bad time for all of us, but we need to talk."

Ramón shook his head. "I have to go find out about Michael."

"Albert will contact us if he hears anything, Ramón. Listen to that crowd down there. We need to use this time to discuss what lies ahead."

Ramón frowned.

"I believe," Elijah said, "that this storm will be the catalyst for change."

"What are you talking about, Elijah?"

"I'm talking about independence!"

"What about it?"

"Ramón, the uproar which will follow this storm could be the final problem that convinces the Crown to rid herself of the nuisance called British Honduras."

"Elijah . . ." Ramón said wearily, "I don't have the time or the energy—"

"Ramón, we must discuss this. Timing will be critical. Those who grasp the opportunity will direct our future."

"Elijah, we'll have to talk about this later."

"It must be soon, Ramón."

Ramón stared down at the storm-ravaged plaza for a moment. Then as he turned to leave he said, "Elijah, if you get control of all of it, I don't think you'll have a God-damned thing."

Downstairs, the crowd watched impassively as Ramón climbed into the dory. He told, Robby, "Let's get on over to the police station."

They paddled past the storm-ravaged open market. The current from nearby Haulover Creek surged through the empty produce stalls. The small fishing boats, usually tied behind the market, were missing—either moved upriver before the storm, or sunk during it.

They passed the swing bridge and glided over the seawall. Ramón looked up Front Street. His two-story, wooden office building had been built at the turn of the century, but appeared to have weathered the storm.

They continued up Queen Street, weaving through the debris until they arrived at the walled police compound. As they entered the main gate, they saw the superintendent of police standing on the second floor landing, shouting orders to three policemen in a skiff. Finally the policemen rowed off.

"Sydney," Ramón called up, "can we be of any help?"

"No, Ramón," he said distractedly. "There's nothing you can do here." He turned to go inside.

"Sydney!" Ramón shouted. "Have you heard anything about Michael Flowers? He was lost in the storm last night."

The superintendent paused in the doorway. "I'm sorry, Ramón. I don't know anything about Michael. We've got thousands of people missing." He disappeared inside.

"Let's try the hospital," Ramón said.

It took half an hour for Ramón and Robby to traverse Queen Street. The concrete buildings on the north side of town had withstood the storm, but those made of wood had been severely damaged. A helicopter passed noisily overhead. Ramón looked up and said bitterly, "U.S. news agencies."

At the next intersection, they turned onto Eve Street. Ramón drew his paddle from the water. "Good Lord!"

Scores of boats jammed the hospital gate—storm survivors, delivering their dead and injured. But the hospital was already overrun; refugees covered the front steps and filled the windows.

Ramón stared at the scene. The dory drifted toward the sea. Finally he said, "We won't be able to get in there for hours. Elijah was right; there's nothing we can do right now. Let's go over to the office."

A half-hour later, they were back on Front Street, paddling against the current from nearby Haulover Creek. The old concrete post office was intact; however, the shops around it had been gutted—either by the storm itself, or the aftermath of looters.

"Mistah Kelley!" called a voice. A Creole waved from a second-floor veranda. "How you making it, sah?"

Ramón halfheartedly returned the wave and was about to respond, when Robby cried out, "Thiefs, sah!"

Two looters were breaking into the Landry Mahogany office building. They were the men who had confronted Ramón earlier that morning. The Creole was downstairs, trying to pry the padlock off the storeroom door with a length of pipe. The Mestizo was upstairs, kicking in the office door.

Ramón and Robby dug their paddles deep into the water. The Creole glanced back over his shoulder and saw them approaching. He dropped the pipe and froze.

"Get away from there!" Ramón shouted up to the Mestizo.

The Mestizo sauntered over to the veranda railing. He gazed down with an insolent grin on his scarred face. "What you want, mon? Huh? What you want?"

Ramón clambered out of the dory. "Get down from there, God damn you!"

The Mestizo's features contorted. "You don't curse me, white motherfucker!" He hurried across the veranda and started down the stairway.

The Creole waded forward and stopped him at the foot of the stairs. "Make we go," the Creole said, grasping the Mestizo's arm.

"Fuck you, mon!" the Mestizo said, angrily pulling his arm away. He waded over to their dory and withdrew a long machete.

"Bwy!" Robby cried. "This is mistah Kelley! Put down that machete!"

Ramón glanced back at Robby and gestured for him to stay back. A crowd of onlookers had formed in the street.

The Mestizo also noticed the crowd. He waded toward Ramón and stopped just a few feet away, menacingly slapping the side of the blade against his palm. "You don't curse me, white motherfucker!"

Ramón's pulse accelerated. He sensed the crowd's presence was waxing the Mestizo's hatred.

The Creole stepped in front of the Mestizo. "Come, mon! It for him this place. Make we go!"

The Mestizo looked at the Creole, then back to the growing crowd. A man's voice from the street cried, "That's mistah Kelley, mon! Put down your machete!" Others echoed the cry.

The Mestizo struggled with indecision, then finally allowed the Creole to take the machete from him. A murmur of relief went through the crowd. The Creole turned toward Ramón with the machete. "Can we go now, sah?" he said softly, so the crowd wouldn't hear.

Before Ramón could respond, a guttural voice snarled, "You God-damned blacky!" Karl Schrader, the German pilot, shouldered past Ramón.

The Creole raised the machete defensively, but hesitated in confusion. In a single swift movement, the stocky German caught his wrist and wrenched the machete from his grasp. The Creole's eyes widened with terror as the blade flashed above him. He lifted an arm to protect his head. The machete severed it at the forearm.

"Karl, no!" Ramón gasped. But the blade flashed again, this time splitting the man's skull.

Everyone stood in stunned silence. The Creole's body floated face down. Blood from the stump of the arm and the mortal head wound colored the water. Schrader turned toward the dazed Mestizo.

"Karl," Ramón choked, "for God's sake! Stop!"

Schrader waved him off with the bloody machete. His eyes never left the Mestizo, who stood motionless.

"Put down the machete, mistah Schrader!" boomed a voice from behind Ramón. "Put it down, or we will shoot!"

A sergeant and two other black policemen, armed with rifles, approached in a skiff.

Ramón stepped between Schrader and the Mestizo. "Karl!" he barked. "That's enough!"

Schrader reluctantly let the machete slip into the water at his feet.

"Him kill the bwy!" a woman cried. A hostile murmur passed through the crowd.

"Take him to headquarters!" the sergeant barked at his men. "Quickly!"

The policemen hustled Schrader into the skiff. As they rowed away, the Mestizo stared after them, fear still etched in his face. When they were out of sight, he looked at the now silent crowd. His fear turned to shame.

Leaving the corpse of his companion behind, he climbed into his dory and paddled away. Before he disappeared between two buildings, he looked back at Ramón and uttered a shrill curse: "White!"

The sound of electricity returning to the Fort George Hotel snapped Ramón out of a fitful sleep. He lay still for a moment, trying to clear his mind of chaotic dreams. Then he reached over and found a lamp on the side table. A low-wattage bulb illuminated the room in an amber glow. He looked at his watch; it was 8:47. He had checked into the hotel six hours earlier and had collapsed on the bed, fully clothed.

He lay back again. Kay must be home by now. He closed his

eyes and tried to imagine her in her parents' house, secure again in the Louisiana town where she had been raised. But instead, the past twenty-four hours rushed back at him—the storm, the loss of Michael, the devastation, the killing. He sat up and reached for the phone. The line was dead. He got up and opened a window. The Caribbean had receded across the seawall; the night sky was clear.

He entered the bathroom and tried the faucet. Rusty water sputtered through the pipes, finally clearing enough that he could wash his face and rinse his mouth. He turned on the shower. Cold water only. After he bathed, he would have to put on the same filthy clothes. They were his only possessions.

Ramón entered the hotel lobby and found it crammed with storm refugees. Some had even been assigned the commercial stalls normally used as airline ticket counters.

A Creole desk clerk looked up with a tired smile of recognition. "Ah, mistah Kelley. Can I help you, sah?"

"All these people lose their homes?"

"Most of them, sah. They began arriving late this afternoon. We've had to put them everywhere. Even the hallways and the bar are full."

"I can share my room, if necessary."

"Thank you, sah."

"I need to contact the States. Are the phones working?"

"No, sah, they are still broke down."

Ramón nodded. "I'm going out for a while. If the phones get fixed and anybody tries to contact me, please take a message. Tell them I'm okay, and I'll call them when I get back."

"Yes, sah."

Ramón descended the hotel stairs and struck out for town on foot. A moist gray silt covered the deserted parking lot. The surrounding neighborhood reeked from the muck that the storm surge had drawn from the open canals and dredged up from the harbor floor.

As Ramón walked up the deserted lane, he tried to organize his muddled thoughts. First, he needed to find out if there was any word on Michael. Then, he had to see what the police had done with Karl. Later, he would check on Bernice. And as soon as he could get through to Louisiana, he would call Kay in Hammond and the Landry Mahogany Company main office in New Orleans.

He passed a large concrete home. A black Rottweiler raced up to the wrought-iron fence, barking ferociously. Ramón's thoughts turned to the violence of the morning. Had Karl come to his defense, not realizing the threat had passed, or had he simply seized the opportunity to commit a senseless murder?

He arrived at Front Street and found it nearly deserted. The Pickwick Club, the century-old gathering place of the colony's white elite, had been leveled. He continued on, evaluating the damage to the shops and offices on the block. Behind the buildings, a billow of orange smoke suddenly rose into the night sky.

Ramón jogged up to the next intersection and looked up Queen Street. British troops were setting fire to the city! Then he realized the soldiers were simply burning a large pile of rubble in the middle of the street. They were hosing down the nearby buildings to prevent the fire from spreading.

He walked up the street and passed through the high-walled entrance to the police station. Lights shone from the second floor office windows. He crossed the compound and climbed the stairs.

"Good evening, Ramón," said a familiar voice as he arrived at the landing. Assistant Police Inspector Bradley walked toward him, hand extended.

"Any news about Michael?" Ramón said as they shook hands.

"No. One of my men just returned from the hospital. It's still quite hectic there, but they don't think he's been admitted."

"Damn. Well, I won't bother them tonight. I know it's a mess over there. Robby and I couldn't even get through the front gate this morning."

"It got worse," Bradley said. "By afternoon, there were too many bodies to bury. They began burning them."

"Are we getting foreign help?"

"Of sorts," Bradley said cryptically.

"Like what?"

"Helicopters dropped supplies earlier this evening."

"U.S. helicopters?"

"Guatemalan helicopters dropped medical supplies. The U.S. helicopters dropped . . . beer."

"Beer? You're not serious."

Bradley nodded. "I saw it myself. I was with George Price. If George would have had a weapon, he probably would have shot them both down for embarrassing him—the Guats by helping, and the Americans by *not* helping."

"How about the British?"

"So far, all we've got from abroad are their sympathies. But locally, a Lieutenant Faulkson showed up about midday with four truckloads of soldiers. They've been hard at it ever since."

"Really?" Ramón said. He had underestimated the young British officer.

"Our local politicians will probably never acknowledge their efforts, though," Bradley continued. "Praising the British is almost as unpopular as accepting gifts from the Guats. They'll probably credit the Americans with coming to our rescue."

"What's been done with Karl Schrader?" Ramón said.

"We've held him here in the office. The magistrate just gave the order to release him. Since the man he killed was a looter, there won't be charges . . . unless there is something else you can add to the statement you gave earlier."

Ramón shook his head. "It was like I told you, the man lifted the machete, and Karl took it away from him and killed him with it."

"He's not disturbed by what he's done," Bradley said. Then he added, "Have you heard the talk, that in Germany he was a Nazi?"

"I've heard it. I don't know if there's any truth to it. One time, when he'd been drinking, he told me he'd flown with the Luftwaffe during the final days of the war. Said he was nineteen at the time."

Bradley looked off, then turned back and gazed intently at Ramón. "Did he have to kill that bwy today?"

"I honestly don't know, Albert. It appeared to me that it was over, but I'm not sure what was going to happen. And neither of us knew that your men had arrived."

Bradley hesitated, then said, "Come in. I'll release him to you."

Ramón followed Bradley into the office. Schrader sat behind an unused desk, sleeping.

"See what I mean?" Bradley said. "No remorse."

Ramón walked over to the rumpled figure and barked, "Karl!"

Schrader raised his head slowly, as if he had been awake all along. "I can go?"

"Yes, mistah Schrader," Bradley said, "you can go."

Then turning to Ramón, he said, "Do you have a place to stay tonight?"

"Yeah, I managed to get a room at the Fort George."

"I'll contact you there then, if we hear anything about Michael."

Ramón and Schrader left the office. As they exited the compound onto Queen Street, a black policeman approached. He eyed Schrader as they passed.

"Do you need a place to stay?" Ramón said.

"No, I have a place." Schrader didn't elaborate.

They arrived at the swing bridge.

"I go this way," Schrader said, gesturing down the street where the killing had occurred.

"I don't think that's a good idea."

Schrader gave him a quizzical look, then laughed in genuine amusement. "Should I be afraid, Ramón? Of what? A blacky with a machete?"

"Karl, that guy just wanted to get away. And you killed him!"

Schrader laughed again, then turned and headed down the dark street.

5. TAWNYA

Five days had passed since the hurricane. Ramón rode in silence, as Assistant Police Inspector Bradley maneuvered his battered Morris Minor along the Northern Highway. The raised, potholed road separated the churning sea on one side, from a stagnating mangrove swamp on the other.

They rounded a sweeping bend and saw a police Land Rover parked on the shoulder of the road. Bradley pulled in behind it, and they climbed out. A half-dozen king vultures circled lazily overhead in the late afternoon breeze. Four policemen stood at the edge of the swamp, looking down at a corpse. Two enormous, blue-gray crabs picked at the rotting remains. So little flesh was left that Ramón could only recognize Michael from the print of his mud-stained shirt. He gagged at the stench. Grabbing a large rock, he crushed the crab that was feeding on Michael's head. As he fumbled for the rock again, the other crab lifted its large pincer and scurried to safety of the dark, stagnant water.

"Ramón!" Bradley said, moving protectively toward him.

Ramón's shoulders slumped. He let Bradley take the rock from him.

"Deliver the body to the morgue," Bradley told the policemen.

"No!" Ramón said, turning with tears in his eyes. "Bernice mustn't see him."

Bradley amended his order. "Burn the body here, like we've done the others. Then take the remains directly to the burial ground." He placed a hand on Ramón's shoulder. "Come, mon. They'll see to it."

Ramón allowed Bradley to lead him up to the shoulder of the

road. He paused and looked up at the vultures, now circling lower. "Carrion crow pick who is to die," he said softly, repeating Michael's premonition.

The policemen unloaded a five-gallon can of kerosene and a military flamethrower from their Land Rover.

"Let's go, Ramón," Bradley said.

Ramón reluctantly followed him back to the car.

They drove in silence, until Ramón regained his composure. Finally he said, "How'd you find him?"

"A taxi driver was going out to the airport this morning and stopped to take a piss. He saw the body and reported it. There have been so many that my men couldn't get out here until about an hour ago. When they pulled the body out, they discovered that it was Michael from papers in his wallet. They contacted me straight away."

"So far from the city . . ." Ramón said dully.

Bradley nodded. "Two days ago we found a woman even farther up the highway."

Ramón rubbed his eyes. "What's the death toll so far?"

"We've buried more than three hundred," Bradley said. He gestured toward the mangroves. "But many will never be found."

"Have you notified Bernice?"

"No. It won't be easy. I knew them both."

"I'll tell her," Ramón said.

With apparent relief, Bradley accelerated the car toward town.

They pulled up to the house on Regent Street where Bernice had stayed since the morning after the storm. She had spent most of her waking hours searching for Michael. With each passing day, as the likelihood of his survival had diminished, the elderly homeowner had become increasingly protective of her.

"Don't wait for me," Ramón told Bradley. "I'll be here a while."

He glanced up as he struggled out of the tiny car. The old woman stood on the veranda, looking down at him. Ramón lowered his eyes and pushed through the wooden gate. A mongrel dog that had been sleeping under the house began to bark, as it did each time Ramón entered the yard. This time the old woman made no effort to quiet it.

When Ramón reached the top of the stairs, she was waiting for him. "You found her husband?"

"Yes. He's dead. They found him this morning on the Northern Highway."

She looked away, and said softly, "Man di walk; death di watch."

Ramón didn't reply. The adage was true: death in Belize often came unexpectedly.

The old woman turned back. "Where have they taken him?"

"Bernice won't be able to see him. The crabs had already . . ." He couldn't continue.

The old woman nodded. "Wait here. I'll tell her." She entered the house.

Moments later, Bernice appeared at the doorway. Tears rolled down her haggard brown face. She looked to Ramón for confirmation of what the old woman had told her. When she received it from his expression, her knees buckled. Ramón caught her as she fell. He helped her back into the house and onto a tattered couch in the living room. He held her as she cried.

Daylight faded; the living room was almost dark. From time to time, Bernice had attempted to compose herself, only to lapse back into inconsolable anguish. Ramón occasionally had heard babies crying in another part of the house.

Finally, the old woman reappeared and helped Bernice to her feet. She nodded to Ramón, and guided Bernice into a bedroom. Ramón got up and went outside.

The pretty light-skinned Creole from the newsstand was leaning against the veranda railing. "Granny will care for her, sah," she said reassuringly.

"You've heard about her husband?"

"Yes, sah. It's a pity, but at least her waiting is over."

Ramón gave a sad nod.

"Have you eaten?" she said.

Ramón shook his head.

"I have some rice and beans in the kitchen," she offered.

"I'm sorry," Ramón said, "we've spoken several times at Alma's Newsstand, but I don't know your name."

"I'm Tawnya Lightburn, sah. But you won't be seeing me at Alma's again; it washed away."

"I'm sorry to hear that, Tawnya. I'm Ramón Kelley."

"I know who you are, mistah Kelley," she said with a quick laugh.

"Ramón," he said.

"Ramón," she repeated with a smile.

He looked down the nearly deserted street. "Do you know if any of the eating places around here have reopened? I need to get away from here for a little while, and it'll probably be better for Bernice if she has some time alone."

"I believe the Conch Shell on Albert Street is open."

"Will you join me?"

"Sure, sah . . . Ramón. Just let me tell Granny to watch the babies while I'm gone."

"Oh, yes. And . . . uh . . . ask your husband to join us."

"I'm not married, Ramón," she said, smiling over her shoulder as she entered the house.

A few minutes later, she returned and preceded him down the stairs. Ramón opened the gate for her. As they stepped into the street, a bicycle bell rang in warning. They paused as a young Creole couple rode by. Then side by side, they crossed the street and started up a dark alley toward Albert Street.

"Tawnya, I appreciate what you and your grandmother have done for Bernice and her baby."

"Hand wash hand," she replied.

Ramón looked down at her and smiled. Tawnya walked with a smooth even stride. Her white cotton dress, trimmed in yellow, set off her straightened dark hair and honey-toned skin. Ramón suspected the dress was her Sunday best.

She caught him looking and smiled.

"You just have the one child?" he said.

"Yes. My baby's name is George. We call him Georgy. I named him after mistah Price."

Ramón was sure that her naming her baby after the local political leader was a sign of respect, not an indication of parentage.

Up ahead, a gate opened and three young Creole men stepped into the alley. Ramón tensed, but they passed without speaking—staring at Tawnya and ignoring him. Ramón glanced back over his shoulder. The men turned the corner and disappeared up Regent Street.

Ramón and Tawnya arrived at Albert Street. A half-block away, the Conch Shell restaurant sign was lighted.

"Looks like it's open," Ramón said.

"A Mestizo man don't miss a chance to make a dollar," Tawnya said with a laugh.

Ramón thought of another Mestizo man—the looter on the day after the storm.

They arrived at the restaurant. The windows and front door of the clapboard shack were open to catch the cooling breeze from the Caribbean, three blocks away. The stain from the storm surge extended nine feet up the pale blue exterior.

Ramón followed Tawnya through the front door. Five mismatched tables completely filled the dingy room. A heavy-set Mestizo came through the kitchen door. "Tawnya!" he cried with pleasure, wiping his hands on a dirty apron.

"Hello, Antonio," Tawnya said. "Do you know mistah Kelley?"

The Mestizo nodded diffidently. "I know your name, sah, but we haven't met."

"Antonio is the owner," Tawnya said.

Ramón extended his hand, and Antonio smiled and grasped it. "Please, sit down," he said. "Can I get you something to eat?"

"What do you have, Antonio?" Tawnya said.

"Fresh snapper, plantain, and breadfruit. It just arrived this afternoon from Dangriga. And I have some rice and beans. There is no fresh water, but I have some orange Fanta."

"It all sounds good to me," Ramón said, checking with Tawnya, who smiled and nodded. Looking back at Antonio, Ramón said, "You seem to be recovering well from the storm."

Antonio looked around the room with entrepreneurial pride. "A businessman must make the best of things, sah." Then he quipped, "At least the crabs will be nice and fat this year."

At first Ramón didn't grasp the reference; then the recollection of the crabs feeding on Michael's corpse struck him, and he stood up, knocking over his chair.

Antonio stepped back, his dark eyes open wide.

"Ramón!" Tawnya said, grabbing his arm. "He didn't know!"

Ramón looked down at Tawnya for a moment. Finally, he nodded. "I'm sorry, Antonio," he said, and righted the chair and sat back down at the table.

Antonio looked at Tawnya for an explanation.

"The Creole lady staying with Granny is a friend of mistah Kelley's," Tawnya said.

"Ah, yes," Antonio said, still bewildered. "The lady has stopped here several times inquiring after her husband." Then his expression changed, as if he were beginning to comprehend. "They found him?"

"Today," Ramón said, "in the mangroves. Crabs were feeding on him."

"I'm sorry, sah," Antonio stammered.

"You had no way of knowing," Ramón said. "Your joke is a bad one, though. I'd forget it."

"Yes, sah."

Ramón forced a smile. "Is your food offer still good?"

"Coming up, right away, sah," Antonio said. He hurried into the kitchen.

Tawnya reached across the table and placed a hand on top of one of Ramón's clenched fists. "Are you all right?"

He looked down at her delicate tan fingers. She started to pull her hand away, but he encompassed it with his other hand. "Yeah, I'm okay. I generally don't lose control like that."

Antonio returned with the orange drinks, and Tawnya slipped her hand from Ramón's.

"I'm sorry, sah," Antonio said, "but we have no ice."

"This will be fine," Ramón said.

"The food will be ready, directly, sah. It looks like you will be my only customers tonight. Dollars will be scarce for some time now."

"If you haven't already eaten, why don't you join us?" Ramón said.

Antonio checked with Tawnya, who smiled and nodded her assent. "Thank you, sah," he said, then went back into the kitchen.

When he reappeared, he was balancing three plates, heaped with food.

"Antonio!" Tawnya laughed, as he placed a plate in front of her. "I can't eat all of this." Turning to Ramón she said, "You'll need to help me."

Ramón ruefully shook his head. "It's Belize City rice and beans that's giving me this," he said, patting his paunch. But then, like the others, he ate hungrily.

When they were done, Antonio cleared the table and returned with two bottles of warm Carta Blanca beer. "I only have two," he said apologetically.

"None for me," Tawnya said.

Over the beer, Ramón said, "How long have you been in business here, Antonio?"

"Nearly three years, sah. I cooked at the Palace Hotel for seven years; then I buy this place."

"Were you born here in the city?"

"No, sah. Corozal. My father sent me here when I finished school. He worked all his life in the sugarcane fields, and he wanted me to live better." Antonio reached inside the top of his apron and took out a crumpled pack of Winsomes. He offered one to Ramón.

Ramón took a cigarette and accepted a light. He seldom smoked, and now puffed without inhaling. As he leaned back in his chair, he noticed a water-stained picture of Queen Elizabeth, hanging crookedly on the front wall. "What do you think of the PUP move for independence?" he said.

Antonio frowned. "It does not concern me."

"Independence does not concern you?"

"The People's United Party does not concern me," Antonio said. "Creoles fancy themselves as dark Englishmen. When they take over, the lives of those of us with Mayan and Spanish blood will not change." He crushed out his half-smoked cigarette and began to collect the plates.

A short while later, Ramón and Tawnya returned to Regent Street. The house was dark. "Looks like everyone's asleep," Ramón said, relieved that he wouldn't have to deal with Michael's death anymore this evening.

He opened the gate. The thin mongrel snarled, then turned tail and ran underneath the house, barking.

"He'll wake everybody up!" Tawnya said, hurrying after him. Ramón followed, carefully picking his way through the storm debris caught between the pilings.

The moon illuminated the muddy backyard. Tawnya pulled her skirt under her and squatted down. She tried to coax the scraggly animal to come to her, but it growled suspiciously and retreated to a far corner.

"Is that your dog?" Ramón said.

"No," she said with a laugh. "Granny fed him one time, and now he thinks he lives here. He only comes to her."

"Ugly dog," Ramón said.

"Meager," Tawnya said, trying to rise without getting her skirt muddy.

Ramón stepped forward and offered his hand. She grasped it and rose into his arms. Ramón stirred as he looked down at her full lips, slightly parted and smiling up at him. He hesitated.

Tawnya looked from side to side in mock seriousness. "No one can see us," she said, and again offered her mouth to him.

Ramón lowered his head and kissed her firm lips. She started to encircle her arms about his neck, but he clasped her wrists and lowered them to her sides. "I'm sorry," he said.

She gave him a teasing look of disappointment, then took his hand and led him back to the street.

A short while later, as Ramón passed through the hotel lobby, the young Creole night clerk called out from behind the front desk, "Mistah, Kelley! I have a letter for you, sah. From the States."

"Has the airport reopened?" Ramón said.

"Yes, sah. The TACA flight made it in this afternoon. We are getting back to normal now."

Ramón took the letter; it was from Kay. He gave the clerk a nod of thanks and headed for his room.

Moments later, he stood in the center of his spartan quarters, reading the familiar handwriting.

October 31, 1961

Ramón,

I may not send this letter. However, it's important to me that I capture my feelings, right now.

It's early morning. Mom and Dad are in the living room, listening for news about Hurricane Hatti. I should be feeling concern for you, and compassion for the city, but I don't. Tomorrow, I'm sure I will, but today I just feel anger and humiliation at your having dispatched me back to the States, like an unwanted obligation, while you see to the things that are truly important to you: your business and the well-being of those damned niggers! Tonight I hate that ghastly country of yours, and I hate you too.

When we first met in New Orleans five years ago, you were so unlike the other men I'd known. You were older, and your Central American upbringing had made you rugged and independent. I was young, and I had no way of knowing that the same traits, which I found so attractive, would prove to be demeaning to me, and destructive to our marriage.

I've tried to live in British Honduras twice now; there will be no third time. I know you don't think I've tried. I have tried, Ramón. I truly have!

You're callous. You've never been able to understand my feelings. Like the time I tried to shop in that squalid open market—seeing the fly-covered iguanas lying with their stomachs split open on the butcher block, right beside the fish I wanted to buy for dinner that night. And those pathetic turtles, flailing helplessly on their backs, awaiting their slaughter. I fled through that sea of grinning black faces and barely made it to the street outside, where I vomited in the gutter in front of the passersby. You'll never understand what something like that does to a person like me.

The people there won't accept me. Whenever you're around, the women are so solicitous. "How are you Mrs. Kelley?" "Why don't we see more of you, Mrs. Kelley?" Damn them! They never call, and whenever you're not around, they treat me with contempt. And everyone knows about the affair you had the last time I left.

I know you think I'm prejudiced; I can't deny that, any more than I can deny I was born here in Louisiana. We may have limited contact with colored people here, but at least when we do, we can understand what they're saying. Down there, their pidgin English, their "Creole", is unintelligible. I know the maids are talking about me when they giggle between themselves. They think it's funny that they can talk right in front of me, and I can't understand what they're saying. It's not my imagination, damn you! I know they're talking about me!

Mom and Dad were stunned when I called them from the New Orleans airport a few hours ago. They were concerned about you, staying to ride out the storm, and concerned about me, saying that I had left you for good. Mom didn't want me down there in the first place, so she's been supportive. Dad always liked you, and he just seems sad.

Ramón, last night I came to you, needing to be held. Just held! Had you been able, I would have willingly sacrificed myself to that damnable storm. If you've got me pregnant, it will be my final humiliation.

Kay

Ramón carefully folded the letter and put it back into the envelope. He walked over to the window and gazed out at the choppy night sea. For the past five days, in the storm's immediate aftermath, he had been preoccupied with pressing, tangible issues. But now, his wife's ringing denunciation and the image of Michael's mutilated corpse forced him to reflect. He turned and looked back at his bleak surroundings. The two new sets of khakis he had bought that morning hung in the otherwise empty closet. "Forty years old . . ." he mused aloud, filled with a sense of abject failure, "and this is what I've got to show for it . . ."

He turned again, and stared back out to sea for several minutes. Finally, he gave an impatient shake of his head. "Chuh!" he said aloud. He crumpled the envelope into a tiny ball, then dropped it into a wicker wastepaper basket and began undressing for bed.

6. AMBERGRIS CAYE

Ramón strolled across the old swing bridge, heading for Battle-field Park. The People's United Party was about to hold its first political rally since the hurricane. It was late afternoon, and the familiar smells of tropical produce and butchered animals wafted across the street from the open market. Ahead, a boisterous crowd overflowed the town plaza. It brought to mind a similar gathering, a decade earlier, which had erupted into a full-scale riot. At issue had been the Crown's devaluation of British Honduras currency.

Ramón stopped in front of the Bank of the Caribbean. The bank was closed, but a light was on in Elijah Ruiz' office. Ramón looked around for a good vantage point from which to watch the proceedings. Across the park, near the Court House stairway, several men readied the PUP sound truck.

A family of Mennonites in a horse-drawn cart passed in front of him. True to their somber religious sect, they stoically stared straight ahead, aloof from the turmoil around them. Their ruddy Germanic features, burned from toiling on their remote farms, contrasted with the animated dark urban mass that filled the plaza. As Ramón watched them cross the swing bridge, the Creole idiom for foreign whites, "bakras", came to mind. It was a jibe at overly-ambitious whites, who foolishly worked in the tropical sun until it burned their "backs raw".

A tattered Mesitzo pushcart vendor approached him. "Fresco, sah?"

Ramón looked down at the filthy cart and started to decline, but the evening was hot. "Yeah, let me have one."

The vendor opened a wooden icebox and pulled back a burlap cloth that covered a small block of ice. He shaved the ice with a metal scoop, until he had enough to fill a paper cone, then drenched it with a thick brown syrup. He reached for a punctured can of condensed milk and brushed away several flies.

"No milk," Ramón said.

The vendor shrugged and handed him the fresco.

"How much?"

"Two coppers, sah."

Ramón gave him two large one-cent pieces.

A familiar voice behind him said, "Just like a day at the circus." Elijah Ruiz descended the bank steps.

"Bigger circuses than this have come to British Honduras, my friend," Ramón replied.

Elijah smiled at Ramón's use of the local adage, which literally referred to a circus that had gone broke in the city decades before, and figuratively expressed skepticism that any major endeavor could ever be successful in the colony.

Ramón took a bite from his shaved ice. "Can I buy you one?"

Elijah shook his head. "Where have you been keeping yourself?"

"I've been busy, getting my office set up again and trucking workers out to our Gallon Jug camp."

"So, back to business as usual."

Ramón nodded, without elaborating. He knew the wily banker was well aware of the difficulties he was having in keeping his mahogany operation solvent. Changing the subject, he said, "I probably won't stay for all the speeches. Will PUP demand that the British get out, as usual?"

"You're in for a surprise," Elijah said with a smile. "George Price plans to announce his new position: PUP will now accept the British proposal for gradual decolonization."

Ramón frowned. "*Gradual* decolonization? PUP has always demanded immediate, outright independence."

Elijah nodded. "Tonight, however, George will begin playing the game by British rules. He will accept their customary, drawn-out schedule for decolonization."

"Why the change in position?"

"Political expediency. George needs to regain the support of the Creole middle-class. His attempts to align us with the Organization of Central American States, rather than with former island colonies like Jamaica and Barbados, have failed."

"I've heard a lot of criticism lately," Ramón said. "Rumors of George having secret meetings with Guatemalan officials and accepting financial backing from them."

Elijah nodded. "The opposition is painting George as a traitor, bent on getting us annexed by Guatemala."

"Any truth to it?"

"Certainly not! You know George, nearly as well as I do. He studied for the priesthood as a young man and is a devout Catholic to this day. The idea of his consorting with communists is nonsense."

"But still," Ramón said, "there are the persistent rumors."

"George broke off negotiations with Guatemala last month, when *Presidente* Fuentes again threatened to cross our border and regain their 'lost province'."

"Is that another reason for keeping the British here?"

Elijah nodded.

"What do the rest of the PUP officials think?"

"It doesn't matter what we think," Elijah said, with a hint of acrimony. "PUP is simply an extension of the will of George Price."

A young voice interrupted them. "Mistah Ruiz! Mistah Kelley!" Tawnya Lightburn waved from across the street. They returned her wave.

"Lovely gyal," Elijah said, as Tawnya started toward them. "You've met her, I take it."

"Yes. She and her grandmother are the people who have been taking care of Bernice Flowers."

"Oh, I didn't realize," Elijah said.

"Hello, mistah Ruiz. Hello, mistah Kelley," Tawnya said with a smile.

"Hello, Tawnya," they responded.

The public address system screeched, and a man at the podium tried to quiet the noisy crowd.

"Ramón, I have to get over there," Elijah said, raising his voice over the hubbub. He started to turn away, but then turned back and said, "Listen, my friend, I'm going out to Ambergris Caye tomorrow afternoon. My wife is already there, and she reports that our house wasn't damaged by the storm. I'm taking several people with me, and there will be musicians and the like. We'll return Sunday night. Why don't you join us?"

"I don't think so, Elijah . . ." Ramón began.

"Come along, mon! We all need to get away from this place."

"Well . . ." Ramón said uncertainly.

"We're leaving from the Custom House wharf at five o'clock. I'll look for you there!" Elijah disappeared into the crowd.

At the podium, George Price stepped to the microphone to a mixed chorus of cheers and catcalls.

"This may not be a safe place to be," Ramón told Tawnya.

"I'm not here for the speeches," she said with a smile. "I work at Brodie's Dry Goods now. I was going home when I saw you standing over here."

Ramón studied her inviting lips and regretted the twenty-year difference in their ages.

"You really should join mistah Ruiz tomorrow, Ramón," she said. "The city is so broke up; it would do you good to get away to the cayes."

"I'll think about it."

She gave him a quick smile, then turned and headed for home.

Ramón watched until she disappeared around the corner. Then he turned his attention back to the podium, where George Price dutifully tried to deliver his prepared speech. However, shouts of "Independence now!" and "Guat communist!" all but drowned him out.

Finally, a dissident near the podium unfurled an American flag, and most of the crowd joined in a chant from the previous decade:

"Dollah fo' dollah, gimmee 'um, gimmee 'um,
Dollah fo' dollah, gimmee 'um, gimmee 'um,
Dollah fo' dollah, gimmee 'um, gimmee 'um, . . . "

'Bigger circuses' Ramón thought, as he turned and headed back to his room at the Fort George Hotel.

The following afternoon, Ramón and a dozen other guests rode in the stern of Elijah's open launch. The hull of the thirty-foot craft pounded against the choppy Caribbean, occasionally sending a fine salt spray over the passengers. An animated rehash of the PUP rally had been underway for the past hour and a half.

Ramón rose from the hard bench, rubbing his backside. "I need to move around." He went forward and gazed out at the horizon. The village of San Pedro on Ambergris Caye came into view.

Elijah joined him. "Almost there, my friend."

Ramón nodded. "Quite a debate you were having back there."

"Why didn't you join in?"

"My Creole's not that good. You folks were speaking much too fast for me."

"I apologize. We forget when we are together that we're speaking a language all our own."

Ramón looked back at the mix of Caribs, Creoles, and Mestizos. "The Creole dialect unites you, doesn't it?"

Elijah reflected a moment. "I suppose you're right . . . at least those of us who live in Belize City. The language we learn in our homes and in the streets does pull us together, more than the language we are taught in school."

They silently watched the approaching caye for a moment, then Elijah said, "Ramón, do you remember the morning after the storm, when I told you that I thought it would be the catalyst for change?"

"Vaguely. Something about whoever acted first would wind up running the country."

"Pretty close," Elijah said with a smile.

"Looks like George Price agreed with you and got started last night."

"He didn't waste any time, did he?" The rancor in Elijah's voice was unmistakable.

"Elijah, what are your reservations about the new PUP policy, and about George himself?"

Elijah sighed. "I think it's a mistake not continuing to press for immediate independence. As for George . . . I'm afraid the Crown is turning him into its kind of man."

In his five years in the colony, Ramón had been too busy struggling with his logging operation to spend much time analyzing the local political intrigues. Now he asked, "And what kind of man is that?"

"An 'enlightened colored man'," Elijah said bitterly, "molded in their own image and likeness. No doubt, in a few years, they'll feel comfortable in turning over the colony to him."

"I still don't understand your concern."

"My concern is that Englishmen will be replaced by light-skinned Creoles. For two hundred years, Creole public servants have learned the ways of the Englishmen, and how to protect their positions, particularly from dark men like myself."

"So what's needed?"

"To be strong," Elijah said, gazing at him intently, "we must unite—Creoles, Caribs, Mestizos, and Maya. If we are not united when the British leave, then we will be vulnerable, not only to Guatemala, but also Mexico. Even the U.S. would be a threat to us. They usually manage to get in the middle of any confusion in Central America."

"Would you like to be prime minister?"

"It is not possible . . . not at this time." Elijah gazed pensively out to sea. "I am too black."

"I don't think—" Ramón began.

"A long time ago," Elijah interrupted, "I developed an understanding of my position. My Carib ancestors were a proud mixture of Africans and South American Indians, who came here from the island of St. Vincent. My father was an ambitious man, but doors were closed to Caribs, so he had to fish for a living. He fished day and night, until he could buy a boat . . . then a next one . . . then a next one. When I was sixteen, he sent me to St. John's College. My father taught me the lesson he had learned, although he didn't know the name for it. It is called 'capitalism'."

Ramón smiled. "Your situation isn't too different from mine, is it?"

"No, it isn't. Like me, you also are unable to participate fully. You have lived your entire life in Central America, but because of your skin color, people here still consider you a 'gringo'."

Ramón chuckled. "So, you're too black, and I'm too white."

Elijah nodded.

"Well," Ramón said, "perhaps we should combine our efforts."

"I would like that, but not in the logging business."

"Why not logging?"

"Wood cutters founded British Honduras, and our forests have sustained us for three-hundred years, but this era is coming to an end."

"I'll admit it's been getting more difficult to find mahogany," Ramón said, "but with modern equipment, companies can log here another fifty years."

"If we were to stay a colony, you may be right. But a national government will be more . . . prudent, than the present colonial one."

Ramón realized Elijah was sharing an insight into the future PUP agenda, and he grew concerned. He had invested the last five years of his life developing his company's logging operation and positioning himself for a partnership.

Elijah continued, "Would you be interested in considering non-logging ventures?"

"Elijah, as much as I respect your opinion, I'm not ready to give up on logging."

Elijah shrugged.

A woman's shout interrupted them. They were within a hundred yards of the caye. Elijah's wife, Esther, happily waved to them from the end of a rickety wooden pier.

That evening, Ramón dozed in a woven cord hammock on the veranda of Elijah's beach house. He was awakened by a young Mestizo couple, returning from a swim. Sitting up, he asked groggily, "What time is it?"

"Half past nine, sah," the young man said.

"Mistah Kelley, will you be joining us at the fiesta?" the young woman said.

Ramón heard the faint strains of music over the steady drone of the wind and sea. He gingerly put his bare feet on the rough wooden floor. "Yeah, I'll see you there."

"See you there!" the young woman echoed as she and her boyfriend banged through the screen door.

Ramón stood up and walked over to the veranda railing to clear his head. His shirt blew open in the soft evening breeze. He heard the sea churning against the barrier reef, a few hundred yards away. The stars in the clear Caribbean sky seemed quite near.

The music grew louder, punctuated by applause. Ramón descended the stairs to the soft sand and walked around to the rear of the house. Flickering kerosene lanterns lighted the area. A crowd of thirty or more people had already gathered for the party. A few danced, but most simply sat beneath the palm trees, listening to a calypso band.

Ramón reached the edge of the crowd. The band finished a song and the audience clapped enthusiastically. The lead singer was a Mestizo who worked at Karl Schrader's airplane hangar. The effeminate young man clearly enjoyed the crowd's response to his ribald songs. As soon as the applause died down, he started another:

"One Sunday mornin' I got up late
A monkey was standin' outside me gate

When I went out to investigate
It started this tale that now I relate
I don't know what to tell this monkey wan' do
I don't know what to tell this monkey wan' do"

Elijah and his wife waved from the other side of the crowd. Ramón returned their wave and leaned comfortably against a coconut tree.

"This monkey now was gettin' me down
So I think that I go see Sally Brown
When I start out and pick up me stride
The monkey was right there by me side
I don't know what to tell this monkey wan' do
I don't know what to tell this monkey wan' do"

A movement to the left of the musicians caught Ramón's attention. Tawnya Lightburn rose from the shadows where she had been sitting. She wore a bright yellow sleeveless blouse and white shorts. Her tan skin glowed in the lantern·light as she approached.

"Hello, Ramón," she said with a mischievous smile.

"Well, hello," he said, returning her smile.

She raised a coconut to her lips and took a sip from a straw. Then she offered it to Ramón.

Putting his hands around hers, he tried the sweet concoction of rum and coconut water.

"I mean I kiss her
The monkey kiss her too . . ."

She put her mouth close to his ear. "I was afraid you had decided not to come."

"I mean we jump bed
The monkey jump bed too . . ."

Ramón responded to her closeness.

"I mean I feel her
The monkey feel her too . . ."

"I fell asleep on Elijah's veranda," Ramón said huskily. "Why didn't you tell me you were going to be out here?"

"I wasn't sure if I could arrange an invitation."

"Who did you come out with?"

"Tony," she said with a smile.

"Tony?" Ramón said, disappointed.

"That Tony," she said, nodding toward the singer. "We went to school together."

"Oh."

She looked up at him with amusement. "I assure you, Ramón, he's not interested in me . . . or any other gyal."

Tony looked at them, as he defiantly sang:

"I mean I FUCK her
The monkey fuck her too . . ."

The crowd had anticipated the final lyrics and roared with delight. Ramón and Tawnya joined the others in the last refrain:

"I don't know what to tell this monkey wan' do
I don't know what to tell this monkey wan' do
I mean I don't know what to tell this monkey wan' do
I don't know what to tell this monkey wan' do!"

Ramón and Tawnya strolled hand in hand along the narrow beach. Behind them, the calypso strains grew more faint. As they entered the outskirts of the tiny fishing village of San Pedro, a voice from a dark veranda greeted them with a friendly, "Good night."

"Good night," they both responded.

Tawnya led him away from the houses. They paused by a bent coconut palm, and Tawnya reclined on its curve. Ramón pressed against her. Just as their lips met, the moon burst from behind a cloud high overhead. Through half-closed eyes, Ramón realized that they were in an old cemetery. He started to pull away to get his bearings.

"Ramón!" she said petulantly, pulling him back to her. They kissed passionately, and she tugged at the clothing between them.

He reluctantly grasped her wrists. "I didn't bring any . . . protection for you."

"We don't need it," she said with a poignant smile.

"We can't risk—"

"There's no risk," Tawnya interrupted. When he didn't respond, she said, "There was a . . . problem when Georgy was born last year. I can't . . . become pregnant again."

He released her wrists and pulled her close. They kissed again. She drew back for a moment. In the moonlight, he saw her white shorts slide down her tan legs to the sand.

The moon was now directly overhead, and Ramón could make out the weathered markers in the tiny cemetery. "I wonder how old these graves are," he said.

"Some are very old," Tawnya said.

Ramón stooped by a mottled stone marker, but the inscription had long since eroded away. "How old do you think?"

"Baymen times." She stooped beside him and kissed the back of his neck.

"When?"

"Baymen times."

"Oh, yes, the baymen." Ramón was familiar with the legendary feats of a handful of Englishmen and a few hundred slaves—forefathers of the Creoles—who had driven off the final Spanish armada at the end of the 18th Century. "You're not afraid of ghosts?" Ramón teased.

"Not the ghosts on this caye."

They stood up. "What ghosts *are* you afraid of?" Ramón said.

Tawnya gazed down the coast for a moment, then said, "I won't go to St. George's Caye."

"Why not?"

"Old Gray Lady."

"Who?"

"Old Gray Lady. And don't you tease me, Ramón!"

"Tell me about her," he said, not sure if she were serious.

"All right. But you don't laugh. If you had grown up here, you would know about her too."

How young she looks, Ramón thought as Tawnya began to recount the tale from her childhood.

"In time past," she said, staring out at the sea, "a mother and father brought their two children to St. George's Caye on holiday. The big storm came, and the children got lost. The father got afraid and sailed away. But the mother stayed to look for them. She stood on the beach, wrapped in a sheet, calling for her children. The waves splashed sand and mud on her. Then the big wave took her."

Tawnya looked at Ramón, who remained solemn. She concluded, "And on stormy nights, on St. George's Caye, you can still hear Old Gray Lady calling her children."

Ramón took her in his arms, as he would a child. "Do you believe this story?"

"Chuh," Tawnya said, drawing back from him. Then she added with an impish smile, "But I never go to St. George's Caye."

Ramón laughed.

"Come along, Ramón!" she said, tugging at his hand.

"Come along, where?" he said, still laughing.

"To our tree! I want a next one."

When they returned to the party, only a few couples remained, reclining in the shadowed seclusion of coconut palms. The musicians had left, except for the singer, who softly strummed his guitar. He nodded to Tawnya and Ramón as they sat down in the sand and leaned against a tree. He began a plaintive song, popular throughout the Caribbean:

"Anything to keep me from sleepin'
A lot of sailor bwys they were leavin'
And everybody there they were jumpin'
To hear the sailor bwys in our chorus singin'
Brown skin gyal stay home and mind baby
Brown skin gyal stay home and mind baby
Poppa's gone away in a sailing boat
And if him don't come back
Stay home and mind baby"

The young Mestizo, who was staying at Elijah's house, left his girlfriend and dropped down beside Ramón and Tawnya. He held up a freshly gathered coconut and a half-empty bottle of rum.

Ramón smiled and nodded.

The young man carved out the coconut eyes with a pocket-knife and poured in a measure of rum.

"The white mon made an invasion,
We thought it was a help to the island
Until they left for home off vacation
They left the native bwy home to mind their children
Brown skin gyal stay home and mind baby . . ."

Ramón and Tawnya each drank from the jagged opening. Ramón nodded his appreciation, and the young man returned to his girlfriend.

"Make I tell you a story 'bout Millie
She made a nice blue eyed baby
They say he fancy the momma
But the blue-eyed baby they know he foddah
Brown skin gyal stay home and mind baby . . ."

Ramón took Tawnya in his arms and leaned back against the tree. The singer stared into the darkness as he sang:

"Now the white mon all had their pleasure
While the music played to their leisure
And everybody there they were jumpin'
To hear the sailor bwys in our chorus singin'
Brown skin gyal stay home and mind baby
Brown skin gyal stay home and mind baby
Poppa's gone away in a sailing boat
And if him don't come back
Throw away that DAMN baby!"

Early the next morning, Ramón stood alone on the veranda of Elijah's beach house, watching the sun rise from the sea. He wore a swimsuit, and a towel hung from his neck. Offshore, an island dweller dived for conchs. A few hundred yards farther, the Caribbean churned against the barrier reef. Ramón shook his head. The cayes were a fisherman's paradise, but no one promoted them.

The screen door behind him opened, and a smiling Elijah stepped onto the veranda. "Good to get away from that Goddamned city, isn't it, Ramón?"

Ramón nodded.

"I'm a bloody fool for not packing my belongings and moving out here permanently," Elijah said.

"And make your living diving for conches?" Ramón said, pointing to the diver.

"Yes, God damn it! I did it before, you know!"

"You were younger then," Ramón said with a laugh. "You'd better stay at your bank desk."

"That's what my wife told me two days ago."

Ramón laughed again, then said, "I was just thinking, Elijah, with a hundred cayes off our coast, there must be at least ten like this one that would be ideal for tourism."

"Possibly, Ramón. But I don't want to see these beaches covered by hotels and the citizens of San Pedro turned into waiters. If we're going to develop tourism, it should be on the mainland."

"Belize City is too dirty," Ramón said. "No one would come there."

"I'm not so sure about that. There's talk that an American named Jack Nicklaus plans to build a golf course to the south of town."

"If he does, he'll regret it. Elijah, to Americans, Belize City is a slum. Plus, it has no beaches. To compete with places like Jamaica and Cayman, resorts would have to be out here on the cayes, or down the coast around Stann Creek."

They were interrupted by the sound of someone pumping water from the rain vat.

"Esther is up," Elijah said. "Let's not talk any more about putting hotels on her lovely island." He clapped Ramón on the shoulder and went back inside.

Ramón descended the wooden stairs and walked across the

damp sand. At the edge of the water, he climbed onto Elijah's pier. Seagulls cried overhead. A pelican, perched on a piling, lunged into ungainly flight as he approached.

Ramón stopped at the edge of a rectangular swimming crawl. A cord net secured the enclosure from man-of-wars and the larger fish. Thin, transparent needlefish darted through the netting. Ramón took a deep breath and dived into the cool green sea.

He surfaced. The salt water blurred his vision, but he caught a brief glimpse of a tan body diving off the ledge toward him. Before he could react, strong fingers dug into his ribs, then playfully pulled at his swimsuit. A laughing Tawnya surfaced.

"Gyal!" he gasped.

"Your brown skin gyal!" she said, then kissed him.

7. RIO SARSTOON

Ramón walked up Marine Parade Street, carrying everything he owned in a single duffel bag. Ahead stood the wood-frame house that would be his new home. A carpenter hammered on the roof. Storm repairs were not quite completed; however, after the expense of three weeks at the Fort George Hotel, Ramón had decided to move in anyway.

He climbed the outside stairway and paused on the veranda. Across the street, the Caribbean lapped at the low seawall. He opened the front door and stepped into the living room. Through a jagged opening in the ceiling, he saw the clear blue sky. The Creole carpenter leaned over the edge and called down, "Mistah Kelley, how you making it?"

"Okay, mon. You keep the rain off me, uh?"

"Yes, sah!" the carpenter said with a laugh.

Ramón entered the bedroom. Its simple furnishings would meet his needs. He dropped his duffel bag onto the bed and walked to the rear of the house.

The kitchen hadn't been damaged. He checked the rusty refrigerator; it was empty, but operating. He rummaged about the cabinets and found that his landlord had provided some mismatched plates and utensils.

A manual water pump stood over the kitchen sink. He tried the handle, and water sputtered up from a large wooden vat in the backyard. In the more affluent neighborhoods, rain water was collected off the corrugated iron roofs. In the poorer areas, people without rain vats had to line up with buckets at community hydrants.

He looked out the window and saw four king vultures perched

on the rooftop next-door. Thousands of these scavengers inhabited the city. Ramón frequently reminded his maids to boil his drinking water, but he knew they seldom did. A local adage said: "Once you have drunk our water, you will always return." Buzzard shit must be addictive, he thought as he put his mouth under the spout and took a drink.

He opened the rear screen door and stepped onto the wide veranda. An enormous scarlet macaw perched on the railing. It eyed him suspiciously and stretched its yellow and blue wings. Next-door, two German shepherds began to bark. The bird fluttered down to the veranda floor and waddled menacingly toward Ramón, barking like a dog.

"Mind the bird, sah!" called down the carpenter. "She don't like no one on her veranda."

Ramón held his ground. As a boy in Panama, he had trapped birds like these to sell to the wealthy. The macaw stopped her ungainly charge in front of him; her head came to his knees. She threateningly flexed her powerful beak. "Pretty girl," Ramón said softly.

The bird barked again and was joined by the dogs below.

"Pretty girl," Ramón repeated, and the bird quieted. He reached down to pet her. She responded with a squawk, but allowed him to stroke her feathers. The dogs quieted.

"That's some girlfriend you're getting here, sah," the carpenter said with a laugh.

"For true, mon. For true."

Ramón stood barefoot in his living room, speaking to his employer on the telephone. "Damn it, Milburn! Don't you Americans realize the condition this place is in? What do you mean, you've moved up our next shipment?"

There was an echo-filled delay in the international telephone line before young Landry's voice came back from New Orleans. "Ramón, we know about the storm damage. But a ship is available at an excellent rate, and we've contracted for it. We only need 500 logs for a shipment."

"Delay it!" Ramón snapped.

"Impossible. It's only available now, and we're saving $30,000. The ship will arrive in Belize City in two weeks. Your shipment of logs has to be ready to go."

"Damn it, Milburn! If the trees are still growing in the jungle, I can't load them onto your God-damned ship! We've got less than 300 logs collected at Burrel Boom."

"I understand that, Ramón. I received your last report. So I've contracted for an additional 200 logs on consignment."

"When are they supposed to arrive at the boom?"

"They won't be delivered to Burrel Boom. They're coming from Guatemala, so they'll be turned over to you on the Sarstoon River."

Ramón shook his head in exasperation. The Sarstoon was 150 miles to the south. He would have only two weeks to send a tug down the coast, raft 200 logs together, and tow them up to the city. Finally he said, "I'll see what I can do."

"We must have a shipment in two weeks," Landry said.

"I'll take the tug down myself. We'll bring up as many as we can."

"I know you'll do whatever is possible, Ramón." The line went silent for several seconds, then Landry's voice came back, "And Ramón, . . . as soon as the ship is loaded . . . we need you up here in New Orleans for a meeting."

Ramón waited for an explanation, but none was offered. "Okay, Milburn," he said, "I'll see you in a couple of weeks."

"Goodbye, Ramón." The line went dead.

Ramón stood staring out the window at the choppy Caribbean.

Tawnya padded barefoot into the living room. "Ramón, you must get rid of that bird."

"What?" he said distractedly.

"I gave her a banana," Tawnya said petulantly, "and she tried to bite me."

"Tawnya, leave that God-damned bird alone! I'm the only one she'll let come near her."

Tawnya pouted. "Whoever heard of a bird that barks like a dog?"

"Tawnya," Ramón said with a sigh, "I've got problems."

"I know. I heard you shouting."

"Then what's this shit about the bird?"

"Foolishness," she said with a laugh, and motioned for him to follow her into the bedroom.

Two days later, Ramón awoke on the aft deck of the Landry Mahogany tugboat. The powerful launch had no sleeping quarters, or even a head. The only enclosed areas were the cramped wheelhouse, forward, and the engine room, below. The aft deck was open and piled high with logging chain.

Ramón sat up and grimaced with a residual headache from breathing diesel fumes. It had rained during the night, and for a brief time he had tried to sleep in the engine room. The morning sea lay calm. He looked toward shore; they were within a quarter-mile of the mouth of the Sarstoon, the river that formed the colony's southern boundary with Guatemala. Over the roar of the twin Caterpillar engines, he heard an unusual knocking coming from beneath the water line.

He got to his feet and picked up the duffel bag he had used for a pillow, then entered the wheelhouse and threw the bag into a corner.

"Good morning, sah!" his Creole captain shouted over the engines. "I'm afraid there is a problem."

"You mean the noise in the stern?"

"Yes, sah. I think the bearing is broke. When we get to the trading post, we must stop and take a look."

"Damn! Robby, if we need to get another tug down here, I need to know right away. We're already working against a tight deadline."

"Yes, sah."

Ramón went over to a pile of old *Clarion* newspapers, grabbed a few pages and stepped outside the wheelhouse. The boat's two

Creole deckhands sat on the bow, watching the approaching shore-line.

Ramón walked over to the leeward side. Clenching the news-paper between his teeth, he dropped his trousers and shorts, and grasped a length of rope tied to the wheelhouse. Securing his feet on the edge of the deck, he lowered the upper part of his body, hand over hand, until his backside skimmed just above the emer-ald-green sea. The deckhands turned and gave friendly waves. Ramón responded with a grudging nod.

When he finished, he struggled to hold his weight with one hand, and quickly used the newspaper with the other. Then he hauled himself back on deck. He pulled up his trousers, just as the boat entered the mangrove swamp at the mouth of the Sarstoon.

A thatched hut, built on pilings, stood nestled in the man-groves. All four members of the Ketchi Indian family who ran the tiny trading post had assembled on its narrow pier. As the tug drew near, the husband and wife smiled and waved. Their teenage daughter and her younger brother caught the mooring lines thrown by the deckhands.

Robby shut down the engines, and the desolate outpost fell silent. Then slowly, the cries of countless birds, hidden in the mangroves, rose to fill the void.

"*¡Capitán! ¡Capitán!*" the young boy cried, as Robby came out of the wheelhouse and stepped onto the pier. Robby stooped and hugged the youngster, then produced chocolate bars for him and his sister.

Ramón stepped off the boat and shook hands with the father. The mother smiled and nodded shyly. "It's been almost two years since I was here," Ramón said. "These can't be the same two chil-dren."

The family, who spoke little English, looked at each other in confusion and talked among themselves in Ketchi. Finally, they grasped his joke and laughed. The mother pantomimed how quickly her two children were growing.

"You . . . come . . . inside?" the father said.

Ramón shook his head. "The boat is . . . broke down."

Robby went back aboard the tug and disappeared into the engine room. He emerged a few moments later, stripped down to his shorts. He sat down on the stern and lowered his feet into the river. There was no mistaking his reluctance to enter the mangrove-blackened water. Finally, with a socket wrench in hand, he eased over the stern.

For nearly a minute, there were only the muffled sounds of Robby working below. Then there was silence. Suddenly he broke the surface, gasping and waving the boat propeller over his head. Ramón grabbed the propeller, and a deckhand took the wrench and three large bolts.

Robby clambered onto the boat. "The bearing was broke down, sah," he said, still gasping for breath. "The casing was cracked. It slip away from me and I lose it, but it could not be fixed."

"Is a new bearing all we need?"

"Just the bearing, sah. The shaft is good."

"Do we have a spare?"

"At the office, sah."

Ramón checked his watch; it was just past 8:00. His clerks should be monitoring the shortwave for the logging camp's morning report.

He went into the wheelhouse and powered up the two-way radio. Keying the transmitter, he called, "Tugboat *Falcon* to Landry Mahogany . . . come in please . . . over."

He turned up the volume on the receiver, but only received static.

He repeated, "*Falcon* to Landry . . . *Falcon* to Landry . . . come in please! Over."

No answer.

"Robby!" Ramón snapped, "did you check out this Goddamned radio before we—"

He was interrupted by the voice of one his clerks, 150 miles away, ". . . hear you, *Falcon*. Over."

"Landry, this is *Falcon*. We're at the trading post on the Sarstoon, and we need a new stern bearing. Over."

"Roger that, *Falcon* . . . at the Sarstoon . . . need a stern bearing. Over."

"Landry, this is *Falcon*. We have a bearing there in the storeroom. Get hold of Karl Schrader. Tell him that I need him to fly it down to me, immediately. This morning! Confirm. Over."

"Roger that, *Falcon*," the clerk responded. "Have mistah Schrader fly the bearing down to you, directly. Over."

"Roger that," Ramón said, feeling a measure of relief. "I want someone to monitor this frequency day and night, until we're underway again. Confirm. Over."

"Roger that, *Falcon*," the clerk responded. "Day and night. Over."

"Roger that, Landry. Out." Ramón powered down the radio and stepped onto the pier. Robby and the two deck hands waited attentively. "It'll be a few hours," Ramón said. "There's nothing we can do until Karl arrives."

"Sah," Robby said, "can we count on mistah Schrader?"

"We have to. There's nobody else who can get an airplane in here."

Ramón awoke with a start; he had been napping in a twine hammock at the rear of the trading post's single room. The sun was now directly overhead, but a cooling Caribbean breeze circulated through the hut's open windows.

The Indian girl sat on the floor, grinding corn on a stone tablet. She was bare to the waist, a custom of Ketchi women when indoors. Her parents slept nearby in another hammock. There had been no other customers that morning; they often went for days without visitors in this desolate region.

Ramón sat up. Through the open door, he saw Robby and the boy fishing from the pier. He checked his watch; three hours had passed since the radio transmission. His mouth was dry, and he scanned the meager supplies that lined the shelves behind the counter: coffee, tea, condensed milk, canned fruit, flour, rice, sugar, salt, powdered milk—all imported, labels written in both Spanish and English. Behind the cracked counter glass lay a sparse assortment of unwrapped bread.

"Do you have something to drink?" he said, pantomiming drinking.

The girl rose, went over to a clay urn, and ladled a milky gruel into a calabash gourd. She shyly brought it to him, then returned to her grinding.

Ramón sat sipping the sweet corn mixture, while he watched her work. The peaceful scene before him, the sea breeze rustling through the thatch, and the birds' muted calls from the mangroves made him sleepy again. He was about to recline back into the hammock, when he heard the faint sound of an engine. The boy jumped up and pointed to the sky. Robby looked back and nodded.

As Ramón stepped through the doorway, a pontoon plane passed noisily overhead. He recognized the silver and black markings of one of Karl Schrader's Cessna-180s. The single-engine aircraft banked over the mangroves and flew upriver, so it could descend into the wind.

Moments later, it set down lightly and taxied up to the trading post. The Ketchi couple secured the airplane to the pier. Schrader shut down the engine, then climbed out of the cockpit and onto a pontoon, holding the new bearing. Robby took it from him, and Ramón helped him onto the pier.

"Glad to see you, Karl," Ramón said. "Thanks for getting down here so fast."

"Certainly, Ramón," Schrader said, looking past him to the young girl. She shyly offered him a gourd of her corn mixture. He shook his head, not taking his eyes off her. Uncomfortable under his intent gaze, she went back into the hut to cover herself.

"I need to come back here again," Schrader said with a malevolent smile. "But today, I have a charter to Campeche. Is there anything else you need, Ramón?"

"No, the bearing should do it. I'll radio the office; they'll have a draft ready when you get back to the city."

"I don't charge you, Ramón. It all evens out."

"We can discuss it when I get back," Ramón said.

Schrader responded with a curt nod and climbed back into the cockpit.

Moments later, the Cessna sped down the river toward the sea, pontoons slamming against the water. Finally it struggled into the air, banked to the north, and flew out of sight.

Ramón stepped onto the tugboat's stern, where Robby and the two deckhands had already assembled. The Ketchi father tied his son's heavy fishing line to a pier piling, and the entire family came over to watch the repair effort.

"All set?" Ramón asked Robby.

Robby, new bearing in hand, nodded uneasily and lowered himself into the murky water. He perched on the rudder for a moment, then took a deep breath and disappeared beneath the surface.

Ramón lay on his stomach, head and arms hanging over the stern. He couldn't see Robby, but he heard the muffled sounds of his working below.

Suddenly Robby broke the surface, pulling himself onto the stern in a single motion. "I have the bearing in place, sah!" he gasped. "I almost dropped the new one. You can't see a bloody thing down there!"

Ramón climbed onto the pier and picked up the loose end of the fishing line. He pantomimed that he needed a three-foot length, and the Ketchi father cut it for him. Ramón tied one end around the propeller blades and the other into a loop.

Robby eased back into the water, and Ramón slipped the noose around Robby's wrist and handed him the propeller. A deckhand gave him a bolt. Robby took several deep breaths, then disappeared beneath the surface again.

The sound of muffled scraping emanated from below; then it stopped. Robby broke the surface, his eyes wide and the propeller and bolt still in his hands. The two deckhands grabbed him and pulled him on board.

"Are you okay?" Ramón said.

"Yes, sah," he gasped, "but I couldn't find the propeller holes. It is too dark down there."

Ramón stood up and stripped down to his shorts.

"Just give me a minute, sah," Robby said, still breathing hard.

"Let me try it," Ramón said. Robby protested, but Ramón eased over the stern. Perched on the rudder, he understood Robby's earlier hesitancy; the mangrove-darkened water was the color of coffee. He took the propeller line from Robby and pulled the noose around his wrist. Then, with the propeller in one hand and a bolt in the other, he took a deep breath and slipped beneath the surface.

He opened his eyes. Although only a few feet under water, he couldn't see the transom. He pulled himself down the rudder until he felt the propeller shaft. Something brushed against the back of his thigh. He froze.

Whatever it was didn't return. Concentrate! he told himself. He slid the propeller onto the shaft and slowly rotated it, while turning the bolt and feeling for threads. His throat contracted. Need air! The threads caught. He managed to give the bolt a complete turn, then in near panic, he fumbled the line loose from around his wrist and shot to the surface.

Robby and the two deckhands pulled him on board. He sat on the stern, gasping for air. "The first bolt's in place . . . barely . . . needs to be tightened down. How many more?"

"Two, sah," Robby said. He picked up the second bolt and lowered himself into the water.

"Robby, wait! There's something down there."

Robby froze. "Sah?"

"It rubbed against my leg. It might have been something floating underwater, but it felt like it was alive."

Eyes wide, Robby looked down at the river.

"I'll go," Ramón said.

"No, sah. It is my time." Robby clambered over the stern and slipped beneath the surface.

Again, muffled sounds emanated from below. Finally, Robby broke the surface and they pulled him on board. "The second one is started, sah. I don't feel nothing down there."

Ramón climbed over the side with the third bolt. He took a deep breath, then lowered himself to the propeller. The bolt started easily. He screwed it in as tightly as he could with his fingers, then tightened down the other two. As he began his ascent, he felt a torrent of water rush past his feet. He shot to the surface.

"Damn it!" he said, as they pulled him onto the deck. "There's something down there!"

They all gazed over the side, as the dark river flowed silently by. Finally, Ramón straightened up. "The bolts are in place, but need to be tightened down."

Robby picked up the socket wrench. "It is my time." He lowered himself into the water, hesitated, and then disappeared beneath the surface.

As Robby ratcheted down the bolts, suddenly the water churned.

"What the hell's that?" Ramón said.

A dark form exploded into the air, twisting and splashing, then disappeared beneath the surface. A moment later, Robby appeared, scrambling onto the rudder. Ramón grabbed him and pulled him onto the fantail. Ashen faced, but unharmed, Robby gazed back at the river.

On the pier, the Ketchi father took several feet of slack out of the heavy fishing line. The water churned again. The dark form twisted into the air, then plunged back into the river. The Ketchi waved off offers of assistance. He positioned the line across his shoulders and behind his head. Then he heaved with his left arm, while he wrapped the slack around a piling with his right. The wet line pressed into his bunched shoulder muscles, as he slowly inched the struggling fish toward the pier. It began to tire and its bursts to the surface grew less frequent. Finally, it quit, and the exhausted Ketchi pulled the enormous black grouper onto the pier.

"Biggest jewfish I ever see," Robby said in awe.

Ramón nodded.

The Ketchi boy leaned down, laughing, then retreated as the fish gave a final, violent thrash. Its mouth gaped open, displaying a cavern large enough to swallow a man's leg. The Ketchi father dispatched it with a single thrust of his machete.

The following morning, Ramón piloted the tug along the Sarstoon, twenty miles upriver from the Ketchi trading post. Robby worked in the engine room below, and the deckhands reclined on the bow. Dense jungle pressed to the river's edge; trees on one bank nearly touched those on the other. Iguanas, four and five feet in length, scurried through the branches, disturbed by the engine noise.

Ramón worried about the tight schedule. As a rule, he avoided doing business with Milburn Landry's Guatemalan suppliers. They usually arrived late and often failed to deliver the contracted number of logs. Ramón estimated he and his crew needed three days to chain 200 logs together, and then a week to tow them down the river and up the coast. The freighter was due in Belize City in ten days. It would be close, but they could make the delivery, if there were no more problems.

His thoughts turned to his upcoming trip to New Orleans, and he recalled his first meeting with the two Landrys, father and son, five years earlier. For some time, their British Honduras subsidiary had been losing money. They still used the techniques developed by the original British settlers: cut the trees down and drag them through the jungle to a river, then raft them to the sea. To be competitive in the future, he would need heavy equipment.

His musing was interrupted by a large iguana racing through the branches on the southern side of the river. It leaped out of the tree, froze for an instant in midair, then landed on an overhanging limb on the northern side. Ramón smiled. You're now a British subject, my friend.

The smile faded, as he resumed his contemplation. The Landrys had signed him to a five-year contract and had promised to invest capital to modernize their logging operation. The contract called for him to receive a twenty-five percent partnership in their British Honduras subsidiary, if he could turn a profit with it. Over the past five years, he had produced a thirty-one percent return, despite their not having supplied the promised capital.

The upcoming meeting in New Orleans apparently was to negotiate his new contract. Somehow, he needed to convince them to put money into the operation. Production costs had risen, and would continue to rise, particularly in light of Elijah's prediction of future governmental restrictions.

Robby entered the wheelhouse. "Everything's fine down below, sah."

Ramón nodded and relinquished the wheel. "The boom's just up ahead, isn't it?"

"Yes, sah."

They rounded a bend; a lagoon lay off the left. Ramón took one look at the logs clustered against the far bank and shook his head in disgust. "Damn these people!"

"No more than a hundred logs there, sah," Robby said.

A stocky Indian, clad only in tattered trousers, watched from the river bank. The tug gently ran aground, and the two deckhands leaped into the shallow water and secured it to two trees. The Indian made no move to help.

Ramón jumped off the boat and approached him. *"¿Hablas español?"*

The Indian nodded that he spoke Spanish

"How many logs do you have?" Ramón said.

"I don't know," the Indian said.

"Where is the boat that brought them?"

"Gone. Now I go too." He climbed into a dugout and paddled away.

"As usual," Ramón said angrily to Robby, "when they're short on the count, the bastards leave an Indian behind, and the rest go upriver and hide."

"They don't want to face you, sah," Robby said, as the Indian disappeared around the river bend.

"All right," Ramón said with a resigned shake of his head, "let's get started. I want to get underway at first light tomorrow. Robby, get me a log count. You guys, start the chaining."

Robby walked out onto the floating logs. The two deckhands returned to the tug. One unfastened a long pole from the wheelhouse roof, then jumped into the water and waded out to the logs. The other opened a hatch and piled ten-inch spikes onto the aft deck. Four-inch rings dangled from the spikes' blunt ends.

Robby called out from the far end of the lagoon, "I only count seventh-two, sah!"

"Bastards!" Ramón said.

Robby crossed back to where Ramón stood. "But at least they are big ones, sah."

Ramón nodded. Most of the half-submerged logs had at least three feet of mahogany exposed above the water.

The deckhand in the river had climbed onto the first log. He stood up and poled it over to the tug. The deckhand on the stern, using the flat end of a wedge ax, hammered a spike into the top of the log, close to one end. Then he fastened a heavy logging chain to the ring.

The man in the water returned with the second log. After he had spiked it, he threaded the chain through the ring. "You want ten across, sah?" he asked Ramón.

"Make it seven, since they're big and we've got so few."

Ramón went on board the tug and returned with a pole and an ax. Handing the ax to Robby, he dropped into the water and waded out to the logs.

Night had fallen. The neatly rafted logs now tailed behind the tug, ready for the morning trip down river.

Ramón finished hanging a set of khakis on a makeshift clothesline in the wheelhouse. He had washed his clothes in the river, Indian fashion, while he bathed. Robby and the two deckhands sat around a campfire on the bank. Their shadows danced against the black backdrop of the jungle, and their muffled conversation blended with the sounds of birds and insects, hidden by the darkness.

Ramón jumped off the boat and approached the fire. He smelled an unwelcome odor and looked over Robby's shoulder. Iguana strips sizzled in the pan.

"The bwys catch two, sah," Robby said with a smile.

"What a day, mon!" Ramón said. "First the Guats fuck me, and now you're going to feed me 'bamboo chicken'!"

Robby laughed, then turned serious and asked, "What you think is going on, sah?"

"I don't know what to make of it, Robby. The Guatemalans have been short before, but never by this much."

Robby dished up the iguana and slices of fried breadfruit on metal plates. The four men ate with their fingers, washing down the meal with rain water brought from the city.

When they had finished, Robby asked, "How was the 'chicken', sah?"

Ramón belched. "I think I prefer fish for breakfast tomorrow."

A week later, Ramón and Robby stood in the wheelhouse. Ramón squinted into the bright morning sun, as the tug labored across the placid Caribbean, the log raft trailing lazily behind it.

The freighter loomed ahead, anchored near low-lying Drowned Caye. Since Belize City had no deep-water harbor, logging ships used this offshore mangrove swamp as a staging area. One of the freighter's booms swung over the side with a loud groan.

Ramón said, "Looks like they're already loading the logs from Burrel Boom."

"Sah," Robby said, "that ship looks bad."

Ramón nodded; he had been thinking the same thing. The name on the rusty bow was indistinguishable; a tattered and faded Panamanian flag flew from the mast.

"It looks like the ships that mistah Landry used before you took over, sah," Robby said.

They approached the ship from the windward direction and pulled alongside the Burrel Boom rafts.

A light-skinned Creole ran across the logs toward them, shouting, "Mistah Kelley, sah!"

"It's Clifton, sah," Robby said.

Ramón noted a hint of disdain in Robby's voice. Clifton was the young clerk Ramón had promoted to replace Michael Flowers. It would take time for the workers to accept him. A deckhand threw the bow line to Clifton, who secured it to a raft chain.

Ramón climbed over the side of the tug and onto the raft. "How's everything back at the office?"

"Fine, sah!"

"How many logs did you bring out?"

"The final count was 287, sah."

"How long have you been loading?"

"Since yesterday morning."

"Are you having problems?" Ramón said, nodding toward the listing ship.

"Yes, sah. One boom is broke down. Sah, why are we using such an old ship?"

"I don't know, Clifton."

Ramón walked across the raft to the ship. He paused at the foot of the boarding ladder, as the boom lifted a huge log from the water and slammed it against the hull. It teetered precariously, then tumbled over the side and rumbled into the hold.

The captain waited for him at the top of the ladder, his uniform as shabby as his ship. *"¿Señor Kelley?"*

"Sí, soy Ramón Kelley." They shook hands.

"I am Luis Hernandez," the captain said in Spanish. "I understand you only have seventy-two logs."

Ramón nodded, then replied in Spanish, "The total will be 359, not the 500 we had planned. How many have you loaded so far?"

"About fifty."

"Load my raft next, before we bring any more out of the caye." The captain nodded.

"How long before you can get underway?"

"Probably, day after tomorrow. We only have one boom working."

"How many trips have you been contracted for?"

"Just this one."

Ramón eyed the derelict freighter. Why had the Landrys interfered in his operation?

8. BAYOU ROADS

Ramón stepped outside the terminal building of New Orleans' Moisant Airport. He hesitated, letting his eyes adjust to the darkness and the flickering fluorescent lights that illuminated the passenger pickup area. Rain fell in a steady drizzle.

A Yellow Cab waited at the curb. Ramón started forward, but a man and woman pushed past him and climbed into the back seat. The driver leaned over and lowered the passenger-side window a few inches. "You goin' downtown, mister?" he said, in an accent that sounded more Brooklyn than southern.

"No," Ramón said, glaring at the couple in the back seat, "I'm going out to Harahan."

The driver rolled up the window, and drove off into the night. The taxi lane was empty, except for an old maroon Chevrolet, down at the far end of the terminal. Ramón saw a driver sitting behind the wheel and waved him forward. The car didn't move. Ramón waved again. The driver picked up a newspaper and put it in front of his face.

"God-damned Americans," Ramón muttered. He walked down to where the car was parked. "Ed's Cab" was stenciled in white on the side. Ramón opened the back door, threw his duffel bag onto the seat, and piled in after it. The black driver turned and stared at him. "I need to go to Harahan," Ramón said.

"This is a colored cab," the driver responded sullenly.

"It's a what?"

"A colored cab."

Ramón shook his head in disbelief.

"This cab is for colored folks only," the driver said. "You have to get a white cab."

Rain pounded on the roof. Ramón looked down the still empty taxi lane, then back to the driver. "I'm a British Honduran. It's okay for us to ride in colored cabs."

"You a what?"

"I'm not an American. I just look and sound like one. Now, take me out to Harahan . . . over by the Mississippi River bridge."

The driver scowled, then turned and checked the deserted terminal entrance. Apparently deciding to risk the fare, he started the engine and pulled away from the curb.

Ramón settled back in the worn seat and gazed out the side window. The heavy nighttime traffic along the gaudy motel-row was unsettling. Driving on the right side of the road also seemed unnatural.

The driver turned off the Airline Highway and onto a side street. They entered an old neighborhood, jammed with narrow wood-frame houses. The few residents out on the street were black. Americans probably consider this a slum, Ramón thought, but not by British Honduras standards.

The neighborhood street turned into open road, and the driver picked up speed. Ramón stared into the darkness, his thoughts drifting to the upcoming meeting.

The Landry Mahogany Company's annual budget meeting had prompted his last visit to the States, eight months ago. The Landrys had received him warmly and given him full credit for the success of their British Honduras subsidiary. This current trip was not part of the annual schedule, and Milburn Landry's recent communications had not been warm.

As the cab sped along the deserted road, Ramón wrestled with his ongoing problem: how to produce more mahogany, despite diminishing resources and outdated equipment.

Finally, the driver interrupted his musing. "We're almost to the bridge."

The rain had stopped. Ramón saw the Landry Mahogany Company entrance up ahead. Floodlights illuminated the rear of the facility. The sawmill was in operation. A ship, probably the

Panamanian freighter, unloaded logs from its Mississippi River mooring.

"Give a bend here, bwy," Ramón said as they neared the entrance.

"What?"

Without thinking, Ramón had addressed the black man in Creole patios. "I mean . . . turn in here," he said.

The driver turned, then stopped at the guard house that stood in the middle of the plant driveway. A fat Jefferson Parish deputy sheriff, moonlighting as a gate guard, sauntered over to the cab. He shined a flashlight in the driver's face. "What you want, boy?"

"I got a fare for here."

The deputy shined the light in the back seat.

Ramón shielded his eyes. "I'm Ramón Kelley. I work for Landry."

"Put your hand down. Who you say you are?"

"Ramón Kelley. I work for Landry."

"I ain't never seen you before," the deputy said suspiciously.

"I don't work here at the plant," Ramón said, squinting into the light. "I work in British Honduras."

"Where you say you work, boy?"

"British Honduras!" Ramón said, growing exasperated.

The deputy yanked open the back door. "Don't get huffy with me, boy!"

The driver eased the gear shift into reverse.

"Wait," Ramón said, putting his hand on the driver's shoulder.

"Get out of that car!" the deputy ordered.

Ramón grabbed his duffel bag and stepped outside. The deputy flicked off the flashlight and shifted it in his hand, holding it like a club. The driver slowly backed the cab away from the guard house.

"Hold on!" Ramón said, reaching for his wallet.

The driver paused, looking back and forth between Ramón and the deputy. The deputy gave a subtle gesture with his flashlight. The driver backed into the intersection, turned, and disappeared down the Jefferson Highway.

The deputy sneered. "Looks like you're going to have to walk back to wherever it is you say you come from, boy."

Ramón shook his head in frustration.

The deputy took a step toward him. "Now, boy, I'm gonna tell you one time . . . get yo' ass outta here!"

"Call the operations supervisor," Ramón said. "Or if one of the Landrys is here, call him."

A look of uncertainty crossed the deputy's face, and he stopped hefting the flashlight.

"Is one of the Landrys here?" Ramón demanded.

The deputy nodded, barely perceptively.

"Is it Milburn?"

The deputy nodded again.

"Call him."

The deputy went into the tiny guard house. He picked up the phone and dialed. After a moment, he said into the mouthpiece, "Mr. Landry? Sir, I got a feller out here, says he's from . . . British Hindu . . . and that he works for you."

"Give me the phone!" Ramón said, snatching it out of the deputy's hand. "Milburn, this is Ramón. Tell this ignorant son of a bitch to let me in!"

The deputy glared, but took the receiver when Ramón thrust it back at him. "He do, huh. Okay, sir . . . I just wanted to be careful, you know."

Ramón picked up his duffel bag and started down the drive toward the plant.

"What was you doing in a Ed's Cab?" the deputy called after him. "That's a colored cab."

Ramón kept walking.

"Well, at least I saved you the fare, huh?" the deputy said, hoping to get a laugh.

Ramón ignored him. The cab driver hadn't wanted to pick him up in the first place. Ramón regretted sticking him for the fare.

He continued up the rain-slick drive. A huge metal building loomed to his left. The screams of sawmill equipment echoed into the night. Up ahead, he saw the derelict Panamanian freighter, unloading logs by floodlight. He turned up the sidewalk that led to the company's one-story office building.

Milburn Landry stepped through the doorway. The short humorless man attempted a smile as they shook hands. "Sorry about the mix-up out there, Ramón. I would have left word with the guard, but I wasn't expecting you until tomorrow morning."

"I figured you'd probably be out here unloading the ship," Ramón said, "so I thought I'd check in."

"I was just about to take a walk down there and see how it's going."

"I'll join you," Ramón said, setting his bag inside the office door.

"Where are you staying?" Landry said as they started toward the river.

"Probably at that motel down the highway. I planned to have my cab driver wait for me, but that idiot at the gate ran him off."

"Ran him off?"

"Yeah. He got bent out of shape because I arrived in an Ed's Cab."

"What the hell were you doing in a colored cab?"

Ramón frowned at his employer. "Milburn, if you'll recall, I come from a 'colored' country."

A look of annoyance crossed Landry's face, but he didn't reply. A ripsaw engaged in the sawmill, preventing further conversation.

They arrived at the river bank. Ramón frowned. He'd never seen the holding lagoon so filled with logs.

The freighter rode at anchor about fifty yards offshore. The ship's single boom pulled a log from the hold, hoisted it over the side, and released it into the river. Two men in an outboard moved forward and secured it with a grappling iron. As they approached the lagoon, the log caught the current and broke free, almost capsizing the boat. It took several minutes for the men to recapture the log and herd it into the lagoon.

Landry shook his head. "Tough way to make a living."

Ramón responded with a tight smile, wondering if the log, giving so much trouble to two men with an outboard on the Mississippi, was one that he moved by pole on the Sarstoon. "Are you about through unloading?"

"No, they had engine problems crossing the Gulf. We just got started this evening."

"Where did all these other logs come from?"

"Most are from the Philippines; we received a shipment last week. The rest came in from Africa, the week before." Landry turned abruptly and started back up the drive.

Ramón caught up with him. "What time's the meeting tomorrow?"

"Eight o'clock. I've got some work I need to do before I leave. Do you mind taking a cab to your motel?"

"Cab's fine."

"I'll call one for you from the office."

As they approached the sawmill, Ramón detoured off the roadway and stopped in the brightly lit entrance. The shrill screams of the equipment hurt his ears. On his immediate left, a circular saw quarter-sliced a twenty-foot log. On his right, an enormous lathe pealed off thin sheets of mahogany veneer. The familiar odor of freshly cut mahogany filled his nostrils. He noticed the duplicate pieces of equipment in the rear of the building were idle. Ramón frowned. The lagoon was full, but Landry wasn't running a full shift.

Landry had continued toward the office building. "Milburn!" Ramón shouted. "Why did we contract for that floating piece of shit out there, when we already had so much wood and we're obviously not in a hurry to cut it?"

Without breaking stride, Landry called back, "Economics, Ramón. You'll get the details at tomorrow's meeting."

At 8:15 the following morning, Ramón waited in the company conference room. The Landrys were late. He took a sip from his coffee and grimaced at the biting chicory taste.

Footsteps echoed down the hallway. Moments later, Milburn Landry entered the room, followed by two other men: Jack Hanson, the plant supervisor, and Max Stein, the company attorney.

"Well, look who crawled out of the jungle!" Hanson boomed. He walked around the table and thrust out his hand.

"Hello, Jack," Ramón said, forcing himself to be cordial. The blustery southerner made three or four trips to Belize City each year, supposedly to measure timber. However, he spent most of his time in the town's dingy bars, pursuing local women. He showed little respect for the black colony's people or their customs. Ramón's staff usually wound up doing the work that Hanson had been sent to do, while he pursued liaisons forbidden in Louisiana. Occasionally, Ramón had to spend his own time smoothing over Hanson's indiscretions.

"Hello, Ramón," Stein said from across the table.

"Hello, Max." The dour attorney always reminded Ramón of an undertaker.

"Well, let's get started," Landry said.

"Will your father be joining us?" Ramón said.

"Dad's in Cleveland." Landry took a deep breath. "Ramón, we're closing down the British Honduras operation. Max will go down next week to conduct an inventory and oversee the disposal of assets."

Ramón stared at Landry in disbelief. Landry looked away. Ramón turned to the operations supervisor.

"Sorry, Ramón," Hanson said. "I'll really miss that place."

Ramón looked over to the attorney, who stared back impassively.

Ramón turned back to Landry and said bitterly, "So you had me squeeze out one final shipment, huh, Milburn?"

Landry didn't respond.

"Why, Milburn?" Ramón pressed, his anger building. "Why shut it down now? I've got that operation running in black. Invest in the proper equipment, and we can log there for another twenty years!"

Landry shifted uncomfortably in his chair. "Due to the political instability down there, I've decided to get out."

"Political instability! British Honduras has the most stable government in Central America!"

Landry said haltingly, "I believe the British are about to pull out . . . and I don't think the colored people there have what it takes to govern."

"Have what it takes to govern!" Ramón exploded. "Milburn, do you read the God-damned newspapers? Last year, that half-wit you people elected governor of Louisiana, and call 'Uncle Earl', was wandering around Tijuana, Mexico, trying to adopt whores."

Landry lapsed back into stony silence.

Ramón struggled to regain control of his temper. "Your father has taken risks in Central America in the past, and now he's making money. I can't believe he's suddenly lost his nerve and wants to get out. I want to talk to him."

The company attorney interjected, "The elder Mr. Landry's role is now strictly an advisory one. Legally, Milburn has had the sole authority for running the company for the past six months."

The disclosure surprised Ramón. After a long pause he said, "What about my contract?"

"Your contract calls for you to receive twenty-five percent of the British Honduras operation," Landry said. "As of now, there is no British Honduras operation."

"When was the decision made to close it down?" Ramón demanded.

Landry didn't answer.

Ramón shook his head. That son of a bitch! He'd decided to renege on my contract as soon as he took over. "What are you offering me in the way of a financial settlement?"

The attorney interjected again, saying, "None is required."

Ramón took a deep breath, having difficulty containing his rage. Finally he said, "You're both aware that I've taken far less than the salary I was entitled to, with the understanding that I'd be given a partnership if I met the terms of the contract. Well, I've met those terms. And now you're saying you have no financial obligations?"

The attorney responded firmly, "The Landry Mahogany Company has no obligations to you."

The young owner rose. "I believe that's all we have to discuss."

"Our next discussion is going to be in court," Ramón snapped.

"Litigation in British Honduras will accomplish nothing, Ramón," the attorney said over his shoulder, as he followed the two other men out of the room.

The following afternoon, Ramón stared out the window of a Greyhound bus. A sign on the shoulder of the two-lane highway read, "Hammond - 15 Miles". The name of his wife's hometown contrasted with the French names of the bayou communities he had seen on the mileage markers: Vacherie, Thibodaux, Plaquemine, Maurepas . . .

The bus passed over the bridge that spanned Bayou Manchac. The scene prompted him to think of his father. At the turn of the century, Patrick Kelley had built bridges in southern Louisiana, Mississippi, and down into Florida. Then in 1908, at the age of fifty, he had gone to Panama to work on the Canal. He had married a young Panamanian woman, Ramón's mother, and had never returned to the United States. He had been an uncommunicative man, and now Ramón wondered if his father had ever crossed Bayou Manchac.

The Hammond city limits sign brought him out of his musing. The bus sped past the car dealerships, junk yards, and drive-ins on the outskirts of town, then rumbled through the four-block business district. It turned down a side street. Ahead stood a beige stucco bus station, with two front doors. Over one, a sign read "White"; over the other, a sign read "Colored".

The bus pulled into the dusty parking lot behind the station. Ramón saw his in-laws' station wagon parked off to the side. His wife got out on the driver's side and scanned the bus windows. When she saw him, she gave a hesitant wave.

Ramón stood up and reached for his duffel bag on the overhead luggage rack. An elderly black couple, who had been assigned seats in the rear of the bus, stood in the aisle, patiently waiting. Ramón gave them enough room to pass, but they didn't move. He pulled down his bag and made his way to the door.

Kay waited for him at the bottom of the stairs. "What are you doing in a short-sleeved shirt?"

Ramón gave her an awkward hug, and they walked toward the car.

"Aren't you cold?" she said.

"Yeah, it's a little chilly. I meant to pick up a jacket in New Orleans, but I got busy."

"Did you forget to bring yours?" she said as she went around to the driver's side.

"I lost it in the hurricane, along with everything else." He threw his bag onto the back seat and got into the car.

They pulled away from the bus station. "How bad was it, Ramón? The Landry people notified me as soon as they knew you were all right, but I never got any details."

They headed down a magnolia-lined neighborhood street. "The house was destroyed," Ramón said, "and Michael Flowers drowned."

"The Landry people told me about poor Michael," she said sympathetically. "How did it happen?"

"He and his family were riding out the storm with me, and Michael was swept away." Ramón realized his responses were curt, but so much had happened since the night of the storm, he felt as if he was recounting a tragic event that had taken place years before.

"What about his family?"

"Bernice had a complete breakdown. Even after we found the body, she couldn't accept the fact he was dead. She kept wandering the streets, looking for him. Finally, they had to confine her."

"Oh, no. And her baby?"

"Foster home."

"Oh, dear."

They stopped behind a yellow school bus and waited as a dozen or so youngsters burst from the side door and scattered across the neighborhood yards. The simple scene impressed Ramón; he thought how lucky American children were, to be taken to and from school.

They drove on in silence for another two blocks. Then Kay said, "Mom and Dad have gone down to Grand Isle for a couple of days. They thought we'd need some time alone to work out what we're going to do."

"Kay, I may not be able to send you as much money as I have been . . . at least for a while. Landry fired me yesterday."

"Ramón! Can they do that?"

"They think they can."

"Don't you have a contract or something?"

"I thought I had one," he said bitterly.

"Do you have any recourse?"

"I met with a lawyer in New Orleans this morning. He thinks I have grounds to sue, but he's not confident enough to take it on a contingency basis."

"What about you? Do you think you can win?"

"I don't know, but I'm going to try. And I've decided to raise the stakes. I'm going to file suit here in the States."

"Here?"

Ramón nodded. "My chances of winning would probably be better in Belize City. I'm well-known, and taking on a large American company might get me some sympathy in the courts there. But if I won, I'm afraid a judgment wouldn't amount to much."

"Why not?"

"Jurors there wouldn't understand the amount of money I'd be asking for." He gave a wry shake of his head. "Our largest denomination of currency is a $10 bill, remember?"

Kay turned down the quiet tree-lined street where her parents lived. "When do you think your case will come to trial?"

"My lawyer said he'd try to accelerate things, but it may take a year or more."

"What are you going to do in the meantime?"

"I don't know. Somehow, I've got to raise the money for the legal fees. But to tell you the truth, Kay, right now . . . I'm kind of lost. I really don't know what the hell I'm going to do."

They pulled into the shaded drive of her parent's home. Kay shut off the engine and turned toward him. "Ramón, I know the timing's bad, but there's something I have to tell you."

Divorce, Ramón thought, remembering the letter she had written the night of the storm.

"I'm pregnant," Kay said.

They sat in silence. Ramón gazed out the window. A half-block away lay the college where Kay's father taught. The campus looked deserted; apparently classes had already let out for the Christmas holidays. "Are you going to have it?" he said.

"Of course I'm going to have it!" she said indignantly. "What are you thinking?"

Ramón heaved a sigh of relief. "Your letter . . . I was afraid you might be considering . . ."

"Don't be ridiculous!"

"Will you come back to British Honduras?"

"Absolutely not. Ramón, I've done a lot of thinking. I still love you . . . but I can't go back there again. It's like a prison for me . . . I just can't go back."

"I know that the Tropics are tough on American—" Ramón began, but caught himself.

They sat in silence again. Finally Kay said, "You're not tied to Landry Mahogany now. Why not get a job here?"

"Kay, I was awake most of the night, considering doing that . . . at least while I wait for my lawsuit. But I can't. I'd be as out of place here, as you are in British Honduras. Hell, I almost started a race riot last night over a cab ride."

She frowned.

"There's something else," Ramón said. "I don't expect you to understand it . . . I'm not sure I do myself. He hesitated, then continued, "I've spent my whole life in the Tropics. I know it's harsh down there, but it's . . . it's my life."

Kay responded with a restrained smile.

"Do you want a divorce?" Ramón said.

"Do you?" she countered.

"No."

"Then let's leave things as they are for now."

Ramón reached for her hand. "Kay, I'm *glad* we're having a baby."

"*I'm* having the baby," she said, pulling her hand away. "You're going back to British Honduras, remember?"

Ramón smiled. Kay's assertiveness had returned, now that she was back in familiar surroundings. "It may be a couple of months before I can send you any money," he said.

"I can stay here with Mom and Dad until the baby arrives, but then I'll need my own place."

Ramón nodded.

They sat in silence for a long time. The late fall breeze rustled through the trees. Finally Ramón said, "I need to get back home as soon as possible."

"There's a bus back to New Orleans in less than an hour."

Ramón settled back in the seat, and Kay started the engine.

Ramón gazed out the window, as the TACA Airlines DC-3 lined up on Belize City's single runway. Just before they touched down, he caught a glimpse of the usual handful of British soldiers, patrolling the fence between the airport and the army camp.

The airplane landed with a series of bounces, then reverberated as they rolled down the cracked tarmac. They stopped directly in front of the beige terminal building, and the Mexican pilot revved his engines as if to announce their arrival. The sign over the terminal building entrance read: British Honduras International Airport. Ramón smiled. They were definitely behind the times. Only a single door for both whites and coloreds.

A few minutes later, a blast of tropical air buffeted him as he stepped onto the portable stairway. He smiled when he saw Tawnya Lightburn, wearing a bright yellow dress, push her way through the crowd gathered at the entrance.

She met him at the bottom of the stairs with a firm kiss. "Why are you back so soon?" she asked with a laugh. "Did you miss me too much?"

"Did my house burn down while I was gone?" he asked in mock seriousness.

"No," she said with a frown.

"Are we at war with the Guats?" he said, encircling her waist and guiding her toward the terminal building.

"I don't think so," she said, wrestling his duffel bag from him.

"And do you have money for a taxi to get us to town?"

"I have a few shillings," she said with a saucy smile.

"Then, make we go, gyal!"

9. GALLON JUG

Ramón was alone in the Landry Mahogany office, loading his personal belongings into a cardboard box. In the distance, St. John's cathedral bells called Anglican parishioners to Sunday morning worship.

Footsteps thumped up the outside stairway, then across the veranda. Someone fumbled with a key in the lock and the outer office door flew open. Max Stein, the Landry attorney, hesitated in the doorway.

"Come in, Max," Ramón said. "I'm done here."

Stein crossed the room and glanced into the box. "Your attorney contacted us on Friday. We were surprised you decided to file suit in New Orleans."

It was more a question than a statement, and Ramón chose not to respond.

"Milburn and I have discussed the possibility of a settlement," Stein said.

"Did you discuss a figure?" Ramón said, masking his keen interest.

Stein cleared his throat. "Milburn has agreed to . . . $10,000." The attorney squinted shrewdly at Ramón, awaiting his response.

"Ten thousand, U.S.?"

"No, B.H.."

"That's $5,000 U.S.," Ramón said, "or about $1,000 per year." Stein nodded.

"I'll settle for $25,000—U.S.," Ramón said.

"Out of the question!"

"I'd have cost you an additional $5,000 a year in salary, if you hadn't promised me the partnership."

"Milburn will never approve a cash settlement even close to that figure."

"Then we'll go to court," Ramón said. He picked up the cardboard box and dropped the office keys onto the desk.

Ramón and Elijah stood at the banker's second-floor office window, watching the Monday morning activity around Battlefield Park.

"So, Landry has offered to settle," Elijah said.

"For twenty cents on the dollar," Ramón said bitterly.

"Well, at least, they're thinking settlement."

"Probably thought I was so hard up that I'd jump at their offer."

"Are you?"

"Hard up? Yeah . . . I'm pretty hard up. Forty is damned old to be starting over in the Tropics, unless you've got some capital. For the past five years, all my time and energy has gone into making their God-damned logging operation profitable. If I'd have known that Milburn had gained control of the company, I'd have positioned myself differently."

"So, you may have to accept their offer."

Ramón didn't respond.

"Any other prospects?"

"That's what I wanted to talk to you about this morning," Ramón said. "I understand that Brandon Morrow has gone back to England."

"Yes, apparently for good. He left last week, while you were in the States."

"Probably the best thing for him."

Elijah nodded. "His drinking got out of hand after his wife left. It's a shame; Hawkesworth Distributors went to a lot of trouble to recruit him."

"He's not the first foreigner we've seen screw up his life here. We send 'em back, don't we, Elijah?"

"Yes, Ramón, we send them back."

"Do you think I might be able to land the job?"

"Managing the dealership?" Elijah said, obviously surprised. "Well . . . possibly. However, I believe they were only paying Brandon about $1,000 a month—B.H."

The figure was half what Ramón had been paid by Landry. While it would cover his local expenses, it wouldn't be enough to support Kay in the States. However, it might tide him over until he settled his lawsuit. "I'd like the job," he said.

"You're sure?"

In the street below, tattered pushcart vendors filed down Albert Street, hawking oranges, mangos, and papayas. "Damn it, Elijah," Ramón said, "I'd rather push one of those carts down there, than let that son of a bitch get off with the settlement he's offering!"

Elijah gazed down at the street for a moment, then turned and said, "The profits of Hawkesworth Distributors have been marginal for several years now, and my bank has been underwriting them for the past two. With the luck they've had with English managers, I think that I can persuade them to try a sober Central American."

"Thanks, Elijah," Ramón said as they shook hands.

Ramón pulled his blue International Harvester pickup truck into the Fort George Hotel parking lot. The stencil on the truck door read "Hawkesworth Distributors". He entered the lobby and returned a wave from the Creole desk clerk. He mounted a short flight of stairs and walked down a long hallway to the hotel lounge.

The bar area was filled with a mix of browns, blacks and whites, as it had been each afternoon since the storm had leveled the Pickwick and Belize clubs. Hurricane Hatti had torn down the last vestiges of the colonial caste system.

Ramón searched the room and spotted Max Stein, seated at a table overlooking the swimming pool. As he crossed the room, a voice from the bar called his name. Karl Schrader, disheveled as usual, slouched on a stool at the end of the bar. "I'll be with you in a minute, Karl," Ramón said.

When he reached Stein's table, the attorney didn't extend his hand, just smiled dourly and said, "I appreciate your joining me on short notice, Ramón."

As Ramón sat down, he noticed one of his manila office folders lying on the table. He couldn't make out the label. "How did your inventory go, Max?"

"It all went fine, Ramón. Everything was in order. It's a shame Milburn didn't transfer you to one of our other foreign operations; you're a damned good manager."

Ramón thought the comment strange, coming from a man who would be disputing just that issue in court.

"While I've been down here this week," Stein said, "I formed an idea for a possible settlement. I've cleared what I'm about to propose with Milburn." He tapped the manila folder with a bony forefinger.

Ramón leaned forward; however, a young Creole waitress interrupted them.

"Hello, mistah Kelley."

"Hello, Marva," Ramón said. "What'll you have, Max?"

"Plain tonic water, please."

"And the usual club soda and lime for you, mistah Kelley?"

Ramón nodded and the waitress left.

Stein squinted across the table. "Few men can take this place sober, Ramón."

"You were about to make me an offer, Max."

"The situation is this. Milburn wants to get out of this country, and you apparently plan to stay. We're prepared to offer you Landry's seventeen-acre parcel in Stann Creek Town for a settlement."

Now Ramón recognized the file; he had acquired the Stann Creek property, on behalf of Landry Mahogany, four years earlier.

"Of course," Stein continued, "we'll require a guarantee that you'll make no future claims."

Ramón studied the offer. He had purchased the land for $9,000, U.S.; it now was worth at least twice that much.

"I had the property appraised this week," Stein said, as if reading his thoughts. "Its present value is about $21,000, U.S.."

Ramón's mind raced, looking for pitfalls, while exploring the possibilities. Milburn Landry apparently thought Ramón had a good chance of winning his lawsuit. Assuming that Landry was truly pulling out of British Honduras, he may have decided to make this offer, both to resolve the suit and to quickly dispose of the land. Property moved very slowly in the colony.

"I realize you'll need time to think it over," Stein said.

Ramón sensed an opportunity was at hand. Both local political parties promised to develop industry and promote tourism. The Stann Creek property was on the southern coast and was accessible by the Hummingbird Highway. When he had bought the land, he felt it would be an ideal site for a sawmill, or perhaps even tourism.

The waitress returned. While the attorney paid for the drinks, Ramón considered the drawback to the offer: the land was a long-term investment and his obligations in Louisiana would soon require ready cash. But, on the other hand, court litigation could drag on for a year or more . . . and he might lose. He pointed to the folder. "Can I take a look at this?"

Stein pushed it across the table to him. "On top is the property deed. You're familiar with that. Under it, is a simple release, in which you waive any past or future claims against Landry Mahogany, members of the firm, or members of the family."

Ramón scanned the deed, then studied the release. They were straight forward. There was a third document; Ramón read it, then looked up. "Milburn gave you power of attorney?"

"In matters relating to liquidating his holdings here."

"Max, you've got a deal. Shall we sign the papers right now?"

The attorney responded with his dour smile. "We should have kept you on, Ramón."

Ramón turned in his chair and called out, "Karl!" The German eased off the bar stool.

When Schrader arrived at their table, Ramón said, "Karl, this is Max Stein."

"We've met," Stein said. "I used Mr. Schrader's flying service this morning."

Ramón wondered where Karl had taken the attorney. "I'm acquiring some property," he told Schrader. "I need a witness."

Schrader nodded.

Ramón signed the release and handed the pen to Schrader. The German bent over and quickly scrawled his signature where Stein pointed. Then Stein signed the deed and had Schrader witness that too.

Stein gave the deed to Ramón and put the release into his brief case. As he rose to leave, he said, "Milburn has little confidence that this country can be run by Negroes."

"What do you think, Max?" Ramón said.

"Frankly, I would tend to agree with him, except I see you do not."

The following afternoon, Ramón had chartered one of Karl Schrader's Cessna-180s. They had left the coastal terrain behind and now flew low over the far western rain forest, retracing the route that Stein had taken the previous day.

"Any idea what he was looking for?" Ramón shouted over the engine noise.

Schrader pointed out Ramón's window. "He was interested in this region above the Western Highway. He had his own map, and he had me fly back and forth between here and Gallon Jug for about an hour."

They passed over the village of El Cayo, and Ramón said, "Head north toward Laboring Creek."

Schrader banked the aircraft to the right, and the Mayan ruins of Xunantunich sprawled beneath them. Ramón could make out several people on a scaffold, apparently restoring a frieze near the top of the main pyramid.

Schrader leveled off at 1,800 feet. The uninterrupted tropical forest spread out beneath them, uninhabited, like most of British Honduras.

"Laboring Creek, up ahead," Schrader said.

A river wound eastward through the forest. "Follow it until we leave Orange Walk District," Ramón said.

Schrader switched on the airplane's radio and adjusted the squelch level.

Ramón stared down at the undulating green canopy, but his thoughts had returned to a conversation that had taken place at Government House, a few weeks earlier. A hard-drinking scion of a local family had let slip that the Belize Estate and Produce Company was considering selling its vast land holdings. The logging syndicate owned more than 900,000 acres in this region. Another family member had quickly changed the subject. Ramón wondered if Stein somehow had got hold of the information. He turned back to Schrader. "Do you still fly in supplies for Belize Estate?"

Schrader nodded.

"Did Stein ask about their operation?"

Schrader nodded again. "He was very interested in what they were doing . . . particularly their experimental farm."

"What did you tell him?"

"Nothing. Ramón, what are *you* looking for?"

"I'm not sure. But I believe one day there's going to be a lot of money to be made in this country, and I'm trying to figure out how and where. What do you know about Belize Estate's farm?"

"Their crops aren't as good as the Indians'."

Ramón smiled at Schrader's reference to the illegal marijuana crops, which flourished beneath the jungle canopy.

"Ramón, my impression is that Belize Estate may be closing down. They used to charter my airplane every week; now, it's once a month."

An urgent voice broke in, overriding the radio squelch. "Any station within hearing . . . come in please!" The radio lapsed into static, then the voice returned, "Any station within hearing . . . come in please!"

"Sounds like someone in trouble," Ramón said.

Schrader shrugged.

"Answer the call."

Schrader keyed his radio. "This is Schrader Airways. Over."

There was a pause, then the scratchy voice came back, "Schrader Airways, this is Landry Mahogany. You must help us! We have an injured man. Over!"

Ramón took the handset. "This is Ramón Kelley. Give me your position. Over."

"Mistah Kelley, we are at the Gallon Jug camp. We have a badly injured man! Over."

"Gallon Jug, what kind of injury? Over."

"Sah, a man has been hit in the head with an ax!"

"Blackys!" Schrader sneered.

"Can you set down there, Karl?"

Schrader frowned. "Landry Mahogany fired you, Ramón. Why bother?"

"Damn it! Can you set down there?"

Schrader gave a resigned nod. "There's a logging road I can use, if it's not too muddy."

"Gallon Jug, stand by," Ramón said. "We're heading your way. Over." He gave the handset back to Schrader.

The voice on the ground frantically pleaded for them to hurry. Schrader switched off the radio.

They passed over a cluster of forested hills, and Schrader said, "There it is, straight ahead."

Ramón saw a narrow gash in the dense forest, lined with thatched huts.

Schrader put the airplane into a slow descent and switched on the radio, and they heard the end of a transmission, ". . . can see you now, sah!" Schrader keyed the radio. "Gallon Jug, is the road smooth?"

"Oh, yes, sah," the voice came back. "The road is smooth."

"And is the road dry?"

"Oh, yes, sah! The road is dry."

Schrader switched off the radio, muttering, "Lying blacky." He lined up on a short stretch of straight road, throttled back, and eased the airplane down toward the treetops. The stall buzzer sounded and a red light on the instrument panel flashed.

Up ahead, Ramón saw rain puddles in the road. Then suddenly the road was beneath them, and the seat seemed to drop out from under him, as they rapidly descended the final hundred feet.

The aircraft touched down lightly, but immediately began to vibrate and fish-tail on the rough, muddy road. The engine roared, as Schrader skillfully brought it under control. "Lying black bastards!" he swore. They taxied off the road to the shade of a large mahogany tree.

Ramón recognized the young Creole who ran to meet them. His name was Hemsley Ebanks; Ramón had trucked him out to the jungle from Belize City, a few days after the hurricane.

"Mistah Kelley, sah!" Ebanks shouted. "Thank you for coming to our rescue!"

Ramón and Schrader climbed out of the airplane.

"You humbug me, mon!" Schrader exploded in Creole patois, slamming the palms of his hands into the Ebank's chest. The Creole landed on his back in the mud.

Ramón quickly stepped between them. He helped Ebanks to his feet. "Where's the man who's hurt?"

Ebanks pointed to a nearby thatched hut. "In there, sah." He warily kept an eye on the angry German as they started toward the hut.

"You said he got hit in the head with an ax?"

"Yes, sah."

"Was it a fight?"

"No, sah. It was an accident."

Schrader snorted.

"It has been very hot," Ebanks said, "so we were working at night. Gilroy come up behind me. I never saw him, sah."

"I told you people not to cut at night, until I got generators and floodlights out here!"

"Yes, sah. But the other camps work at night, and you are . . . gone now, sah."

Ramón shook his head in annoyance. Generators and flood-lights had been at the top of his list of needed improvements, but Milburn Landry had repeatedly turned down his requisitions. He should have pushed harder!

He stooped and entered the hut. The tightly-thatched roof and walls retained the stifling midday heat. Ramón gagged on the odor of rotting meat. Two Indian women sat beside a bed made from branches and palm leaves. They moved aside so Ramón could examine the unconscious victim, who also was a laborer Ramón had trucked out from the city. Ramón touched his ashen cheek; the man was in deep shock. His forehead had been laid open. Someone had stemmed the flow of blood with tree moss, and flies now crawled over the saturated, makeshift dressing.

Ramón shook his head. "There's no hope for him."

"Sah!" Ebanks cried. "He is my sister's husband. I must get him back to Belize City!"

The victim gasped. Ramón felt for a pulse at the side of his throat. The man had died.

Schrader exploded, "You bring me here for a dead man?"

"Get the airplane ready, Karl," Ramón said.

Schrader turned on his heel and stalked out of the hut.

"He is dead, sah?" Beaks said in disbelief.

Ramón nodded, then stood up and started for the doorway.

"Sah!" Ebanks cried.

Ramón stopped and looked back.

"You must take him with you!" Ebanks implored. Tears streamed down his face.

Ramón hesitated, then said, "Help me load him onto the plane."

10. ROYALTY

Ramón looked up from the stack of invoices he had been checking. The Hawkesworth Distributors office was a hive of activity, but no one else was working. Clifton, the young office manager he had brought with him from Landry Mahogany, was out on the veranda, hanging a banner. Ramón's three clerks fidgeted at their desks and chattered like school girls. Prince Philip's motorcade was due within the hour.

Ramón stood up. "Okay," he said, raising his arms in mock surrender, "I give up. We're through for the day."

The young women cheered, then followed him out onto the veranda. They all leaned over the railing and admired Clifton's banner, which read: "Welcome Prince Phillip".

"It looks good, Clifton," Ramón said, making no mention of the extra "L" in the prince's name.

Hawkesworth Distributors sat at the foot of the swing bridge, squarely in the center of town. On the other side of Haulover Creek, a large banner spanned the open market. And a block farther, several more had been strung between the trees in Battlefield Park. Spectators filled the verandas and crowded the sidewalks.

One of his clerks leaned over the railing and called down to a young Mestizo, strolling down the street with two Creole companions. The other two women also joined in the flirtation.

Ramón leaned over the railing and yelled, "Come on up!" The young men clumped up the outer stairs. When they arrived on the veranda, they nodded respectfully to Ramón, then joined the women at the railing.

Ramón turned to his office manager. "I'm surprised there's this much excitement over the prince's visit."

"It's been several years since the royal family has come to British Honduras, sah."

"I know, but with the clamor for independence, I wouldn't have thought he'd be so popular."

Clifton frowned and didn't reply.

Ramón let the matter drop. Clifton obviously was content with his life. The "Independence now!" rhetoric of local politicians meant nothing to him.

Ramón looked up Front Street and recognized Tawnya's loose athletic stride. Two Creole men stood in front of the fire station across the street. One of them called to Tawnya as she passed. She flashed her saucy smile, then waved up at Ramón. The man looked up and said something to his companion that evoked raucous laughter.

Moments later, Tawnya stepped onto the veranda.

"Glad you could make it," Ramón said with a smile, thinking how pretty she looked.

"Thank you so much for inviting me, mistah Kelley," Tawnya said in mock formality. Color was a matter of personal preference in British Honduras; however, relationships between whites and Creoles usually weren't flaunted in public. Ramón's clerks exchanged knowing smiles among themselves.

Tawnya joined Ramón at the railing; their arms touched lightly. "You got here just in time," he said.

She smiled up at him. "I know. The procession is forming at the Customs House."

They were interrupted by three resonate booms from a bass drum, followed by an irregular commencement of brass. The Defense Force band was barracked on a dusty road near the Customs House. Each afternoon, their discordant music echoed throughout the city. Now, they signaled the parade was underway.

The music grew louder. Far down Front Street, Ramón saw the first wave of school children—small dark figures in tattered clothing—running toward the swing bridge and stumbling over each other as they looked back at the approaching band. Ramón looked down at Tawnya; she responded with an excited smile.

The band marched into view. The dark soldiers strutted proudly, the din of their music reverberating off the storm-ravaged wooden buildings. They headed straight toward Ramón's office, then veered to the left and marched smartly across the old swing bridge.

Behind the band came more school children, these neatly dressed in parochial school uniforms. Some solemnly tried to march in step with the band; others straggled from curb to curb, waving happily to the spectators.

A large flatbed truck rolled into view, decorated with bunting and flowers, and carrying the reigning "Miss British Honduras" and her court. Ramón's clerks waved and called to the queen by name. The lovely Creole waved back.

Ramón's company pickup truck came next, driven by Brian Hawkesworth, son of the Englishwoman who owned the dealership. The clerks waved and shouted, and the distracted teenager almost ran down a pedestrian. Several community leaders sat precariously on folding chairs in the bed of the truck, including Elijah Ruiz, who hung on to a side panel. He glanced up at Ramón and gave a rueful shake of his head as the pickup bounced onto the swing bridge.

Ramón shouted after him, "The price of leadership, my friend!"

Next, came an open Land Rover. Standing shoulder to shoulder were a pale gaunt figure in a gray double-breasted suit and a dark man in a casual guayabera shirt—the Duke of Edinburgh and the leader of the People's United Party.

"It's him!" cried one of the clerks, and all three jumped and clapped as the vehicle approached. The prince glanced up and gave a tight smile. Ramón suspected it was seeing the extra "L" in his name, but the women interpreted it as recognition and screamed with delight.

When the last vehicle finally passed, the spectators on the sidewalks stepped into the street, as if caught in the wake of the procession heading toward Government House.

Ramón told his clerks, "We're done for today."

"Thank you, sah!" they chorused. Moments later, they and their young men ran across the swing bridge to join the procession. Clifton stayed behind with Ramón and Tawnya.

"Didn't the prince look handsome?" Tawnya said happily.

"Very dignified," Clifton said.

"To tell you the truth," Ramón said, "he looked tired and out of place to me."

"Ramón!" Tawnya said. "Don't you like the prince?"

"I like him fine. The last time he was here, I had the opportunity to speak with him and was quite impressed. But the royal family's continuing popularity makes me wonder if we're really ready to cast off colonialism."

Neither Tawnya nor Clifton replied.

Front Street and the swing bridge were deserted now. Holding hands, Ramón and Tawnya stared down Haulover Creek and out to the Caribbean. Clifton began taking down his welcome banner.

Ramón and Tawnya pulled up in front of her grandmother's house on Regent Street.

"Come back after the prince's reception," Tawnya said, opening the pickup truck door. "I want to hear all about it."

"I'll stop by, if it breaks up before midnight. Otherwise, I'll give you the details tomorrow."

She responded with a playful pout. "I don't want to wait until tomorrow."

"Okay," he said, smiling. He personally found formal functions boring, but he knew how important the prince's visit was to her.

"I'll want to know what people said."

"Yes, Tawnya."

"And what the ladies were wearing."

"I'll keep an eye on the ladies," he said with a laugh. "Anything else?"

"You look very nice," she said, and gave him a quick kiss.

He smiled as she climbed out of the truck. An hour earlier, she had re-ironed the shirt and trousers that his maid had laid out for the evening, and she had insisted that he shave for a second time that day. "See you in a little while," he called after her.

She turned at the gate and gave a quick wave.

Ramón drove the two blocks to Government House. Vehicles lined the street in front of the venerable mansion. The guard at the gate gestured for him to park in the alley, beside the old Anglican cathedral.

Ramón navigated the pot-holed lane and parked in front of a rusty Jeep. The church and its grounds were unlighted, as was the cemetery across the street. He climbed out of the truck and paused, letting his eyes adjust to the night. He glanced to his right. A solitary figure stood amidst the headstones, silently watching him. Although Ramón couldn't distinguish the man's features, there was something vaguely familiar about him. Ramón called out, "Hello there!"

The man's head jerked at the sound of his voice. Then he turned and disappeared into the cemetery. From the darkness, Ramón heard a shrill curse: "White!" He was sure it had been the Mestizo looter.

Ramón made his way up the alley, then crossed the street to Government House.

The guard greeted him, saying, "Good night, mistah Kelley."

"Good night," Ramón said. "Looks like there's a big turnout tonight."

"Yes, sah."

As Ramón walked up the circular drive, he noticed a polished British Army personnel carrier parked near the front door. The officer corps evidently had arrived early.

Wilford, the aging head of the governor's household staff, met him at the front door. "Good night, sah. Sir Peter has a group meeting with Prince Philip in the study. You're invited to join them."

"Thanks, Wilford."

Ramón walked down the hall and stopped in the study doorway.

Prince Philip, Governor Stallard, and PUP leader George Price were engaged in earnest discussion. Several businessmen and politicians, including Elijah Ruiz, surrounded them and listened intently. Elijah stood out from the whites and varying shades of brown.

Elijah saw Ramón enter the room and stepped back from the group. As they shook hands, he said, "You missed the announcement a few minutes ago, Ramón. Colonel Saunders created a stir by reporting that the Guatemalans are again massing troops on the border near El Cayo."

Ramón looked across the room; the graying garrison commander stood apart from the others. Beside him was the young lieutenant Ramón had met the day after the hurricane. "How serious is the threat supposed to be?" Ramón said.

"The colonel seems concerned. But to me, it just sounds like Guatemalan politics. They have an election next month, and *El Presidente* is probably trying to impress the voters with a display of resolve and might."

Ramón nodded.

"Sir Peter seemed embarrassed that the matter was brought up in front of Prince Philip," Elijah said.

At that moment, Sir Peter spotted Ramón and called out, "Ramón, glad you could make it!" He motioned for him to come forward.

Ramón worked his way through the group and shook hands with the governor.

"Prince Philip," Sir Peter said, "may I present one of our leading businessmen, Ramón Kelley."

The prince smiled. "We've met before, have we not?"

"You've got a good memory, Prince Philip. It's been almost five years."

"As I remember, we discussed timber cutting at great length . . . mahogany wasn't it?"

"Yes, we did."

"I understand the mahogany business has fallen off," the prince said.

Ramón nodded. "The company I worked for the last time you were here has pulled out altogether. At the end, we were shipping wood from Guatemala."

"We were just discussing Guatemala," the prince said. "What are your views on this latest bit of saber rattling?"

Sir Peter cleared his throat, as if about to change the subject, but the prince silenced him with a cutting glance.

"I just heard about it," Ramón said. "The issue is probably the same: Guatemala's contention that Great Britain reneged on the 1859 treaty that granted them a road through British Honduras to the Caribbean."

Prince Philip gave a tight nod.

"What do *you* think, Elijah?" Ramón said, turning to his friend and offering him this rare forum to present his views. The rest of the group also turned toward the Carib.

Elijah paused, selecting his words, then said, "Ramón has stated the underlying problem: the road to the sea. This basically hasn't changed over the past hundred years. However, I have a more immediate concern."

"And what is that, Mr. Ruiz?" Prince Philip said, studying him intently.

"Local reaction to these frequent threats. They should serve to unify us, but they do just the opposite."

"Interesting proposition," the prince said. "How so?"

"Guatemala's threats usually occur whenever there are rumors of our gaining independence. And our local leaders respond by retreating to the security of colonial status."

On these words, George Price entered the discussion. "The People's United Party is leading the movement for independence," he said defensively, "but we don't have the military to go it alone against the Guatemalans!"

"If we truly want independence, we must have the courage to grasp it," Elijah responded. "We can't continue to put it off, hoping some day that it will be handed to us, completely without risk."

"Listen to you, and we will all be speaking Spanish by this time next year!" George Price said acridly.

"Gentlemen, gentlemen . . ." the governor interceded. The meeting was over.

As the governor herded the group into the main reception room, the prince fell in step with Ramón and said under his breath, "Perhaps you Yanks would like to take responsibility for this lot."

11. EL CAYO

Ramón trudged up the outside stairway of his seaside home. It was late and he was tired, having spent the past two days in Stann Creek Town surveying his recently-acquired property. He inserted his key in the door and was disturbed to find it already unlocked. He switched on the living room light. Tawnya lay on her back on the couch, her forearm across her eyes. She lifted her arm to identify him, then covered her eyes again.

"Tawnya?" he said.

She didn't reply.

Ramón put down his duffel bag and survey instruments. He went over and sat on the edge of the couch. "Are you all right?" he said, gently moving her arm.

She gazed up at him expressionlessly.

"Tawnya, are you sick?"

She shook of her head, then reluctantly sat up.

"What is it?" he said. Tawnya was not a moody person.

Tears welled in her eyes. "I'm pregnant."

"But you told me you couldn't get pregnant again."

She buried her face in her hands. "My doctor says . . . he made a mistake."

Ramón pulled her to him; she felt lifeless in his arms. "Tawnya, is it . . . safe for you to be pregnant?"

She shook her head. "My doctor is worried . . . because of the problem last time. He will . . . take the baby if I ask him to. But I can't wait much longer. It has been nearly four months."

"Maybe . . . taking the baby . . . would be best. I don't want to lose you."

She pushed him away. "I will not kill your baby!"

"But if you're in danger . . ."

"The doctor said it is *my* decision."

Ramón drew her back into his arms.

She took a deep breath. "I don't want to have our baby here in the city. If you will give me enough money . . ." she faltered. Despite their relationship, she obviously found it difficult to ask for his help. "If you will give me the money," she began again, "I would like to go to that place in the mountains, where you took me last month."

"El Cayo?"

She nodded.

Ramón thought for a moment. The niece of a longtime friend ran a Catholic mission there. "I might be able to arrange something," he said slowly, "if you're sure that's what you want to do."

"I'm sure. And I want little George there too."

"Wouldn't it be better if you left him with your grandmother?"

She shook her head. "Granny is too old . . . and she will be angry that we are having another baby . . . without a husband. She has been embarrassed enough."

"Listen, Tawnya, you're not the first woman—"

"No, *you* listen, Ramón," she interrupted. "I never knew my father, only that he must have been white. My mother ran after him to the States, and she never came back. Granny had to raise me." She paused, taking a deep breath.

Ramón waited quietly. He had never seen Tawnya so resolute.

"And my Georgy will never know *his* father," she continued. "Roland worked on a tugboat. He was crushed between two logs and died before Georgy was born. We never married; I just took his last name."

"But, Tawnya, here in Belize City—"

"I *know* about the talk on the street, Ramón! I know what they will say about me, and about our child. I don't want to hear that talk. And I don't want Granny to have to hear it again. But mainly, Ramón, I don't want my children ever to hear it!"

They sat in silence for some time. Finally, Ramón said, "We'll do it your way." He got up and switched off the light, then came back and took her in his arms.

The following afternoon, Ramón's truck rattled along the potholed, single-lane Western Highway. Tawnya held her infant son and stared out the window. As they neared the end of the seventy-mile journey, the vegetation grew more dense and the terrain changed from low plateau to rolling hills.

Ramón gripped the vibrating steering wheel and strained to see through the dust-covered windshield. Traffic was light in this desolate region, just an occasional bus or logging truck. However, since the road was only one lane wide, approaching vehicles had to see each other well in advance, so eastbound traffic could pull into one of the passing bays, located every mile.

Ramón glanced at Tawnya. "We're getting close."

She gazed ahead, not responding.

"Are you feeling all right?"

She nodded.

"It'll be okay," he said, trying to reassure her. "I've made all the arrangements with the mission, and I'll drive over every weekend to check on you."

She nodded again.

Ramón lapsed back into silence. He was having second thoughts about the secretive trip; he was used to facing problems head on.

A few minutes later, they entered the outskirts of Santa Elena, the tiny village across the Macal River from El Cayo. Ramón slowed; ahead, an Indian couple strolled down the middle of the road. Residents of this remote area considered roads to be wide walkways. Ramón tapped his horn. The couple unhurriedly drifted toward the shoulder, then smiled and waved as he passed.

Santa Elena sat perched atop a hill. Ramón downshifted as they started up the incline. At the top, they passed between the scattering of clapboard shops and houses. Below, the Macal River sparkled in the late afternoon sun. And on the other side of the river, lay the town of El Cayo. They descended to the one-lane suspension bridge that spanned the slow-moving stream, then waited as a dilapidated bus crossed from the other side.

Ramón gazed upriver at the tranquil scene of a half-dozen women washing clothes in knee-deep water. A grinding of gears brought him back from his brief reverie; the bus had crossed the bridge and now headed up the hill. Ramón gave the customary tap of his horn to alert the bridge pedestrians, then crossed into El Cayo.

The park at the foot of the bridge was deserted, and the shops had already closed down for the day. They drove past the white-washed town hall, then turned up a steep, rocky incline. Wood-frame houses lined both sides of the dirt street. Although the town was modest in means, it didn't have the slum atmosphere of Belize City.

Halfway up the hill, they passed a ramshackle cantina. A peeling sign over the door read: Club Cayo. A sad Spanish song drifted through the open doorway. Inside, several men idled away the afternoon, drinking beer and playing billiards.

A stark cinder-block building stood at the top of the hill, contrasting with the wooden shacks that surrounded it. Ramón stopped in front of the building and shut off the engine.

Tawnya clutched her infant to her breast and gazed fearfully at the mission. Georgy began to squirm, uncomfortable at being held so tightly.

"Tawnya," Ramón said, "if you've changed your mind, we can go back right now."

"No," she said quickly.

Ramón climbed out of the truck. As he withdrew Tawnya's tattered suitcase from the back, a young Mestizo nun came out of the mission.

"*Hola, don Ramón!*" she called, approaching with a cheerful smile.

"*Hola, Sor Claudia,*" Ramón replied. Switching to English, he said, "Sister Claudia, this is Tawnya Lightburn. As I told you on the phone, her husband, Roland Lightburn, was killed recently. Tawnya needs some time to get over her loss and to have the baby she's expecting."

Tawnya climbed out of the truck, clutching her infant.

"Welcome, Mrs. Lightburn," Sister Claudia said warmly. "We have been expecting you." She held up her hands to take the baby. Tawnya hesitated, then let her have him.

Switching back to Spanish, Sister Claudia said to Ramón, "I think it will be easier if you say goodbye here." She took the suitcase from him.

Tawnya stared at the mission.

"I'll be back to check on you next weekend," Ramón said.

"That won't be necessary, don Ramón," Sister Claudia assured him. "We'll take good care of her." She took Tawnya's elbow and guided her toward the mission.

As they approached the door, Tawnya suddenly broke away and hurried back to Ramón. She looked up at him and said urgently, "I don't want you to come back here, until after I have the baby."

"Don't be silly," Ramón said.

Tawnya glanced over her shoulder at Sister Claudia, waiting in the mission doorway. "If you come every week," she said, "she will know you are the father."

"I don't give a damn—"

"But I *do* give a damn! You must promise me that you'll stay away and not tell anyone about this. Promise me!"

Ramón gazed at her, unable to respond.

Suddenly Tawnya's determination vanished; her shoulders slumped and tears filled her eyes.

Ramón looked away. A slight breeze stirred the hot afternoon air. A stocky Indian woman walked by with a large basket of produce balanced on her head and a baby strapped across her back. From a house down the hill, came the sounds of children playing. "Okay," Ramón said, turning back to her. "I'll only come when you call for me."

She heaved a sigh and looked up at him with gratitude. "And promise me, you won't tell anyone about this . . . ever."

"If that's what you want, then I promise."

"That's the way it must be, Ramón. Always." She turned and hurried back to the waiting nun. They disappeared inside the mission.

12. COLLET CANAL

The Royal Petroleum representative had just left the Hawkesworth Distributors office, and Ramón leaned back in his chair. Clifton, his young office manager, immediately appeared in the doorway. "How did it go, sah?"

Ramón gave a weary but triumphant smile. "It went fine, Clifton. It took me a week to wear down that damned Englishman, but I got the contract."

"Well done, sah!"

"We're not going to make a hell of a lot of money the first couple of years," Ramón said. "But if we deliver everything I promised, within three years we'll be the sole distributor of their product line and the primary supplier of parts and materials for their local operation."

"Damned fine, sah! Mrs. Hawkesworth will be pleased when she returns." A phone rang in the outer office, and Clifton left to answer it.

Ramón settled back in his chair again, pleased with the recent turn of events. Soon after he had taken over the dealership, Mrs. Hawkesworth had confided that she was tired of eking out a living in the colony and longed to return home to England. With Elijah's help and financial backing, Ramón had arranged to buy her out over the next ten years. The agreement he had negotiated with Royal Petroleum ensured the success of the venture.

He wished Tawnya was here to celebrate with him. She now had been in El Cayo for four months. At her insistence, he neither visited nor telephoned the mission. Each Sunday, while the nuns attended morning mass, she called him at home, collect. Although she never complained, he could tell from her tone, particularly the past two Sundays, that she was having a rough time. And by the doctor's reckoning, the baby was not due for another month.

He got to his feet. Maybe Elijah was available for lunch to celebrate.

The telephone awakened him at 6:15 the next morning. When he answered it, a faint voice said, "Mistah, Kelley?"

"Yes, this is Ramón Kelley!" he shouted into the mouthpiece. "Speak up, please!"

"This is telephone central in El Cayo, sah," the voice said. "Will you accept a collect call from Sister Claudia?"

"Yes, central, I'll accept the call."

A faint voice came on the line, *"¿Don Ramón?"*

"Sí, Sor Claudia."

"I am sorry to disturb you, don Ramón, but Mrs. Lightburn had a very difficult night."

Ramón straightened. "What's the matter?"

"The baby is coming early . . . and the doctor fears it may be breached."

"But she's not due for another month!"

"We can't control these things, don Ramón."

"Where is she?" he demanded. "Who's taking care of her?"

"Don Ramón, we are doing all we can for her. She is in the hospital, and her doctor is with her."

"I'm sorry, Sister. I'm sure you're doing your best. Does the doctor have everything he needs?"

Sister Claudia hesitated, then said, "Our medical facilities here are . . . limited."

"Sister," Ramón said, his voice breaking, "is there a possibility she might . . . that she won't pull through?"

"The doctor says it is very serious."

Ramón's mind raced. The Northern Highway was too rough for him to bring Tawnya back in his truck. Finally he said, "I'll fly over as soon as I can charter a plane."

"That won't be necessary, don Ramón. I'll keep you informed."

"I'll be there in a couple of hours. I'm bringing her back."

Ramón searched the city for Karl Schrader. First he had unsuccess-fully tried his house on Hydes Lane. Then he had driven out to Schrader's makeshift hangar and landing strip on Barracks Road. The effeminate Creole singer, who lived and worked in the hangar, had reluctantly given Ramón the address of Schrader's mistress.

Now, Ramón sped through the narrow streets of the city's slums, searching for Allenby Street. He stopped his truck beside one of the wooden footbridges that crossed the Collet Canal. The stench from the excrement-laden, open sewer wasn't new to him, but still he had difficulty in suppressing the urge to retch. He looked about, trying to get his bearings.

Three light-skinned Creole boys stood on the other side of the narrow canal, watching him. They carried composition notebooks and wore the uniforms of a Catholic primary school. The oldest appeared to be about ten.

A darker Creole youngster paddled under the bridge in an old dory. A half-block away, another boy jumped into the filthy canal and swam toward Haulover Creek. The sight of the impoverished children of the neighborhood triggered a contrasting recollection of the yellow school bus in Hammond, Louisiana.

Ramón climbed out of his truck and called across to the young-sters on the other side of the canal, "Can you tell me where Allenby Street is?"

The oldest pointed down the canal.

Ramón walked across the rickety bridge to where they were standing. "Straight ahead? How far?"

"A next bridge . . . and a next one . . . and give a bend, sah," the youngster said, gesturing that Ramón needed to go down two bridges and turn to the left.

A loud splash interrupted them. Ramón turned and saw an elderly Creole woman bend over the edge of the canal to rinse out a slop bucket. Black catfish churned the surface and devoured the filth the woman had emptied into the water.

Ramón looked up the canal. The swimmer climbed into the

other youngster's dory. Ramón turned back to the three boys standing in front of him. "Are you on your way to school?"

"Yes, sah," the oldest replied solemnly.

"Are these your brothers?"

"Yes, sah."

Ramón reached into his billfold and took out a dollar bill. "You listen to Sister today, uh?"

The youngsters chorused, "Yes, sah!"

Ramón handed the bill to the oldest. "And you buy your brothers a fresco after school, uh?"

"Yes, sah," the boy said, smiling.

Ramón got back in his truck and drove slowly along the edge of the canal. The neighborhood was typical of the ramshackle city. The storm surge, nine months earlier, had swept away most of the flimsy dwellings; however, shacks made of the same scrap lumber and rusty corrugated iron had immediately reappeared.

Finally, Ramón saw a flaking sign nailed on the side of a shack, which read: "Allenby Street". The clapboard homes that lined the narrow lane had no street numbers. An elderly Creole woman approached, lugging a pail of water from the community hydrant. Ramón stopped the truck and leaned out. "Can you tell me where Ethlin Evans lives?"

The old woman gave him a snaggletoothed smile and pointed to a nearby shack.

Ramón nodded his thanks and parked his truck beside an open gutter that carried sewage from the houses to the canal. As he stepped from his truck, a window opened on the other side of the street. A black couple appeared and watched him curiously.

Ramón paused at the front door; there were no sounds from within. He knocked and got no response. He knocked again, this time slamming the door with the flat of his hand.

A woman's husky voice said, "Left me, mon!"

"Karl, are you in there? It's me, Ramón!"

He heard movement behind the door. It opened, and Karl Schrader stood in front of him, barefooted, with his pale pot belly hanging over his unzipped khaki trousers.

"Good morning, Ramón," the German said, showing no surprise at seeing him. He gestured for Ramón to follow him inside.

Leaving the door open, Ramón stepped into the room and recoiled at the reek of musky sweat and stale marijuana smoke. A large black woman lay naked on an uncovered mattress on the floor. She raised up on one elbow and strained to focus her eyes. She gave up and rolled over, turning her bare back to him. With a deep sigh, she appeared to lose consciousness.

An open bundle of marijuana, the size of a loaf of bread, lay at the foot of the mattress. Ramón asked Schrader, "Have you been smoking that shit?"

Schrader shook his head. "I brought it in from the bush for that black cow there."

"I need to fly up to El Cayo, right now," Ramón said, still trying to determine the pilot's condition.

Schrader nodded and sat down on the mattress beside the woman. As he pushed his bare feet into a pair of muddy boots, he said, "What's going on in El Cayo?"

"A friend of mine is in serious condition there. I need to bring her back to the hospital here."

Schrader struggled to his feet and pulled on a wrinkled khaki shirt. "I'm ready."

Ramón gazed down at El Cayo from Schrader's Cessna-180. A large athletic field, wedged between the town and the Macal River, served as a makeshift landing strip. Schrader circled until a group of soccer players moved out of the way.

A few moments later, they taxied across the field. The soccer players waved as they passed, then returned to their match.

Schrader parked at the base of the bridge that led into town and switched off the engine. "Unless you need me," he said, "I'll wait for you here."

Ramón nodded. "I ought to be back within an hour." As he climbed out of the airplane, Schrader reclined his seat to take a nap.

Ramón scrambled up an embankment and was met by several elderly Mestizos, who had left their customary park benches to watch the landing. They greeted him with smiles and chattered in Spanish as they escorted him into town. When they arrived at the park, they returned to their benches.

Ramón started up the steep side-street to the mission. He planned to meet with Sister Claudia, then have Tawnya brought to the airplane. The tropic air was already sultry, and he quickly broke into a sweat. Halfway up the hill, he stopped in front of Club Cayo to catch his breath. The rundown cantina was shuttered and locked. He looked down at the shops below. Several horse-drawn carts unloaded produce at the outdoor market. Between the town and the river, Karl Schrader's silver and black Cessna shined in the midmorning sun. Ramón turned and continued up the hill.

As he approached the mission, the door opened and Sister Claudia came out to meet him, her features drawn. *"Buenos días, don Ramón.* I heard the airplane and have been watching for you."

"Buenos días, Sor Claudia. Is there any change in Tawnya's condition?"

"I am sorry, don Ramón. She passed away an hour ago."

"Passed away?" Ramón said in disbelief.

"The baby came. It was breached, as they thought. They fought to save Mrs. Lightburn, but they were unable."

"Damn them!"

"Don Ramón . . . they did everything humanly possible. I was with her."

Overwhelmed, Ramón turned away and stared down the hill. Tawnya . . . Tawnya . . .

After a long pause, Sister Claudia said, "Her body is still at the hospital. We didn't know if she was to be buried here, or in the city." She added apologetically, "I'm afraid something must be decided quickly."

"What about the baby?" he said numbly.

"The baby is fine. It is a boy. Although he came early, he was a good size."

Ramón struggled to collect his thoughts. Finally, he turned back to her. "Where's Tawnya's other baby, Georgy?"

"An older couple has been caring for him. The Polancos were never blessed with children of their own, and they have enjoyed having him. They brought him to the mission every day so Tawnya could see him. They also grew very fond of Tawnya. They were at her bedside . . . at the end."

Ramón turned away again.

"Don Ramón," Sister Claudia said, "this morning, when they learned that Mrs. Lightburn had passed away, they asked if there was any possibility that they could adopt Georgy . . . or perhaps even both babies."

"Adopt the babies?"

"Yes. They are poor, like most people here, but they are good Catholics and are sure the Lord would help them."

Ramón fought past his personal pain and struggled with the decision that apparently was his. Tawnya's grandmother was far too old to raise the two infants. He would have to place them in a foster home—either in Belize City, or here. As he gazed down the hill at the sparkling Macal River, he remembered the children he had seen in the city that morning, swimming in the filthy canal. He turned back to the nun. "Could the Polancos raise them both, if I sent . . . $100 each month?"

"Oh, yes! We have been giving them $25 from the money you have been sending us, and they have been getting along quite nicely."

"You say they're a good couple?"

"Oh, yes, don Ramón. And we would be here, of course, to check on them from time to time."

He nodded. Then, remembering the vow he had made to Tawnya, he said, "I'd prefer to remain anonymous. I'll send the money to you, and you pass it along."

"But, don Ramón . . ." she began. She studied him for a moment, then said, "I can't wait to tell the Polancos that their prayers have been answered."

Ramón heaved a deep sigh. "Sister Claudia," he said, "bury Tawnya here. Her only relative is a grandmother, who is very old. So bury her here . . . where her children will be raised."

"That would be best," Sister Claudia agreed. "When they are old enough to understand, I will take them to visit her."

"I appreciate all you've done, Sister."

"You are the one who is doing so much, don Ramón."

Ramón shook his head despondently. "Is there anything else you need right now?"

Sister Claudia thought for a moment. "The new baby will need a name."

Ramón again shook his head, unable to respond.

"Will it be all right if I give it Father Clive's name?" Sister Claudia said.

"I'm sure that'll be fine," Ramón said hoarsely.

"Clive Lightburn," she said. "I like the sound of that!"

"Anything else, Sister?"

"Don Ramón, I can't think of anything. Will you come to the hospital now, so you can see the baby?"

Tears welled in his eyes and he turned away again. He had never had a child, and the full realization that he now had a son swept over him. He struggled with the vow he had made to Tawnya. He wavered, but said, "No, I need to get back to the city."

Sister Claudia looked disappointed. "Will you come back soon?"

"Yes," he lied. He gave the nun a quick embrace and started down the hill.

That evening, Ramón, who never drank, sat alone in his living room with a bottle of Scotch. The phone rang again; he had ignored it all afternoon. This time it kept ringing, and he finally picked it up.

A vaguely familiar man's voice on the other end said, "Ramón, is that you?"

"Yeah."

"Congratulations! You're a father!"

"What? Who . . . who is this?" Ramón stammered.

"Sorry, lad," the voice said. "Sounds like I must have awakened you from a siesta. This is Vance Anderson—Kay's father—calling from the States. I've been trying to reach you all day. Kay made me a grandfather last night. You have a son!"

PART II: RITES OF PASSAGE

Time longer than rope.

—Belizean Proverb

13. SAN IGNACIO

November 18, 1980

Clive Lightburn leaned on his pool cue and stared through the open window of Club Cayo. The late afternoon breeze barely stirred the humid air inside the shabby cantina. Down the hill in the village, only a few shops remained open. Past the shops, the banks of the Macal River were deserted; the washwomen had left for the day.

The young Creole turned back to the faded, stained pool table, where a middle-aged Mopan Indian studied his next shot. The Mestizo bartender and the only other customer, a thin Jamaican, watched from the bar. The Jamaican's dreadlocks snaked down to his shoulders.

"Come, mon!" Clive said impatiently. "We just playing for shillings."

The Indian glanced up at Clive, but didn't respond. He unhurriedly walked over to the bar and took a sip from his bottle of Belikin. Then he returned to the table and resumed his deliberation.

Clive gazed out the window again. Down the hill, his older brother, George, stepped through the doorway of Buckley's General Store where he worked. He and the white store owner chatted amiably at the curb. The sight of his industrious brother annoyed Clive, who recently had been fired from his service station job for missing work. Clive turned back to the pool table and said irritably, "Look, mon, I got a basketball game tonight. Shoot, no sah?"

Unperturbed, the Indian carefully lined up a long rail shot. After several practice strokes, he finally shot and missed.

"Chuh!" Clive said, striding from the window to the table. He chalked his cue and rapidly pocketed the five remaining balls.

The Indian stared at the table for a moment, then reached into his pocket and withdrew some coins. He slowly counted out fifty cents and handed it to Clive. "Have a next one?"

"No, mon. Not today," Clive said. He walked over to the bar.

"How much you make, Tall Bwy?" the Jamaican said with a grin.

"Two bloody shillings," Clive said in disgust. Turning to the bartender, he said, *"Una Coca, Emilio."*

The bartender brought over a Coca Cola.

"Tall Bwy," the Jamaican said, "I need some help tonight. I pay you twenty dollars."

Clive studied the Rastafarian for a moment. Miles Slusher had arrived in the village six months earlier. He idled away most afternoons at Club Cayo. At night, he pandered to the guests of the San Ignacio Hotel. Clive didn't trust him; however, he was curious how Slusher lived so well, without working.

"What kind of help you talking about?" Clive said.

"I got business in Guatemala, and I need someone to translate for me."

"What kind of business?"

"I am picking up some . . . merchandise."

"What merchandise?"

"You asking a lot of questions, bwy. Are you interested, or not?"

Clive checked the clock behind the bar. "I got a game tonight," he said. In the mirror, he saw his older brother enter the club, carrying a crumpled paper sack. Studying their reflections, Clive again was struck by their contrast. Since they were children, he had questioned whether they actually were brothers. His own complexion was tan, with dark freckles across his nose, and his eyes were green. His brother was much darker and his eyes were nearly black. Although George was tall, Clive was several inches taller.

"What you want, George?" Clive said, turning and facing his brother.

George Lightburn looked awkward and out of place in the cantina. He acknowledged Slusher and the bartender with hesitant nods.

George's diffident manner aggravated Clive. "What you want?" he said again.

"You have a game tonight, no true?" George said.

"Yes, mon. I'll be leaving directly."

George handed him the sack.

Clive frowned. Inside, he found a new pair of canvas basketball shoes. He looked at George for an explanation.

"They're Converse All-Stars . . . from the States," George said.

"Where did you get them?"

"Mistah Buckley let me order them . . . at cost."

"How much you want for them?"

"I bought them for you, mon! They're for the new season."

Clive glanced over at Slusher, who looked on with a bemused smile. Clive put a hand on George's shoulder and guided him toward the door.

As they left the cantina, Slusher called out, "Tall Bwy! Meet me here, after the game!"

Three hundred people jammed the outdoor basketball court behind the San Ignacio Hotel, watching the local team play the visitors from Belmopan. Seven minutes remained in the game. Clive relaxed on the bench; the scoreboard read: Home 72 - Visitors 35. Clive had scored 41 points before his coach had taken him out. With Clive off the court, the two teams now played evenly.

"*Qué tal*, Tall Bwy," said a soft voice.

Clive turned. A young woman who worked in the hotel had slipped into a seat behind him. "*Qué tal*, Ninette. Did you just get here?"

"Uh huh," the pretty Mestizo replied. "I had to work at check-in tonight, and we just closed down. Did you get to play?"

"Yes," Clive said, smiling, "they let me play."

"I heard the crowd calling your name. I'm sorry I missed seeing you."

Clive gazed into her dark eyes for a moment. Then he stood up and walked over his coach. "Make I go back, one time."

His coach looked up, frowning. "Go back? Game almost over, Tall Bwy."

"Ninette miss the first half."

The coach glanced at the young woman, then said with a wry smile, "All right, Tall Bwy."

A San Ignacio player committed a foul, interrupting play. Clive trotted onto the court, and the crowd broke into applause. "Tall Bwy!" shouted a spectator. Others picked up the cry.

The Belmopan player's free throw hit the back of the rim, and the ball caromed toward Clive. He leaped high above an opposing player and slapped the ball to a teammate. He received a return pass as he crossed mid-court, dribbled three times, and slammed home a dunk. Few players in the entire country could play above the rim, and the crowd roared its approval of their hometown hero.

At the defensive end, Clive blocked a Belmopan player's shot. The ball bounced toward the sideline, but Clive caught up with it and threw a long behind-the-back pass to a teammate for an easy lay-up. The crowd roared again.

The Belmopan team was demoralized, and Clive slammed home three more dunks in rapid succession. On the last shot, a frustrated Belmopan player fouled him. Clive made the free throw and left the court to a standing ovation, having scored an even fifty points for the evening.

Ninette smiled and clapped as Clive sat down in front of her. She leaned forward and whispered, "Tall Bwy, where are you going after the game?"

"I'm meeting someone."

"A gyal?"

"No, a mon about some business."

"Chuh!" Ninette said in disbelief. She jumped up and headed back to the hotel.

A short while later, Clive stepped out of the hotel's makeshift locker room.

A voice called out, "Clive!" His brother George bounded down the concrete stairway from the hotel. He thrust out his hand. "Damn fine game, Clive!"

Clive grudgingly accepted the handshake and gave his brother a curt nod. George had been sucking around mistah Buckley so much, he was beginning to talk like a bakra.

"I'll walk home with you," George said.

"I'm not going home."

"Club Cayo?"

Clive nodded and started up the hotel stairway.

"Clive!" George called after him.

"What, mon?" Clive said impatiently.

"That Rastamon is no bloody good!"

Clive shook his head and continued up the stairs. When he reached the top, he found Ninette waiting for him. She opened her slender fist and showed him a hotel key. "Room empty tonight," she said shyly.

Clive took the key and put his arm about her waist. As they headed for the rear of the hotel, he smiled down at her. The Rastamon must wait tonight.

14. HAMMOND

A car door slammed outside Ray Kelley's bedroom window, awakening him from his nap. He listened, wondering if the arrival next-door was Bobbi Sue Mitchell, home from her day of classes at Southeastern Louisiana University. A screen door banged shut, and the driveway was quiet again.

The bedroom was uncomfortably warm. Ray sat up and tossed the blanket onto the floor. Then he lay back again and thought about Bobbi Sue, with the usual result. He heard approaching footsteps in the hallway and flipped onto his side.

The bedroom door cracked open. "Ray," Kay Kelley said, "it's six o'clock. You wanted me to wake you."

Ray raised his head off the pillow, as if he had been asleep. "Okay, Mom. Thanks."

"What would you like to eat?"

"We're not supposed to eat dinner on game nights."

"Honey, that doesn't make sense. How can you play basketball on an empty stomach?"

"They fed us before they let us out of school this afternoon—poached eggs and green peas. Coach said for us to go home and rest up for the game, and not eat anything else."

"They fed you poached eggs and green peas for lunch?"

"Yes, ma'am."

"Whose idea was that?"

"Mom, this is my first varsity game. I don't know who decides these things. Coach Hebert, I guess."

"I'll fix you some fish sticks and macaroni."

"If I ate that, I'd puke on the court."

"Ray! What kind of talk is that!"

The phone rang in the kitchen. His mother temporarily set aside the food debate and left the room. Ray rolled onto his back; the sheet lay flat. He stretched his lanky frame. He wondered how many people would be at the game tonight. The thought of performing before a large crowd brought a pang of anxiety, but it quickly passed. After having been relegated to the junior varsity bench the past two seasons, it was unlikely he would get to play, even though he was a senior.

He climbed out of bed and went into the bathroom. In the mirror, he saw the telltale sign of a pimple forming under his right cheekbone. It was still hidden by freckles, so he left it alone. He ran his hand over his chin, decided there was no need to shave again, and just splashed water in his face.

Back in the bedroom, he pulled on a clean pair of jeans, a new V-neck sweater, and a worn pair of moccasins. He opened his duffel bag and double-checked to be sure he had all of his equipment.

Moments later, he entered the kitchen and found his mother still on the phone. "I'm going, Mom. I'll be back about 11:00 or 12:00."

She put a hand over the mouthpiece. "Do you need a ride?"

"No ma'am. I'll walk."

"Okay, honey," she said with a smile. "I hope y'all win."

"Thanks, Mom," he said as he banged out the screen door.

He walked down the driveway. Just as he reached the sidewalk, a soft voice said, "Hi, Ray." A cigarette glowed in the shadows of the Mitchell's front stoop.

"Bobbi Sue?"

She stepped out of the shadows so he could see her. "Where you going?"

"Got a game tonight." He crossed the lawn to her.

Bobbi Sue sat down on the porch steps and gazed up at him through a wisp of cigarette smoke. She was twenty-one, but looked younger in jeans and a sweater. Her blond hair was pulled back in a ponytail. "My brother's already over at the gym, setting up the P.A. system. He told me you made the varsity this year."

"Uh huh," Ray said, pleased that she knew.

"It's about time," she said, "after all that practicing. I swear, I don't think a day's gone by the past year that I haven't heard you out there in the driveway, bouncing and shooting that ball."

Ray smiled and nodded.

"Who y'all playing?"

"Ponchatoula."

"Ponchatoula! When I was a cheerleader, Ponchatoula was our biggest game!"

"Still is, I guess," Ray said, torn between needing to get to the gym and wanting to make the most of this rare opportunity to impress Bobbi Sue.

She took a deep drag from her cigarette. "Are y'all going to beat 'em?"

"We should. We've got a pretty good team this year."

"Tommy says the team is almost all blacks now."

"Yeah, there's only me and one other white guy."

"Do you play center?"

"No, guard."

"Guard? Tall as you are!"

"We've got a tall team this year," he said, "And we've got some real good jumpers."

"I ought to come watch."

Ray grew apprehensive; he had been talking like he was going to be playing, not just sitting on the bench.

"I'd better not, though," Bobbi Sue said. "I've got an English paper due tomorrow morning."

"That's too bad," Ray said, relieved.

"Well good luck. Don't let those Ponchatoula boys beat y'all!"

"No way!" Ray said, as if he would have something to do with the outcome.

Soul music from a portable radio reverberated off the locker room tile. Ray sat on the concrete floor with his back against a wall, awaiting Coach Hebert's instructions before the team took the court.

The coach climbed onto a bench. "Tyrone, turn off that damn noise!"

Hammond High's starting center laconically reached over and switched off the radio.

The coach looked over at Ray. "Get off that cold concrete, boy! It'll give you hemorrhoids!"

Ray jumped up, although he wasn't sure what hemorrhoids were.

"We're gonna start Tyrone at center," the coach said. The three-year letterman stared disinterestedly at the floor. "Now, Tyrone, tonight I want you to . . ."

As the coach droned on, Ray's attention drifted. All this time in the locker room was taking away from his limited time on the court—the warm-ups.

". . . and finally, at shooting guard," the coach intoned, "we're gonna start Ray Kelley."

Ray felt his stomach turn. The other players, particularly the black letterman he was replacing, looked at him in surprise.

"All right, gentlemen," the coach said, "get out there and get warmed up!"

In a daze, Ray stumbled toward the locker room door. He felt a slap on his back and turned to see the grinning face of the other white member of the team, a gangling sophomore.

The gym was already full, and the hometown crowd cheered as Hammond High jogged onto the court. Ray had never played before a large crowd, and his pulse raced. He wished he was somewhere, anywhere, else.

"All right!" the coach bawled. "Gimmee two lines for lay-ups!"

Ray found himself at the head of the shooting line. The equipment manager fired a ball at him, and Ray fumbled it. The ball bounced off his foot and rolled toward the nearby stands.

"Come on, 'token', wake up!" Tyrone snarled. He pushed past Ray and glided toward the goal with another ball.

Ray jogged stiffly about the court during the lay-up drill, only vaguely aware of the pregame music and cheers. He had spent countless hours practicing on this goal, but now it was foreign—his shots hit the iron and fell away. Jesus! What the hell was going on? He couldn't even make a lay-up. Shit!

"All right!" the coach yelled. "Starters only! Shoot some free throws!"

Ray remained on the floor with his four black teammates. When it was his turn to shoot, he still felt tight and awkward. The goal looked too far away. His first shot barely touched the front of the rim. His second shot rattled in, but he had forced it.

The buzzer sounded, signaling that the game would begin in one minute. Ray and his teammates jogged off the court and huddled around their coach.

"Has everybody checked in with the scorekeeper?" the coach said.

"I haven't," Ray said, confused.

"Then get over there, boy!" his coach snapped. The four veteran starters exchanged glances; Tyrone shook his head.

Ray approached the table and searched for the scorekeeper among the several people seated there. He saw Bobbi Sue's younger brother, Tommy, who did the P.A. announcements. "Tommy, who do I check in with?"

"Are you starting, man?"

"Yeah, who do I check in with?"

"Man, that's great!"

"Tommy, tell me who the hell I check in with!"

Tommy turned to an official seated on his right. "Mr. Harris, Ray Kelley is our other starter." Then he turned back to Ray. "He's got you, man. Good luck!"

His team was impatiently waiting for him as he ran back to the huddle. "All right, gentlemen," the coach said, "this is the first game of the season, so we're gonna keep it simple. We're gonna come out in a man-to-man defense, and we're gonna get on 'em like stink on shit!"

Ray and the reserves chorused, "Yeah!" The four veteran starters stared at the coach impassively.

The buzzer sounded again. Ray and the other starters stacked hands and jogged out to mid-court.

"Get 'em, 'Gun'!" Tommy called out to him, as if it was one of their driveway games.

The Hammond center-jump play assumed that Tyrone would be able to out jump the opposition, and called for Ray to break for the Hammond goal as soon as the referee tossed up the ball. A split second before the toss, Ray got confused and broke toward the wrong goal.

Tyrone jumped late and the opposing center slapped the ball to a teammate who dribbled for the Ponchatoula goal. Ray, already heading in the same direction, raced to stop him. At the goal, Ray leaped and cleanly blocked the Ponchatoula player's lay-up attempt. The Hammond crowd roared its approval.

The other Hammond guard picked up the loose ball and leisurely started up court. Ray, adrenaline flowing, raced down the sideline, past the other players. His teammate saw him and lofted a lob pass toward the goal. Ray followed the flight of the ball through the bright ceiling lights. Oh, shit! Too high! He leaped at the last moment, caught the ball above the rim, and drove it through the net. The gym exploded.

Tommy's voice on the P.A. boomed over the crowd noise, "Ray Kelley!"

The Ponchatoula guard carelessly threw the ball inbounds. Ray wheeled, intercepted it, and drove for an uncontested lay-up.

"Ray Kelley!" boomed the P.A..

"Pick 'em up!" Ray screamed at his teammates, who were jogging back to the other end of the court. They hesitated, then raced back to join him in a full-court press.

At mid-court, the two Hammond forwards trapped the Ponchatoula dribbler and stripped him of the ball. Ray led them in a three-on-two fast break. He stopped at the free throw line and hit a clean jump shot.

"Ray Kelley!" boomed the P.A..

"Pick 'em up!" Ray screamed. "Full court press!"

The Ponchatoula players got the ball across mid-court, but missed their shot, and Tyrone snared the rebound. The Hammond team raced back to the offensive end. Ray got the ball on a dead run and launched a jump shot from twenty-five feet, which knotted the net around the rim.

The gym was in bedlam, and the stunned Ponchatoula players called for a time out.

As Ray led the other Hammond players off the court in a dead run, Tommy's voice boomed, "Ray . . . MACHINE GUN . . . Kelley!"

15. BELIZE CITY

Ramón paced the living room of his modest wood-frame home, awaiting the dawn. Now nearing sixty, he found it increasingly difficult to sleep through the night. He paused at an open front window and listened to the Caribbean lapping at the low seawall on the other side of the street. The sound triggered a recollection of the hurricane that had struck the city twenty years earlier. In the storm's aftermath, there had been an atmosphere of promise, both for the colony and for himself—promises as yet unfulfilled.

He thought of Tawnya Lightburn, as he frequently did. Had she lived, she would be forty now. He shook his head, annoyed with himself. Recently he had become preoccupied with his reminiscences.

He padded into the kitchen and snorted when he noticed his new maid hadn't put the bread in the refrigerator. The loaf lay on the counter, loosely wrapped in plain white paper. He opened the wrapping and checked for insects and mold. Finding none, he cut off a thick slice and put the remainder in the refrigerator.

He passed through the living room and stepped out onto the front veranda. The sun's first rays lighted the horizon. He took a bite from the stale bread; its tough crust brought back memories of his childhood in Panama. On Sunday mornings, his mother often took him to a thatched-roof hut, where a San Blas Indian woman baked bread in an outdoor clay oven—*micha* the bread had been called.

Footfalls of an approaching runner drew his attention. A familiar solitary figure jogged past, throwing jabs aimlessly into the morning haze. The runner was a former Golden Gloves fighter, now detached from reality.

As the fighter passed from view, Ramón thought back to his early days in the city, when the morning streets had been filled with runners, training for Golden Gloves fights. A young British Honduran of that era had risen from the local competition to become the sixth-ranked heavyweight in the world. He had been slated to fight Rocky Marciano, but had been stabbed to death in New York's Harlem, just months before the championship bout.

Ramón again shook his head in annoyance. An old man's musings. He turned and went inside to shower and dress for the coming day.

Ramón was working in his private office, when he heard Elijah Ruiz' resonant laughter. He rose from his desk and walked over to the doorway. His old friend was teasing his secretary. "Watch out for that old mon, Mavis!" Ramón said.

Elijah turned with a broad smile. "Ramón!"

"Good to see you, Elijah," Ramón said as they shook hands. "How are you feeling?"

"Like a bloody school bwy! Those American heart surgeons know their business!"

"You look trim enough," Ramón said, ushering him into his office.

"I've lost thirty pounds," Elijah said. He took a chair across the desk from Ramón. "Unfortunately, I have to stay on a strict diet from now on."

"I need to get on one myself," Ramón said, patting his paunch.

"Mine's not too bad, actually," Elijah said. "Fish and rice are allowed, but no beans or sweets."

"We thought the Belize Defense Force might have to invade Houston to get you back."

Elijah smiled. "After they discharged me from the hospital, Esther and I flew to Los Angeles and spent a week with Jovita."

"How's your daughter doing?"

"Quite well. She's in her second year of nursing school. She's become quite Americanized. She may stay there."

"We're losing so many of our best young people," Ramón said.

"Ramón, I considered staying there myself. I could afford to, you know, and I think I may be a bloody fool for not doing it."

"Because of your health?"

"That's part of it. But mainly, for the first time in my life, I'm beginning to see Belize like outsiders do—not quaint, simply backward and rundown."

"You're seriously thinking of leaving?"

Elijah got up and walked over to the window. He looked down at Haulover Creek for a moment, then turned back and said, "Still a city of open sewers, after all these years!"

Ramón joined him at the window. "One day we'll close them."

"You know what I mean, Ramón. Twenty years ago, the future of our nation looked so bright!"

Ramón smiled. "I was having similar thoughts myself, just this morning. I'm afraid we're getting old, my friend. We're having old men's regrets."

"True enough, we're getting old. However, the fact remains that damn little has changed over the years. The British offered us complete independence in 1964, but our clever politicians held out for limited self-rule. Now, nearly twenty years later, the British are still here. For all practical purposes, we're still their colony."

"Well," Ramón said, "at least we made them let us drive on the right side of the road."

Elijah smiled ruefully. "Yes, and we've changed the names of everything, like we were bloody Africans. Renaming the country 'Belize' was reasonable enough, but now every little bush town insists on being renamed."

Ramón smiled. "I still have trouble calling El Cayo, San Ignacio."

"And renaming Stann Creek Town, Dangriga!" Elijah said with a derisive snort.

For a moment they stood in silence, watching two fishermen in a dory cast their nets into the river. Elijah turned away and said irritably, "This country has the best bloody fishing in the world, and those lazy coolies are out there catching the shit-eating catfish of Haulover Creek!"

A car horn blew from the parking lot below.

"That's Esther," Elijah said. "Probably afraid I'm overdoing it. Will you join us for dinner this evening, Ramón?"

"For Esther's fish and rice? Sure, mon!"

"Maybe she'll fix boil-up, since we're having a guest," Elijah said wistfully.

Ramón smiled at his thin friend's craving for the rich Carib dish of fish, yams, cassavas, and plantains. They shook hands, and Elijah left the office.

Ramón went back to his desk. He leaned back in his chair, pleased that his friend was up and about. However, their conversation had again left him with the hollow feeling of unfulfilled promise.

Ten years after coming to work at Hawkesworth Distributors, Ramón had bought out the owner; six years after that, he had paid off the bank loan. But then the country's economy had stagnated, and now he felt dissatisfied. Kelley Distributors wasn't enough to show for the twenty-five years he had labored in Belize. His time was running out.

Mavis entered the room. "The bwy brought the *Belize Times*, mistah Kelley."

"Thank you, Mavis."

He disinterestedly thumbed through the local tabloid. On a back page, devoted to news from the interior, the name "Lightburn" caught his eye. There was a one-paragraph account of a Tall Boy Lightburn, who had started San Ignacio's new basketball season by scoring fifty points in a game against Belmopan.

Ramón reread the paragraph several times, then set the paper aside. He leaned back in his chair again, remembering the one time he had seen Tawnya's sons, six years earlier. He had traveled to San Ignacio on business and had stopped by the old mission to pay his respects to Sister Claudia, who over the years had handled the funds to care for Tawnya's children. She had been reserved and had insisted on taking him over to the mission's athletic field, where the two boys were playing soccer. Ramón had watched for several minutes as a tall, light-skinned Creole dominated the game. Ramón had glanced down at the nun and caught her studying him intently. Remembering his vow to Tawnya, he had left before the game was over, without making direct contact with the boys. He hadn't been back to the mission since.

Time's running out, he thought again. If he was to accomplish anything in this God-forsaken place, he would need a son. He leaned forward and picked up the phone. When the operator responded, he said, "Central, I want to place a call . . . to the States . . . to Hammond, Louisiana."

16. EL PETEN

Clive was already awake when the family rooster crowed. He stretched, then lay still, listening to the familiar sounds of morning. Other roosters crowed from both sides of the Macal River. A stove lid dropped in the kitchen. Across the cramped bedroom his brother George snored on.

Clive got up and pulled on the trousers he had left piled beside his bed, just two hours earlier. He padded into the kitchen and found his foster mother toiling over the old wood-burning stove. Preoccupied with her morning ritual, she didn't hear him enter the room. She was nearly seventy now. Her husband had died seven years earlier.

"Buenos días, Mamacita," Clive said.

The diminutive Mestizo turned and looked up at her tall Creole foster son. *"Días, mijo,"* she said with a smile.

"The coffee smells good," Clive said in Spanish. He poured a cup from the dented metal pot on the stove, then dropped into a chair at the kitchen table.

His foster mother carved off two thick slices of homemade bread and put them onto the hot griddle. "The black man came to see you last night," she said in Spanish.

"The black man?"

She cracked two fresh eggs and dropped them onto the griddle. "The one with hair like snakes."

Clive smiled. "His name is Miles Slusher, Mamacita."

"I don't need to know his name," she said irritably. "He looks evil. I made him leave."

"He's just a man with long hair, Mamacita."

She flipped over the toast and eggs. "I smelled the scent of the smoking herb on his clothes."

"It's part of his religion," Clive teased, knowing the comment would draw her ire.

"Religion!" she snorted.

Clive took a sip from his coffee. "He worships an African god."

"A pagan god?"

"An African god. Slusher is a Rastamon. They worship the king of Ethiopia. The king's name is Haile Selassie."

His foster mother scowled. "I've never heard the priests speak of this pagan god."

"Ethiopia is in Africa, Mamacita. And Haile Selassie is still alive."

"Still alive! The snake-haired one worships a pagan god who is still alive?"

"Yes. And smoking ganja is part of their religion. They use it . . . like you Catholics use wine."

His foster mother glared at him. Then, realizing he was amusing himself at her expense, she scooped an egg off the griddle with her spatula and turned to throw it out the window.

"¡Mamacita! ¡Mamacita!" Clive laughed, jumping up and pinning her frail arms against her sides.

The old woman looked up at Clive and shook her head in annoyance, but finally dropped the egg onto a piece of toast.

"¿Qué pasa?" said a voice behind them. The exchange apparently had awakened George.

Clive ignored his brother. He took the eggs and toast from his foster mother and sat down at the table to eat.

"Buenos días, Mamá," George said, as he stooped and kissed the old woman's temple. He gave Clive a disapproving look and said in English, "What time did you get home?"

Clive continued to ignore him. He knew George was envious of his having spent the night with Ninette.

"Well?" George demanded.

"It's no big thing, mon," Clive replied in English.

"With Papá dead, I'm responsible for you."

"Chuh!" Clive retorted.

The old woman frowned. Although she spoke little English, she understood enough to recognize the tension between her two foster sons.

"What time did you get home?" George pressed.

"I'm not sure, George. Ask Ninette when you see her."

George glared, then turned and stalked out of the kitchen, banging the screen door behind him.

"*¡Jorge!*" the old woman shouted after him.

George quickly reappeared in the doorway. "*¿Sí, Mamá?*"

"Come back and eat," she ordered.

"*Un momento, Mamá,*" he said, then hurried across the back yard to the family outhouse.

"Will you come to mass with us this morning, Hijo?"

"Not today, Mamacita," Clive said with a smile. He had stopped going to church when he was twelve.

The old woman gazed at him for a moment. "Be careful, Hijo," she said softly.

Clive responded with an indulgent nod.

That night, Clive stood beside Miles Slusher in front of a Guatemalan border official. The dingy office smelled of unwashed bodies. Several other travelers sat on a bench against the far wall, awaiting their turns to negotiate their clearances.

The official looked up from Slusher's Jamaican passport and snarled a string of invectives in Spanish. Clive took a step back. Although he had lived near the border his entire life, this was the first time he had ever tried to cross over into Guatemala.

"What's he saying?" Slusher asked Clive.

"He don't like your looks. He's not going to let us pass."

"Tell him I want to see Captain Benavides!"

Clive was about to translate, when a heavily accented voice said, "Why you no come last night?" A slovenly captain walked up behind them.

"Change of plans," Slusher said. "Tell this mon to let us pass."

"Why you no come last night?" the captain repeated.

"What difference does it make, mon?" Slusher said. "I'm here tonight. This bwy has come with me."

The captain rubbed his unshaven chin with the back of his hand. Finally, he nodded for the other official to let them pass.

"Why was that mon so angry?" Clive said as they emerged from the customs building.

"Because I'm a day late," Slusher said. "But I couldn't come last night, because you were greasing the crease of that spry stucky at the hotel."

They climbed into Slusher's ancient Land Rover. He turned the ignition key several times before the engine started. Moments later, they sped through the dirt streets of Melchor de Mencos. The border village's meager shops had already closed for the evening.

"What business you got over here?" Clive said. "Getting herb for the tourists?"

"Bwy!" Slusher said with a snort. "I don't need to come to Guatemala for ganja. Belize has an ample supply."

"Then why are we here?"

"I have some important customers . . . customers who buy . . . antiques."

"Antiques?"

"Mayan antiques."

"Talk straight, mon."

"An American at the hotel buys Mayan relics," Slusher said. "He is an archaeologist, but he also is a thief. He pays for jade."

Clive grew uneasy. In Belize, there were heavy penalties for looting Mayan ruins. "The Guats don't mind us taking their relics?"

"Bwy!" Slusher snorted.

They left the dusty village streets behind them, and had to slow. The rock-covered road to the interior was so rough that Slusher seldom shifted out of first gear. Clive strained to see through the cracked, dirty windshield. The old Land Rover's single, dim headlight barely penetrated the dark, uninhabited surroundings.

After a quarter-hour of incessant pounding, Clive leaned over and shouted, "How much farther?"

Slusher dismissed the question with an impatient wave of his hand. As they crested a hill, the moon disappeared behind a cloud. They descended to the bottom of an arroyo and stopped in front of a dilapidated bridge.

"Get out and lead me across," Slusher said. The Land Rover engine died as Clive climbed out. It took Slusher several tries to restart it.

Clive gingerly started across the wooden structure. In the headlight's dim beam, he saw that the left side of the bridge had been washed away. He motioned for Slusher to keep to the right. The old timbers groaned under the weight of the Land Rover.

Clive made it to the other side and stepped onto the shoulder of the road. The Land Rover sputtered as Slusher negotiated the final few feet. He gunned the engine and accelerated past Clive.

"Slusher!" Clive shouted.

The vehicle gathered speed as it roared up the incline. At the crest of the hill, the brake lights flashed and the gears ground. Then there was only darkness and silence. Clive ran up the dirt road, stumbling over unseen rocks. He stopped when he reached the top of the hill. The moon emerged from behind the cloud. Slusher walked toward him from a stand of trees.

"What the fuck!" Clive exploded.

"Shut up!" Slusher hissed. "The bloody Land Rover was about to die back there."

The moon went behind another cloud, again plunging the area into darkness. Clive reached out to be sure that Slusher was still close by and felt the Rastafarian jump at his touch. "What are we doing here?" Clive whispered.

"Waiting for someone," Slusher said tersely.

"Tell me what the bloody hell is going on!"

"Keep your voice down," Slusher said. "We're waiting for a guide."

"A guide? To take us where?"

"To meet a Belize bwy named Wilman."

"A Belize bwy? Out here?"

"Wilman killed a mon in Belize," Slusher said, "and now he can't go back. He lives out here with a Guat gyal. Last year, he found a hidden pyramid and began selling the relics. He pays Captain Benavides to let his customers cross the border."

The moon emerged again. An Indian of the Peten forest stepped from the trees. He appeared to be in his fifties—short and stocky, clad only in tattered trousers. He stared at them impassively.

"This is the bloody fool who guided me last time," Slusher muttered. "He almost lost me in the bush. He doesn't speak English. That's the reason I brought you."

"*¿Hablas español?*" Clive asked the Indian.

The Indian nodded that he spoke Spanish.

"What is your name?" Clive said.

"Tzul."

"Tell him to take us to the pyramid," Slusher said.

"*Guiemos a la piramide, Tzul,*" Clive said.

The Indian turned and disappeared into the trees.

"Quick, mon!" Slusher said. "Don't let him out of your sight. The bloody fool runs like a jaguar!"

The Indian trotted effortlessly down a narrow path. The dense forest forced Clive and Slusher into single file behind him. Slusher struggled to keep up. The canopy of trees blocked the moonlight, and Clive lost all sense of direction; he simply concentrated on keeping the Indian's shadowy form in front of him.

Finally, they broke from the forest and started across a wide savanna. The Indian picked up the pace, and Clive broke a heavy sweat. They approached the next stand of trees and Slusher gasped that he had to stop. Clive relayed the order to the Indian, who pulled up just inside the tree line.

Slusher dropped down on all fours; his dreadlocks covered his face. Clive bent forward, hands on knees, trying to catch his breath. Slusher's back arched twice, then he vomited between his hands. The Indian looked on impassively—mouth closed, breathing through his nose.

Clive straightened and gazed across the savanna, undulating

in the night breeze. He estimated they had run for more than a mile. "How much farther is it?" he asked the Indian.

The Indian stared at him without responding.

Clive looked down at Slusher. "Do you know where we are?"

Slusher, still breathing hard, shook his head without looking up.

Clive's concern increased; if the Indian abandoned them, they'd be lost in the bush. "Who do you work for, Tzul?"

"I am a chiclero."

"Don't you work for a man named Wilman?"

"Yes, I work for him too. He paid me to bring the man with the long hair."

"Where is the pyramid?" Clive said.

The Indian pointed into the stand of trees.

Slusher looked up. "What's he saying?"

"His name is Tzul. He's a *chiclero*. He knows the way to the pyramid, but he won't tell me where it is."

"What's a *chiclero*?"

"They bleed chicle from the sapodilla trees. It was used for chewing gum, but no one buys it any more. This is probably an old chiclero mule trail we're on."

Slusher struggled to his feet, and they took off again in single file. Clive marveled at the old Indian's stamina. Finally, they stopped at the base of a steep hill.

"This is it," Slusher gasped.

Clive nodded; telltale cohune trees grew nearby. The "ancient ones" had always planted the oil-producing palms within their cities. The hill was actually a pyramid, rising fifty feet from the forest floor, hidden by more than five centuries of tropical growth and decay.

"Wait here," the Indian told Clive. "I get the black man." He disappeared into the trees.

"Wilman must live close to here," Slusher said. "Last time, the Indian wasn't gone long."

"Bloody lonely place," Clive mused, looking about at the dark forest. "Is there a looter's trench into the pyramid?"

Slusher shook his head. "The relics aren't in the pyramid; they're down in a cave. Come, I'll show you."

They walked over to a clearing and stopped at the edge of a twenty-foot bluff. Slusher pointed to a boulder that protruded from the undergrowth, about halfway down. "The cave is next to that big rock."

"What's it like inside?"

"I don't know. I didn't go in."

"Why not?" Clive said. He and his brother had explored all the caves around San Ignacio.

"I saw a duppy."

"A what?"

"A duppy, mon. I saw a duppy come from the cave."

"What the bloody hell is a duppy?"

"You don't know about duppies?"

Clive shook his head.

"A duppy can look like a mon, but a duppymon can turn his head back to front."

"Chuh!"

"For true. Duppymon can hide a mon's shadow."

"Bwy! What a lot a rot."

"No, mon. True word. If a duppy come after you, it can kill you!"

"What makes you think you saw a duppy here?"

"After a mon has been dead three days, his spirit mist rises from the grave. I saw a spirit come from the cave last time."

"Chuh, bwy! You just see steam coming from water in the cave. I see it all the time."

A twig snapped, and the Indian appeared from the forest. "No one is at the black man's hut."

Clive translated for Slusher.

"Tell the Indian to go inside and get us some jade," Slusher said.

Clive translated the order, but the Indian refused. "He says he won't go in by himself."

Slusher gazed down at the cave entrance for a moment, then said, "You think it just steam, uh?"

"Sure, mon," Clive said.

Slusher took a deep breath. "Make we go." He dropped into a sitting position on the edge of the bluff, then slid down the embankment.

Clive and the Indian followed.

Slusher pulled back the fronds of a large fern, exposing an opening wide enough for a man to enter.

"We need a light," Clive said.

Slusher handed him a plastic cigarette lighter.

Clive pushed his head and shoulders through the opening. The first whiff of the ammonia odor of bat droppings brought tears to his eyes. He flicked the lighter. From what he could see in the amber glow, the cave was similar to those he and his brother had explored—a limestone cavern, formed eons earlier by an underground river. A stream wound across this cave's floor, probably the remnant of such a river.

Clive extinguished the light, then gingerly pulled himself through the opening and clambered down the steep muddy slope to the cave floor. He flicked the lighter again and raised it above his head. Several bats, directly overhead, released from their perches and fluttered back into the shadows at the rear of the cavern. Roach-like beetles swarmed over the bat guano that covered the floor.

"Come, mon!" Clive shouted up to Slusher. "There ain't no duppies down here!"

The Rastafarian descended into the cave, followed by the Indian.

"Tell him we want the small green statues of the gods," Slusher said.

Clive told the Indian, who nodded and threaded his way through the wet stalagmites to the rear of the cave. Clive and Slusher followed him to an opening that led to an inner chamber. The Indian stopped at the entrance. Clive moved past him and entered with the lighter. Clay urns littered the floor—most broken, but many intact. Slusher pushed past Clive and rummaged through the pottery shards, looking for jade. He excitedly held up a figurine, about three inches high—a Mayan princess with a large headdress.

Clive picked up what looked like a coin. It was an amulet, carved from bone. He spit on it and scrubbed it with his thumb. A figure emerged—a male captive, bound with ropes. Clive dropped it into his pocket.

A bat fluttered down from the ceiling, coming close to his face. Clive recoiled. He followed its flight back into a far recess of the cavern, and something in the shadows caught his eye. He took a step closer. "Shit, mon!" he gasped.

The body of a man lay draped backward across a large boulder. Its arms and legs were bent unnaturally, as if all the major bones had been broken. Vacant eyes stared from the battered head.

"It's Wilman," Slusher whispered.

The Indian bolted from the chamber.

"Don't let him leave us here!" Slusher cried.

They hurried after him, arriving at the muddy slope in time to see his legs go through the cave entrance.

"¡Párate!" shouted a voice outside the cave. Rifle shots rang out, and someone screamed in pain.

Clive extinguished the lighter.

Above, someone shouted orders. "Soldiers," Slusher whispered.

Then there was silence. A flashlight beam suddenly pierced the darkness and a voice boomed, "Slusher!"

Clive and Slusher backed away from the entrance. "Who knows you're here?" Clive whispered.

"Only Captain Benavides and Wilman . . . Wilman must have told them."

"Slusher!" the voice boomed again. Someone entered the cavern.

Clive and Slusher turned and stumbled toward the inner chamber. A flash and deafening roar filled the cave. "Jah!" Slusher cried out to his god. Another shot rang out and ricocheted around the cavern. As Clive plunged into the inner chamber he heard Slusher fall. Clive flicked the cigarette lighter and frantically searched for an escape route. He bumped into the corpse, and in panic backed away from it. The lighter went out, then slipped from his shaking hand when he tried to relight it. He dropped to his knees and groped through the broken pottery. He couldn't find it!

Flashlights played across the chamber entrance. Clive scurried across the floor and located the stream.

"¡*Muchacho!*" snarled a menacing voice.

Clive followed the shallow water away from the chamber entrance until his head struck a stone surface. The stream ran off into what felt like a small tunnel, perhaps two feet in diameter, located beneath the wall.

"¡*Muchacho!*" snarled the voice again.

Terrified, Clive eased into the tunnel feetfirst; it dropped off at a steep angle. Only his head and hands were exposed. The water rushed past him, saturating his clothes and threatening to pull him into oblivion.

A flashlight played across the cavern wall. It was on him! He took a deep breath and released his grip. As he hurtled down the rough conduit, a scream lodged in his throat. Suddenly he plunged into a water-filled chamber. He opened his eyes and panicked, finding himself submerged in a black void. He swam up with powerful strokes, but his hands hit solid rock overhead. He frantically pulled himself across the limestone, searching for air. He inhaled water and screamed in terror. He was still screaming when he broke the surface.

Treading furiously, he gasped for air. His choking echoed through the dark chamber. He swam until his hand struck rock. Then he pulled himself onto a narrow ledge and sat with his back against the cavern wall, drinking in the cool air. Clive had seldom known fear and had never faced death. Now he cringed in the dark like a terrified child.

Then in the silence, he heard the faint cry of a tinamou bird. Tears of relief filled his eyes. He struggled to his feet and groped his way along the winding cavern wall. Finally he looked up and saw the night sky through a narrow opening. He clambered up a muddy incline and pulled himself into the bright moonlight.

He hesitated, listening for the soldiers. A giant mahogany tree stood a few yards away. Clive crawled over and pulled himself into a sitting position, hiding between its enormous root fins. Again, he listened for the soldiers.

Time passed, then the tinamou cried again. Folklore said that the tinamou whistled at half-hour intervals. Had it been that long? Then off in the distance, he heard muffled shouts. He jumped to his feet.

"*¡Párate!*" ordered a voice behind him.

Clive whirled. A Guatemalan army officer walked toward him, rifle in the firing position.

Clive threw up his hands. "Don't shoot!" he cried in Spanish.

"Stand still!"

Clive remained motionless.

"We expected you last night," the officer said as he approached.

"Expected me?"

The officer stopped in front of Clive and smiled malevolently. "The black man told us you were coming. He died during interrogation. We made it last several hours, although he was eager tell us everything . . . as you will be."

Clive's stomach tightened with fear.

"You black thieves provide my men with excellent training."

A shout echoed from jungle, and the officer's head reflexively jerked in the direction of the sound. Clive stepped forward, grabbing the rifle muzzle and driving a knee up the smaller man's crotch. The officer gagged in agony. Clive jerked the rifle out of his hands; it landed somewhere behind him. He spun the struggling officer around and pulled a forearm across his throat. The officer tried to cry out, but Clive lifted him off his feet, crushing his air passage. The officer kicked frantically. Finally he went limp, and Clive let him slump to the ground. For a moment, Clive gazed in disbelief at the dead Guatemalan, then he turned and fled into the jungle.

By the time Clive arrived back home, the stars that had guided him across the border had faded into the predawn light. He entered the shack quietly; his foster mother wasn't up yet. He limped down the narrow hallway and stumbled into his bedroom.

George sat up in bed. "What the bloody hell!"

Clive dropped onto his own bed, too exhausted to respond. His shoulders slumped and he stared down at the canvas basketball shoes George had given him, just two days earlier. They were now torn and filthy from his trek back from the Peten.

"Speak to me!" George said. "Where have you been?"

"George . . . I must leave San Ignacio. Can you give me some money?"

"What trouble have you gotten into now?"

"The trouble's not here in Belize . . . it's in Guatemala."

"Guatemala? What were you doing in Guatemala?"

"George, . . . trust me, mon. It's better you don't know anything. Just help me get away."

"Get away? To where?"

"Belize City."

"Belize City! Why?"

"It's large . . . many people . . ."

"But you don't know anyone!"

"George . . . I can't stay here. Help me, mon."

George gazed at his younger brother for a moment, his concern evident. "I have $45," he said finally.

"Thanks, mon," Clive said. "I'll return it as soon as I can." He forced himself to his feet. "I'll catch the nine o'clock bus. Now I need to bathe."

"Mamá will be sad," George said. "You have always been her favorite."

17. CELEBRITY

Ray took a shortcut through Southeastern Louisiana University's magnolia-covered campus. Coach Hebert had been pleased with the win over Ponchatoula High the night before and had canceled the after-school practice. On his way home, Ray planned to stop by his grandparents' house to be sure that his grandfather had seen the *Times Picayune* write-up of the game.

The fall afternoon was unusually warm, and college students lolled under the trees. Ray passed the liberal arts building where his grandfather taught literature. Several coeds sat on the front steps, watching a touch football game. A half-block off campus, he saw his mother's car parked in front of his grandparents' house.

A familiar voice called out, "Ray! Ray Kelley!"

Bobbi Sue Mitchell waved to him from the other side of the makeshift football field. He hesitantly returned her wave.

"Come here!" she called impatiently.

Ray felt himself redden as he approached. Seated in the midst of the other coeds, Bobbi Sue looked like a queen among her princesses. Ray managed to affect a casual, "How y'all doing?"

"Hey, y'all!" Bobbi Sue said. "Know who this is? This here's 'Machine Gun' Kelley!"

Ray shifted his books awkwardly.

A petite brunette said, "You're who?"

"I'm . . . ah . . . Ray Kelley." He began to perspire.

"He's *Machine Gun* Kelley," Bobbi Sue corrected. "He scored 36 points last night for my old high school!"

"Oh, high school," the brunette said. She returned her attention to the football game, calling out, "Come on, David!"

"Well . . . be seeing you," Ray mumbled.

"See you, Ray," Bobbi Sue said. "Good game last night!"

As Ray crossed the street that bordered the campus, he shook his head in annoyance. At school that day, he had enjoyed his new prominence. But in a matter of minutes, the coeds had him feeling awkward and unsure of himself again.

He approached his grandparents' house and saw his grandfather and mother sitting on the front porch.

"Hello, lad," his grandfather said.

"Hi, Grandpa. Hi, Mom." He dropped onto the porch swing. "Did you see the paper this morning, Grandpa?" As a rule, his grandfather paid little attention to athletics; however, Ray knew he was avidly interested in anything involving his only grandchild.

"I saw it. Fine job, lad!"

"Thanks, Grandpa. Where's Grandma?"

"She's inside, getting dinner started. She's proud of you too. Of course, this morning, I had to explain the difference between basketball and tennis. She had the two confused, and had a little trouble understanding the newspaper's account of what you'd done."

"Who explained the difference to you?" Ray teased.

His grandfather chuckled. "I'll have to admit, I'm not much better informed. But I am proud of you, lad. I know that making the team was important to you, and that you worked hard to accomplish it."

Ray smiled; his grandfather's approval was important.

"You must get your athletic ability from your father's side," his grandfather said. "We've never had any 'machine guns' on ours."

"Oh, Ray, by the way," his mother said, "your father phoned from British Honduras this afternoon."

"Belize," Ray's grandfather corrected.

"Oh, yes," she said. "Well, I still think of 'Belize' as being that squalid city, not the whole country."

"What did he want?" Ray asked, not really interested. Over the years, his father's trips to Hammond had been infrequent, and usually uncomfortable for everyone.

"He'd like you to spend the summer with him."

"No way!"

His mother nodded. "I told him I didn't think you'd be interested. Well, I'll go see if Mom needs some help." She got up and went inside.

"Were you nervous last night?" his grandfather said.

"Scared shitless, Grandpa."

The old man grimaced at Ray's language. "But you did it anyway. And by the newspaper accounts, you did it in fine fashion."

"Thanks, Grandpa."

After a pause, his grandfather said, "Ray... I think you should accept your father's invitation."

"Why, Grandpa? Mom's told me what it's like down there."

"I know, lad, but . . . the man's your father."

"Bull, Grandpa! He's never had anything to do with me."

"Nothing?"

"You know what I mean. He's never been around. Like basketball . . . like you said a few minutes ago . . . I did it myself!"

"He's provided financial support for you and your mother all these years."

"Well . . . that's not enough."

"Ray, the man's your father. Your name is Ramón Kelley, and one day you'll want to know about the man you were named after."

Ray looked away. He had been called "Ray" since he was an infant; even his closest friends didn't know that "Ramón" was his given name.

"You can't wait too long, lad," his grandfather said. "Your father is nearly as old as I am."

"I don't like him," Ray said flatly.

"Well, I *do* like him, Ray. He's a strong man who has survived in a region that most men would find unbearable."

"Belize sucks, Grandpa!" Ray said, wanting to drop the subject.

The old academician again winced at Ray's choice of words. "It's a rugged land, true enough. But I think a summer down there would be a grand experience."

"I don't want to go, Grandpa."

"At least give it some thought."

Ray looked up in time to see a squirrel leap from one magnolia tree to another. He turned back to his grandfather and said unconvincingly, "I'll think about it, Grandpa."

18. OUTCAST

Clive struggled to keep his eyes open, as the crowded bus rattled across the Western Highway. The billboards alongside the road indicated they were nearing the end of the seventy-mile journey from San Ignacio to Belize City. His legs ached from the trek back from the Peten and from being bent in the same position for the past three hours.

An overweight Creole woman sat next to him, wedging him against the side of the bus. They hit a deep chuckhole, and Clive grimaced as his knees banged against the seat in front of him.

They passed a mangrove swamp, and he let his mind drift to his only other trip to Belize City. His San Ignacio basketball team had won their league title and had been invited to play against Team Belize. As they had neared the city, his teammates' boisterous chatter had abruptly quieted. The youths from the far western village had been intimidated by this metropolis of 40,000. Clive smiled, remembering the city girls who had waited for them in front of the Civic Auditorium. Spry stuckys, he thought, then winced. He had picked up the expression from Miles Slusher.

The recollection of his terror in the cave flashed into his mind. He couldn't believe he'd killed somebody! He fended off the disturbing memory by focusing on the current danger. Would the Guats come after him? The border official, Captain Benavides, could identify him. However, if he did, he would implicate himself for taking bribes and letting looters into the country.

The soldiers, on the other hand, would likely pursue the incident; they would have to account for their dead officer. However, they might not want a full investigation, because of what they had done to Wilman.

The bus rumbled into the outskirts of the city, interrupting his musing. The unpainted shacks, standing on stilts, looked similar to those that dotted the hills of San Ignacio; however, crammed together on this flat terrain, they appeared destitute and forbidding.

The woman seated beside him had been gossiping with a friend across the aisle. Now she turned and spoke to him for the first time. "Are you coming here on holiday, bwy?"

"No," he said uneasily, "to . . . work."

"What kind of work do you do?"

"I . . . ah . . . don't know, exactly."

"Do you have family in Belize City?"

"No." She frowned, and he quickly lied, "I'll be staying with some friends." He turned away from the inquisitive woman, hoping to avoid further questions.

The bus crossed Central American Boulevard and weaved through twisting, dirty streets until they arrived at a shack that served as the bus station. He waited as the passengers in front slowly filed off. Finally the fat woman beside him struggled to her feet. He painfully stood up and followed her down the aisle.

Outside, the driver was on the bus roof, handing down luggage. The bright sun blazed overhead, and the humid air was saturated with the stench from a nearby canal. Clive felt light-headed. The driver picked up his woven hemp bag and threw it at him. Clive caught it and moved away from the bus. The fat woman stood watching him.

He slung the bag over one shoulder and took off down the street. As he crossed the canal on a narrow footbridge, he looked with revulsion at the open sewer below. On the other side, he headed up a narrow street, jammed with people on bicycles and on foot. In spite of his jeopardy, the hubbub of the city excited him.

He passed a grocery shop and considered getting something to eat, but then remembered he only had the $45 his brother had given him. He decided to wait.

The street came to a dead end at a tree-filled park. It reminded him of the one in his village, where the old men idled away their afternoons. A large open market stood off to the left. And on the other side of the plaza loomed a two-story white building, crowned with an ornate clock. From photographs, Clive knew that this was the court house.

He entered the park and walked over to a two-tiered fountain. There was no water. Hot and thirsty, he sat down on a concrete bench. Nearby, a man in ragged clothes slept under a tree.

A push-cart vendor approached him. "Fresco?"

"How much?"

The vendor glanced down at Clive's hemp bag. "Shilling."

"Chuh!"

"Five cents," the vendor said.

"Make I have one."

The vendor shaved off the ice and added the brown syrup. "Milk?"

"Sure, mon!"

The vendor brushed the flies off the condensed milk can and poured the thick yellowish liquid over the syrup and ice. He handed the paper cone to Clive, who gave him a five-cent piece. The vendor turned without thanking him and pushed his cart on down the path.

Rude motherfucker, Clive thought. He settled back on the bench and took a bite of the sweet concoction.

A middle-aged Mestizo approached him from the other direction. The man's clothes were in tatters, and his battered face showed signs of countless beatings. He stopped in front of Clive, thrusting out a dirty hand. "Give me shilling, no?"

"Give you shilling for what, mon?"

"Just give me shilling."

Clive frowned; the poor of San Ignacio didn't approach people, demanding money. "I got no money for you."

The beggar didn't move.

"Left me, mon!" Clive said.

"White mon's baby," the Mestizo sneered.

"What you call me?" Clive said angrily, jumping to his feet. He had dealt with similar taunts all of his life.

The beggar stepped back. "White!" he cursed, then turned and shambled away. He disappeared down an alley.

Clive sat down again. The emotion of the moment passed, and he suddenly felt very tired. His fresco melted rapidly in the mid-day sun. He finished it and dropped the paper cone amid the other debris strewn around the bench.

A Creole his own age approached from the direction of the court house. The youth stopped in front of him and glanced down at his bag. A wide smile crossed his face. "How you making it, mon?"

"All right," Clive said warily.

"Make I join you?"

Clive shrugged.

"I haven't seen you here before," the youth said, sitting down.

Clive nodded noncommittally.

"Where are you from?"

"Cayo District."

"San Ignacio?"

Clive nodded.

The youth looked around, then back to Clive. "Do you need a hit on the herb?"

Clive got to his feet. "I don't smoke that shit."

"Don't rush off, bwy!" the youth said. He grabbed Clive's fore-arm.

Clive pulled his arm away.

"Easy, mon!" the youth said. "Tell me what you want. A gyal?"

"I don't want nothing from you, mon," Clive said. He swung his bag over his shoulder and started off in the direction of the open market.

A haggard Mestizo woman hurried toward him. "Give me shilling, no, sah!" she croaked.

Clive stepped off the sidewalk to get around her. A horn blew, and an ancient lorry missed him by a scant few inches.

A ragged middle-aged Creole, leaning against the market wall, said with a grin, "Mind yourself, tall bwy."

The familiar nickname caused Clive to break stride. He stumbled on the cracked sidewalk, distracted by all the unwanted attention. He ducked inside the market and found himself in the midst of a large produce area. Past the open back wall, several fishing boats bobbed at river moorings. As he walked through the market, women behind the wooden counters held up mangos, breadfruit, plantain, and papayas.

He arrived at the rear of the market. The fishing boats were all unattended. Close by, a fat Mestizo butcher chopped the tail off a live iguana. Flies covered the stained cutting block.

"Sah," Clive said, "can you tell me where these fishermen are?"

"They done for today," the butcher said contemptuously. "They only fish in the morning. Now they down on Water Lane Street, getting drunk."

"Do you need some help, sah? I'm looking for work."

"No, bwy," the butcher said, pulling another iguana onto the cutting block. "Try again this afternoon. Some other fishermen will be coming back from the cayes."

Clive slumped down on the seawall and leaned against a mooring stake. Debris and raw sewage floated down the river and out to sea. The flies from the market swarmed about his face. He leaned forward, lowered his head between his arms, and dozed off.

Clive walked across the swing bridge. He paused midway and looked back at the now nearly deserted market. He had spoken to the fishermen returning from the cayes, but none had needed help the next day. Discouraged, he turned and continued across the bridge.

On Queen Street, he passed a young Creole woman. He caught her inviting look, but kept his attention focused on the unfamiliar surroundings. It would be dark soon; he needed a place to stay.

Ahead a weathered sign read: "Police Station". As Clive passed the high-walled compound, he stole a look through the open gate.

Two Creole policemen struggled with a Mestizo in handcuffs. They drove him to his knees and beat him with their nightsticks. One of the policemen looked up. Clive averted his eyes and continued down the street.

A half-block farther, he paused in front of a grocery shop. He glanced back; there were no policemen in sight. He stepped inside the store.

A Lebanese woman stood behind the counter. "Yes?"

"Ah . . . do you have a newspaper?" Clive said. He had never purchased a newspaper before, but he needed to find out if the incident in Guatemala had been reported.

"Yes, the *Belize Times* just arrived." She handed him a copy of the tabloid. "One shilling, please."

As Clive reached into his pocket for change, one of the policemen from the compound entered the store.

"Make I have some Winsomes, Jasmin," the policeman told the clerk.

A ten-cent piece slipped through Clive's fingers and clattered onto the glass countertop.

The policeman looked at Clive, then glanced down at his hemp bag. "Where you from, bwy?"

"Ah . . . Cayo District, sah."

"So you've come to the big city, eh, bwy?"

"Yes, sah."

"Where you staying?"

"Ah . . . I don't know. I just arrived . . . I haven't found a place yet."

"Try Barracks Road, bwy. There is a boarding house up by the clock tower." Without waiting for a reply, he pocketed his cigarettes and left the store.

Clive paid for his newspaper and stepped outside. The policeman was already out of sight. Clive walked up to the next corner and saw the clock tower, two blocks away. Although it was late afternoon, the clock said 10:17.

Halfway up the next block, he ducked into a deserted alley.

His hands shook as he unfolded the newspaper and flipped through the pages. He saw no mention of the Guatemala incident. He turned back to the front page and methodically went through the entire newspaper again. Nothing. Relieved, he stepped from the alley and continued up Barracks Road in search of the boarding house.

A quick shower had revived Clive. As he entered the boarding house dining room, he felt alert for the first time that day. Three men were already seated around the long wooden table—two elderly Creoles engaged in conversation and a middle-aged white man reading the *Belize Times*. Clive dropped into one of the five unoccupied chairs. The Creoles nodded to him; the white man ignored him.

A pale young woman with dark hair emerged from the kitchen, balancing a tray of food. "You're late," she told Clive.

"Hurry up, girl!" the white man said irritably.

She set the food in the center of the table and returned to the kitchen. She reappeared a moment later with a plate and flatware for Clive. "We eat promptly at 7:00," she said.

Clive nodded and reached for what remained of a bowl of rice and a plate of fried plantain. The other dish was something he didn't recognize; it appeared to be fried corn meal, held together by strands of meat. He took the last slice, tried it, and found it tasted similar to his foster mother's tamales. "What is this?" he asked the young woman.

"Stuffed heart."

"Heart?"

"Yes. You stuff the heart with seasoned corn meal and cook it, then cut it into slices."

"It's good," Clive said.

The young woman smiled.

"It's cheap shit," the white man sneered.

"If the food here doesn't suit you, sah," said one of the Creoles, "why don't you stay at the Fort George?"

The white man glared, but said no more.

Clive surmised the Fort George must be a hotel for the wealthy. The comment reminded him of his own limited assets. Tomorrow, he would need to find a cheaper place to stay. The old woman who ran the boarding house had charged $2 for the night's lodging and three meals. His $45 wouldn't last long at that rate.

The men finished their meal without further conversation. The young woman passed in and out of the room from time to time. She was full-figured and looked white enough to be English, but her speech was clearly Belizean.

Fatigue swept over Clive again. He pushed his plate away and struggled to his feet, nearly knocking over his chair.

The young woman reentered the room with a large wooden bowl, filled with mangos. "No fruit?" she said to Clive.

"No . . . thank you." He unsteadily made his way through the dining room door.

He climbed the uneven stairs to his room on the third floor. The musty smell hit him as he stepped inside. He crossed the room and opened the single window. A cooling breeze blew in from the Caribbean. A reggae song drifted up from a radio next-door. Clive barely had enough energy to pull off his clothes and lay them across the solitary wooden chair. He stretched out on the cot and fell asleep instantly.

The sun had already risen when Clive awoke the next morning. He stretched, then lay still, listening to the unfamiliar sounds of morning in the city. Reggae again came from the radio next-door, and shouts and bicycle bells rang out from the street below. His mouth was dry; he had slept without waking for almost ten hours.

He closed his eyes again. The music ended and Radio Belize relayed the news from the British Broadcasting Corporation. The British announcer droned on about events that had no meaning to Clive. He put his forearm across his eyes and was about to drift off to sleep again, when a crisp Belizean voice came on the air:

And now, the local news. Guatemalan authorities have filed a formal protest with the governments of Belize and Great Britain, over the alleged looting of Mayan ruins near the Belize border . . .

Clive sat bolt upright.

. . . reported that a Lieutenant Luis Alvarez was murdered by two men described as Belizeans . . .

Clive leaped to his feet and rushed to the open window.

. . . and authorities in Cayo District say that . . .

Clive suddenly turned away from the window and looked down by his feet. His belongings lay on the floor in a pile beside his hemp bag. He spun around, saw his trousers in a heap beside the chair, and crossed the room in a single stride. His wallet was gone!

He futilely searched the pockets again and again, as he stared at the open window through which the thief had entered during the night.

. . . brought to you by Klim powdered milk and . . .

Clive had left the crowded neighborhood behind him, and now trudged up a deserted road that meandered alongside the sea. He was still stunned at losing all his money his first night in the city. He had counted on his brother's loan lasting for at least a month, while he found work.

A lorry sped up behind him and blew its horn. Clive veered onto the grassy shoulder. The truck rumbled past, spewing exhaust smoke. Clive held his breath until he was clear of it. He glanced to his right; the sky was darkening on the horizon. A squall was heading for the coast. Bad luck *ta raas!* he thought.

He passed a roadside food stand. He was hungry, having bolted from the boarding house without eating.

A block farther, he came upon a large white building. A sign in front read: "Belize Pickwick Club". A light-skinned Creole stood on a tennis court, overseeing three black laborers who were cutting weeds with machetes. Clive went up to the wire-mesh fence and called out, "Sah, I am looking for work!"

"I got no work for you, bwy."

Clive continued on. Ahead, he saw a battered Plymouth sedan

parked on a grassy area beside the road. The hood was open, and a man leaned into the engine compartment. Another man stood nearby. Their clothes were filthy, and they wore their hair in matted dreadlocks. They appeared to be Rastafarians. As Clive approached, the one standing off to the side shouted, "Bwy! Come here, no?"

Clive warily approached.

"What you know about cars, bwy?" the man said.

"I know a little," Clive said. The Mestizo who owned the San Ignacio service station had taught Clive to drive and to make minor repairs, before he fired him.

"The bloody thing died in the night," the man said. "It was running good when we stopped. But this morning, it cough one time, and now it don't do nothing."

Clive leaned over the fender and checked the battery cables. They were secure on the posts, but the braided ground strap had rusted through at the chassis. "You got a busted cable," he said.

"You can fix it?"

"Yes, but I need a wrench," Clive said, hoping they might give him a dollar or two.

The man went around to the rear of the car, opened the trunk, and returned with a pair of pliers.

A few minutes later, Clive secured the cable to a chassis bolt closer to the battery. "Try it, no?"

The engine started and assumed a rough idle.

"You a good mechanic, bwy," the man said.

"I . . . could use some money," Clive said.

"We have no money to give you, bwy," the man replied. "The magistrate took it all. Me and Nesta been locked up since Saturday."

"Why were you locked up?"

"Selling herb."

"Shit," Clive muttered. Heavy raindrops began to fall. He picked up his hemp bag and turned to leave.

"Bwy!" the man called after him. "At least make we take you where you going."

"I'm not sure . . . where I'm going."

The one called Nesta gave him a shrewd look. "Are the police looking for you, bwy?"

When Clive didn't respond, the other man said, "We going to Corozal. You can come, if you want."

"I got no money," Clive said.

"We find something for you, bwy" the man said with a laugh. The one called Nesta laughed too.

It was midmorning, and Clive sat on the dirt floor of an open lean-to, staring out at a steady drizzle. It had rained continuously since he arrived in Corozal three days earlier.

The lean-to nestled into a stand of trees; the front faced a large sugarcane field. Puddles had formed in several places under the leaking roof, and a small stream wound across the floor. The trees and the rain muffled the sound of the surf from the nearby bay.

Clive glanced over his shoulder at the two Rastafarians sleeping on the ground at the rear of the shelter. They had begun a liturgy immediately upon arriving—smoking marijuana and praying to Haile Selassie. For the past two days, they had continued to smoke, but there had been little praying.

Clive shook his head in frustration. In Belize City, they had promised him work; however, immediately upon his arrival, he had discovered they simply wanted him to tend the marijuana plants they had hidden among the sugarcane stalks.

He stood up and stretched. He hated the thought of wasting another day, waiting for the rain to stop. For three days, all they had eaten was the fish he had caught in the nearby bay and the coconuts he had picked up off the beach. At least you can't starve here, he thought grimly.

Nesta rose unsteadily to his feet, gave Clive a vague nod of recognition, then lurched to the edge of the lean-to and urinated out into the rain. Clive turned back to the sugarcane field. The rainfall slackened. He reached over and pulled down his hemp bag from a support pole. He slung it across his shoulder and stepped from the shelter.

"Where you going, mon?" the Rastafarian called after him.

Clive ignored him and walked into the dense sugarcane. The stalks swayed high above his head. He plunged ahead. The sod clung to his tattered basketball shoes, and the cane leaves slapped at his face and arms.

He plodded along for several minutes, then emerged from the field and found himself standing at the edge of a muddy road. From the sun's position in the overcast sky, he knew the bay was to his right and the town of Corozal was to his left. The Rastafarians had told him there was a resort on the bay, but they had cautioned him that the foreigners who stayed there were dangerous.

The rain fell harder. He stood at the side of the road, undecided which direction to go. Then he heard the sound of an approaching vehicle and watched as a mud-splattered Land Rover approached from his left. The driver weaved erratically from side to side, avoiding the large water-filled potholes. The vehicle veered toward Clive, and he retreated to the edge of the sugarcane field.

The driver brought the vehicle to a skidding stop. Lowering the passenger side window, he called out, "Hey! Come over here!"

Clive went over to the vehicle. The driver was a white man, tanned from the sun and smiling under a neatly trimmed gray mustache.

"Yes?" Clive said.

"Are you going this way?" the man said, gesturing toward the bay.

"Ah . . . yes."

"Come on. I'll give you a ride."

Clive opened the door, then hesitated. "I'm wet and dirty."

"Get in," the man replied brusquely. "Let's get going."

Clive climbed inside, and they pulled away. The man hunched over the steering wheel, struggling to see through the mud the wipers smeared across the windshield. "Are you from around here?" he said. His accent sounded American.

"Ah . . . no," Clive said.

"Corozal?"

"No," Clive said evasively, "Cayo District."

They hit a deep water-filled hole, and Clive and the driver both hit their heads on the canvas roof. "God damn it!" the man swore.

A few moments later, the road came to a dead end. The turbulent bay churned in front of them. A scattering of thatched-roof huts lay off to the right; a barbed wire fence enclosed the property on the left.

"Okay," the man said, "where you going?"

"I . . . ah . . . I'm not sure. I've never been here before. I'm . . . looking for work."

"You're not going to find any work over there," the man said, gesturing toward the huts. He turned the vehicle to the left and drove toward the fenced property.

They passed through an open gate. A guard, standing under a tree with a rifle slung over one shoulder, waved to the driver.

"This area is guarded, day and night," the man said. "Don't try to get in here on your own."

Clive nodded.

"What kind of work are you looking for?"

"Any kind. I just need work."

"How old are you?"

"Twenty-two," Clive lied.

"I may have something for you up at the inn, if this damned rain ever stops."

Clive's hopes rose. He looked out the window with interest. They passed the most luxurious homes he had ever seen, built from stucco and set back from the road on large lots. Wrought-iron fences surrounded the houses, and large dogs rushed to the gates as they passed. Clive wondered who these rich people were.

Ahead loomed a large white building, set on a point of land that protruded into the bay. They passed through the wrought-iron gate. A neatly lettered sign read: "La Posada don Carlos".

"Do you work here?" Clive said.

"I own the place." The man stopped the Land Rover beside a

utility building, shut off the engine, and extended his hand. "I'm Charlie Westerfield."

"I'm Clive Lightburn, *don Carlos.*"

"Speak Spanish, do you?"

"Yes, sah."

"That comes in handy around here . . ." Westerfield's voice trailed off. He frowned, listening intently. "The God-damned generator's stopped!" He threw open the door, jumped out, and disappeared into the utility building.

Clive climbed out and waited uncertainly in the doorway.

"Come in here!" Westerfield shouted.

Clive entered the room and found the inn owner standing beside a generator, holding a gasoline can.

"Somewhere around here," Westerfield said heatedly, "there's a God-damned Indian that thinks I'm in town, and he's wandered off and let this generator run dry. And as soon as he gets back . . . I'm going to fire his ass!"

Clive didn't risk responding.

"I need somebody I can count on," Westerfield said. "Somebody to keep the generator running, do the yard work, keep the pool clean, and stuff like that. You think you could handle it, boy?"

"Yes, sah!" Clive grabbed the gasoline can and began filling the generator tank.

"It only pays $10 a week, but you get your meals in the kitchen, and there's a bunk through that door there."

"Thank you, don Carlos!"

"What did you say your name was?"

"Clive, sah. Clive Lightburn."

"Okay, Clive. You've seen how quickly I'll fire your ass if you fuck up, right?"

"Yes, sah!" Clive said, emptying the last of the gasoline into the tank.

"Okay, pay attention. Here's the choke and here's the starter. If the generator ever stops and you have to restart it, you pull out the choke and push this button. But it had better never stop, just because it's out of gas!" He pressed the starter, and the generator fired noisily.

Westerfield strode toward the door and motioned for Clive to follow him. When they were back outside, he said, "Clive, the guests I get here in my inn, and those that live in those houses you saw, are important men. Do you understand that?"

"Yes, sah."

"No, you probably don't. But take my word for it. I mean, they're *real* important. There's no guests here right now, but if there had been, I'd be in deep shit." He stared down the road in silence for a moment, then added, "They don't have patience with people who fuck up. Take my word for it."

19. HEART DRUM

Ramón walked across the old swing bridge, annoyed by the heavy traffic. When he had arrived in Belize, there had been less than a hundred vehicles in the city. Now, more than 2,000 cars and trucks careened about its narrow streets.

On the north side of Haulover Creek, he passed the dilapidated fire station. "Mistah Kelley!" called out a voice from the shadows. "How you makin' it, sah?"

"Fine, Lloyd," Ramón said with a wave. "And you?"

"Gettin' along, sah."

Ramón continued up Front Street, feeling uncomfortable after his lunch of fish, rice, and beans. His weight was up to 250 pounds. Elijah Ruiz had begun to lecture him about the need to get on a diet.

He crossed the street and recognized several of the vehicles parked in front of the ramshackle Palace Hotel. The new bunch didn't seem to have much to do, except hang out at the Palace bar. He was tempted to walk on, but he had told Kendall Foster that he would meet with him and some of his associates.

Ramón entered the hotel bar and spotted Foster and three other young men, seated at a table in the rear of the room.

"Mistah Kelley," the Creole bartender said, as Ramón walked past, "what can I bring you?"

"Club soda and lime, Edmund," Ramón called back.

Foster stood up as he approached. "Thanks for coming, Ramón."

"Certainly," Ramón said, as they shook hands. Foster, a white Creole, was the scion of one of the wealthiest families in Belize. Ramón nodded to the three other men, who were Americans and relatively new in the country. Two ran a small flying service; the third was a partner in a Houston travel agency. Full ashtrays and empty glasses cluttered the table, although it was early afternoon. Foster pulled up a chair for Ramón.

Ramón sat down, thankful that he was positioned under a ceiling fan. The bartender brought over his club soda, along with another round of rum and cokes. Not wanting to waste his entire afternoon with heavy drinkers, Ramón got to the point. "You said on the phone that you wanted to discuss your plans for developing tourism."

Young Foster took a long swallow from his drink. "We haven't worked out all the particulars. However, we're far enough along that we're looking for someone to manage the venture."

"I'd need to know something about your plans, before I could recommend anyone."

"I've already recommended you, Ramón."

The offer didn't come as a complete surprise. "I have my dealership," Ramón said.

The American travel agent snorted. "That little chickenshit operation can barely be keeping you in rice and beans!"

"Well," Ramón said, belching softly, "I happen to like rice and beans."

"Ramón," Foster said, "I believe we've got an idea that can't miss."

"Tell me about it."

Foster's face lighted up. "We're going to build a tourist lodge in the jungle!"

Another circus come to Belize, Ramón thought. His interest in the conversation waned. "You plan to build a tourist lodge in the jungle?"

"Yes, mon. On my family's property in Cayo District."

The mention of the vast Foster holdings near the western border recaptured Ramón's interest. "What does your father think about this venture?"

"I tried to discuss it with him, but he wouldn't hear me out. He says there's no future for tourism in the interior."

"Just maybe, your father knows what he's talking about."

"Chuh!" Foster said.

"Kendall," Ramón said, "I agree with your father. I don't think Cayo District has much to offer tourists."

"Shit, Kendall!" the Texan interrupted with a sneer. "I told you these old guys all think the same. It's the reason this country's so fucked up. These old farts never had the balls to do anything with it!"

Ramón stood up. "Kendall, if you'd like to stop by my office sometime, I'd be glad to discuss this further."

"Tell me something, man," one of the pilots said with a slur, "do you know anything about that area?"

"I'm familiar with it," Ramón said levelly.

"Buddy," the pilot said, "I fly over Cayo District once a week. I *know* what I'm talking about!"

Ramón gazed at the man, eyes narrowed. "Asshole . . . I tramped through that God-damned jungle . . . bringing out mahogany . . . before you were born!"

The pilot sat motionless. Ramón turned and stalked out of the hotel bar.

He had started down Front Street, when he heard Foster's voice. "Ramón! Wait a minute!" Ramón stopped and waited until Foster caught up with him.

"Look, mon," Foster said, "I'm sorry for the words that were passed back there. They'd been drinking."

"They're always drinking, Kendall. That's the reason I avoid them."

Foster said plaintively, "Why are you so sure our plan won't work?"

"I can't say for sure it won't work, Kendall. Before I could advise you, I'd need to hear more about it. But my initial reaction is, I don't see Cayo District as a tourist attraction. Other than the Mayan ruins at Xunantunich, there's nothing out there."

Foster glanced toward the hotel.

"But the main thing that concerns me, Kendall," Ramón continued, getting the young man's attention again, "is your choice of associates. For any plan of yours to work, you'd better steer clear of the drunken cowboys that hang out at the Palace."

Kendall stared down the street for a moment, then turned back and said sullenly, "There's more to my plan, Ramón."

"Stop by my office sometime, and let's discuss it."

The young man gave a tight nod, then turned and headed back to the hotel.

Ramón sat on the veranda of Elijah Ruiz' home, sipping a pineapple drink and looking out over the choppy afternoon sea.

"'Old farts' are we?" Elijah said with a chuckle.

"According to the cowboys at the Palace."

"Questionable authorities."

"True," Ramón said, "but I'm not sure we can deny the charge altogether. Our generation doesn't have much to show for our years of trying to develop Belize."

"Don't be too hard on us, Ramón. In the last twenty-five years, we've moved away from colonialism, and we've seen a fair amount of economic growth."

"Yes, but on the other hand, we're still not completely independent, and too many of our people live in poverty."

A silence followed, as both men stared out to sea. Finally, Elijah muttered, "Old farts for true, uh?"

"You and I are running out of time, my friend," Ramón said. "If we're going to accomplish something, we'd better get a move on."

"What do you think it would take to develop this bloody country, Ramón?"

Ramón thought for a moment. "I believe we'd need a stronger commitment to develop tourism."

"Such as what young Foster is proposing?"

"Possibly, but I don't see the jungle ever being a tourist attraction."

"The cayes then?"

Ramón nodded. "American investors apparently think so, the way they're buying up Ambergris Caye."

"For true. Small hotels are going up all around my property. I told Esther last week that we ought to rent out rooms ourselves."

"I think when we built the inland capital at Belmopan, twenty years ago," Ramón said, "we moved away from our strength. The sea can be dangerous, true enough; however, I think it's the biggest asset our country has."

"But the agriculture, the timber . . ."

"We're too under populated to exploit our inland resources. That's the reason our imports exceed our exports. Our only chance to gain a favorable balance of trade is to expand tourism."

"Why not leave the cayes alone and promote tourism in Belize City?"

"Potential investors, particularly Americans, see it as a slum. In the States, our whole city would be classified as a ghetto."

"I'm sure it would be, since most of us are dark skinned."

Ramón shook his head. "American prejudices aside, the city's filthy and most of our people don't earn a decent wage. That's why we lose our best young people. The kids we send to the States for an education, usually don't come back."

"Unfortunately, you're right, Ramón. My own daughter told me—"

Elijah was interrupted by the sound of his wife's car pulling into the driveway. The two men got up and walked over to the veranda railing. Ramón saw an attractive white woman get out on the passenger's side.

"Come, Ramón," Elijah said. "There's someone I want you to meet. She's come down from the States for a visit."

Ramón followed Elijah downstairs, where the two women struggled with a large suitcase.

"Let me give you a hand with that," Ramón said.

"Ramón!" Esther Ruiz said with delight. "I'm so glad you're here. I want you to meet a dear friend of mine. Dawn Peterson."

"How do you do," Ramón said.

"Hi, Ramón," the woman said, thrusting out her hand. "Good to meet you. God, is it always this hot here? This is real humidity . . . even compared to Houston."

Ramón shook her hand. He guessed her age to be early-forties. Her reddish hair shone in the sun; a sprinkling of freckles adorned her pale cheeks. Her grip was firm, like the rest of her body. Ramón drew in his stomach. "I'm afraid you've arrived in the middle of our rainy season," he said. "This is our worst time of year."

"Dawn is a social worker at Methodist Hospital in Houston," Esther said happily. "We met her when Elijah was there. She promised to come down on holiday, and she did!"

Later that night, Ramón and Dawn stood on the seawall behind Elijah's house, looking out at the moonlit Caribbean. Over dinner, Dawn had captivated Ramón with her healthy femininity and straightforward ideas. Ramón savored the return of an emotion he had feared he had lost.

"How long have you lived down here, Ramón?"

"I've lived in the Tropics my whole life. I was born in Panama, and came to Belize about twenty-five years ago."

"Twenty-five years? You must like it here."

"It's just . . . where I wound up. Belize is pretty primitive—always has been. When I came here, I felt there was tremendous potential. I still do."

She gave him an understanding smile. "Are you married?"

"Yes . . . well, yes and no."

She waited.

"My wife lives in the States. We never divorced, but it's been nearly twenty years since we lived together."

"Then why on earth do you stay married?"

"It's hard to explain. I'm a Central American. We have different ideas about . . . families . . . and . . . responsibilities."

"Mmmm," she said.

"What about you? Is there a Mr. Peterson waiting for you in Houston?"

"There's a Mr. Peterson in Houston, but he's not waiting for me. We divorced four years ago. Mr. Peterson was my second attempt at marriage, and I don't plan on there being a third."

Ramón was pleased that she wasn't married. "How long will you be down here?"

"About a week. I've really been looking forward to it. Esther and I became good friends in Houston. We'll probably sit around and talk for a day or two. Then, she has some people here she wants me to meet—women involved in social work. Also, I hope to get out and see some of the surrounding countryside."

"I don't think Elijah and Esther go out of town much nowadays, since Elijah's heart attack. But I'd be glad to show you around."

"Well, thank you, Ramón. I'd like that."

"In fact," Ramón said, "I'm driving down to my property near Dangriga on Monday." Then he added, "But that probably wouldn't be a good trip for you; the Hummingbird Highway is in terrible condition."

"Ramón, I grew up in place called Bandera, Texas. Believe me, I can handle any road Belize wants to throw at me."

"Just remember those words next week," Ramón said with a laugh. "You said you'll be here for a week?"

"A week . . . maybe longer," Dawn said, then turned and started toward the house.

Ramón trudged through the soft sand toward the thatch-roof cabin, carrying a crumpled paper sack. The late afternoon sea churned nearby. He climbed the wooden steps and paused at the rusty screen door. Dawn had undressed and lay on her stomach. She had pulled the sheet across her, but left her bare shoulders exposed to the cooling breeze.

Ramón opened the door, and Dawn turned quickly toward him. Recognizing him, she said, "Mmmm . . . I dozed off. The sound of the surf affected me like a sleeping pill."

"Is your back feeling any better?" Ramón said. He sat down on the other bed and set the sack on the floor.

"No. There's no hot water, and the cold shower made it feel worse. God, this is embarrassing! I can't believe I'm such a sissy that I can't take a Jeep ride!"

"Not just a Jeep ride, but a five-hour ride down the Hummingbird Highway. Your muscles probably locked up, tensing against the bumps. I think I'd better take you to a doctor."

"Oh, Christ no! This is embarrassing enough. Let's not bring all of Dangriga in on it." An attempted smile turned to a grimace when she tried to move.

Ramón reached into the sack and withdrew a stalk of bananas. Then he pulled out a small unlabeled bottle. "Would you like to try a local remedy?"

"Looks like moonshine. Good God, Ramón, moonshine and bananas. You Central Americans really know how to wine and dine a woman!"

Ramón laughed. He unscrewed the cap off the bottle, took a whiff, and wrinkled his nose. "It's a . . . liniment . . . external use only. The woman who owns the grocery shop down the beach is also the local *buyai*."

"The local what?"

"Buyai. She's a spirit medium—like a shaman, or an obeah woman. She conducts rites that invoke the spirits of the dead. She also specializes in bush medicine. I told her about your problem, and she gave me this."

"Oh, God," Dawn groaned, "voodoo medicine."

Ramón screwed the cap back onto the bottle.

"Well, what are you waiting for?" she said.

"Want to try it?"

"Seems to be all we have, unless you know a cure involving bananas." She slid the sheet down to her waist.

Ramón sat down on the bed beside her and poured some of the thick amber fluid into his palm. He slowly applied it to the middle of her back.

"God, Ramón, I don't know what she's got in there, but it smells like she started with a kerosene base!"

"Is it burning you?"

"No . . . it feels . . . kind of like Ben-Gay . . . warm, but it doesn't burn. A little lower, please. The pain's near the base of my spine."

Ramón massaged her back with the oily fluid for several minutes.

"Lower, Ramón," Dawn murmured.

He filled his palm with the fluid again and rubbed it across the top of her hips.

"Lower, Ramón," Dawn whispered.

Ramón cleared his throat. "Lower?"

"Ramón, my back feels fine now. Lower . . ."

After Dawn had dozed off, Ramón had moved to the other bed. Now, he lay on his back, hands behind his head, gazing up at the thatched roof.

"You look very pleased with yourself, Mr. Kelley."

Her voice startled him. He sat up and smiled at her. "I feel like a teenager."

"What are you doing over there?"

"Giving you some room."

"Come back," she said, lifting the sheet invitingly.

Ramón self-consciously moved from his bed to hers. His weight caused her to roll toward him, and she enfolded him in her arms and kissed him passionately.

"See?" he said with a grin. "I'm too big to share a bed."

Dawn patted his ample stomach. "We'll need to do something about this."

"Too late. Too many years of Belize rice and beans."

"It's not healthy for you to be this big. It has to come off."

Ramón was pleased; it sounded as if she were making long-range plans, which included him. "Is your back okay?"

"I feel wonderful!" she said, hugging him.

"The buyai knows her stuff," Ramón said.

"The buyai woman . . . and the banana man."

They both laughed, then lay quietly, listening to the sound of the surf. The evening light faded.

"Ramón, does this place have electricity?"

He shook his head. "We'll have to use that kerosene lantern over there. Or, if you prefer, we can move to the hotel in town."

"Absolutely not! I love this place."

Ramón smiled. Dawn was shattering his notion of American women.

"I'd like to meet the buyai woman and thank her," Dawn said.

He nodded. "She won't be at her store tonight. She'll be resting for the *dugu* she's performing in the morning."

"What's a 'dugu'?"

"It's a healing ceremony. There's a woman from the village who supposedly is possessed by an evil spirit."

"And the buyai is going to heal her?"

"Healed you, didn't she?"

"Seriously, Ramón."

"Caribs maintain close ties with their ancestors, not only those buried here in Belize, but also those buried in their previous home, the island of St. Vincent. Sometimes, the spirit of an ancestor possesses a member of the community. The dugu is the ceremony where the buyai appeases the spirit and returns the person to the living."

"Have you ever seen one of these ceremonies?"

"A couple of years ago. The same buyai let me attend. Matter of fact, she invited me to attend the one tomorrow."

"Ramón!" Dawn said, sitting up. "Can we go?"

"Are you sure you feel up to it?"

"Ramón, I just had a back spasm. I'm fine now. Come on, help me get this kerosene washed off."

At first light, Ramón and Dawn walked through a cluster of palm trees. Twenty yards away stood a thatched hut, built facing the sea. Several Caribs milled about the entrance.

"That's the cult house," Ramón said.

The Caribs turned and stared at them.

Dawn stopped. "Ramón, they don't seem to want us here."

He took her hand. "It's okay."

She didn't move. "I think we should leave."

A stocky Carib woman emerged from the cult house.

"That's the buyai," Ramón said.

The woman looked at them, then spoke briefly to her followers. She gave Ramón a quick nod and reentered the cult house. The others followed her inside.

"That was our invitation," Ramón said. "The dugu is about to begin. It's for a village woman, who moved to Belmopan. She's a school teacher and has been possessed by an ancestor. She's come home to be cured."

"A school teacher practicing this superstition?"

"Her Carib doctor in Belmopan recommended it."

"Look," Dawn said, pointing out to sea. Several fishing dories circled offshore. The fishermen wore crowns fashioned from palm fronds.

The resonant first beat of a large drum caused Ramón and Dawn to jump. At the sound, the fishermen turned and paddled their dories toward shore. The villagers, led by the buyai, marched from the cult house to meet them. The buyai shook a gourd rattle; three drummers followed her cadence.

Ramón whispered to Dawn, "The fishermen are bringing the ancestors from the afterworld."

The procession stopped at the edge of the sea. They sang as the dories approached.

"I know this refrain," Ramón said.

Our journey has been sad, my grandchild,
We have searched for our grandchildren.
We have crossed the deep ocean,
Because our descendants are far away.
We have stood on the shore of Aurayana,
On the beautiful shore of Aurayana,
shedding tears.

The boats arrived at the beach, and several villagers waded into the surf and unloaded baskets of fish and crabs.

"Gifts for the ancestors," Ramón said.

The fishermen beached their boats and joined the procession, as it reformed and marched to the cult house.

When the last villager disappeared inside, Ramón took a step forward, but Dawn held back. "Ramón, I don't think we should go in there."

"It's okay," he said. "The buyai has given her approval."

Dawn reluctantly followed him over to the cult house. They stepped inside. Drums reverberated through the thatched enclosure, and the congregation kept time to the staccato beat with a vigorous hip-rolling dance.

Ramón led Dawn around the outer perimeter until he found a good vantage point to watch the ceremony. He put his mouth near her ear. "The woman wearing the yellow scarf is the one who's possessed."

A young Carib woman stood in the center of the room, arms at her sides and head thrown back. Only the whites of her eyes showed. Abruptly, the drummers stopped playing. The woman began to speak, softly at first. Then her arms flailed and her voice rose. Her words rang out, anguished and beseeching.

Dawn dug her fingers into Ramón's forearm. "What's she saying?" she whispered.

"I don't know. She's speaking in Garifuna."

"Where's the buyai?"

"It's not time for her, yet."

Finally, the possessed woman's harangue trailed off. Again, she gazed at the thatched roof, and her eyes rolled back. Suddenly she crumpled to the dirt floor. Dawn moved toward the woman, but Ramón restrained her.

No one stirred for several seconds, then the rhythmic sound of gourd rattles broke the silence. The buyai entered the room from an alcove off to the side. A drummer took up the rhythm, as the buyai moved through the congregation to the center of the room.

"That large drum in the center is the 'heart drum'," Ramón whispered. "It draws the ancestors from the earth below."

The congregation began to chant to the beat of the drums. The other two drums joined in, and the congregation resumed their hip-rolling dance to the throbbing rhythm. The buyai and her assistants moved about the cult house to predetermined points, conducting a ritual of chanting and dancing. The possessed woman frequently would revive, rise, and dance as if in a trance. Or she would stand and hysterically beseech the congregation. Then she would slump to the dirt floor.

After more than an hour, Ramón led Dawn out of the cult house.

As they walked up the beach to their cabin, Dawn was noticeably disturbed. Ramón put his arm around her. "Are you okay?"

She nodded without replying.

"These dugus often go on for a week," Ramón said. He wanted to allay her concern. "Since we won't be here for the end, I'll predict it for you: everybody will be exhausted; the ancestors will be appeased; the school teacher will be healed; and buyai will gain ten more converts. Eleven if you convert."

Dawn gave him a cutting glance.

Ramón stopped and turned her toward him. "Dawn, I wouldn't have taken you there if I had thought it was dangerous, either for you or for the villagers. Consider it . . . like you've attended someone else's church service."

"Church service! Calling up dead ancestors?"

"Not that different from Christianity," Ramón said. "They're just more closely related to the deceased."

Dawn reluctantly smiled, then took his hand. They strolled on in comfortable silence. As they came within sight of their cabin, she stopped and turned to him. "God, this is an exciting country!"

20. PEARL RIVER

"Easy, man!" Ray called out from the rear seat.

Tyrone Johnson's recently-acquired Pontiac Trans-Am drifted dangerously close to the shoulder. The headlights played across the dense pines that lined the desolate country road.

Tyrone regained control and grinned at Ray in the rearview mirror. "Stay cool, Token!"

Tyrone's girl friend, Caroline, looked back. "Bobbi Sue, you all right?"

"Uh huh," Bobbi Sue said, nestling under Ray's arm. Her lips brushed against his ear, as she whispered, "If Daddy could see me now! Going out with my little brother's friend and tearing through backwoods Mississippi with nigras."

Ray pulled her face between his neck and shoulder, so Tyrone and Caroline wouldn't hear. She drew back, giggling. When she started to speak again, Ray silenced her with their first kiss. Bobbi Sue put her arms around his neck and probed his mouth with her tongue.

"Hey, man!" Tyrone said. "This ain't no time to be gettin' leg. You got a game tonight."

Ray opened his eyes and again saw Tyrone's grinning face in the rearview mirror. He reluctantly released Bobbi Sue. In the car's dimly-lighted interior, he saw a smile of conquest on the young woman's face. He cleared his throat. "How much farther, Ty?"

"We're there, man. See the lights up ahead?"

A yellowish aura lighted the night sky.

"Is this Pearl River?" Bobbi Sue said.

"Must be," Ray said as they approached a clearing in the pines. "And that must be Pearl River Consolidated."

Tyrone turned up a gravel drive, then bounced into a freshly mowed field that served as a parking area.

"It's big!" Bobbi Sue said. "What's such a big school doing out here in the middle of nowhere?"

"Tyrone says the kids are bussed here from miles around."

"Now tell me again, Ray," Bobbi Sue said, "who's holding this tournament?"

"I'm not sure. I've never played here before. Ty told me there'll be a few company teams entered, but mainly it'll be former college players from towns around here. To enter a team, you just have to put up $200."

"I've never heard of anyone holding tournaments after regular basketball season is over," Bobbi Sue said.

"Me neither, 'til Ty asked if I wanted to play." Ray leaned forward. "Hey, Ty, how long they been holding these tournaments?"

"Years, man." Tyrone pulled into a tight parking space between two pickup trucks and shut off the engine. "My daddy played here in the Fifties. He said they'd have a white tournament one weekend, and a black one the next. There ain't a hell of a lot to do out here in the boondocks. These farmers love to put on their best overalls and come out to watch B-ball."

Tyrone and his girl friend slid out of the car on the driver's side. As Ray pushed the passenger's seat forward, he glanced out the side window. A farmer stared down at him from the cab of an old pickup truck. Ray carefully opened his door and eased out. He made sure the door didn't hit the truck as Bobbi Sue climbed out. They went around to the rear of the car, where Tyrone was unloading equipment bags

The pickup truck's doors opened, and two white men in overalls stepped down. Ray and Tyrone exchanged glances. The farmers sauntered back to where they were standing. "You boys playing here tonight?" the driver drawled.

"Uh huh," Ray said uneasily.

"Who y'all play for?"

"Hammond," Tyrone said.

"Hammond," the farmer said thoughtfully. "Over in Luziana?"
Ray nodded.

"Y'all a long way from home," the other man drawled.

Ray nodded again, although the trip had been less than forty miles.

"That means y'all playin' the first game," the driver said.

Ray frowned at Tyrone, who responded with a tight nod.

A grin broke across the driver's face. "Well, hell! We'll pull for y'all tonight then. We're from Pearl River, and our team don't play 'til nine o'clock. Good luck!" The two men turned and headed toward the gym.

When they were out of earshot, Tyrone said to Ray, "You'd a been hell on the freedom rides, boy."

Ray sighed with relief. "You were looking kinda pale yourself there, buddy."

Ray and Bobbi Sue followed Tyrone and Caroline through the parking lot. Several young men lounged around the gym entrance. One of them said something that Ray didn't catch, and the rest laughed.

The familiar sound of basketballs hammering the floor echoed into the concession area. An elderly man collecting tickets at the door recognized they were players and waved them through. A surge of excitement hit Ray as he stepped into the brightly-lighted gym. At least 1,000 people were already on hand. Several players had arrived early and were warming up.

"Home boy!" Tyrone called out to a player at the near end of the court.

"Wha's happenin', outlaw?" a tall black player in his early thirties called back. He languidly flipped up a jump shot and jogged over to Tyrone.

"It's all right, bro'," Tyrone said. They exchanged grips.

"Hear you be playin' for Memphis next year," the player said.

"Signed, sealed, and delivered," Tyrone said with a grin.

"Yeah, I seen you drivin' through the quarter in that Trans-Am. The 'man' must be payin' better than he did ten years ago."

Tyrone grinned again.

The player nodded to Ray and said to Tyrone, "So you brought the 'Gun' with you, uh?"

"Yeah. He ain't bad . . . for a white boy."

"Yeah, I know. I watched him fill it up against Bogalusa a few weeks ago." He extended his hand to Ray. "I'm James Brodman."

"I've seen you too," Ray said as they shook hands. "I used to go out watch you when you played for Southeastern."

"Long time ago, boy," Brodman said. He picked up a loose ball and arched a shot from twenty-five feet. He turned to Ray before it ripped through the net. "Where you goin' to college?"

"LSU."

"How they payin'?"

Ray shook his head.

"They ain't payin', or you ain't talkin'?" Brodman said. His wide grin exposed a gold tooth.

Before Ray could answer, Bobbi Sue said, "Where we supposed to sit?"

"They'll make room for you over there," Brodman said, pointing to an area where several black women were seated. Turning to Tyrone and Ray, he said, "The dressing room's through that door. You outlaws go get dressed."

A few minutes later, Ray and Tyrone walked back onto the court in makeshift uniforms. Tyrone had given Ray a faded green T-shirt with a barely discernible "22" stenciled in black.

Ray glanced around at his teammates. All were black and most were in their thirties. He didn't recognize anyone except James Brodman. A ball rolled across the floor. Ray scooped it up and flipped in a soft jump shot. He eased into the pregame shooting ritual.

Moments later, Brodman walked over to where Ray and Tyrone were loosening up in a slow-motion game of one-on-one. "I'm goin' to start you two, since you're used to playin' together. Tyrone, you'll be at a forward, since I play center. Gun, you'll play shootin' guard." Then he pointed to the scorekeeper's table. "You two outlaws go ahead and check in."

As Ray and Tyrone walked off the court, Ray said, "What's this 'outlaw' stuff?"

Tyrone frowned. "You ain't serious, are you?"

"Yeah. What's it mean?"

They had arrived at the table. "Names?" the scorekeeper said.

"Shit, man," Tyrone said to Ray, "you ain't kiddin', are you?"

"Names?" the scorekeeper demanded.

Tyrone turned and said with a deadpan expression, "Wallace, sir. George Wallace."

The scorekeeper shook his head. "And yours?" he asked Ray.

"What's going on here, Ty?" Ray said.

Tyrone stepped between Ray and the scorekeeper. "Ain't you never heard of 'outlaw ball'?" he whispered.

"I don't know what the hell you're talking about."

"Son, if you're plannin' on playin'," the scorekeeper said, "you got to give me your name."

"Make up a name," Tyrone said under his breath.

"What?"

"Make up a name . . . any name."

"What?"

Tyrone turned to the scorekeeper. "His name is . . . Gunner, sir. Booker T. Gunner. He used to play for the Covington School for the Deaf."

The scorekeeper shook his head again, but dutifully entered the names into his book.

Ray and Tyrone walked toward their bench. "Amateurs aren't supposed to play in these tournaments, are they?" Ray said.

"I thought you knew, man," Tyrone said. "Can't believe you lived in Hammond all your life and never heard of outlaw ball. Why don't you go get dressed and wait over there with the ladies?"

They arrived at the team huddle. Brodman had begun his pregame instructions. Ray scanned the boisterous crowd. A nasal voice on the public address system gave the starting lineups, including one Booker T. Gunner. Behind the bench, Bobbi Sue leaned forward in eager anticipation. Ray turned to Tyrone. "Fuck it. Let's run and shoot!"

It was past midnight when the two couples arrived back in Hammond. Tyrone drove slowly through the dark streets of Ray's neighborhood. Ray slouched down in the rear seat, and Bobbi Sue faced him. Her legs were drawn up and the zipper of her jeans was open. Ray ached from the past hour of heavy petting.

"We're almost there, y'all," Tyrone said.

"Let's go park someplace," Ray said huskily.

"No, Tyrone," Bobbi Sue said. "I can't stay out. Daddy's working swing shift tonight, and he'll be home any minute."

Ray helped her sit up. One thing he didn't want was trouble with Mr. Mitchell. As long as he could remember, the entire neighborhood had tiptoed around Thomas Mitchell. He worked odd hours and made a long commute to and from the Todd Shipyards in New Orleans. He was always irritable, and occasionally violent.

Tyrone turned onto the street where Ray and Bobbi Sue lived. He flipped off the lights and coasted to a stop across the street from Bobbi Sue's house.

"Daddy's truck isn't in the drive," Bobbi Sue said. "Good, he isn't home yet."

"Give us a minute to say good night," Ray told Tyrone. "Then I need to get my stuff out of the trunk."

"Yeah, man. I got to give you your money too."

"Money?"

"Yeah. Brodman gave me mine and yours."

"What money?"

"For the game tonight," Tyrone said. "Man, you don't know nothin', do you? The way the tournament works is: each team puts up $200, and they get $200 back for every game they win. Your share for tonight is $25."

"I didn't know we got any money—"

"Ray, come on," Bobbi Sue interrupted, pushing him. "Daddy's due home in a few minutes."

Outside the car, Bobbi Sue put her arms around Ray's neck. "I wish I didn't have to go in," she said.

"Me too."

"If you and Tyrone hadn't stayed to watch the second game," she said petulantly.

"Brodman wanted us to see what the Pearl River team looked like. He says they usually win their own tournament. If we get through tomorrow night's game, we'll probably play them in the finals on Saturday."

"Good as y'all are, it shouldn't matter who you play. And you, 'Mr. Gunner', with your thirty-five points. Those two rednecks from the parking lot had everybody cheering for you, like you were the local hero or something!"

"Crazy, wasn't it?" Ray said with a grin.

"Will you take me back for the rest of the games?"

"Sure, if you want to go."

"Of course I want to go! I can't believe you're so bashful. I'm glad you got up the nerve to ask me to come along tonight."

"Somebody's coming!" Tyrone said.

Ray glanced over his shoulder and saw headlights approaching.

"Quick!" Bobbi Sue said. "Run!" She shoved him in the direction of his house.

Ray jogged across the street. As he arrived at the end of his driveway, he heard Caroline call out, "Bobbi Sue, your purse!"

Bobbie Sue hurried back to the car.

Ray continued up the driveway. The rear door was unlocked, as it always was. He let himself in, then quietly threaded his way through the dark house to his bedroom. He dropped onto his bed and listened intently.

Tires screeched away from the front of his house. The side door to the Mitchell residence opened and closed. A truck door slammed and Mr. Mitchell's voice boomed out, "Bobbi Sue! Get back here!" Then heavy footsteps echoed up the Mitchell driveway. The side door was thrown open and Mr. Mitchell shouted, "Bobbi Sue!" The door slammed shut.

Ray jumped up and hurried over to his bedroom window.

Lights went on throughout the Mitchell residence. Muffled shouts came from the kitchen.

Ray's mother burst into the bedroom and rushed over to where he was standing. "Ray, honey, what's going on over there?"

Before he could respond, Bobbi Sue shrieked, "No, Daddy!" Mr. Mitchell shouted something unintelligible. Bobbi Sue screamed in pain. She screamed again, and Ray bolted toward his bedroom door.

"Ray, honey!" his mother cried. "Don't get involved with those trashy people!"

Ray banged out the kitchen door and ran across his back yard to the Mitchell residence.

"What were you doin' with that God-damned nigger?" Mr. Mitchell demanded.

Ray heard the sound of a slap and a scream from Bobbi Sue. He pounded on the Mitchell's side door. The house went silent. Then Mrs. Mitchell pleaded, "Please, Thomas, don't hit her again!" Bobbi Sue's younger brother, Tommy, cried, "That's enough, Daddy!"

Ray's mother caught up with him. "Come back, honey," she implored.

Ray shook his head.

"I'm going to call the police," his mother said. She rushed back to the house.

"What were you doin' with that God-damned nigger?" Mr. Mitchell hollered.

"I wasn't with him, Daddy! Please . . ."

"I seen you run from his car. And I seen the nigger son of a bitch haul ass out of here, when he seen it was me!"

"Honest, Daddy . . . No!" Another slap, and a scream from Bobbi Sue.

Ray burst through the door. Bobbi Sue cringed on the floor, trying to hide under the breakfast table. Her father stood over her with a wide leather belt. Mrs. Mitchell and Tommy cowered near the kitchen sink.

Mr. Mitchell turned to Ray. "You! Get out of here!"

"She was with me, Mr. Mitchell," Ray said fearfully.

"Get out of here, I told you!"

"Mr. Mitchell, Bobbi Sue was out with me!"

"What are you talkin' about, boy?" Mr. Mitchell said, approaching him.

"She was with me, sir!"

"Bullshit! I seen that nigger she was with!"

Ray heard a siren approaching. "No, sir!" he said, his voice breaking. "She was with me. She just went to see me play basketball."

"You're a God-damned liar! You kids finished your damned basketball weeks ago!"

Flashing lights shone through the window. "Yes, sir, we did. But this was a special tournament, over in Pearl River. The boy you saw drop us off is a member of the team I play on."

Two policemen burst into the kitchen. Mr. Mitchell ignored them and glared at Ray. "'Special tournament', huh? Special tournament, like one of them outlaw tournaments? You tellin' me you was playin' outlaw ball over in Pearl River, and you and some nigger took my girl over there!"

Ray nodded, caught a glimpse of a huge fist, then lost consciousness.

The following afternoon, Ray walked home from school. The policemen who had responded to the disturbance call apparently had spread the story around town. By midday, the source of Ray's split lip had been common knowledge around Hammond High. At lunch, he had told Tyrone that he was dropping out of the Pearl River tournament. "With only three weeks to go 'til graduation," he had said, "I don't need this shit."

Now, he felt uneasy as he approached his house. The policemen had not arrested Mr. Mitchell. They simply had warned him that they would be back for him if there were a recurrence.

Ray turned up his driveway. There was no sign of activity next-door. Mr. Mitchell's truck was gone. He had probably already left for his shift at the shipyard.

Ray entered his kitchen. The screen door banged shut behind him. His mother called out from the living room, "Ray, honey, is that you?"

"It's me, Mom," he said. He put his books on the counter and opened the refrigerator.

His mother entered the kitchen. "Ray, a Mr. Butler called—" She stopped in mid-sentence when he turned and looked at her. "Oh, honey! Your poor lip looks terrible!"

"Who's Mr. Butler, Mom?"

"Who's . . . ? Oh, yes, Mr. Butler. I had just come in from shopping, and I couldn't understand what he was talking about. Wait a minute; I made some notes." She picked up a piece of paper off the kitchen table. "Let's see . . . he said he's an assistant to the Athletic Director at LSU . . . he'd been contacted by an alumnus in Hammond . . . some outlandish report that you'd taken part in 'outlaw' activities."

"Damn!" Ray said under his breath.

"Ray," his mother said, looking up with a frown, "Thomas Mitchell was shouting something about outlaws last night. What are they talking about?"

"Mom . . . the game I played in last night was sort of . . . semi-pro. The players on winning teams get paid a few dollars for each game they win. Amateurs aren't allowed to take money, so they play under phony names . . . like aliases. The other players call us 'outlaws'."

"You took money you weren't supposed to?"

"Yeah . . . but I didn't do it for the money. I got to the gym there and just . . . wanted to play. Now please, Mom, this Mr. Butler. Did he say anything about me . . . and LSU?"

"He said for you to contact him right away. I have the number here. Oh, Ray!" she said, putting her hands to her face. "Do you think they might revoke your scholarship?" .

21. LA POSADA

Clive skimmed leaves off the Posada don Carlos swimming pool. The ten-room inn was unoccupied, as it often was. Neighborhood residents and transient marijuana traffickers made it profitable for don Carlos to keep it open, despite the low occupancy.

Clive sweated heavily in the late afternoon heat. He paused and pushed his hair away from his face. He hadn't cut it since arriving in Corozal, five months earlier. A woman friend in the nearby village now kept it braided in dreadlocks.

Clive gazed across the emerald-colored bay to a peninsula of Mexican territory. Three steep hills protruded from the low-lying coastline. The Indian cook had told him they were unexplored Mayan pyramids.

Gravel crunched nearby, drawing his attention. A dusty Ford taxi pulled into the parking lot. A middle-aged white man climbed out of the back, then pitched headlong onto the ground. Three young Creole women scrambled from the car, laughing uproariously. The driver, an unshaven Mestizo in his thirties, got out and watched with a tolerant smile.

The white man sat up and looked about with a sheepish, drunken grin. He fumbled with his shoelaces, and the girls squatted down to help him. Still laughing, they told him they had switched his shoes while he was asleep.

The driver helped the man to his feet. He swayed, then shoved the driver away and beckoned the girls. Two took positions under his arms and walked him toward the inn. The third ducked into the car and collected their purses.

"Clive!" shouted a voice behind him.

Clive turned and saw the inn owner hurrying across the patio to meet the arrivals.

"Help the driver with the bags," Westerfield said.

Westerfield and his guests noisily greeted each other. Clive walked up to the driver. "Bags?"

"We don't have no bags," the driver muttered, pushing past him. Clive smelled rum on his breath.

From the group's appearance, they had been on the road for more than a day. A shrill burst of female laughter erupted from inside the inn. Belize City whores, Clive thought with contempt, then returned to his tasks.

That night, Clive cleaned the supper mess from a pool-side table. The five guests had moved inside and resumed drinking. A cassette player blared, punctuated by bursts of raucous laughter. Occasionally, the white guest's voice rose in drunken petulance, followed by other voices placating him. Clive gathered the last of the dirty plates and entered the inn.

No one looked his way as he crossed the polished tile floor. Westerfield and the white guest sat at the bar, engaged in earnest conversation. The taxi driver had a glass in his hand, as he half-heartedly slow-danced with one of the young women. Another woman sat at the bar, staring at her drink. The prettiest of the three rummaged through the inn's cassette collection.

Clive passed through the open kitchen door. The Mayan couple who prepared and served the food were cleaning up.

"Do you know who those people are?" Clive said in Spanish.

The husband shrugged indifferently. His wife said, "I've seen the American before, but not the women."

The music in the next room came to an abrupt stop. Then a heavy punta beat echoed from the tiled room. The tan woman who had selected the music shouted, "Come! Make we rock!"

Clive leaned against the sink and watched through the open doorway. The taxi driver and his dark Creole partner came alive and vigorously undulated their hips to the throbbing punta. The tan woman pulled Westerfield onto the dance floor. Clive was surprised at how well the inn owner danced to the music of southern

Belize. Punta rock was a modern interpretation of Carib cultural dances.

The chubby, light-skinned woman at the bar tried to coax the American guest onto the floor. He pushed her away and gazed intently at the woman dancing with Westerfield.

Clive shook his head, angry at the foreigner for disrespecting Belizean women, but angrier at the complaisant women.

The two couples danced for the length of the tape, pausing only long enough to change partners between songs. The surly American guest swayed unsteadily on his bar stool. The light-skinned girl sat silently beside him.

The music paused while the tape changed direction. Westerfield, out of breath, took the opportunity to return to his bar stool. "Enough for me!" he said. The taxi driver also returned to the bar.

The music resumed, this time with the slow ballad, "Nothing Lasts Forever". The two young women stood alone on the dance floor. When none of the men approached them, they turned to each other and began to sway in a slow, sensual punta.

The tall black woman took the male lead. In time with the rhythm, she aggressively pursued the slight tan woman, who danced away, rejecting her advances. Finally, the black woman appeared to lose interest. The tan woman danced back, within inches, and began to mirror her movements. They swayed in unison to the slow drum beat, without touching, then bent their knees and slowly undulated down.

Clive shifted uncomfortably.

"We're leaving now," the cook said.

Clive turned and nodded. The Mayan couple quietly left through the screen door on the other side of the kitchen. Clive returned his attention to the dance floor. The women now danced back to back, still not quite touching. They gazed over their shoulders at each other, and again bent their knees.

A bar stool scraped on the tile, and the American guest staggered onto the dance floor. The tan woman was unaware of him, until he grabbed her wrist and yanked her to a standing position. Then he pulled her in the direction of the guest rooms.

The black woman stood alone in the center of the floor, looking toward the doorway where her partner had disappeared. The taxi driver got up and took her in his arms. They finished the dance in a close embrace.

Clive strode across the kitchen and banged out the screen door, into the night.

Clive had just dropped off to sleep when the door to his alcove creaked open. He sat up and was blinded by the light from the generator room.

"Get up," said a figure silhouetted in the doorway.

For an instant Clive thought the generator must have stopped, but then heard it running in the next room. He swung his legs over the side of the cot and fumbled for his trousers. "What time is it, don Carlos?"

"A little after eleven. Some guests have arrived. I need you to help me get them settled in."

Clive dressed quickly, then followed the inn owner through the generator room and out into the quiet night. As they walked across the manicured courtyard to the main building, Clive's mind cleared. He had grown accustomed to late arrivals. From don Carlos' demeanor, these must be marijuana traffickers.

"One of the guests is a pilot," Westerfield said as they passed the swimming pool. "In about five hours, he'll need you to drive him out to his airplane."

Clive understood without having to ask for details. The inn owner allowed marijuana traffickers to conduct their deals in his establishment, but he never personally went close to their operations.

Clive and Westerfield entered the inn. An elderly white man sat sipping a whiskey at the bar. Clive hadn't seen him before; however, he did recognize the three Mestizos seated at a nearby table. They were frequent guests, who drove up from Belize City.

"*¡Qué tal, joven!*" one of the Mestizos called out with a grin. He picked up a set of car keys off the table and tossed them to Clive.

"*Qué tal, don Luis,*" Clive said as he caught the keys.

"Mr. Schrader," Westerfield said to the man at the bar, "this is Clive. He'll get your things from the car, and he'll be your driver in the morning."

The old man set down his whiskey glass and eased off the bar stool without replying. He shuffled toward the door.

Clive followed him outside. A dusty Mercury sedan sat beside Westerfield's Land Rover. The Mestizos apparently had picked up the pilot at the landing area. Clive walked around to the rear of the car and opened the trunk. He took out a valise and set it on the ground. Then he pulled out three garment bags and threw them across his shoulder. The pilot reached down for the valise. "I'll take that for you," Clive said.

"I take my own gear, blacky," the man snarled.

"Take it ta raas!" Clive said. He slammed the trunk lid and walked away. He had reentered the inn and started across the tile dance floor, when the pilot called out, "Blacky!"

Clive turned.

The old man stood in the doorway, the valise at his feet. He withdrew a sheathed hunting knife from the bag. "You need some manners, blacky!"

Clive glanced around the room. Neither the Mestizos nor Westerfield moved to intercede.

Clive gazed into the pilot's washed-out blue eyes. This old man was a killer. Fear rose in Clive's throat and his hand instinctively went to the bone amulet he wore around his neck. He rubbed his thumb across the carved image of the Indian slave. The fear left him; he kept the old man fixed in his gaze.

Several seconds passed. The old man was the first to look away. He put the knife back into the valise. "Put my bag away too, boy," he said, kicking it across the floor. Then he returned to his whiskey at the bar.

Before first light, Clive and the old pilot headed south on the Northern Highway. The Land Rover's headlights played across the cane fields on either side. Fifteen-foot steel poles stood along the shoulders of the road. Government agents had erected them at hundred-yard intervals to clip the wings of marijuana smugglers, who used the narrow highway for a landing strip.

Clive searched for a particular pole, one which had been bent at a sharp angle to mark the location of the hidden airplane.

The pilot spoke for the first time that morning. "You almost died last night, boy."

Clive didn't reply. He smelled the whiskey on the old man's breath.

"Do you know what it's like to be dead, boy?"

Again, Clive didn't respond.

"Do you?" the man demanded.

Clive glanced down at the valise between the old man's feet. "No, mon," he said uneasily, "I don't know what it's like to be dead."

The pilot gazed out the side window and said softly, "It's just like . . . before you were born."

They drove in silence for a while. Finally, the pilot said, "What's your name again, boy?"

"Clive."

"What's your last name, Clive?"

"Lightburn," Clive said, wishing he were free of this strange old man.

"Were you born around here, Clive Lightburn?"

Clive shook his head.

"Belize City?"

"No," Clive said abstractedly, looking for the subtle landmark. "I'm from San Ignacio."

"San Ignacio, you say?"

Clive spotted the bent pole ahead, and ignored the question. He slowed, then turned into a dense sugarcane field. They drove thirty yards down a freshly-graded dirt road, then made a sharp turn. The Land Rover's headlights played across an old silver and black Cessna-180. Clive stopped and shut off the engine.

"Did you say you were from San Ignacio?" the old man said.

"Yes, mon," Clive said impatiently, "San Ignacio." He wanted the old man to get out of the vehicle and let him be on his way. A malevolent smile formed on the old man's lips. He suddenly burst into a rasping laugh.

"You find that funny, uh?" Clive said.

"Last night, you reminded me of somebody, but I couldn't remember who. Now I do. I know your father, boy."

"My father's dead," Clive said automatically. Sister Claudia had told him that his father had been killed in a logging accident.

"Dead?" the old man said, then laughed again. "I'm telling you, boy, I know your father." He opened the door, climbed out, and shuffled over to his aircraft.

Clive had never met anyone who had actually known his father. Now, as the pilot climbed into his aircraft, Clive struggled even to recall the name the nun had told him. Roland! He threw open the Land Rover door and jumped out. "Did you know Roland Lightburn?" he shouted.

The old man opened the airplane's side window and leaned out. "Your father's not dead, boy!" he shouted. "And whoever Roland Lightburn was, he wasn't your father!"

The propeller spun. A dim light illuminated the cockpit. The old man was still laughing, enjoying his private joke. The airplane pulled around the corner and headed down the dirt road. The nearby straight stretch of highway would serve as a runway.

Clive heard the old man rev his engine for takeoff. The airplane had started its dash down the highway, when Clive suddenly realized the sound was moving in the wrong direction. The marijuana growers had knocked down the steel poles to the north, but not to the south.

Clive jumped into the Land Rover, but froze when he heard

the airplane's engine abruptly shut off. A large fireball illuminated the predawn sky. Then he felt the concussion.

It's just like . . . before you were born.

Clive sat alone at the bar of the Posada don Carlos. He heard his telephone connection being made to San Ignacio, then the ringing. A familiar voice at the other end said, "Buckley's Dry Goods Store."

Clive didn't respond.

"Buckley's Dry Goods," the voice said impatiently.

Clive cleared his throat. "George . . . it's me, mon."

"Clive! Where are you, bwy?"

"Corozal."

"Corozal! What are you doing there?"

"I work at a place called La Posada don Carlos."

"Why didn't you call us before?"

"George . . . how are things there?"

"Mamá is fine. But she worries about you."

"What about the problem in Guatemala?"

"Guatemala? Oh, yes. If you had contacted me, I could have told you. The Guatemalans notified authorities here that one of their soldiers and two Belizean looters had been killed in a shootout. They refused to return the bodies of the Belizeans."

"Is that all?"

"That seems to be the end of it."

Clive felt relieved, but wondered if the Guatemalans had truly put the incident aside.

"When will you be coming home?" George said.

Clive's mind raced. Even if the Guatemalans weren't looking for him, he couldn't simply return to San Ignacio and resume his old life. Too much had happened during the past six months. And, there was the old pilot's taunt. "George," he said finally, "I'll send you the money I owe you."

"Forget about the money, mon! When the bloody hell will you be coming home? What can I tell Mamá?"

"Tell her . . . I'm well . . . and that I'll visit her in a few months. But first, I have to go back to Belize City."

22. ARRIVAL

Ray had a window seat on the TACA Airlines flight from New Orleans to Belize City. For the past hour he had stared down at the metallic dark-blue Gulf of Mexico, 35,000 feet below. He checked his watch. They must be getting close.

The Boeing-737 passed over a large cloud, obscuring his view. He shook his head; he couldn't believe his grandfather had talked him into this. Two nights earlier, he had still been dejected over Louisiana State University's having withdrawn his scholarship. On the spur of the moment, he had agreed to his grandfather's suggestion that he get away from Hammond for the summer. His grandfather immediately had called the airport in New Orleans and made the reservation.

The cloud below faded away, and Ray got his first glimpse of the Yucatan Peninsula. He felt a pang of apprehension as the plane crossed the coastline and he eyed the dense jungle canopy. For the next three months, he would be in a foreign country, under the charge of the stranger who was his father.

A Mexican stewardess strolled down the aisle, passing out slips of paper. She handed one to Ray and explained it was an immigration form that had to be filled out to enter Belize. Ray pulled his duffel bag from under his seat and took out a pencil.

"Help me no, sah?" said an elderly black man, seated next to him.

Ray had tried to chat with the man earlier in the flight, but the Belizean's pidgin English had been too difficult to follow. "Need to borrow my pencil?" Ray said.

"No, sah. I cannot write. You must do it for I."

"Oh . . . okay. Let me fill out mine first."

Ray completed his form, except for the passport number. His grandfather had assured him that he wouldn't need a passport, since he was just going down for the summer. Now he wondered if there would be a problem because he didn't have one.

The plane slowed and began a gradual descent.

"Help me no, sah?" the man said again.

It took Ray several minutes to complete the form. He was sure he had misspelled much of what the old man had told him. Place of birth had been particularly difficult. Ray had finally entered "Dan Greega". He handed back the completed form. The Belizean nodded gratefully.

Ray looked out the window and discovered they were over water again, flying low and parallel to the nearby coast. He marveled at the contrasting colors—the marbled greens and blues of the Caribbean, the luminescent yellow of the coastal waters, and the deep green of the jungle in the distance. He looked up the coast and saw few signs of inhabitants, only a scattering of shacks along a solitary road that wound north.

The plane banked sharply. Off in the distance lay an airport with a single landing strip. The landing gear lowered, and a stewardess gave final instructions in both Spanish and English. Ray pulled his seat belt tighter.

Moments later, the jet touched down. The engines roared, as the pilot braked. Ray braced himself against the seat in front of him. The plane stopped just short of the end of the runway.

They taxied over to the stained, stucco terminal building. A crowd of dark people clustered around the entrance. Several more perched on the railing of a second-floor veranda. Ray had the curious feeling that he had somehow landed in Africa.

The other passengers stood up and retrieved their luggage from overhead. Ray remained seated, looking for his father in the crowd outside. Finally, he grabbed his duffel bag and joined the last of the passengers filing down the aisle.

A blast of hot tropic air hit him when he reached the door of the aircraft. He descended the portable metal stairway, squinting into the bright sunshine. He still didn't see his father. He perspired freely as he followed the other passengers across the tarmac.

Inside, the immigration area was crowded and noisy. He futilely scanned the room for his father. The other passengers crowded around a side door, apparently waiting for their luggage. Ray went over and joined them.

When the baggage cart arrived, he located his suitcase and followed the other passengers to an inspection line. He searched for his father as the line crept slowly forward.

Ray put his suitcase and duffel bag on the counter. "Passport!" demanded the black immigration officer.

"I . . . uh . . . don't have one."

"You must have a passport to enter Belize."

"Nobody told me I needed one."

"You must have one."

"I'm telling you, man," Ray said, his voice breaking, "I don't have one!"

"What's the problem?" said a deep voice behind him.

Ray turned. For an instant, he didn't recognize the overweight man who now stood beside him. It had been nearly three years since his father's last visit to Hammond.

"The bwy says he has no passport, sah."

"Where's your passport?" his father said.

"I don't have one," Ray said, his voice breaking again. Now both men stared at him. "If it's such a big problem," Ray snapped, "just put me back on the damned airplane!"

His father frowned, then said to the immigration officer, "This is my son, visiting me from the States. We'll get him a passport before he goes back, through the American consul here."

"Very good, mistah Kelley," the officer said.

Disoriented, Ray followed his father outside. The front of the building teemed with people; taxi drivers aggressively competed for fares. Ray's father started across the unpaved parking area. A car rumbled past, covering Ray with a cloud of dust.

"This is it, here," his father said, pointing to a grime-covered Jeep.

Ray threw his bags into the rear and climbed into the passenger seat. His father started the engine and pulled away from the terminal. Four black men strolled down the center of the road. His father impatiently tapped the horn. The men meandered to one side, allowing just enough room for the Jeep to pass.

At the end of the airport driveway, they turned onto a rough asphalt road. They picked up speed, and his father glanced over and said, "Why don't you have a passport?"

"Yeah, Dad," Ray said sarcastically, "it's real good seeing you too."

His father turned, eyes narrowed. "Son, I don't put up with smart talk, like your mother evidently does."

Ray fought back tears of frustration. His father wouldn't have to put up with any talk at all. He was getting out of here, as soon as he got that damned passport!

They drove on in silence. Ray stared out at a passing mangrove swamp.

Finally they entered the city itself. Even his mother's description of Belize City hadn't prepared him for this level of poverty. They bounced across a narrow canal bridge. Ray recoiled at the stench.

"We have open sewers here," his father said, breaking the long silence.

They passed a parochial school. Paint peeled from the one-story wooden structure, and vultures perched on its rusty corrugated roof. Children in ragged clothing played outside on packed bare dirt. Through the open windows, Ray heard children reciting lessons in unison. A black toddler, clad only in a dirty T-shirt, urinated into the gutter.

"Is the whole city like this?" Ray said.

"Like what?"

"Like . . . a slum."

"Some of it's cleaner, but most of it's even worse."

"Why would anybody want to live here?"

"Some of us do it to support families in the States."

Ray didn't respond.

"Most foreigners can't handle it down here," his father said. "The men turn into drunks, and the women go back home . . . like your mother."

"I don't blame her."

"You're evidently a lot like her, Son."

Ray lapsed back into silence.

They turned a corner and stopped beside a two-story wooden building. A peeling sign read: "Kelley Distributors".

"This is my dealership," his father said. "We've already shut down for the day, but I need to pick up some papers. Do you want to come up?"

Ray shook his head.

His father climbed out of the Jeep. "Wait for me here then. It's 5:30. You'll get a chance to see the bridge swing."

The rusty metal bridge sat nearby. A uniformed policemen stepped into the street and blew a whistle. Vehicles and pedestrians came to a stop. Six men positioned themselves behind a long lever in the middle of the bridge. They pushed, and the bridge slowly pivoted away from the street. It took several minutes before the bridge was parallel to the river. Then a horn blew, and a line of boats filed past in either direction.

Some of the waiting pedestrians looked at Ray; he felt uncomfortable under their dark scrutiny.

His father returned and climbed into the Jeep. "They swing the bridge twice a day," he said, "for the boats that are too tall to go under." Then he pointed to a squat gray boat, tied behind his office building. "While you're down here, Son, I'm going to have you work on that tug over there."

Ray was unaccustomed to anyone dictating his activities. His mother and grandfather always made him a part of their decisions. Screw that tug! He was getting out of here!

"Hello, Ray. I'm Dawn Peterson."

Ray set his suitcase and duffel bag down on the living room

floor and awkwardly shook hands. His father hadn't said anything about a woman living with him.

"I'm Ray . . ." he began, then flushed. The woman obviously knew who he was; she had just called him by name.

"I've been looking forward to meeting you," she said with a warm smile.

Ray looked at his father.

"Dawn's staying here with me," his father said. He looked as if he were expecting a reaction.

Ray picked up his luggage. "Where's my room?"

"Come on, I'll show you," Dawn said.

Ray followed her into a sparsely furnished room. A breeze blew through the open windows. Offshore, a sailboat knifed through the choppy Caribbean.

"Ramón usually uses this room for his study," Dawn said, "but I had him clear it out for you. It's got a terrific view. I thought you'd enjoy it."

"Thanks," Ray said. Another stranger was making decisions for him.

"Your father's really been looking forward to your visit, Ray."

"Yeah, I could tell. He wasn't at the airport to meet me, and every time I open my mouth he gives me one of those looks . . . like I crawled out from under a rock."

Dawn laughed. "Give him a chance, Ray. You're as strange to him, as he is to you."

"How long have you and Dad . . . uh . . ."

"Been living together? For a couple of months now."

"Are you from here?"

"Lord, no! I'm from Houston. I came down to visit a friend, and stayed because I like it here."

"You like it?" Ray said in disbelief.

Dawn laughed. "Yes, believe it or not, I really like it. Most 'foreigners'—your father's term for people like you and me—find it too primitive. But once you learn your way around, it can be incredibly exciting. The people down here are all . . . larger than life. And I particularly like your father."

"I don't think I'll be staying long," Ray said.

"Don't decide too quickly, Ray. Your father's delighted that you've come down. We're having dinner tonight at the Fort George Hotel with some of his friends. He can't wait to show off his *hijo*— his son."

Ray realized it would be impossible to dislike this woman. "Okay," he said finally, "I'll give it a shot."

23. THE AMERICANS

Ramón sat at the head of the table in the Fort George Hotel dining room. The waitress brought the after-dinner coffee, interrupting Elijah Ruiz' discourse on Belizean ethnicity and its effect on local politics. Ray sat next to him, obviously engrossed in Elijah's views. Esther Ruiz and Dawn sat at the far end of the table.

Ramón smiled as he studied the two Americans—a love he had met so late in life and a son he had never known. He had an overwhelming sense of well-being, and a desire to live much longer.

When the waitress completed her rounds, Ray asked Elijah, "Have England and Guatemala ever had talks and tried to settle their dispute?"

"Several times over the past hundred years. But they've never been able to resolve the issue. Recently, George Price, leader of the People's United Party, tried his luck—unofficially of course. Unfortunately, the opposition party got wind of it."

"Unfortunately?"

Elijah nodded. "They're resurrecting an old charge that George plans to sell us out."

"Couldn't the U.S. be of some help in settling the dispute?" Dawn interjected.

Elijah cleared his throat. "Well . . . you see . . ."

"Dawn," Ramón said, coming to his old friend's assistance, "we view you Americans with as much concern as we do the Guatemalans."

Elijah chuckled. "I'm afraid that's true. But enough politics. Ray, tell us about your plans for the future."

"Well . . . I just graduated from high school. I guess college is next."

"Is that so? I have a daughter attending the University of Southern California. She's becoming a nurse. What do you intend to study?"

"I'm not sure . . . probably literature."

"Literature, you say?"

"Uh . . . my grandfather . . . teaches at the college in my hometown and . . . I've been thinking about taking literature."

As Ramón to listened his son's hesitant responses, the concern he had felt at the airport returned. Why was Ray so damned unsure of himself?

"Will you be going to school where your grandfather teaches?" Elijah said.

"Uh huh."

"Ray," Ramón said in surprise, "I understood you were going to school in Baton Rouge."

"Uh . . . yeah. I'd planned to go to LSU, but . . . it didn't work out."

"The last time I spoke with your mother, she said they'd given you an athletic scholarship that would pay all expenses."

Ray shook his head.

"What happened?" Ramón pressed, sensing his son was sidestepping something.

"They took it away from me," Ray said, barely audibly.

"Took it away?"

"Uh . . . yeah."

The waitress reappeared and asked Ray if he wanted more coffee. He shook his head.

"Why did they take your scholarship away?" Ramón said.

"They ruled me ineligible." Ray looked down at the table.

"Who ruled you ineligible?" Ramón said, irritated by his son's evasiveness. "Why?"

"Ramón," Dawn said, "would you like more coffee?"

He gave her an annoyed look and waved the waitress away from his cup. "Ray," he said, "explain this business about losing your scholarship."

Ray looked up. "Dad, you don't know the first thing about basketball . . . or athletic scholarships . . . or anything!"

Ramón glared at his son, his lips pressed together in a thin line. "Then you explain it to me."

Ray took a deep breath. "I took some money . . . for playing in a game. It made me ineligible for any NCAA school."

"Who gave you money? What's 'NCAA'?"

"Ramón, we can pursue this later!" Dawn said.

Ramón saw by her expression that he apparently had gone too far. God-damned Americans!

Later that night, Ramón padded into the bedroom. Dawn sat up in bed waiting for him, arms folded.

"How could you embarrass the boy like that!" she snapped.

Ramón climbed into the bed. "He shouldn't embarrass so damned easy. And besides, the issue isn't that he got embarrassed; it's why the hell he lost his scholarship!"

"If he had a scholarship, he earned it on his own. And if he lost it, he lost it on his own. And it's none of your business!"

"None of my business! He's my son. I pay for his education."

"You hardly know the boy. What's he ever asked you for?"

"Well, if he's going to live down here, he damned well better toughen up!"

"Live down here! Ramón, that boy wants to be on the first plane out of here tomorrow!"

"Good! I put up with this crap from his mother. I sure as hell don't plan to put up with it from her kid!"

The sound of a door slamming let them know that their heated exchange had carried into the next room.

At first light the next morning, Ramón stepped onto the front veranda. He found Ray leaning against the railing. The youth turned with a resentful look.

"Son," Ramón said, "I'm sorry about last night."

"What?"

"I said I'm sorry about last night."

His son looked him straight in the eye. "Did Dawn tell you to say that?"

"Well . . . yeah."

Ray blinked, then responded with a tight smile and a nod.

They both turned and gazed out to sea, in uneasy truce.

24. RETURN

Clive stepped off the bus at the Belize City terminal. The stench from the nearby canal triggered the recollection of his last arrival. Only six months had passed, but it seemed much longer. He walked around to the side of the bus and waited for the driver to throw down his hemp bag.

A city youth pushed in front of him. Clive grabbed him by the shoulder and yanked him back. The youth turned with a hard look, but it quickly faded. "Excuse me, bruddah," he mumbled.

Clive nodded. People in this bloody city had fucked him last time. This time he'd fuck back.

The driver held up his bag.

"Here!" Clive shouted. The driver carefully handed it down to him.

Clive struck out toward the center of town. As he crossed the Collet Canal bridge, two small boys ran by, shouting, "Rastamon! Rastamon!"

Clive caught his reflection in a dirty shop window: reddish-brown dreadlocks, shapeless rural shirt and trousers, and open sandals. He looked like a Rastamon, for true.

A few minutes later he arrived at Battlefield Park. A banner hung across the entrance, announcing a political rally the following week. Clive turned and entered the Bank of the Caribbean.

A lobby guard hurried over. "What you want here, Rastamon?"

"Bank business," Clive said, pushing past him. Don Carlos had taught him about banking.

The guard followed him over to a teller window. A young Creole woman frowned at him through the bars. Clive pulled out his wallet and withdrew the bank draft that had closed out his Corozal account. He slid it across to the teller.

"$1,742?" the woman said in apparent surprise.

Clive nodded. The amount represented six months of salary and tips, plus bonuses for special guest services.

A distinguished looking Carib stepped into the teller cage. "Is there a problem here?"

"This bwy has a draft for $1,742, mistah Ruiz," the teller said, handing him Clive's check.

The man studied the check, then looked up at Clive. "I'm Elijah Ruiz, president of this bank. What is it you wish?"

"I want $100 cash, and I want to put the rest in your bank." Clive knew they were disturbed by his appearance, but their opinions meant nothing.

"Do you have some form of identification?" the banker said.

Clive took out his creased driving permit.

The banker studied it, then handed it back. "Your check will have to clear before you can withdraw against it, mistah Lightburn."

Shit! Clive thought. He hadn't anticipated the delay; he only had a few dollars in cash. It would be like last time: no bloody money!

"However," the banker said, "if you need the cash straight away, I'll be glad to ring your bank in Corozal and verify assets."

Clive nodded.

The banker returned a few minutes later and handed the check to the teller. "Glad to have you with us, mistah Lightburn," he said with a smile. He nodded to the teller to conduct the transaction. The guard held the door for Clive as he exited the bank.

Clive strode up Albert Street, passing the open market and ignoring the beggars who cried out to him. He crossed the swing bridge and approached a two-story building on the other side. A pealing sign read: "Kelley Distributors". A fat white man descended the stairs, followed by a tall white youth. From his clothes, Clive could tell that the younger man was an American. Probably another bloody Peace Corps worker, he thought as he headed up Queen Street.

A few minutes later, he arrived at the boarding house. The

pale young woman he remembered from last time was sweeping the front porch. He climbed the stairs. "Do you have a room?"

She nodded.

"How much by the week?"

"Ten dollars. In advance."

"I spent a night here before."

She nodded.

"Last time, someone came in during the night and took my money."

She shrugged.

"I want a room with locks on the door and windows."

"Come this way, sah."

Clive sat at the dinner table with the young woman and her mother. He was their only guest for the night. The older woman was also light-skinned, although not as light as her daughter. She had said little throughout the meal. As her daughter went into the kitchen with a load of dirty dishes, she asked, "Where are you from?"

"Corozal."

"Are you a Rastamon?"

Clive shook his head. "I don't believe in that shit."

She seemed taken aback by his language. "Are you a Christian then?"

"No, I don't believe in that shit either."

She stood up, glared at him, and stalked into the kitchen.

The younger woman came into the dining room. "What did you say to Mama?"

"We were discussing religion."

The young woman smiled.

"Dorla," he said, calling her by name for the first time, "when I came out of the Bank of the Caribbean this afternoon, I saw a cinema next door. Have you seen the film there?"

"*Shaft?* No, it just arrived at the Majestic this week. Why were you in the bank?"

"Opening an account. Will you come with me to the cinema tonight?"

"Generally . . . I don't go out," she said.

Clive frowned. She probably thought some white motherfucker was going to show up here tonight and carry her off to the States. "Come, gyal," he said, "you can't work all the time."

She hesitated, then smiled and said, "All right. Let me finish the dishes."

Later that night, they stood on the boarding house second-floor landing.

"Thank you for the cinema," Dorla said.

"Is your room this way?" Clive said, nodding down the dimly lighted hallway.

"Yes," she whispered, "and Mama is directly across from me. Be quiet or you'll wake her."

Clive slipped his arms around her waist. She came to him with her face uplifted and allowed him a brief kiss. "Good night, Clive," she said with a smile. She turned toward her room.

Clive started down the hallway with her. She stopped and shook her head. Clive started to speak, but she pressed her pale fingers across his lips. He moved her hand and took her in his arms again. She allowed him a long kiss.

She opened her eyes and seemed to have trouble focusing. Before he could kiss her again, she whispered, "I must go to my room now."

She turned and started to tiptoe away, but Clive moved with her. She stopped and shook her head again. Clive smiled and placed a firm hand on the small of her back. She put a finger across her lips, imploring him to be quiet, then allowed him to guide her to her bedroom door.

Frowning, she pointed toward the door across the hall. Clive gave her another lingering kiss. As they separated, he reached behind her. He quietly opened her bedroom door and gently pushed her through the doorway.

"You must leave," she whispered in the darkness.

Clive closed the door behind them, pulled her close and kissed her again.

"Not with a coolie bwy . . ." she implored herself. Then she took his hand and led him to her tiny bed.

25. DANGRIGA

Ray stood on the seawall, unsure what was expected of him. After only forty-eight hours in Belize, his father was sending him down the coast on a three-day trip.

Robby, the old Creole captain, started the tugboat engine. A young deckhand scrambled about the gasoline-filled barge, securing the tow lines.

"Give 'em a hand, Ray!" his father shouted down from the veranda of Kelley Distributors, loud enough to attract the attention of the crowd that had formed for the morning swinging of bridge. "You're not there to watch!"

Ray jumped from the seawall onto the rusty barge. He looked around, still uncertain what he was supposed to do. He had never been on a boat larger than an outboard.

"Cast off!" the Creole deckhand shouted.

Ray hesitated. Cast off what?

The deckhand impatiently moved past him and released the barge from its fore and aft moorings.

"Come up here, mistah Kelley!" Robby called to Ray from the wheelhouse.

As Ray put one foot up onto the seawall, the barge began to drift. For a moment, he was caught with one foot on the seawall and one still on the barge, as the space over the sewage-laden water slowly widened. He lunged forward, striking the shin of his trailing leg on the edge of the concrete wall. He managed to regain his balance and stand up. Robby waved him forward, and Ray jogged down the seawall, ignoring the pain in his shin. He jumped onto the tugboat's wet aft deck. His basketball shoes slipped out from under him, and he landed hard on his backside.

"If you'll take the wheel, sah," Robby shouted, "I'll cast off the bow line."

Ray shook his head as he struggled to his feet. No way he was going try to drive the damn boat! "Is the bow line the one in front?"

Robby grinned. "Yes, sah. It is the one in front."

Ray climbed back onto the seawall and hurried over to the mooring stake. He tried to untie the line, but the knot was too tight.

"Just pull the end, sah!" Robby shouted.

Ray frowned, but pulled as he had been instructed. The knot magically slipped apart.

"Push the bow free, sah!" Robby shouted.

Ray dropped into a sitting position on the edge of the seawall and pushed against the side of the boat with both feet. The tug slowly moved away from the wall. He jumped up and threw the line onto the bow. Then he took a couple of quick running steps and leaped onto the stern, slipping awkwardly again, but this time managing to catch himself. The engine roared, as Robby fought to gain control of the drifting barge.

They were underway. Ray looked back at the Kelley Distributors building. The veranda was empty.

Late that afternoon, Ray stood alone in the wheelhouse, steering the tug along the dense coastline. His head ached. He knew what the problem was, but he wasn't ready to hang over the side of the boat from a rope to remedy it.

Robby entered the wheelhouse. "A bit more to starboard, Ray."

Ray gave the wheel a half-turn. He smiled, pleased at how much he had learned his first day at sea, and at having been accepted by the two Belizeans. Robby had even stopped addressing him as "sah".

"We'll be coming up on Dangriga directly," Robby said.

Ray gazed at the coastal vegetation off to the right and saw nothing to distinguish it from the miles that had preceded it. Off

in the distance loomed a chain of desolate hills, covered with jungle.
"How can you tell where we are, Robby?"

"Bwy," Robby said with a laugh, "I've captained your daddy's
tugboats for more than twenty years. And for fifteen years before
that, I was first mate on the Heron H, delivering people and goods
up and down this coast. I know it better than I know my wife's
body."

The young deckhand entered the wheelhouse. "Chuh, old mon.
You done long forgot what you ever knew about a woman's body."

"You, bwy!" Robby retorted in mock anger. "Don't you be
talking about bodies. Got fathers looking for you from Corozal to
Punta Gorda!"

The deckhand grinned at Ray, clearly pleased with his reputa-
tion. He opened the door leading to the engine room, and disappeared below.

"Allan is a good bwy," Robby said, lowering his voice so the
deckhand wouldn't overhear. "His father was Michael Flowers.
Michael worked for your father before you were born."

"Is that right?"

Robby nodded. "Michael drowned when Hurricane Hatti hit
your father's house. Last year, Allan got in trouble, but your father
got him out of jail and gave him this job."

A wave of bitterness swept over Ray. Nice to know Dad gives a
shit about *somebody*.

Three hours later, they had docked at a harbor to the south of
Dangriga, and workers from the Royal Petroleum Company were
pumping out the tug's gasoline cargo.

"Robby," Allan said, "make we go to town, no, sah?"

"Not me, bwy."

Allan turned to Ray. "How about you, mon?"

"Is it okay if I go, Robby?" Ray said.

Robby hesitated, apparently uncertain what authority he was
supposed to exercise over his employer's son.

"Do you need me here?" Ray pressed.

"No, bwy . . ."

"How long are we going to be gone, Allan?" Ray said.

Allan shrugged.

"You must be back by dawn," Robby said firmly.

Ray laughed. "I'm sure we won't be gone that long . . . will we?"

Allan shrugged again.

"Don't get this bwy in trouble, Allan," Robby said. "You hear me?"

Allan had already climbed off the boat and was headed down the pier. Ray gave Robby a quick wave and took off after him.

By the time Ray and Allan reached the outskirts of Dangriga, darkness had fallen. The few street lights barely illuminated the jumble of weathered clapboard shacks that pressed against the dusty road.

Ray's first impression was that Dangriga was a miniature Belize City. Stann Creek ran through the middle of town, spanned by a one-lane bridge. Fishing dories lined the muddy river bank.

They crossed the bridge and started up a wooden sidewalk on St. Vincent Street. Shops and vendor stalls crowded the potholed main thoroughfare. The residents here were noticeably darker than in Belize City. Elijah Ruiz had told him that his African-Indian ancestors had landed here in the early 1800s. He had said that Caribs were a close-knit culture, who seldom married outside their ethnic group, as Creoles did.

Allan turned down a dark alley. Ray followed, and had second thoughts about the excursion. "Where we going?"

Allan pointed up the alley to a dilapidated shack. A rusty Coca Cola sign hanging crookedly over the front door read: "Havana Nite Club". A heavy drum beat grew louder as they approached.

The door of the club flew open and the music blared into the street. A Carib laborer stumbled out. He blocked the doorway, looking first at Allan, then at Ray. Finally, he lurched past them and staggered up the alley.

"I don't think this is where we ought to be," Ray said.

"Come, mon," Allan said, opening the door.

They stopped inside the doorway, letting their eyes adjust to the dim lighting. The Caribs seated at the bar and scattered around the half-dozen tables watched Ray with interest. He was ready to leave, but wasn't sure they would let him.

Allan moved forward, and Ray followed, stumbling on the warped flooring. They stopped at a table where two Carib women sat drinking beer.

"Good night, ladies," Allan greeted them with mock formality. "Can we join you?"

Both women stared up at Ray. Allan dropped into one of the two unoccupied chairs.

"Is it okay?" Ray said uncomfortably. The thin woman shrugged; the chubby one smiled and nodded. Ray sat down.

"Well, ladies," Allan said, "how are you this evening?"

"Very well, thank you," the chubby one said. The other woman gazed across the room indifferently.

"I'm Allan, and this is Ray."

"I'm Perlene," the chubby one said. "And this is Noema."

Noema said something to Perlene, which Ray couldn't understand.

"Speak English please, ladies," Allan said with a smile. "We don't speak Garifuna."

"Why do you bring a bakra here?" Noema demanded.

"He is my friend. He comes from the States."

"Why is he here?"

"To make a movie," Allan said glibly. "He is a big movie star in the States."

"Chuh!"

"For true!" Allan said.

"Don't vex me, bwy!" Noema said. She slid her chair back to leave.

"How about a next beer, ladies?" Allan said quickly.

Perlene smiled and nodded; Noema settled back in her chair. Allan got up and went over to the bar to order the drinks. The women stared at Ray.

"Uh . . . nice town y'all have here," he said.

"How long have you been in Dangriga?" Perlene said.

"Uh . . . just a couple of hours," Ray admitted.

They stared at him again.

"I . . . uh . . . met a guy from here on the plane coming down, though . . . and he . . . uh . . . said it was nice."

"What was his name?" Perlene said.

"I . . . uh . . . don't remember . . ."

They sat in silence again, until Allan returned with the beer.

Ray wondered about the drinking age in Belize, but didn't ask. He judged the women to be about his and Allan's age. Noema was sullen, but Allan obviously found her attractive. Perlene was a bit too plump, but at least she was friendly.

Ray looked around the room. The other customers had lost interest in them. He began to relax. He lifted his beer bottle and read the name: Belikin. He took a swallow; it tasted similar to the Dixie 45 he and Tyrone drank in Hammond.

Allan spoke earnestly to Noema, but the jukebox was too loud for Ray to hear what he said. Three couples moved about the dance floor, vigorously undulating their hips to the repetitive rhythm of drums and gourds. Ray leaned forward and said to Perlene, "I like the music. What's it called?"

"Punta rock," she said with a smile. "We make it up here in Dangriga and in Punta Gorda." She reached over and took his hand. "Come, make we dance."

Ray shook his head. "I . . . uh . . . don't know how to do that stuff."

Perlene shrugged, but continued to smile, and rested her hand on his thigh.

Two hours later, Ray had consumed four bottles of Belikin and was now completely at ease. Allan and Noema returned from the dance floor, hand in hand. Allan was sweating. Noema sat down and took a long swallow from her beer. Allan slid his chair close to hers. She tilted her head back and allowed him a kiss.

A slow song came up on the jukebox. "That's pretty," Ray said.

Perlene smiled. "It's called 'Nothing Lasts Forever'. The singer is Andy Palacio. He comes from here. Do Americans know about him?"

Ray shook his head. Perlene leaned toward him, inviting a kiss. Ray quickly stood up and said, "Uh . . . I think I can handle this slow stuff."

Out on the dance floor, Perlene turned to him and Ray placed his hand on her firm waist. She hesitated long enough to pick up his unfamiliar dance step, then moved in close against him. Ray closed his eyes and swayed to the plaintive sound of the Belizean singer.

The club had closed at midnight. Now the two couples walked along the narrow beach, north of town. Most of the nearby houses were dark. Ray assumed that he and Allan were taking the young women home.

Allan and Noema walked up ahead, arms about each other's waist. Perlene held Ray's hand. When the other couple stopped to kiss, she squeezed it, indicating she wanted to stop too.

"Is that a cemetery over there?" Ray said, trying to fill the pause.

Perlene, not to be put off, pulled his head down and pressed her full lips against his. Ray closed his eyes and kissed her firmly.

The couples resumed walking along the beach until they came to a makeshift footbridge. They carefully picked their way across it, then passed in front of a darkened hotel. There were no houses up ahead. Ray suddenly realized that they weren't taking the women home. "Where are we going?"

"There is a quiet place around the next bend," Perlene murmured.

Ray panicked. He'd never done it before!

Allan and Noema left the narrow beach and took a few steps down the sheltered side of a low escarpment. They sank to the ground in a passionate embrace.

"Leave them," Perlene said, tugging at Ray's hand.

Reluctantly, he followed her farther up the beach, then over the escarpment.

They stopped near a clump of trees. Perlene sank to her knees. "Come," she said, pulling his hand.

Ray's mind raced. How could he get out of this! "Uh . . . I . . . need to get back to the boat."

"Chuh," Perlene said with a laugh, pulling him down in front of her and pressing her lips to his.

After a long kiss, Ray said huskily, "I can't . . ."

"Chuh," she said softly again. She had unzipped his trousers, and now opened her dark fist and showed him that he could, and would.

The morning sun rose from the Caribbean, as Ray and Allan strolled down the dirt road to the harbor.

I did it! Ray kept thinking. I finally did it!

"Looks like the old mon is awake," Allan said as they started down the rickety wooden pier.

Ray heard the low rumble of the tugboat engine.

Robby stepped from the wheelhouse. "Where the bloody hell have you been, bwy?" he asked Allan.

"Laying pipe, old mon," Allan said, jumping aboard. "We were in town, laying pipe."

"Are you all right, Ray?" Robby said.

"I'm fine, Robby," Ray said, as they entered the wheelhouse. "Sorry if we worried you." Then he added with a grin, "We were just in town, laying pipe."

26. HAULOVER CREEK

Ramón and Elijah sat on the veranda of the Four Fort Street Restaurant, watching the midday bustle. A horn drew their attention, and two British Army trucks rumbled by.

"I guess you've heard," Elijah said, "the Guats are at it again."

Ramón nodded. He picked up a stained menu. He was more interested in lunch than the latest Guatemalan threat to invade Belize. Dawn had fixed breakfast for him: toast and fruit juice. Now, five hours later, everything on the menu looked good.

A young Creole waitress came over to their table and set a loaf of homemade bread between them. "Good morning, sahs," she said with a smile. "Our special today is baked chicken with rice and beans."

Ramón gazed longingly at the "mosquito toast" entry on the breakfast page—French toast stuffed with cream cheese and honey—but finally said, "I'll take the special."

"I'll have the chef's salad," Elijah said, "with the dressing on the side." When the waitress left with their orders, he said, "I thought Dawn had you on a diet."

Ramón nodded ruefully, as he buttered a thick slice of bread. Obviously, Elijah had been sticking to his. "You said on the phone, today's lunch was more than social."

Elijah took a sip from his water. "I've received word that Glenn Foster is relocating to Miami."

"Miami?" Ramón said in surprise. Glenn Foster was the aging autocrat of one of Belize's wealthiest families. "You mean permanently?"

Elijah nodded. "Apparently, Glenn has decided to live out his final years in the comfort of the States."

"Any idea what's going to happen to his Cayo District property?"

"I've been told he intends to turn it over to his son—all 390,000 acres."

"Damn!" Ramón said. "Kendall Foster can't be thirty years old."

"Twenty-nine to be exact."

"Remember a couple of months ago," Ramón said, "when I told you Kendall and some Palace Hotel cowboys had a half-baked scheme to develop tourism in the jungle?"

Elijah smiled. "The land will be Kendall's now, to do whatever he likes."

"Do you think he might part with some of it?"

"What do you have in mind?"

Ramón shook his head. "Nothing specific . . . maybe clearing some forest for citrus or cattle."

The waitress returned with their orders. However, Ramón was no longer thinking of food; he was assessing the opportunities that this changing of the guard might bring to Belize. He needed get hold of Kendall—right away.

"There's another young capitalist," Elijah said, gesturing toward the street.

Ramón turned. A tall, light-skinned Creole strode toward them. "Another Rastafarian," he muttered, turning back to Elijah. "There's more and more of them these days. You can't hire them to work. They sit on their asses, smoke marijuana, and listen to that reggae crap."

"I don't think that applies to this one, Ramón. He's one of my newest depositors. He just moved down from Corozal and opened up an account a few days ago. Very businesslike, despite his appearance. His name is Lightburn."

Ramón quickly turned back to the street. The youth disappeared behind a corner of the restaurant, heading in the direction of the Fort George Hotel. Ramón already knew what Elijah was about to say next.

"I believe his first name is Clive."

Ramón sat behind his office desk, trying to concentrate on a pile of invoices. However, his thoughts kept returning to his and Tawnya's son. He took off his reading glasses. The boy's opening a bank account suggested that he planned to stay in Belize City. If so, somehow he'd need to keep an eye on him. And what the hell had he been doing in Corozal?

Outside, he heard gears grind as the bridge began its afternoon swing. He rose from his desk and walked over to a window that overlooked Haulover Creek. A line of boats waited to come upriver. At the far end, he saw his tug. He wondered how Ray had fared on his first trip. He had seemed so out of place when they cast off three days ago. Out of place . . . like his mother.

Ramón looked back at his desk. He had several hours work to do, but it would have to wait. Dawn expected him home at a reasonable hour. It was hard to stay caught up, now with her in his life. He smiled. God, she was worth it, though! He pocketed his glasses and headed for the door.

Out on the second floor veranda, he locked his office and looked back at the river. His tug passed the open bridge. He frowned; Robby was following too closely behind a large launch. Then he saw Robby and Allan standing on the stern. Ray was at the wheel!

"Back off!" Ramón shouted. Realizing that Ray couldn't hear him, he waved frantically for him to steer away from the launch.

Ray looked up. He smiled broadly and waved back.

The pitch of the launch engine alerted Ramón that it was slowing. "Ray! Move away—"

Ray suddenly understood, but reacted too late. He swerved toward the seawall, but clipped the stern of the launch with the bow of the tug.

"God damn it!" Ramón exploded. He hurried across the veranda and down the stairs.

Robby rushed into the wheelhouse. Ray threw the tug into reverse and steered it toward the seawall.

"Take the wheel, Robby!" Ramón shouted as he ran across the parking lot.

The prow slammed into one of the tires that served as a sea-wall buffer.

Ramón jumped on deck and stormed into the wheelhouse. "Robby!" he yelled, pushing Ray away from the wheel. "What the hell do you think you're doing?"

The old Creole stood by, as Ramón completed the docking maneuver. The deckhand secured the tug to the landing.

Ramón stepped outside the wheelhouse. The launch had continued upriver. A figure at the stern waved, indicating that no serious damage had been done. Ramón went forward and found the damage to the tug also was superficial. He whirled around and demanded of Robby, "Where's Ray?"

Robby nodded toward the fire station.

Ray stalked around the corner and out of sight, fists clenched.

"God damn it, Robby!" Ramón snapped. "All I need is to sink somebody's boat. What the hell were you thinking about, letting Ray bring the tug in?"

Robby looked down at the deck.

"Answer me!"

"The bwy can drive the boat, sah."

"He's never been on a tug before!"

Robby looked up. The whites of his dark eyes were milky tan. "The bwy can drive the boat . . . sah!"

In the more than twenty years that Robby had worked for him, Ramón had never seen him angry. "I'm sorry, Robby," he said. "You probably wanted to give him a chance to show off for me. You don't understand though; the boy has been living with his mother."

"The bwy did just fine, sah," Robby said, holding Ramón's gaze. "He learns very quickly."

Ramón frowned. He suspected that Robby was being less than truthful. "Would you be willing to take him out again?"

"Anytime, sah."

Ramón smiled. At least Ray had what it took to make a friend of the old Creole.

27. U.A.P.P.

Clive entered the boarding house dining room and found Dorla and her mother relaxing over Sunday morning coffee. Dorla smiled up at him; her mother gave him an angry glance. He took a seat at the head of the table. Dorla had come up to his room again during the night. The old woman probably knew.

"It's after 9:00," the old woman said. "We don't serve breakfast after 9:00." She rose from the table and clumped upstairs.

"What do you want to eat?" Dorla said.

"Just some toast and coffee will be fine, gyal."

She gave him a shy smile, then went into the kitchen.

Clive picked up a scattered copy of the *Belize Times* and reassembled it. He scanned the meager help-wanted section, as he had all week. The ad for a handyman at the Fort George Hotel was still in the paper, although he had been given the job, the day before. The Fort George manager knew don Carlos and had hired Clive as soon as he saw the inn owner's letter of recommendation.

Dorla returned from the kitchen. "I brought you some papaya too."

"Thanks, gyal."

She sat down at the table. "When do you start work?"

"Tomorrow."

"Clive . . . where do you come from?"

"Corozal. Before that, San Ignacio."

"Do you have family?"

He spread orange marmalade on his toast. "I have a brother and foster mother in San Ignacio. My mother is dead."

"What about your father?"

Clive didn't answer. Since returning to Belize City, he had

contacted all the Lightburns in the telephone directory. None had known of a Roland Lightburn, who had died in a logging accident twenty years earlier. One person, however, had suggested that he contact a man named Ramón Kelley, who had run a large mahogany operation during that period.

"Clive?"

"My father is dead too," Clive said. The taunt from the old pilot came to mind, but he dismissed it.

"Do you have a gyal friend in San Ignacio?" she said shyly.

"No, chica," he said with a smile. "I got no gyal, just a mother and a brother." His answer apparently satisfied her. She got up and went into the kitchen.

Clive returned to the newspaper. The headline heralded a People's United Party rally to be held the following week in Battlefield Park. A one-page ad accused the opposition candidates of dishonesty and incompetence. Several articles followed the same theme.

Clive stood up and walked over to the kitchen door. Dorla was bent over the sink, the backs of her pale legs tensed. Clive cleared his throat. "I'm going out, gyal."

She turned and gave him her shy smile.

Out on the street, Clive paused at the foot of the boarding house stairs. The quiet Sunday morning made him think of his foster mother. She would be at mass soon, and would probably pray for him.

He strolled along the row of locked storefronts, undecided how to fill his last idle day. Then he remembered seeing an outdoor basketball court next to the fire station.

As he approached Hydes Lane, two Creole men suddenly came around a fence corner. One slammed Clive with his shoulder, then pushed him away. Momentarily stunned, Clive almost stepped into an overflowing gutter.

The man who had bumped him snarled, "Get out the way, Rastamon!"

Clive held his ground. The two men wore black berets over

long hair, cut in the Afro style of the 1960s. The man who had bumped him was stocky and muscular; the other was tall and thin.

"I said, get the fuck out the way, Rastamon!"

Clive touched the amulet that hung from his neck. "Fuck you ta raas, fat bwy!"

"Earl!" the thin one said, moving between them. "Mind! Policemon coming!"

Clive glanced over his shoulder. A policeman, a half-block away, strolled toward them.

"Rastamon," the stocky man said, "we settle this one next time."

"Any time, motherfucker."

The man gestured for Clive to follow him down the side street.

Clive's adrenaline still raced as they walked around the corner. The stocky man veered across the narrow lane toward a one-story shack. A crude sign painted across the front read: "Headquarters— United African People's Party". A graying Creole stood in the doorway, also wearing a black beret.

"Come, Rastamon, make we go out back!" the stocky man said. He started through the doorway.

"What's going on here?" the older man demanded, grabbing the stocky man by his arm.

"I'm going to kick this bloody Rastamon's ass!"

"Hold on!" the older man said. He turned to Clive. "What kind of trouble you making here, Rastamon?"

"I ain't no Rastamon! That mon there is making the trouble!"

"Earl and the Rastamon catch collision," the thin man interjected. "Now the Rastamon wants to fight."

The older man turned Clive. "There ain't going to be no fight, bwy. But come inside."

"I ain't taking no shit off no Rastamon," the stocky man said belligerently.

"Shut you mouth, Earl," the older man said. "The bwy said he ain't no Rastamon." He extended his hand to Clive. "I'm Garth X. Wade."

"I'm Clive Lightburn." They shook hands.

As Clive passed through the doorway, Earl muttered under his breath, "There be one next time coming for we, Rastamon."

Clive scanned the shack's gloomy interior. Two old desks occupied the front of the single room, piled high with paper and pamphlets. A neat row of canvas cots lined the rear. Percy took a seat behind the smaller desk. Earl slumped onto the floor with his back against the wall. He scowled up at Clive.

"Have a seat, bwy," Wade said, gesturing to a backless wooden chair. Then he took a seat behind the larger desk.

Clive sat down. "What kind of place is this?"

"Headquarters for the UAPP—the United African People's Party. I'm the leader."

"I haven't heard of your party."

"It's new. Our mission is to unite all African people living in Belize—Creole and Carib alike." Wade's voice rose. "Our mission is to free ourselves from the oppression of Europeans and Americans, and govern Belize as a black nation!"

Clive frowned. "But the *Belize Times* says, we will be independent in a few years."

"*Belize Times!* Don't you know that's a PUP newspaper? Listen to me, bwy. Independence is too long coming. And if the English do leave, PUP won't help the poor. George Price and the rest will just feather their own nests. Then they'll go hat in hand to the United States, like good little slave children."

"What would you do?"

Wade gazed at him intently. "Do it the black mon's way. Apply the black mon's values . . . not those of the British . . . not those of the Americans." He paused, as if awaiting Clive's response.

"How many members do you have?" Clive said.

"In Belize City, not too many. But we're growing. Our strength is in the villages."

"In San Ignacio?"

"We just formed a unit there. Why do you ask?"

"That's my home."

"Bwy," Wade said with a smile, "make I tell you about the UAPP."

Clive stepped outside UAPP headquarters. He paused, letting his eyes readjust to the midday sunlight, then turned and headed up the narrow lane toward Barracks Road. His mind raced with the information he had received. For two hours, Garth X. Wade had recapped the Black Power movement in the United States and outlined his plans to use similar tactics to form a militant party in Belize. The rural poor and the urban underprivileged were to be his membership base. Clive had little knowledge of politics and had never personally spoken with a truly motivated leader, other than an occasional overzealous priest. Garth X. Wade had left him inspired.

A few minutes later, he passed in front of the fire station. Next-door, a basketball goal had been erected on the concrete foundation of a razed building. A two-on-two basketball game was in progress. Clive watched the final plays of the one-sided contest.

When the game was over, a player on the losing team walked off the court. The other player shouted, "Hey, tall bwy! Want to play?"

Clive hadn't had a basketball in his hands for more than six months. He jogged onto the court.

28. ONE ON ONE

Ray walked along Front Street in the midday heat. It was Sunday, and the downtown area was nearly deserted. He carried a letter in his hand, asking his mother for plane fare to return home. As he approached the old post office, he glanced across the street to a makeshift basketball court. A two-on-two game was in progress. He stepped under the post office arcade and dropped his letter into the airmail slot.

An elderly Creole woman sat nearby on the filthy sidewalk. She held up a hand. "Give me shilling, no sah?"

Ray reached into his jeans and found a twenty-five-cent piece. She bobbed her head in thanks.

Ray crossed the street. The basketball court was the uneven foundation of a razed building. The backboard had been nailed together from odd-sized boards. A remnant of an old fishing net hung from the rim.

Ray leaned against a nearby building and watched the game. A tall Creole with long braided hair was clearly the best player on the court. For a while, he was content to pass off to his teammates and rebound their errant shots. The game dragged on. Finally he grew impatient and dunked three straight shots to put an end to it.

A player on the losing team called over to Ray, "Want to play, white bwy?"

Ray hadn't touched a basketball since the Pearl River tournament. Primitive as this game was, he suddenly felt like playing. He pulled his shirt over his head, exposing his pale skin and freckles.

"White-speckled-banana," one of the players said in a lilting voice. The others laughed.

The tall Creole fired a pass at Ray. "You can take it out . . . Banana."

Ray spun the ball on his index finger. It was light and slightly out of round, but he had played with worse. He threw it in bounds to his teammate, who feinted toward the basket, then passed it back.

"Come pop me, Banana," the tall Creole goaded.

Four days of frustration welled up in Ray. He took two deceptively slow dribbles toward the Creole, then blew by him for an easy lay-up.

"Good move . . . Banana!" the Creole said, as he retrieved the ball from under the goal.

"I got your banana," Ray said, "swinging between my legs!"

The Creole fixed him in an unblinking stare—greenish eyes, behind lion-mane dreadlocks. A primitive charm lay against his bare chest.

Uh-oh, Ray thought. He hesitantly reached for the ball.

"You don't get the ball, bwy!" the Creole snarled. "You just scored the points."

"In the States we play 'make-it, take-it'."

"You not in the States now, Banana. Now you come to Belize."

The Creole threw the ball in bounds to his teammate and assumed a center's position with his back to the goal. Ray took his defensive position behind him. The ball came in. The Creole faked right, then spun left. He took a leaping step toward the goal, hung above the rim, and drove the ball through the tattered net. Ray had never played against anyone, including Tyrone Johnson, who could dunk on him from a standing start.

Ray's teammate threw him the ball, then moved off to the side to let the two go at it, one on one.

"Come pop me, no, sah!" the Creole taunted.

Ray took two slow dribbles, as he had the first time, but this time hit a jump shot from fifteen feet. The Creole had played him loose, anticipating another drive, but still almost blocked the shot.

The Creole received a pass and faced the basket. He feinted left, then went right. Ray didn't take the fake, but still couldn't block the shot. The Creole soared over him and drove home another dunk.

Ray got the ball again, twenty-five feet from the basket. The Creole waited for him, ten feet away. Ray took a long set shot, which ripped through the net.

"Chuh!" the Creole said. He took the ball and drove for the goal. He slammed into Ray, but still managed to get high enough to drive the ball through the net.

Ray was stunned from the impact, but realized there would be no fouls called here. His teammates threw him the ball, and he buried another long set shot.

"Motherfucker," the Creole muttered. He received a pass at the baseline. Ray dropped into his defensive stance, trying to block the path to the goal. The Creole powered past him, first veering away from the goal, then leaning back and dunking over the front of the rim.

Ray stood in a stationary dribble, twenty-five feet from the goal. On defense, he couldn't stop this guy!

"You finished, Banana?" the Creole goaded.

Ray felt a surge of adrenaline. He shifted the ball to his left hand and dribbled slowly down the left side of the court. The Creole moved up to stop him. Without interrupting his dribble, Ray bounced the ball behind his back and into his right hand. He had a step on the Creole as he drove across the middle. He leaped high at the goal, but felt the Creole soar above him to his left. Ray swung the ball far out the right, then brought it over his head with all his strength. The Creole blocked the shot cleanly. Ray instinctively caught the rim, pulling it loose from the backboard. He and the Creole fell in a pile beneath the goal.

Ray scrambled to his feet and offered a hand back to the Creole. "Good block, man."

The Creole ignored the hand and slowly got up, fists clenched. "You fuck up our goal, bwy!"

"I didn't mean to—" A horn blew. Ray turned. His father's Jeep sat parked at the curb.

"Who the bloody hell is that?" the Creole snarled.

"My father."

"Go to your daddy, bwy," the Creole said contemptuously.

Ray hesitated, then turned and walked off the court. He picked up his shirt and went over to where his father was parked.

His father gazed past him, to the tall Creole who was surveying the damage to the basketball goal. "Do you know that boy?"

"No, but the son of a bitch is good."

His father started the engine. "Like you said the other night, I don't know much about basketball. But it looked to me like you were holding your own."

29. NEW ALLIANCES

Ramón finished drying off and pulled the towel around his waist. He paused in front of the bathroom mirror, deciding whether he needed to shave before he and Dawn went out for the evening.

"Ramón," Dawn called from the bedroom, "do you know if Ray's feeling okay?"

Ramón walked out of the bathroom. "As far as I know. Why do you ask?"

"I just remembered. Esther Ruiz said she saw him coming out of Dr. Castillo's office this morning."

Ramón frowned. "He's supposed to be at the boat yard today, working with the shipwrights."

"She said she saw him."

"I'll talk to him when he gets home."

"He probably won't be going with us to the PUP rally tonight," Dawn said. "He told me at breakfast he was going fishing with Robby after work."

"I hadn't heard about the fishing trip. Robby's really taken a liking to the boy."

"Everybody has."

Later that evening, Ramón and Dawn had joined Elijah and Esther Ruiz on the second floor of the Bank of the Caribbean building. Ramón sat across the desk from Elijah. Dawn stood beside Esther at an open window, watching the crowd form for the political rally in Battlefield Park.

"Do you miss being on the podium?" Ramón asked Elijah.

"Not a bit. I wasted too much bloody time down there the past twenty years."

Esther turned from the window. "Now that I've finally got him off the podium, my next goal is to move him out to Ambergris Caye." Elijah smiled and shook his head. Esther turned back to the scene below.

"You may have got out just in time," Ramón said. "A lot of people think that PUP's going to lose this election."

"Unfortunately," Elijah said, "that may be true. We've been the party in power during this damnably slow move toward independence. The people hold us, not the British, responsible for Belize's social ills."

Shouts from the park interrupted their exchange. The two men rose and joined the women at the open window. George Price, the PUP leader, stood at the raised podium. Opposition party hecklers shouted that he was a communist and called for his resignation.

"Ramón," Dawn said, "I don't like the looks of this."

He put an arm around her waist. "Usually, it's all just rhetoric." Movement near the podium caught his attention. Several men, dressed in khakis and black berets, pushed their way through the crowd. Among them was a now familiar figure: Clive Lightburn, shorn of his dreadlocks. How the hell had he gotten involved with that group!

The militants arrived at the podium. The younger members cleared a path and allowed their aging leader to mount the steps. He turned to the throng and lifted his arms. "Black people! Arise! Unite!"

A murmur went through the crowd, then a spontaneous cheer went up. George Price signaled to a Belize Defense Force detail, deployed nearby. The troops pushed their way through the crowd toward the podium.

"Arise! Unite!" the old man cried again from the steps. Then general pandemonium drowned out his call.

The black power advocates struggled to hold their position against the government troops, and the spectators near the podium stampeded away from the confrontation.

Ramón lost sight of Clive and turned from the window. "I need to get down there!"

"What?" Elijah said. "Don't be foolish, mon!"

Dawn dug her fingers into his arm. "Ramón, stay here!"

Ramón turned back to the scene below. The troops had gained control. Clive stood quietly in the custody of two soldiers.

Two hours later, Ramón and Dawn returned home.

"I'm going to talk to Ray," Ramón said.

Dawn nodded and went into their bedroom.

Ramón opened his son's door. "Ray, are you awake?"

"Yeah. I heard y'all coming up the stairs." He switched on the nightstand lamp and glanced at the clock. "Y'all were out late."

"There was disturbance over at the rally tonight. We waited until it was safe to be on the streets."

"Was anybody hurt?" Ray said, sitting up.

"Apparently not. It got ugly for a few minutes, but I don't believe there were any injuries. I don't even think there were any arrests."

"Sorry I missed all the excitement. Robby and I went fishing."

"So I heard. Ray, I also heard you went to see a doctor today."

Ray looked surprised. "How did you hear about that?"

Ramón sat down on the foot of the bed. "It's a small town. Are you having some kind of problem?"

"It's taken care of," Ray said. He reached over to turn off the light.

"Leave the light on. What's the problem?"

"Nothing serious."

"What's the damned problem?" Ramón said, annoyed by his son's evasiveness.

Ray avoided eye contact. "I've got a . . . social disease."

"Social disease! You mean from sex?"

Ray nodded.

"How did you get it?"

"How did I get it? How do you think I got it?"

Ramón took a deep breath, suppressing his irritation at his son's sarcasm. Finally he said, "Does the girl know?"

Ray shrugged.

"Well, does she?" Ramón demanded.

"I don't know," Ray said, still not looking at him.

"You've got a responsibility here, Son. You have to be sure she knows."

"There's no way I can do that, Dad," Ray said, scowling. "I'll probably never see her again."

"You have to be sure she knows, or she's liable to spread it around."

"I wouldn't know how to get in touch with her."

"We'll have to call your mother."

"Call my mother! Why?"

"So she can contact the girl's parents."

"Contact the girl's parents!"

"Damn it, Ray, you've got a responsibility here," Ramón said, disappointed that his son didn't see it for himself. "The girl may be spreading it all over Hammond, while you're down here in Belize."

A look of comprehension came over Ray's face. "Dad, I didn't get it in Hammond. I got it here."

"Here? When . . . how?"

"Last week. I . . . uh . . . laid some pipe . . . down in Dangriga."

"Laid some pipe down in Dangriga," Ramón repeated softly. He stared at Ray for a moment. "How serious is it? Syphilis?"

"No, nothing like that. It's some kind of fungus . . . on the surface. The doctor called it a . . . yeast infection, or something. He gave me a salve that's supposed to clear it up in a couple of days."

Ramón shook his head, then looked at his son with a bemused expression. "Robby tried to tell me you fit in real well down there."

Ray frowned, then smiled.

Ramón stood up and started toward the door. "Plan to come to the office with me in the morning. I have a meeting scheduled with someone I want you to get to know."

A few minutes later, Ramón climbed into bed with Dawn. "I heard you talking with Ray," she said. "Is he sick?"

"No. He picked up . . . a fungus."

"A fungus?"

"Yeah."

"How did he get it?"

Ramón hesitated, then said with a smile, "Laying pipe, down in Dangriga."

"Laying pipe?" Dawn said in dismay. "Ramón, why do you have that boy doing all this manual labor. You're spoiling his vacation!"

The following morning, Ramón paced in the middle of his outer office. His secretary, Mavis, sat at her desk, taking his dictation. Ray was perched in a window with a ledger on his lap. He was supposed to be learning the Kelley Distributors inventory system, but instead he stared down at the boat traffic on Haulover Creek.

The office door flew open, and in walked an ebullient Kendall Foster.

"Good morning, Ramón," the young Belizean said as they shook hands. "And you, Mavis," he said, bending down and draping an arm across her shoulders, "lovely as ever."

"Mistah Kendall!" she protested, but clearly enjoying his attention.

"Ray," Ramón said, "come over here, Son. I want you to meet Kendall Foster."

Ray walked over and awkwardly extended his hand.

"It's a pleasure to meet you at last, Ray," Kendall said as they shook hands.

"Yeah," Ray mumbled, "nice meeting you too."

"Come this way," his father said, ushering them into his private office at the rear of the building.

"Ramón," Kendall said as they all sat down, "you start your day too bloody early."

Ramón automatically checked his watch. It was after 9:00; he and Ray had arrived at the office at 6:30.

Kendall turned to Ray. "These old men go to bed and get up with the chickens. They don't understand that we young men have responsibilities at night. Have you found a gyal here yet, Ray?"

"Uh . . . no . . . not yet."

Ramón suppressed a smile.

"We'll have to see about that," Kendall said with a conspiratorial wink. "The female drums are alive with the news that an eligible bachelor has arrived in town. My two sisters heard of you days before I did."

Ray smiled uncomfortably.

"Kendall," Ramón said, "I hope you won't mind if Ray sits in on our discussion this morning. While he's down here, I'm trying to give him some idea how his old man earns his rice and beans."

"Certainly I don't mind." Turning to Ray, Kendall said, "Learn all you can from your father, Ray. He's one hell of a businessman."

"Ray," Ramón said, "a few months ago, Kendall told me he wanted to develop tourism in the interior. That's what we'll be discussing here today." Ramón's comment was for Kendall's benefit. Earlier that morning, Ramón had thoroughly briefed his son on the significance of the meeting. He had explained that he was looking for an opportunity to enter into a business venture with Kendall, who had recently become one of the largest landowners in Belize. Ray had seemed uninterested.

"Actually, Ramón," Kendall said, "developing tourism is more a . . . means to an end. My primary goal is to get my property self-supporting. It's all rain forest. To use it for farming or cattle, I would have to clear it. My dilemma is: I can't afford to let my property sit idle, yet I don't want to ruin it."

Ramón leaned forward. "What do you have in mind?"

"I've done some research the past year, and I think there may be crops and livestock that can thrive in the forest, without destroying it. There have been small-scale successes in various parts of the world, such as coffee and fruit in Colombia, and water buffalo in Thailand. These are the kinds of things I'd like to try here."

"Where does tourism fit in?"

"My guess is that it will take five to ten years to find crops and livestock suitable for this region. In the meantime, I'll need a steady source of income. My idea is to sell off a portion of my property—say 25,000 acres—and use the money to set up a tourist lodge and an experimental farm. The lodge itself would require about 3,000 acres and the farm about 47,000. The profits from the lodge would support the experimental farm until it was self-supporting. Then, if I can make the farm profitable, the other 315,000 acres can remain untouched."

"How large is an acre?" Ray interrupted, showing his first interest in the discussion.

"I believe," Kendall said, "an acre is about the size of one of your American football fields."

Ramón nodded.

"Wow," Ray said. "You mean, your property is big enough to hold almost 400,000 football fields?"

The young Belizean smiled. "A neighbor of mine owns a piece of property nearly twice as large."

"And you'd be willing to sell off 25,000 acres?" Ramón said.

"Unfortunately, I have no choice. My father left me land rich, but cash poor."

"How much capital would you need for your venture?"

"I estimate $1,500,000, U.S.—$500,000 for the lodge and $1,000,000 for the farm."

"Any prospective land buyers at this time?"

Kendall shook his head.

Ramón thought for a moment. "Citrus growers or cattle raisers would be the most likely buyers. That means all 25,000 acres would be slashed and burned."

Kendall nodded. "I hate the thought of clearing the forest. But, as I say, I have nothing but land to invest."

"I don't know anyone locally who has the amount of money

you're talking about," Ramón said. "But, I could check with some
of my contacts in the States, if you don't object to an American
investor."

"I'll accept American investors."

"I suspect," Ramón said, "you're going to meet some resis-
tance from some of these environmentalist groups that are raising
hell in Guatemala these days."

Kendall nodded. "I've had some preliminary talks with members of the Belize Audubon Society. I gave them no guarantees,
but I told them I'd do whatever was economically feasible to protect the environment."

Ramón turned to Ray. "Do you see what we're up against
down here, Son? We don't want to sell out the environment, but
this country's so desperately poor our natural resources are often
all we have to barter with."

Ray nodded.

"How soon could you begin looking for investors?" Kendall
asked Ramón.

"I could fly up to New Orleans tomorrow."

"You can't be off traveling, while your son's visiting."

"I'll be fine," Ray interjected. "Actually, I'd kinda like to see
how this thing turns out."

Ramón smiled at his son, pleased with the interest he was
showing.

"Tell you what, Ray," Kendall said, "I'm flying out to my property this afternoon. I'll be working there for a few days. Would you
like to come along and get a firsthand look at this jungle we're
talking about?"

"Sounds great!"

Ramón nodded approvingly.

30. FLORITA

Ray gazed transfixed at the jungle canopy below. This was only his second time in the air. Flying in the co-pilot seat of Kendall Foster's Cessna-206 was far more exciting than traveling as a passenger in a lumbering jet. He glanced over at Kendall, admiring the confident young Belizean. "How long have you been flying?" Ray shouted across the droning engine.

"I learned when I was about fifteen. My father hired an old bush pilot to teach me. He was a friend of your father. His name was Karl Schrader."

"Dad hasn't mentioned him to me."

"He died recently . . . crashed up in Corozal . . . probably smuggling marijuana. He was one hell of a flyer. His aircraft must have broken down."

"I'd sure like to learn how to fly."

Kendall raised his hands from the controls. "Okay, you take it."

Ray shook his head.

Kendall grinned, then gave the altitude control a slight bump and folded his arms across his chest. The airplane began a slow descent.

"Hey!" Ray cried, grabbing the co-pilot controls and easing the plane back onto a horizontal path. After a few minutes, he relaxed and tentatively experimented with a slow bank to the right, then to the left. Grinning, he looked over at Kendall.

Kendall nodded approvingly, then pointed to the compass and altimeter. "Stay at about 2,000 feet and fly due west. We can't risk using too much petrol. There are no landing strips between Belize City and my place, and it'll be a long walk if we go down in the jungle."

"Is that the rain forest down below?"

Kendall nodded. "It's one of the few in the Western Hemisphere that isn't in immediate danger."

"What's happening to the others?"

"In most countries, they're being chopped down so the land can be farmed. That's wasteful, because the land really isn't good for farming. Even citrus growing and cattle raising, like we were talking about this morning, are only marginally successful."

"Why's that? Looks like you could grow anything down there."

"The vegetation is misleading, Ray. Usually, there's only a thin layer of fertile soil. The reason that the jungle is so dense is that nutrients have to be stored above ground in the vegetation itself. When the vegetation is stripped, these nutrients are lost. The people who slash and burn the rain forests often have to move on after a few seasons, because the soil soon becomes leached and eroded."

"Why do they do it then?"

"Some of it is being done by large corporations, out for short-term profits. Poor countries, with little else to offer, are often obliged to sell off their natural resources. That's what your father was talking about this morning. And some of it is being done by peasant farmers—often squatters—whose only means of survival is to clear small *milpas* in the jungle."

They flew on in silence for several minutes, then Kendall took the controls. "We're almost there. Before we land, I want to show you something." He put the plane into a gradual descent, then banked to the right. He pointed through the window on Ray's side. "See that hill over there?"

A steep peak jutted through the jungle canopy. "Yeah, I see it."

They slowly circled. "It's not a hill; it's a Mayan pyramid. There are hundreds of unexplored ruins in Belize. That one happens to be on my property."

"Wow. You own a pyramid?"

The young Belizean nodded and pulled the airplane out of the turn. "It's on my land, but government has strict rules about what can be done with it. Someday soon, with government's consent, I'd like to restore that one and develop it as the centerpiece for my tourist center and wildlife preserve."

Ray smiled. If the kids in Hammond could see him now, flying into a rain forest, with a guy who owns a pyramid.

"That's my house over there," Kendall said, pointing to a structure perched on top of a knoll in a jungle clearing. He banked to the left and lined up on a straight stretch of road. As he put the aircraft into a sharp descent, he glanced over at Ray and said with a grin, "Don't worry, mon, by Belizean standards, this is one of our better landing strips."

Moments later, they bounced to a stop in the midst of the rain forest.

After dinner, Ray stood alone on the veranda of Kendall's wood-frame house, staring into the shadows. Although the site was elevated, he felt immersed in the jungle. As dusk turned to night, a crescendo rose from the unseen forest, as the sounds of birds, insects, and frogs blended with the rush of the nearby river rapids.

Kendall stepped onto the veranda. "Would you like some coffee?"

"Uh, no thanks."

Kendall joined him at the railing. "So, how do you like it out here?"

"Man, it's really different."

"Not like Hammond, Louisiana, aye?"

"It's sure as hell not like Hammond. But it doesn't look like the other parts of Belize I've seen, either."

"You'll get a chance to see more of it tomorrow. We're flying over to San Ignacio Town. Belize is an unusual country, Ray. On our eastern coast, we're like the Caribbean island nations. But here on our western border, we're more Central American. For 300 years, the Caribbean influence has been the stronger, but we may be in for a change."

"Why's that?"

"Most immigrants entering Belize today are coming from other

Central American countries. Many come from El Salvador, and there is also a steady trickle from Guatemala, Honduras, and even as far away as Nicaragua. They come to Belize because our country is stable and peaceful."

"Are these legal immigrants?"

"Some are. In fact, last month a church organization got government's permission to establish a refugee village for Salvadorans about fifty miles from here. I wish it could have been closer; I could have put them to work on—"

A rasping roar from nearby in the jungle interrupted him. The wildlife din also hushed.

Ray's heart pounded. "What the hell was that?" he whispered.

"What did it sound like?"

"A jungle cat."

Kendall smiled. "Many people think they're hearing a jaguar, or 'tiger' as we call them. But what you heard is the sound of a howler monkey. We call them 'baboons'. The baboon is king in our jungle. The ancient Maya worshiped them as gods."

The howler continued to bellow and grunt from the edge of the clearing. Finally it moved away, and its outbursts blended in with the other night sounds.

"You were saying you needed people to work out here?" Ray said.

Kendall nodded. "Belize is badly underpopulated. I've got about fifteen Mayans from this area. My foreman and his wife, the woman who fixed our dinner tonight, are the only ones who live on the premises. The rest come from a nearby village. I'll need a lot more people to fully develop this place." He sighed. "Right now, they're not available."

"When we were flying in, you said you wanted to restore that pyramid."

Kendall nodded. "Hopefully, I won't have to provide the workers for that. I would like to get a U.S. university interested in the project. That's the reason I'm going to San Ignacio tomorrow, to meet with a group from the University of Pennsylvania."

Kendall paused for a moment, as if deciding whether to continue. Finally he said, "Ray, within ten years, this area could be unbelievable! Next to the ruins, I plan to build primitive cabanas. Tourists will come here to see this land as it was hundreds of years ago. To the east, I want to raise crops that don't require stripping the forest. To the south, a herd of Asian water buffalo." He paused again, as if uncomfortable at having shared his vision.

"Wow," Ray said. The young Belizean's dreams were infectious.

The following morning, Kendall and Ray trudged up a steep, rocky street to the San Ignacio Hotel. Ray glanced over his shoulder; Kendall's aircraft, parked on the soccer field below, glinted in the midmorning sun.

Two British Army trucks crested the hill. Ray and Kendall moved over to the shoulder of the road and waited for them to pass.

"How many English soldiers are in Belize?" Ray said.

"About 2,000 troops throughout the country, and a Harrier jet squadron in Belize City. There is also a Gurkha unit, skulking about somewhere in the bush."

They continued up the hill.

"Is there ever any actual fighting between the British and the Guatemalans?" Ray said.

"Oh, occasionally there are some shots fired, but usually it's a mix-up of some sort . . . just enough to keep our politicians on edge. Ironically, the British troops indirectly provide a service for the Guats. They keep the communist rebels from receiving arms supplies. Are you familiar with the basis of Belize-Guatemala dispute?"

"Mr. Ruiz explained it to me. The Guatemalans claim that Belize broke an agreement to give them a road to the sea a hundred years ago, so now they claim the whole country is theirs."

Kendall nodded. "Most Guatemalan maps show Belize as their eastern province."

They arrived at the hotel, a one-story, cinder-block structure.

Ray glanced back at the picturesque village below. Remembering how much his mother had hated this country, he suspected she had never come to San Ignacio.

They entered the hotel lobby, and an attractive young desk clerk cried out, "Mistah Foster! Good to see you again, sah!"

"Good to see you, Ninette."

"Does Delia know you're in town?" she said.

"Not yet, but she will shortly."

The clerk smiled, but Ray thought he detected a trace of disappointment.

"Ninette, this is Ray Kelley. He'll be staying with me here for the next few days. Take good care of him, uh?"

"Hello, mistah Kelley. We're glad to have you with us. Won't you sign in please?"

After they had registered, Kendall led Ray over to the lobby's spacious rear window, overlooking the swimming pool. A basketball court lay off to one side.

"Ray," Kendall said, "uh . . . look, mon . . . I have a gyal friend here in town who I haven't seen in a few weeks. I won't be able to be with her tonight, because of the meeting with the university people."

Ray waited.

"Uh . . . Delia and I . . . will probably be spending the afternoon . . . in my room."

Ray caught on. "Hey, man, that's not a problem. I can find something to do around here."

"If you feel like doing some exploring," Kendall said, "that large pyramid we flew over—Xunantunich—is just seven miles from here. The caretaker out there is an expert on the place and can tell you all about it."

"Sounds good."

"Ninette can give you directions on how to get out there. Studying Xunantunich will help you understand what we'll be talking about tonight. I'm hoping to restore my pyramid similarly."

"Y'all have a good time this afternoon," Ray said with a grin.

Ray descended the stairs of an ancient bus that ran between the villages of San Ignacio and Benque Viejo. The water canteen hanging from his belt banged against the door.

As the bus pulled away, spewing a cloud of smoke and dust, Ray made out the stenciled lettering from its previous life: Rhinelander High School—Rhinelander, Wisconsin.

Ray turned and looked down a steep embankment. Below, lay the Mopan River and the small hand-winch ferry the desk clerk had described. An elderly Indian watched him from the deck of the ferry.

Ray scrambled down the embankment. "Is this the way to Xunantunich?"

"Shu-nan-tu-nich," the Indian said, correcting Ray's pronunciation.

Ray stepped on board. "How much?"

"There is no charge, but we can't leave until a car comes."

Ray was relieved that the man could speak English. He decided to take the opportunity to learn about the ruins. "Are you Mayan?"

The Indian nodded.

"So your people built Xunantunich?"

"*Sí. Los viejos*—the ancient ones."

"They must have been very . . . powerful."

"Yes, only the British race is stronger."

"The British race?"

"Yes," the Indian said sagely. "The British race is always in command. It is that way all through history. After the Mayan race, came the Roman race. Then came the American race. But the British race is always in command . . . like now."

Ray decided not to challenge the old man's understanding of world history. "What can you tell me about Xunantunich?"

"Many things. I know it well. Some nights I sleep in the maiden's chamber."

"What maiden?"

"Xunantunich in Maya means 'stone maiden'."

"You sleep in the pyramid?"

"Sometimes. I look for Xtabay." The Indian shifted his gaze downriver. "One night, many years ago, I see her."

"Xtabay?"

"Yes, the tall, beautiful maiden. My people know her. One night, when I sleep in the chamber, I hear something. At first I think thiefs, but they don't come inside. Then I see a bright blue snake."

"A snake?" Ray said. Jungle vipers concerned him more than Mayan spirits.

The Indian nodded. "Stairs in the chamber go outside. The snake climbed the stairs. I got too much fright to follow. But when I look up, I see her!"

"Who?"

"The beautiful maiden, Xtabay!" The Indian was now lost in his recollection. "She wears a bright blue robe. Her feet are tied with rope, and she raises her hands to the sky." He paused, still staring downriver.

"What happened?"

The Indian turned back with an expression of remorse. "I look away . . . and when I look back . . . she is gone."

After a long silence, Ray said, "How long do you think it will be before a car comes?"

The Indian shrugged.

"How long does it usually take?"

"I don't know. This is not my job. The mon who works here is at a funeral."

Ray took a Belizean dollar out of his billfold. "How about if we go now?"

"There is no guide there. He is at the funeral too."

"I can get by without a guide. I just want to take a look around."

The Indian shrugged and took the bill.

A few minutes later, Ray stepped off the ferry on the other side and headed up a packed dirt trail. Large palms arched overhead, so dense that they blocked the midday sun. A warm breeze rustled the fronds. Ray kept an eye out for snakes, bright blue or otherwise.

He walked for about a mile, then rounded a bend and came to a clearing. Several mound-like structures lay before him. Behind them loomed an enormous pyramid, taller than a ten-story building.

A thatched hut stood off to the right. A sign designated it as the guide headquarters and called for a one dollar entry fee. The hut was empty. Ray scanned the deserted plaza. It appeared he was the only person on the premises. The solitude made him uneasy. He considered turning around and going back, but then he would have to explain his quick return to the Indian.

He started down a trail that wound through the outer structures. As he walked, he gazed up at the main pyramid. The lower half resembled a terraced hill; the upper half looked like a forbidding stone fortress. At the top level, three dark doorways opened onto the plaza. Five enormous stone blocks formed a crown at the summit.

He arrived at the base of the pyramid. The trail branched off in two directions. He chose the one to the right and began the climb up the steep grassy incline. He was sweating by the time he arrived at the stone structure. He stopped to catch his breath and looked back at the plaza below. Still no sign of anyone else. The eerie sense of solitude swept over him again.

A weathered wooden stairway led to the top of the temple. As he took the first step, he glanced up and froze. He raised his hand to shield his eyes from the sun. A tall, dark woman stood at the summit. Her garment was bright blue. Ray turned away from the sun, then looked back. She was gone.

Somebody was screwing with him! He scanned the plaza below. No one in sight. The Indian had set him up for this! No, the old man hadn't volunteered his story of the maiden; Ray had drawn it out of him.

Ray kept checking the summit, but the figure didn't reappear. On impulse, he bounded up the rickety stairs. He paused when he reached the upper level, breathing hard and sweating heavily. He looked inside the closest of the three doorways. The chamber was empty, except for a stone stairway. This must be where the Indian thought he saw the blue snake.

Ray entered the chamber and edged over to the stairway. Through an opening above, he saw the cloudless sky. He edged up the stairs, then stepped out onto a wide ledge. The five massive stone blocks were taller than he was. The one immediately in front of him prevented him from seeing if anyone else was on the summit. He didn't know if he was in real danger, or just in danger of embarrassment. "Hey!" he shouted. "Anybody home?"

A torrid breeze whistled across the rough stone. He squeezed into a two-foot gap between the two closest blocks. Reaching above his head, he grasped the upper surfaces and managed to pull himself up. His canteen scraped against one side. On top, he found the five hewn surfaces to be flat and each about six feet square. He stood up slowly, then cautiously jumped from block to block, searching the summit, but finding no one.

Finally he sat down on the middle block. For a long time, he watched and listened. Off to the north, he recognized the village of San Ignacio. The village to the south apparently was Benque Viejo. To the west lay Guatemala.

Ray knew that Mayan priests had killed millions of people, constructing and consecrating temples such as this. He looked down the side of the pyramid and shuddered, visualizing the human sacrifice that had gone into this one. Mayans had been building these edifices for their gods during the time of Christ. Somebody got the wrong scoop, Ray thought. Maybe they both did.

The sun beat down on him. His mouth was dry. He unhooked the canteen from his belt and unscrewed the cap. What was it that his father had said about drinking the water of Belize? He felt light-headed, and couldn't remember. He put the canteen to his lips and drank thirstily.

The wind gusted, whistling across the hewn stone surface, like a woman's wail. He stood up, and drank again. Water ran from the corners of his mouth and down his neck. He lowered the canteen and looked about. He had never felt so alive!

The engine of an approaching vehicle drew him from his reverie. An old Jeep entered the plaza and pulled up beside the guide hut. A man in a khaki uniform got out.

Ray climbed down from the summit and headed for the stairway. Kendall had told him that the guide was an authority on Xunantunich; however, Ray decided just to pay his dollar and leave. He had been exposed to enough Mayan lore for one day.

Ninette, the hotel desk clerk, looked up as Ray trudged into the lobby. "How was your trip to the ruins, mistah Kelley?"

"Uh . . . interesting." He handed her the empty canteen. "You were right. I needed this out there. Thanks."

"You got sunburned. Your skin is too light. You must get some lotion." She returned her attention to some paperwork.

Ray headed toward his room, thinking about cooling off with a swim. As he crossed the lobby, he glanced through the rear window. The pool area was deserted, except for a single figure, walking along the edge of the water. He stopped in mid-stride. It was the woman from the pyramid. She wore a bright blue swimsuit.

Ray riveted his eyes on her, afraid she might vanish again. She was tall and tanned, and walked with supple, athletic grace. She stopped at the end of the pool, and tied her long black hair away from her face, exposing high cheekbones and full lips. She dipped a foot into the water to test the temperature, then dived in and began swimming laps with powerful crawl strokes.

Ray shook his head. What the hell was going on? Too much sun? He glanced down at his sweat-soaked, grime-covered jeans and T-shirt. He momentarily considered running to his room and changing into his swimsuit, but decided he had better not give her a chance to disappear. He hurried out the lobby door and down the steps that led to the pool.

Ray dropped into a wooden pool chair, next to one with a towel draped across it. On the young woman's next lap down the pool, she saw him. She stopped and wiped the water from her eyes.

God, she's gorgeous! Ray thought. And she's gonna think I'm nuts.

She pulled herself from the water and walked over to her towel.

"Uh . . . hi," Ray said. He began to perspire. "Uh . . . by any chance . . . were you out at the pyramid this afternoon?"

"Yes. I saw you there."

Ray heaved a sigh. "Thank, God."

She frowned.

Ray tried to explain. "I'm not superstitious . . . but you see . . . one minute you were there . . . then you vanished."

Still frowning, she shook her head.

Ray tried again. "You see . . . the old man that ran the ferry told me this story about a blue snake that turns into a princess or something . . . wearing a blue robe . . . then she disappears."

She looked about, as if uncomfortable being alone with him.

"I know this isn't making any sense . . ." Ray mumbled.

"I'm familiar with the story of Xtabay," she said. "It is a common legend of the Mayan culture."

"Well . . . you see, you were wearing blue . . . and disappeared . . ."

She suddenly began to laugh, and dropped into the chair beside him.

"I know it's dumb," Ray said, "but you see, I'm not from around here."

"I'm sorry," she said with a sympathetic smile. "I shouldn't be laughing at you. Before I saw you there, I was feeling uneasy myself. I've done research at that site before, but I've never seen it as deserted as it was today."

She had a marvelous smile. Ray began to relax. "How did you disappear?"

"I didn't know who you were. Since we were all alone out there, I thought it best that I leave. While you were coming up the west side, I went down the old frieze scaffolding on the east side. Then I took the short trail to the river crossing."

"And wearing blue? Like even now, your bathing suit."

She laughed again. "It is known as Maya blue. I wear it because I've been told it looks good on me." She pulled her towel around her, as if preparing to leave.

Ray needed to keep the conversation going. "Uh . . . are you Mayan?"

"I'm Mestizo," she said, settling back again.

"I'm not sure what that means."

"Mestizos are a mixture of Indian and Spanish. My name is Guerrero. My auntie says we are descended from the legendary Spaniard, Gonzalo Guerrero."

"I'm sorry, I've never heard of him."

"Then I must tell you about him. In 1511, a ship of Spanish conquistadors sank off Yucatan. A seaman named Gonzalo Guerrero was captured by the Maya and taken to be their slave. But Guerrero soon earned the respect of the Mayan chief, Nachan Can. Guerrero took a Mayan wife, who gave him three children. He had his nose and ears pierced, and his hands and face tattooed, in the tradition of the Maya. By 1517, when the Spaniards returned to Yucatan, Guerrero was captain of Nachan Can's army. The Spaniards ordered Guerrero to return to them, but he refused. When the Spaniards landed, Guerrero led the army that drove them back into the sea."

"Wow. What a guy."

"Yes, what a guy," she said with a laugh. "He was the first European to set foot in Belize, and his children were its first Mestizos." She started to rise again.

"Uh . . . did you say you were studying archaeology?"

"Not archaeology. I've just completed my first year at Belize College, where I'm studying to be a teacher. Someday I hope to go to school in Mexico and study Mayan history. But for now, I'm learning it on my own."

Before Ray could reply, a voice called out, "So here's where you are!" Kendall Foster bounded down the concrete stairs. "I see you've been making friends, Ray. Introduce us."

"Uh . . . I'm afraid . . ."

"I am Florita Guerrero," the young woman said, smiling at Kendall.

"Nice to meet you, Florita," Kendall said, confidently drawing up another pool chair. "I'm Kendall Foster. Do you live here in San Ignacio?"

"Uh . . . my name is Ray Kelley," Ray said, belatedly introducing himself.

Florita responded with a quick nod and smile, then continued with Kendall, "No, I'm here on holiday. I live in Belize City."

"How can I not have met you?" Kendall said.

"I have heard of you," she said. "I believe you know the older sister of a friend of mine: Maria Gomez?"

"Certainly! And her little sister's name is Estella. Is that your friend?"

Florita nodded.

"Little Estella must not be so little anymore," Kendall said with a smile.

Florita returned his smile.

Ray was uncomfortably aware that the wealthy young Belizean was having no trouble in keeping her from leaving.

"Listen, Florita," Kendall said, "we have a business meeting scheduled tonight, but can we get together tomorrow?"

"I'm sorry," she said. "I'd like to, but I'm leaving for Tikal early in the morning."

Ray was disappointed. He also resented how quickly Kendall had taken over. "Where's Tikal?" he said.

"It's a major Mayan ruin, about sixty miles inside Guatemala," Florita said.

"Who are you traveling with?" Kendall said.

"I'm going alone. I was telling . . . Ray . . . I'm studying Mayan culture. My auntie gave me this trip as a present."

"If you wait two days," Kendall said, "I can fly you there. That Guatemalan road to the west is terrible."

Ray had lapsed into silence, knowing he couldn't compete.

"Thank you for the offer," she said, "but I believe I'll stay on my original schedule."

Kendall looked resigned, then brightened. "Would you like some company then?"

"On the bus?"

"Sure," Kendall said. "Ray here. I'll be busy for two days, and it'll be a bloody bore for him." Turning to Ray, he said, "You ought to go with her, mon. The Guats have done a first rate job with Tikal."

Ray brightened, suddenly finding himself back in the game.

"I'm leaving from the hotel at 8:00," Florita told Ray. "As mistah Foster says, the road to Tikal is quite bad. But you're welcome to join me if you want to come along."

"Sure!"

"Very well," she said. "I'll meet you in the lobby at 8:00." She stood up. "And I hope I'll be seeing you again, mistah Foster. Maybe in Belize City?"

"I'm certain we'll see each other again, Florita," Kendall said.

Ray and Kendall watched her climb the stairs to the hotel.

"You didn't mind me volunteering you, did you?" Kendall said.

"Hell no! Are you kidding?"

Kendall grinned. "Well, she looked like she was getting away, and you weren't saying much."

Ray stood beside Florita in front of a Guatemalan border official. The hand-carved sign on his desk read: "Capitán Benavides".

The slovenly agent looked up at Florita in amusement, while she berated him in Spanish. When she paused, he said with a grin, "*Veinte-cinco quetzals.*"

Florita turned to Ray. "He wants twenty-five quetzals for us to enter Guatemala—five for me and twenty for you. He says you must pay twenty because you don't have a passport. But visitor cards should only cost us one quetzal each."

"I tell you what, *bonita*," the Guatemalan said, suddenly displaying his English. "For you, only one quetzal. But you, *gringo*, you go back to Belize."

Ray had no intention of being separated from Florita. He reached into his billfold and pulled out an American $10 bill. "Is this enough?"

The Guatemalan sneered and handed Ray his card. When Florita reached for her card, he held onto it for a moment. Finally he said, "Another time, *bonita*," then let her take it.

Moments later, Ray and Florita walked across the concrete bridge and into the border village of Melchor de Mencos. A morning breeze blew dust and litter about the main street. Guatemalan soldiers slouched in front of the village's few shops and eyed them as they passed. The soldiers were Indians and appeared to be in their early teens. Ray towered a foot above them.

Florita pointed to a gathering of people on the corner. "We catch the bus over there."

As they approached the edge of the crowd, a battered bus arrived from the other direction. There were several minutes of confusion, as the passengers inside the bus struggled to get out, and those in the street fought to get in. Ray and Florita were among the last to board. Several men already stood in the aisle. An old Indian woman moved over and made a place for Florita on the end of the seat. Ray took a place in the aisle, standing beside her.

Although it was still early morning, the sun's heat radiated through the metal roof. Ray was sweating freely by the time the driver pulled away. They rumbled through the village, covering it's grimy clapboard buildings with yet another layer of dust.

When they finally reached the rocky, open road, the bus began to vibrate like a jackhammer. Ray clung to the hand rails on the backs of the seats, struggling to keep his balance as the driver swerved to avoid the larger rocks and potholes.

After a half-hour of incessant pounding, Ray leaned down to Florita and shouted, "How long a trip is this?"

"Four hours," she said sympathetically.

Ray shook his head. No way he could take this for four hours! Suddenly the bus rapidly decelerated and he pitched forward. As they came to a stop, Ray bent down and looked through the front window. Diminutive soldiers, like those in the border village, surrounded the bus.

A soldier climbed aboard. *"¡Documentarse!"* he shouted, then gestured with his rifle for the passengers to get off the bus.

Ray followed Florita down the aisle. He stepped off the bus and hesitated, confused by the turmoil around him. Several soldiers swaggered about, impatiently shouting orders in Spanish. Several more climbed onto the bus roof and threw down the passengers' luggage. A soldier moved in front of Ray and shouted, *"¡Al otro lado!"*

"What's he want?" Ray asked Florita.

"Follow the other men," she said tersely.

The soldier prodded him with a rifle. Ray stumbled around the front of the bus and found the other male passengers lined up, shoulder to shoulder.

The soldier pushed Ray in line with the others. *"¡Documentarse!"* he shouted.

"I don't speak Spanish—" Ray began.

"¡Documentarse!" the soldier demanded.

The other men pulled out identification. Ray produced the visitor's card he had been given at the border. The soldier snatched it away from him and scrutinized it, upside down.

"¿De donde eres?" the soldier demanded.

"I don't speak Spanish," Ray said.

"¿De donde eres?" the soldier repeated.

"I don't speak Spanish," Ray said, futilely looking about for someone to translate for him.

"¿Gringo?" the soldier said.

Ray nodded.

"¡Pasaporte!"

"I . . . I don't have one."

"¿No tienes?" the soldier said angrily.

Ray shook his head that he didn't understand.

The soldier prodded Ray with his rifle and marched him away from the others. Ahead stood a thatched roof shack; behind it, lay a rushing stream. The initial confusion had worn off; now Ray was scared. He risked a glance over his shoulder.

Florita stepped from the line of female passengers. *"¡Espera!"* she shouted. She broke away from her group and ran toward Ray.

A soldier standing near the bus raised his rifle to the firing position and shouted, *"¡Párate!"*

Ray raised his hands. "Don't shoot!" he begged.

The soldier beside him raised his hands too, apparently concerned for his own safety. The other soldier walked forward, his rifle still in the firing position. They hovered around Ray and Florita, shouting at them.

"What do they want?" Ray asked Florita.

Florita spoke to the soldier who had detained Ray, then said, "His orders are to stop any Americans who don't have passports. I told him they gave you clearance at the border, but he won't listen. They're taking you to their officer."

Ray and Florita followed the two soldiers to the hut. The soldiers gestured for them to enter. There was no one inside. The single room contained only a hewn table and chair, and a dirty folding cot. The soldiers positioned themselves just outside the doorway.

Ray looked out the rear window. A file of soldiers straggled up the slope from a nearby river. They were naked, except for towels pulled around their middles and rifles slung across their shoulders. They apparently had been bathing.

He looked out the front window. The other passengers were reboarding the bus. Past the bus stood a billboard. Someone had painted a primitive portrait of a skull, with blood dripping from its mouth and a bayonet clenched between its teeth. Ray pointed to the billboard. "What the hell is this place?"

Florita read the caption. *"Aqui se Forjan los Mejores Combatientes de los Americas.* Here are trained the best soldiers in the Americas."

The bus engine started.

"They're leaving us!" Ray said.

"*¡Silencio!*" one of the soldiers barked.

The bus pulled away from the checkpoint and disappeared over the crest of a nearby hill.

Time passed. Finally, another soldier approached the hut, clad in a towel and carrying a rifle. He was taller than the others, with light skin and sharp features. The soldiers standing guard outside the door came to attention as he passed, then followed him inside.

The officer set his rifle on the table and spoke briefly with his men. He turned to Ray and gestured for him to face the wall. Ray did so, but glanced over his shoulder. The officer took Florita over to the opposite wall.

One of the soldiers moved behind Ray and kicked the insides of his ankles, forcing him to spread his legs, then pushed him into a leaning position. The other soldier put the muzzle of his rifle against Ray's cheek and forced his face against the wall. The soldier behind him squatted down and checked for concealed weapons.

Florita cried out. Ray whirled, instinctively grabbing the rifle muzzle. He caught a glimpse of Florita—spread-eagled against the far wall with the officer's hand pushed between her legs. The soldier beside Ray fought to regain control of his rifle. Ray threw an awkward overhand right. The soldier who had been searching for weapons drove his head into Ray's stomach, slamming him against the wall and causing him to release the rifle. Ray brought up a knee, sending the soldier in front of him reeling across the room. He caught a glimpse of something coming up from his lower left periphery.

When Ray regained consciousness, he found himself propped in the doorway of the hut. Florita knelt beside him, dabbing at his face with a soiled wet rag. Soldiers meandered nearby, but kept their distance.

"You okay?" Ray said, trying to rise. His words came out strangely slurred.

"They didn't hurt me," Florita said, and gently pushed him

back. "We can return to Belize as soon as someone comes along who will take us."

Ray ran his tongue across the inside of his throbbing cheek. He winced, when he felt jagged edges where two smooth teeth had always been.

"He hit you with his gun. Some of your teeth are broken."

"Why are they letting us go?"

"They had no reason to detain us. The soldiers were ignorantly carrying out orders. And that stupid officer made things worse. Now, because they hurt you, they just want to get rid of us."

A car stopped at the checkpoint, but it was headed in the wrong direction. Finally, an old pickup truck rattled down the hill, heading toward Belize. Still groggy, Ray got to his feet and followed Florita out to the middle of the road. The truck's florid-faced driver was bantering in Spanish with the soldiers. As Ray and Florita approached, the soldiers grew serious again. In Spanish, Florita asked the driver for a ride to the border.

"*Claro, señorita,*" the driver said. Then he looked at Ray and said in a nasal, deep-south twang, "What happened to you, boy?"

"You're an American?"

"Uh huh. Come on, y'all get in."

Moments later, they rattled east toward Belize. Ray's jaw ached.

"What did y'all do to get them boys mad at you?" the driver said. "You ain't involved in none of that marijuana stuff, are you?"

"No, sir," Ray said, having difficulty speaking. "They just fucked with us because I didn't have a passport."

"Watch your language, boy!" the man said sharply. "We got a lady with us." Then he said, "Where y'all from?"

"I'm from Belize City," Florita said.

"I'm from Hammond, Louisiana," Ray said. He felt Florita shift toward him, and thought he saw the driver reposition his leg so it still pressed against hers.

"Hammond, huh. Well, I'm from McComb, Mississippi. You know where that is, don't you, boy?"

"Yes, sir, I do. It's not far from my hometown." The pain and the vibration of the truck were making him sick.

The man nodded. "I've been down here more than twenty years, preaching the Lord's word. Y'all been saved, ain't you?"

Ray felt too sick to respond. Florita stared at the road ahead. Again, she moved her legs away from the driver. Ray shifted closer toward the door to give her more room.

"I'm Reverend Eldon Bodine, minister of the New Bethlehem Congregational Church in El Cruce. I'm going to Melchor to do some baptizing. If y'all ain't already been baptized, you need to be."

The truck slammed into a pothole, and a searing stab of pain shot through Ray's jaw. He closed his eyes, wanting the ride to end.

Finally the road smoothed. Ray opened his eyes and sighed with relief. They had entered the border village.

The driver stopped at the bridge. "Sure y'all don't want to come over to the mission?" He placed a sun-blotched hand on Florita's knee.

"No thanks," Ray mumbled. He and Florita scrambled out of the truck.

As they crossed the bridge, Ray gazed past the customs house. A large billboard read: "Welcome to Belize".

31. THE CORPORATION

"Guatemala!" Ramón roared. "What the hell were you doing in Guatemala?"

Ray set his travel bag inside his bedroom door, then returned to the living room and said nonchalantly, "Going to Tikal."

Ramón looked distractedly at Dawn. She shook her head and continued to stare at Ray's badly bruised jaw.

"What the hell did you do in Guatemala to get in trouble with the damned military?" Ramón demanded.

"Nothing, Dad. They were kids, younger than me. They hassled me because I didn't have a passport."

"Tell me where the hell you got those gold teeth."

Ray grinned, displaying the two shiny bicuspids again. "Kendall took me to a dentist in San Ignacio. Some nerves were exposed that had to be fixed right away."

"Ray," Ramón said, struggling to regain his composure, "when did all this happen?"

"Last week."

"Last week! Why the hell didn't you come back here right away?"

"I was having a good time."

"Having a good time! Getting your God damned teeth knocked out?"

"Don't worry about it, Dad. Really, I'm okay."

Ramón shook his head.

"Dad, I met a really neat girl."

"Met a girl . . ." Ramón mumbled, trying to imagine his wife's reaction, when her only child returned to the States with two gold teeth and a social disease.

"Wait 'til you meet her," Ray said. "Her name's Florita."

Ramón abruptly focused on the conversation again. "You brought back a girl from Guatemala!"

"No, Dad," Ray said with a laugh. "She's from here in Belize City. We were going to Tikal together when the soldiers stopped us."

"Going to Tikal together," Ramón said slowly. He sat down on the couch. "Ray . . . your mother wired the money you asked her for. Her note said for me to put you on the next plane home."

"I don't want to go back early anymore, Dad."

"Son, it might be best to cut short this first visit and—"

"I don't want to go back at all," Ray interrupted.

Ramón studied the firm set of his son's bruised jaw. "Well, call your mother in the morning and tell her you've changed your mind. But you'll have to go back in time to start school."

Ray gazed at him unflinchingly.

"And damn it, boy, take it easy! There's such a thing as fitting in too well down here."

The following evening, Ramón, Ray, and Kendall gathered in Ramón's private office.

Kendall opened Ramón's trip report. He read the executive summary on the first page, then looked up. "The Landry Corporation was your old firm, wasn't it?"

Ramón nodded "It was Landry Mahogany then. They shut down their logging operation twenty years ago. Since then, they've restructured into land development and trade."

"And you kept in contact with them?"

"No . . . at least not directly. Milburn Landry and I split on bad terms. In fact, I had to file suit to get him to make a fair settlement on my contract. But I've kept in touch with his attorney, Max Stein. Max is retired now, but he was willing to serve as intermediary between Landry and me in structuring this offer."

"Dad," Ray interrupted, "if Landry screwed you twenty years ago, why would Kendall want to do business with him now?"

"Down here, Son, we don't have the luxury of just doing business with people we 'want to'."

"True enough, Ramón," Kendall said, "but Ray makes a good point: 'Same knife sticks sheep, sticks goat'."

Ray frowned at Kendall.

Ramón smiled. "There's a Belizean adage for everything, Son."

"Seriously, Ramón," Kendall continued, "considering your past difficulties with this Landry fellow, do you think I could trust him?"

"Trust him? No. But I think you could work a deal with him, if you bound him in a straightforward contract and process it in the States."

"And his offer is?"

"He's offering you $1,000,000 for that 23,000-acre tract that juts out and touches the Western Highway."

Kendall shook his head. "That's one-third what the property is actually worth, and $500,000 less than what I need. Is Landry the only possibility?"

"His was the best of two offers. Max also put me in touch with the US Oil people in Houston. Both Landry and US Oil are interested in the same tract. US Oil's offer is $850,000."

"Does US Oil want to drill?"

"I doubt that's what they have in mind. They've done seismic testing in the area, but oil companies usually don't buy property—only the exploration and recovery rights. I suspect their offer is tied to some kind of diversification program, which they're not willing to disclose."

"How about the Landry people? What do they have in mind?"

"They're also not disclosing their plans. But, judging by their other Central American activities, my guess is that they're looking for a place to raise cattle for export."

"To the States?"

"No, more likely to Caribbean island nations and the United Kingdom."

Ray broke in. "Isn't cattle raising one of the things you said would hurt the rain forest?"

Kendall nodded. "They'll probably slash and burn. But it's

like your father says, Ray, down here we often have to make compromises. Without alternatives, what can we do?"

Ramón picked up a manila folder off his desk. "Kendall, Landry's and US Oil's offers are probably the best you'll get." He passed the folder across the desk to the young Belizean. "However, before you make your decision, here's a prospectus I'd like you to consider."

"What's this?"

"It's a proposal for a corporation. You'll need time to go over it in detail, but I'll summarize it for you. Basically, Elijah Ruiz and I would like to enter into a joint venture with you."

Kendall responded with a bemused smile. "I thought you were opposed to my tourism idea?"

"Not opposed, necessarily. I just couldn't envision a customer base."

"And now?"

"We follow the lead of Mexico. First the Mexicans attract tourists to their seaside resorts, like Cozumel and Cancun. Then they entice them inland to their ruins."

Kendall leaned forward.

"For years, Elijah Ruiz and I have discussed the cayes' potential for tourism. While we've sat around talking, American investors have been taking action."

Kendall nodded.

"Our proposition is, we want to expand your plan. We would lure tourists down to Belize to scuba dive and fish on the cayes, then fly them inland for a jungle adventure."

"That's all well and good, Ramón. But I don't have enough capital to build my jungle lodge, much less one on the cayes."

"Elijah and I believe we can supply the missing pieces. In the corporation we're proposing, you would be the majority shareholder. We estimate your investment would be $3,000,000—the true value of the 23,000 acres you would have to sell to Landry. You also would provide the 50,000 acres for the farming and lodge project. Your other 317,000 acres wouldn't be involved." Ramón paused.

"Go on," Kendall said.

"Elijah would put up his Ambergris Caye property. He has a beach house that sits on a two-acre tract on the windward side of San Pedro. American investors have recently offered him $300,000 for it. Elijah's wife loves the caye and for years has been trying to get him to retire out there. Since he refuses to retire, she agrees that the next best thing would be to have him work out there."

"How large a share would he want?" Kendall said.

"Ten percent. He'd also get an annual salary of $12,000 U.S. for living on-site and managing the caye lodge."

Kendall smiled. "And your involvement?"

"I'd put up approximately $300,000 in cash to cover the cost of building the caye lodge. I have a firm offer of $230,000 for my dealership. I also have seventeen acres of prime coastal property in Dangriga. I don't have a firm offer at this time, but I'm confident I could sell it for something in the $90,000 range. In addition to 10 percent of the corporation, I'd also get a $12,000 per year salary for managing the Belize City corporate office."

Kendall got up and walked over to the office window. He stared down at Haulover Creek for a moment, then turned back. "We could begin immediately!"

Ramón smiled, feeling a surge of excitement, himself.

"The sooner the better," he said. "We'd need to form the corporation and get government's approval before the next election."

Kendall thrust out his hand. "Done!"

For years, Ramón had struggled to build his modest dealership. Now he was about to risk all he had painstakingly accumulated in this single bold venture. He rose from his desk and grasped the young Belizean's hand. "Well," he said, sitting down, "let's work out the details."

"Uh, Ramón," Kendall said, remaining standing, "Ray and I are due at the Belize Club shortly."

Ramón looked inquiringly at Ray.

"I forgot to tell you, Dad. You remember the girl I told you about . . . the one I went to Guatemala with? Kendall and I are meeting her and her sister."

Ramón gave a wry shake of his head. "Okay, business will have to wait until tomorrow. But, Kendall, we need to get together with Elijah, first thing in the morning."

Kendall nodded, and they shook hands again.

"Dawn knows not to expect me this evening," Ray said over his shoulder, as he followed Kendall out of the office.

The outer office door slammed. Ramón walked over to the side window and watched the two young men bound down the steps and climb into Kendall's pickup, laughing at something one of them had said. Ramón smiled with pride. It was like Ray had lived here all his life.

He glanced across the street and his sense of well-being vanished. Clive Lightburn strode across the street and started up his office stairway.

32. SAN PEDRO

As Clive climbed the Kelley Distributors' exterior stairway, two young men pulled away in a pickup truck. He recognized the American he had played basketball against. The youth gave him a tentative nod, but Clive ignored him.

At the landing, Clive hesitated in front of the office door. Having to ask a white man about his father galled him. Finally he opened the door and stepped inside. A fat man stood alone in the center of the room, almost as if he had expected him.

"Mistah Kelley?"

The man nodded.

"I'm Clive Lightburn. I'm looking for information about my father."

The man took a deep breath, but didn't speak.

"My father's name was Roland Lightburn. He was a logger. I was told he might have worked for you a long time ago."

The man frowned. "I'm sorry . . . Clive . . . you took me by surprise. Please, come this way."

Clive followed him to a private office. The man sat down behind his desk and gestured for Clive to have a seat across from him. Clive remained standing. "Did you know my father?"

"I didn't know . . . Roland Lightburn. He didn't work for me. I . . . knew your mother, though."

"My mother?"

The man nodded. "She and her grandmother cared for a friend of mine, after Hurricane Hatti."

"But you didn't know my father?"

"I didn't know . . . Roland Lightburn. But your mother spoke of him."

"I was raised by foster parents in San Ignacio," Clive said. "I know very little about my mother and father, only what a nun at the mission told me."

"And what was that?"

"My mother was originally from Belize City. She moved to San Ignacio and died when I was born. Sister Claudia told me about her, but she never talked about my father."

The man studied him for a moment. Finally he said, "Your mother once mentioned to me that Roland Lightburn died in a logging accident. I don't know the details." He lapsed into silence again.

The man's reticence annoyed Clive. "So Roland Lightburn was my father?"

The man looked away for a moment, then turned back. "Yes."

"Someone told me that Roland Lightburn was not my father."

The man frowned. "Who told you that?"

"A pilot in Corozal. The one who died last month in the plane crash."

"Karl Schrader?"

Clive nodded. "He told me that Roland Lightburn was not my father, and that my father was still alive."

Again the man seemed preoccupied. Finally he said, "Roland Lightburn was your father."

Clive nodded, annoyed with himself for having given credence to the old pilot's taunt. "Is there anything else you can tell me about my father?"

Again, the man seemed to struggle for words. "I believe your father was . . . a good man, Clive."

The sound of the bridge making its afternoon swing echoed through the window.

"I have to go," Clive said. "I am due at work in thirty minutes."

"Where do you work?"

"The Fort George Hotel."

The man smiled for the first time. He got to his feet. "I know the manager there, Greg Harrison. You'd better be on time."

They passed through the outer office. As Clive opened the door to leave, the man extended his hand. "Clive, stop by anytime. Particularly if you ever need help."

As they shook hands, Clive thought the offer of help strange, coming from a white man he didn't know.

Clive's first night shift at the hotel had lasted until 2:00 a.m.; however, he awoke at dawn as usual. He lay in the narrow boarding house bed, recalling the night before. The regular desk clerk was an elderly Creole, who had been promised a daytime assignment as soon as a suitable replacement was found. Clive had quickly discovered that the forty-room Fort George Hotel was far more complex than the ten-room Posada Don Carlos. However, he was confident that he could handle the night desk job, if they gave it to him permanently.

A soft knock on the door interrupted his musing. Then a key rattled in the lock. Dorla stuck her head in. Seeing him awake, she stepped inside and locked the door behind her. She slid out of her house dress and climbed into bed with him. "You've been awake for a while," she said, running her pale hand down his bare chest and finding him relaxed. He responded to her touch.

A short while later, with Dorla lying peacefully in his arms, Clive smiled at the thought of how bold she had become in the short month he had stayed at the boarding house. He shook her gently. "Get up, gyal. Your mother will be looking for you."

Dorla squeezed him and didn't move. Finally she said, "Mama knows where I am."

"And she don't mind?"

Dorla shook her head. "She's afraid for me, but now she knows . . ."

"She knows what?" Clive said, raising her chin so he could look into her dark eyes.

"She knows how I feel . . . that you not just some coolie bwy."

"No, gyal. I'm not just some coolie bwy."

Later that morning, Clive crossed Front Street and walked onto the makeshift basketball court, bouncing a ball he had bought the day before. No one else was on the court. He looked up at the new backboard; it was much sturdier than the old one. A regulation net hung from the orange rim. He wondered if the American who had pulled down the old goal had paid someone to replace it.

Clive tossed up a close-range jump shot. The ball hit the rim and caromed off. The backboard was solid; the rim was strong and tight. Clive retrieved his miss, turned, and drove for a dunk, wrapping the net around the rim.

He warmed up for several minutes with dunks and close-in jump shots. Then recalling the American's fluid outside shot, he moved out to twenty-five feet. He spun the ball in his hands, trying to remember the American's technique. He lofted a shot, and missed everything. He had to hustle to keep the ball from rolling into Haulover Creek. He tried another long shot from the side, and again missed everything. He jogged over, retrieved the ball, and set for another shot.

"Keep your elbow in!" someone shouted.

The American walked onto the court, spinning a basketball on the tip of one finger. He was flanked by two Creole youths. Clive brought the ball down from the shooting position and drove hard for the basket, wrapping the net around the rim with a dunk.

The American and the two Creoles started shooting on the goal with him. Clive fielded a missed shot. The American's ball was brand-new and had "Genuine Leather" stamped across it. Clive threw it back. His new rubber ball now felt too light.

The four youths played two-on-two. Clive and the American guarded each other. Their styles contrasted, as they had in their earlier confrontation. Clive was able to overpower the white youth, but his superior natural ability was offset by the American's polished technique. Clive's team won the first game, but only by a close margin.

Near the end of the second game, the American altered his

style and aggressively established position nearer the goal. It aggravated Clive that the American was picking up his power moves so quickly and was using them against him.

On the final point of the game, the American got a pass down low and wheeled toward the goal. Clive reacted too late. As he futilely went up to block the dunk, the American used his free arm to ward him off, striking him sharply across the nose. When Clive's eyes cleared, he saw a triumphant, gold-toothed grin on the white youth's face. Clive rushed toward him. The other two Creoles moved between them before any punches were thrown.

"Come on, Ray," the Creole named Allan said, "we have to get to work."

The American gazed at Clive for a moment, then followed his companions off the court.

"Bloody pussy clots," Clive muttered under his breath.

Clive bounded up the stairs of the Fort George. After only three weeks, the hotel manager had moved the regular clerk to the day shift and had given Clive the late shift. Though it monopolized his nights, Clive enjoyed the challenge of the job. When he arrived for work each evening, guests were arriving and demanding service. As the evening progressed, he gradually brought things under control. By the time he left at 2:00 a.m., the lobby and phones were silent.

The day clerk looked up from the hotel ledger as Clive approached. "Mistah Harrison wants you to report to him straight away. In the bar."

Clive turned away from the counter and hurried down the hallway.

"Clive!" a waitress called as he passed the restaurant doorway. "Nice shirt, bwy!"

Clive acknowledged her with a quick wave. Dorla had helped him pick out three dressy guayabera shirts at Brodies Dry Goods, just that morning. He entered the bar and spotted the hotel manager seated at a window table. Across from him, sat the Carib who had verified Clive's first deposit at the Bank of the Caribbean.

Clive approached the table. "You wanted to see me, mistah Harrison?"

The hotel manager nodded and gestured toward an empty chair. Clive sat down.

"I'm Elijah Ruiz," the banker said, extending his hand. "Do you remember me?"

"Yes, sah," Clive responded as they shook hands.

"Clive," the banker said, "Ramón Kelley told me about you. I understand that Tawnya Lightburn was your mother."

"Yes, sah," Clive said, wondering why they had been discussing him.

"I didn't know your mother well," the banker said, "but as I recall, she was a lovely young lady."

Clive nodded without responding. He was uncomfortable talking about his mother with these men, since he knew so little of either of his parents.

"Clive," the hotel manager said, "mistah Ruiz has a proposition for you. I'm afraid it's going to cost me a damn good night clerk."

The following morning, Clive and Elijah sat at the bow of a launch, cutting through an unusually rough sea. The boat captain tacked back and forth to keep from burying the bow in the swells.

Clive eyed the approaching caye. It looked more like a mangrove swamp than a firm island. He turned to the banker. "Tell me again, mistah Ruiz, what will we be doing out here?"

"Call me Elijah, bwy. This trip, I just want you to get acquainted with the property. We won't begin construction out here for four months, but I wanted you to get a firsthand look at where you'll be working."

"You said the hotel will have thirty rooms?"

"Eventually. They'll be individual cane cabanas. We plan to have eight the first year. We'll also put up a larger building for the office and a combination bar and restaurant. Later, Ramón thinks we should build a shop for scuba divers and fishermen. We also may invest in diving and fishing boats."

The launch tacked again, then eased around the southern tip of the caye. The surf ground against the nearby coral reef. A fine spray blew across the open deck.

Elijah continued, "We at the Foster Corporation are gambling that fishing and diving around the reef will become a major tourist attraction. We hope to attract Americans here to San Pedro, then get them to extend their vacations and go inland to our jungle lodge."

"How large is San Pedro?"

"About 1,200 people. The population out here has doubled over the past ten years and will probably double again in the next ten. Most San Pedranos are Mestizo and speak some English, but not too well. Your Spanish will be an asset out here. Unfortunately, I never learned to speak it."

Clive gazed at the caye, now passing along the port side of the launch. He had misgivings about having accepted Elijah's job offer. "Mistah Ruiz . . . uh . . . Elijah, why did you choose me for this job?"

"It was Ramón Kelley's idea, actually. But I wholeheartedly agreed with him after I thought it through."

"But why, sah?"

"I'm not sure what gave Ramón the idea. Probably, because your mother and great-grandmother took care of a friend of ours after Hurricane Hatti. My motives, however, are purely selfish. I've had heart trouble recently, and I need a strong body to help get things going out here. I checked your references. Charlie Westerfield thought very highly of you at Posada Don Carlos, and Greg Harrison hates losing you from the Fort George in four months."

"I'm to stay there four more months?"

Elijah nodded. "Ramón and I worked out an agreement with Greg. We pay your salary, and he trains you until we need you out here."

A cluster of low-lying buildings caught Clive's attention. "That's San Pedro, bwy," Elijah said.

Clive approached a ramshackle, seaside bar. It was nearly midnight. Elijah had gone to bed early, and Clive had been walking the sand streets of San Pedro.

He stepped through the doorway of the dimly lit bar and found it nearly deserted. He took a stool at the unoccupied end of the counter. At the other end, a Mestizo bartender talked with three sunburned white youths. From their ages and shaved heads, Clive surmised they were British soldiers on holiday.

The bartender walked down to Clive. "Yes?"

"Belikin."

The bartender pulled the beer from the cooler. "One dollar."

Clive handed him a crumpled dollar bill, then took a long drink.

"I not see you before," the bartender said.

"This is my first time on the cayes," Clive replied in Spanish.

The Mestizo smiled. "Welcome," he said in Spanish. "And how do you like it here in San Pedro?"

"I like it. My employer is building a hotel down the street. I'll be moving out here in four months."

The sound of a glass crashing to the floor interrupted their exchange. A white youth struggled to his feet from a nearby booth. A young Mestizo girl was squeezed into the corner. Clive hadn't noticed them when he came in.

"Soldiers," the bartender said under his breath to Clive.

The soldier staggered over to where Clive was standing. "More of the same," he told the bartender.

The bartender went down to the other end of the counter and mixed two rum drinks.

Clive glanced over his shoulder at the girl again. She appeared tired, and very young. She pulled a compact out of her purse and tried to repair her makeup.

"What you lookin' at, you fucking abo'?" the soldier said. Then he reached up to examine the amulet that hung from Clive's neck.

Clive pushed him away. The soldier regained his balance and lunged, throwing a roundhouse right. Clive easily deflected the blow and drove his fist into the soldier's stomach. The soldier dropped to his knees, then slumped into a heap. Bar stools scraped against the floor. The other three soldiers warily walked toward Clive.

The bartender hurried out from behind the bar. He stepped between Clive and the soldiers. "No fight!" he shouted.

The soldiers advanced toward Clive. The one on the floor gasped for air, then vomited.

"Out, you!" the bartender ordered in English, pushing Clive toward the door. "Too many for you," he said under his breath in Spanish.

Clive let the bartender lead him outside. The soldiers stopped in the open doorway. The bartender gave Clive a fake shove, while saying in Spanish, "In a few months, those soldiers will probably be some of your best customers."

33. HOMECOMING

"Ray," his mother said with a pained tone, "why did you have to wait until the last possible minute to come back from British Honduras?"

"Belize, Mom," Ray said. He got up from the breakfast table and carried his dishes over to the sink.

His mother wasn't to be put off by geographical technicalities. "Why didn't you come home earlier, so we could get your teeth fixed?"

"I like the gold teeth, Mom. I'm going to keep them."

"You are not!"

Ray chose not to argue with her. The gold was there to stay. "I've got to get going. This is the final day for late registration. It starts at 8:00."

"Your grandfather was disappointed that your scholarship to LSU didn't work out, but he's looking forward to having you in his literature department at Southeastern. I just wish we'd had time to get your teeth fixed before school started. Gold teeth look so . . . common."

Ray was tempted to postpone the next bit of bad news, but decided now was the time to get it all out in the open. "Mom, I won't be in Grandpa's department. I've decided to major in business."

His mother looked at him in disbelief. "Ray, you've never expressed the slightest interest in business. Why in the world would you want to major in it?"

"I discussed it with Dad."

His mother blinked, fighting back tears.

Ray pressed on. "Dad and Kendall—he's the guy that Dad's

in business with now—told me that they'd hold a job for me down there, but I needed to learn more about business."

His mother slumped in her chair. When she looked up, tears streaked her cheeks. "Ray, honey," she said in an anguished voice, "you were only down there for three months. What has that man done to you?"

"Dad didn't do anything, Mom. Just the opposite. When I tried to talk him into letting me stay down there, he told me I had to come back and get a degree. But I still plan to spend the summers down there."

"He's turned you against me."

Ray put a hand on her shoulder. "He didn't turn me against you. It's got nothing to do with you."

She didn't respond.

"It'll be okay, Mom. Honest."

She shook her head without looking up.

"Gotta go, Mom, or I'll be late." He banged out the screen door, relieved to have the confrontation behind him.

As he crossed the backyard, Bobbi Sue came out of her house with an armload of books.

"Hey, Ray! When did you get back?"

He walked over to her. "Yesterday afternoon."

"How was it in . . . what's the name of that place?"

"Belize. It was great."

"You got a nice tan," she said. "What did you do, lay out in the sun all day?"

Ray grinned. "No, I didn't do any laying out."

"Ray! What happened to your teeth?"

"I got into a fight with some Guatemalan soldiers."

"Got into a fight?" she said, drawing back. She now seemed ill at ease in his presence. "Uh . . . you'll have to tell me about it . . . but I've got to get to class now."

As Ray watched her hurry over to her car, he thought of Florita. Bobbi Sue looked so . . . white. Downright unhealthy.

Late that afternoon, Ray walked down the outer hallway of the Southeastern gym. He heard the familiar sounds of a basketball scrimmage. The varsity's first practice session was underway. He entered the locker room.

"You want something?" said a reedy voice from inside the equipment cage.

Ray had seen the gaunt, pimpled youth at freshmen orientation that morning. He evidently was the equipment manager. "I need a locker," Ray said.

"Who are you?"

"Ray Kelly."

The manager picked up a clipboard off the counter and studied it for a moment. "I don't have any 'Ray Kelley' here."

"I'm a walk-on."

"Well, I don't have any equipment for you. Nobody told me about any walk-ons."

"I brought my own gear," Ray said. He found an empty locker and quickly changed.

A few minutes later, he stepped from a tunnel and walked onto the brightly lighted gym floor. Coach Bourgeois stood on the side of the court, watching his players scrimmage. The teams raced up and down the court in new green and gold practice uniforms. Ray felt out of place in his old purple and white high school gear.

Coach Bourgois glanced back. "What do you want?"

Ray walked over. "Hi, I'm Ray Kelley."

"Yeah, I know who you are, hotshot," the coach said coldly. "'Machine Gun' Kelley. I asked what you wanted."

"I want to walk on."

"What?"

"I want to try out for your team."

"I kind of half-expected you to show up," the coach said with a sneer, "when I heard LSU shit-canned you."

Ray gave a tight nod, controlling his anger.

"Since we're not an NCAA school, you figure you'll do us a favor and play here at home, huh?"

"I'm not here to do you a favor," Ray said levelly. "I just want to play some ball."

There was a break in the scrimmage, and the players eased over so they could listen to the exchange. The stocky coach played to his audience. "I watched some of your high school games, 'Machine Gun'. I already got me enough pussy shooters. What I need is a banger. I need me somebody with guts enough to pound the boards!"

Ray gazed into the coach's eyes.

"Okay, hotshot," the coach said. "Go in with the green team. Take Theriot's place."

A slender black youth pealed off his green practice shirt and threw it to Ray.

Ray pulled the sweat-soaked garment over his head, then trotted over to the sideline to receive the inbounds pass.

"I told you, I don't need a guard, hotshot!" the coach bawled. "Get under the God-damned goal!"

Ray moved inside and took his position just outside the lane. The hulking white center on the gold team shouted, "Switch!" He assumed a defensive position behind Ray, towering over him by at least six inches.

The guards on the green team brought the ball inbounds. Ray assumed a wide center's stance and raised one arm, presenting a target. The center pushed him in the small of the back. Ray stumbled forward, just as the ball was thrown to him. The center lunged forward, elbowing Ray in the side of the head and intercepting the pass.

"Step forward to meet the pass, hotshot!" the coach yelled from the sideline. "This ain't high school!"

Ray ran unsteadily to the other end of the court. He assumed his defensive position, his ear ringing from the blow to the head. The gold team quickly worked the ball inside, and the center scored easily on a point-blank lay-up.

"Nice defense, hotshot!" the coach bawled.

The guards on the green team set up in the forecourt. Ray

took his position down low. The center drove a forearm into the back of Ray's neck. Ray turned, dazed. "What the hell!" A guard fired a pass that hit him in the head.

"Get off the court, hotshot!" the coach shouted. "Before you get killed!"

The hulking center looked down disdainfully. "You heard the coach. Get off the court . . . pussy!" With a sneer, he turned to say something to a teammate.

Ray drove a fist into the upperclassman's soft midsection. The surprised youth raised his hands to fight, then dropped them and doubled over when he found himself unable to breathe. Ray landed an uppercut to the middle of his meaty face, ripping a nostril away from the cheek. A torrent of bright red blood flowed from the tear. Before Ray could deliver another punch, two players grabbed him from behind.

The center slumped into a sitting position on the floor. The coach and trainer raced onto the court. The trainer stemmed the flow of blood with a towel. The other players gathered around and looked on curiously. Ray pulled himself loose from the two who were holding him. He threaded his way through the onlookers, pulling off the sweat-soaked green shirt as he walked. The player who had given it to him stood off to the side. Ray threw him the shirt.

"Nice shot . . . 'Gun'," the black youth said with a grin.

Ray quickly showered and dressed. He heard the sounds of the scrimmage continuing. The equipment manager busied himself nearby, but avoided direct contact.

A few minutes later, Ray stepped from the dressing room and headed down the hallway that led outside.

Coach Bourgeois stood in his office doorway, arms crossed. "Can you still shoot?" he said.

Ray stopped in front of him. He gazed into the coach's eyes. "Yeah, I can shoot."

"Practice is at 3:00 tomorrow. Stop by here first. I'll have your scholarship papers ready for you to sign."

Without responding, Ray turned and continued down the hall. Outside, he paused on the gym steps. The campus oaks, which had always seemed so stately, now appeared squat and dwarfed, compared to the giant mahoganies he had seen in the jungles of Belize.

"Chuh!" he said aloud, and headed for home.

34. INDEPENDENCE

Ramón and Elijah sat on the veranda of Elijah's home, sipping pineapple drinks and looking out over the Caribbean. Through the open window, they heard Esther Ruiz and her maid packing the kitchen utensils.

"I'll miss this place," Elijah said.

"Having second thoughts?" Ramón said.

"No, my friend. Now that I've separated myself from the bank, I'm looking forward to this new challenge on the cayes."

"Well, don't overdo it out there. We're a couple of 'old farts', remember?"

"Yes, I remember. Six months ago, you and I sat here poking fun at the ambitions of the young. Now we're joining them in their folly."

Ramón smiled and nodded.

"How long will Dawn be gone?" Elijah said.

"I don't know. I spoke to her on the phone last night. She's still in Texas. Says she needs more time to think things over."

"Don't let her get away, Ramón."

Ramón almost confided that he planned to get a divorce and ask Dawn to marry him, but decided the disclosure would be premature. Instead he said, "I'm glad she got out of the country before the rioting began."

"It's maddening!" Elijah said. "Here we are, the day before England grants us outright independence, and local politicians are still threatening to start a civil war over it."

Ramón nodded. "The opposition's making quite an issue over George Price's attempts to negotiate a nonaggression pact with Guatemala."

Elijah shook his head in annoyance. "They're so obsessed with their fear of communism, they interpret any contact with Guatemala as traitorous. On the other hand, George's timing was extremely poor. I spoke to him yesterday. He said he had realized he was taking a risk, but at the time had felt it was worth it."

"Why?"

"Partly idealism and partly politics. First, he sincerely wants to resolve this continuing threat to our national security. Secondly, most Belizeans hold his party responsible for our domestic problems, since PUP has controlled internal affairs for the past twenty years. He felt if he could lay to rest the fears about a Guatemalan invasion, the people would have confidence in his push for independence."

"Instead," Ramón said, "Guatemala broke off the talks and closed down the border again."

Elijah nodded ruefully.

"George's motives are generally good," Ramón said, "but at times he's confident to the point of arrogance. I've heard talk that the opposition party may boycott the independence ceremony tomorrow."

"Hopefully, there won't be anything more disruptive than a boycott."

"Do you and Esther plan to attend?"

Elijah shook his head. "Esther is concerned about my health. We leave for San Pedro, first thing in the morning. I agreed to go, rather than worry her. I'll probably sneak a listen to the broadcast on Radio Belize, though."

After supper with the Ruizes, Ramón headed back to the city. Barracks Road was deserted. Suddenly his Jeep headlights picked up small blue-gray figures, scurrying across the potholed thoroughfare. He had no time to swerve, and heard the familiar, ongoing crunch of crabs smashing beneath his wheels. The spawning creatures covered the road, making their annual migration to the sea. Too dense to avoid, the slaughter lasted until he entered the city.

As he headed down the twisting residential street, the image of Michael Flowers' corpse came to mind, and the huge crab that had pulled the last of the flesh from Michael's skull. It was hard to believe that it had been twenty years.

Then he smiled, recalling the chance meeting with Tawnya in the storm's aftermath. His smile faded as he remembered his recent conversation with their son. Clive had come to him, in search of his identity, and Ramón had to lie to him. Immediately afterward, he had arranged for Clive to join him in the new corporation, as he had anonymously arranged for his care as a child. But when Clive had sought the truth, he had lied to him.

Ramón pulled up in front of his house, but remained seated in the Jeep, looking out across the moonlit sea. Finally with a grunt, he climbed out of the cramped vehicle. He paused and looked across the placid water. Promise, or no promise, he had to tell him.

Ramón shouldered his way through the independence day crowd. A band had set up in Battlefield Park, and their heavy beat reverberated off the surrounding buildings. Thousands of spectators undulated to the throb of the vigorous punta.

Ramón approached the Bank of the Caribbean building and automatically glanced up to the office window, which for so many years had been Elijah's. The shutters were closed. Beneath it, two policemen kept the teeming crowd off the bank steps. Ramón looked around for a place from which to watch the ceremony.

"Ramón!" called a familiar voice.

Ramón turned toward the bank. Police Inspector Bradley stepped through the doorway and waved him over.

Ramón weaved through the crowd and mounted the steps. "How have you been, Albert?" Ramón said as they shook hands.

"Busy as all bloody hell, Ramón. Would you like to watch the ceremony from here?"

"Yes. Thanks."

The inspector nodded his consent to the policemen, then said to Ramón, "I'd better get over there, closer to the speakers. If we get through this business today, several of us plan to get together at the Belize Club. Will you join us?"

"Let's see how this goes first."

The inspector nodded, then plunged into the crowd.

Ramón stood watching the press of people for nearly an hour. The infectious punta reverberated on. People danced wherever there was room. Despite the celebration around him, Ramón found it difficult to believe that independence was finally at hand.

A commotion broke out to his right. Several uniformed members of the United African Peoples Party swaggered into the area and assumed positions off to his right. The spectators moved out of their way. Ramón scanned the militants' unsmiling faces and was relieved to see that Clive was not among them.

He glanced down at his watch. The ceremony was already forty minutes late in starting. At the podium, the local and foreign dignitaries assembled and took their seats. Next to George Price, was Queen Elizabeth's personal emissary, Prince Michael of Kent.

"Communists!" screamed a hoarse voice from Ramón's right. The accusation echoed around the park.

Ramón scanned the crowd, measuring its volatility. Finally the hecklers quieted and the ceremony began.

George Price took the microphone. "There is no need to fear freedom . . ."

A figure moved toward Ramón, drawing his attention. For an instant, he thought he saw Tawnya Lightburn looking up at him. But it was just a pretty young Creole, looking for a place to watch the ceremony. Ramón offered his hand. The girl hesitated, then with a saucy smile, grasped it and climbed up beside him.

The policemen stepped forward.

"It's okay," Ramón said, "She's . . . an old friend."

One of the policemen shook his head, unimpressed.

The girl said something to them in Creole patois, spoken too rapidly for Ramón to follow. The policemen grinned and returned their attention to the ceremony.

"What did you tell them?" Ramón said.

"Creole talk," she said.

"Uh huh," Ramón said in familiar resignation.

While a U.S. Assistant Secretary of State conveyed President Reagan's regards, a fight broke out in the area that had been commandeered by the UAPP militants. The two policemen standing beside Ramón watched with interest, but didn't leave their bank post. The speeches continued from the podium.

The fight ran its course, uninterrupted. One of the combatants, a ragged Mestizo with a profusely bleeding face, staggered off in the direction of the swing bridge.

A skirl of bagpipes drew Ramón's attention to the scene before him. On the flag pole in front of the court house, a color guard slowly lowered the British Union Jack. Then, amid a twenty-one-gun salute, they smartly raised the blue, white, and red flag of Belize in its place.

Unexpectedly, Ramón felt his eyes brim with tears. He looked down at the young girl beside him.

She cocked her head and frowned up at him.

Ramón cleared his throat. "Time longer than rope," he said. The Belizean adage meant, "Justice will finally prevail".

The girl laced her fingers through his, and they stood side by side in rapt attention as the symbol of the tiny new nation flapped in the Caribbean breeze, marking the end of three centuries of British rule.

Silence followed the final thunderous boom. Then a resonant Creole voice not far from the podium cried out, "God save the queen!"

As Ramón walked up the dark and nearly deserted Front Street, he still heard the joyous celebration on the other side of Haulover Creek. The power blackout, which had occurred soon after the conclusion of the formal ceremonies, did nothing to dampen the enthusiasm of the new nation's citizens.

Ramón had left the celebration early, knowing that the following day would be demanding. There was much to do, and the new business venture would be the easy part. He planned to call Clive to his office and have their long-overdue talk. And, after all these years, he planned to write a letter to his wife, asking for a divorce. Then he would call Dawn.

A battered Chrysler rumbled past and annoyed Ramón with a triumphant blast of its horn. So many cars now! He recalled how peaceful the city had been when he had first arrived. People had walked leisurely in the middle of the streets. There had been the cheerful sound of bicycle bells.

Now, television had arrived, emptying the night streets of honest citizens. Lovers, living alongside the foul-smelling canals, no longer threaded their way up the narrow lanes, to promenade along the Southern Foreshore seawall in the clean Caribbean breeze. The night streets had been relinquished to the lawless.

Ramón felt fatigued and wished that he had driven to the ceremony. Because of the threat of rioting, he had left his Jeep secured beneath his house. He passed the venerable Palace Hotel. There was talk that it was to be closed. Just past the hotel was an alley that would shorten his walk home. As he turned up the narrow dark lane, he stumbled and nearly stepped into an overflowing gutter. Will we ever close these damned sewers?

Footfalls echoed behind him. He turned. A ragged, vaguely familiar Mestizo was almost on top of him. A blood-soaked bandage covered one eye.

"White!" cursed an anguished, shrill voice.

Ramón caught a glimpse of a machete blade coming down.

PART III: THE NEW NATION

If ya drink de Belize watta, you mus com bok.
—*Belizean Proverb*

35. VILLA PEDRANO

Present Day

Clive awoke to the sound of someone closing the bathroom door across the hall. Instantly alert, he sat up amid the tangled sheets. The moon illuminated the unfamiliar bedroom in a silver haze. He twisted his arm so he could see his digital watch; it was 3:17. The toilet flushed and the bathroom door opened, followed by the opening and closing of a bedroom door down the hall. The seaside condominium was quiet again.

He looked down at the young American sleeping beside him. Blond and tanned, she had been vivacious that morning on the dive charter; now she was inert. An empty cocaine vial lay beside her compact on the bedside table. Clive shook his head in contempt.

He climbed out of bed and picked up his T-shirt and jeans off the floor. He dressed quickly, making no effort to be quiet. He had dressed under similar circumstances in the past; he knew the girl would be unconscious for hours.

Moments later, he walked barefoot up Barrier Reef Drive, which ran along the windward side of the narrow island. The ramshackle wooden buildings that housed the modest hotels, bars, and restaurants were dark and quiet. After fifteen years on Ambergris Caye, the sand streets of San Pedro were as familiar as those of his native village on the mainland.

He passed the Villa Pedrano Hotel; it too was dark. The framing for seventeen new cabanas was silhouetted against the clear night sky. Elijah had recently offered him the use of a room in the main building, rent free, but Clive had declined. He felt guilty at having turned down the old man's offer. Elijah treated him like a son, and Clive knew he was lonely. Years before, Elijah's daughter had left Belize to live in the States, and last year his wife had passed away. However, Clive preferred to spend his off-duty time away from demanding guests.

He came to an opening between buildings and was hit by a gust from the prevailing trade wind. He looked out to sea and could make out an old sandlighter, passing between the shore and the barrier reef. Its sails were full, as it plowed through the choppy Caribbean. It was too dark to identify the boat, but Clive surmised it was manned by one of the Mestizo fishermen, native to the caye. He was probably going out to work a prime fishing spot, before the charter boats brought out the tourists. Over the past decade, these hundred-year-old, working sailboats had become fewer and fewer, until now they seemed an oddity among the sleek charter crafts.

Clive turned down a narrow alley. Moments later, he crossed Pescador Drive, the spine of the village. A cowardly mongrel broke the silence, barking from behind a house piling. In the distance, another dog picked up the cry. Clive continued down the alley, then turned right on Angel Coral Street, which ran along the leeward side of the island.

A block farther north, he arrived at the stilted shack he had rented for the past three years. He climbed the rickety stairs and walked across the uneven veranda. He unlocked and threw open the door. Before entering, he reached in, flipped the light switch, and scanned the single room. Assured that his spartan furnishings were as he had left them, he stepped inside.

As he undressed, his thoughts returned to the young American diver he had just left. He had run into her at the Hatch Cover Bar. She had begun snorting cocaine in the ladies' room, and he doubted she would even remember who had taken her home. He felt a twinge of guilt, but forced it from his mind. He had seen too many Americans take advantage of Belizean women, to allow himself to feel sorry for one of theirs.

Naked, he climbed into bed. He glanced at his watch; it was 3:45. He had another charter at 9:00.

36. XTABAY LODGE

Ray sat reading the *Belize Times* in the dining area of the Xtabay Lodge, deep in the Belizean rain forest. It was late afternoon. Earlier, he had supervised the clearing of an area around an unexcavated Mayan ruin, but a heavy rain shower had interrupted work.

"Ramón!" Florita called from the lodge's check-in counter. "Leave Gonzalo alone!" She came out from behind the counter.

Ray looked over the top of his newspaper to the next dining table, where his two sons were supposed to be studying their Calvert School at Home kindergarten lessons. The older boy, age five, looked back at him with theatrical innocence; the younger boy, age four, extended a quivering lower lip.

Florita snatched a piece of notebook paper from the table and held it up for Ray to see.

"Tommy Goff again," Ray said with a resigned shake of his head. A few weeks before, he had sat the boys down and cautioned them on the dangers of snakes in the area. One was the tomigoff, an aggressive fer-de-lance that propels itself in short jumps and leaps from trees to attack those who disturb it. Since the lecture, the older boy had used the information to torment his younger brother, drawing pictures of snakes and telling him that "Tommy Goff" was going to jump on him in his sleep.

Florita sat down at the table between them. Her sons jumped up and assumed positions on either side of her.

"Give me *bruddah* lashing, no, sah?" the younger boy said to Ray.

Ray, who had tried to keep a stern countenance, lost it to Gonzalo's Creole patois. Laughing, he asked his wife, "Make we give him bruddah lashing?"

Florita shook her head and reluctantly smiled. She gave both boys affectionate swats on their backsides.

Ray gazed at his brown family, feeling like a fortunate outsider, whom they allowed to live with them. "Get to work, boys," he said.

Ramón dropped into his chair and lowered his head to his book.

"But, Daddy!" Gonzalo implored.

"No 'buts'. I'm going to test you two on your numbers in an hour. If you pass, you can come into San Ignacio with me. If you don't, you stay here and study some more."

Gonzalo warily pushed his older brother's snake rendering to the other side of the table, then furiously scribbled his numbers.

"I forgot this is a basketball night," Florita said. "Do you have a game?"

"No, just a practice session."

"Will the road to San Ignacio be passable?"

"It'll be safe enough. The rain this afternoon didn't last too long. As dry as it's been, it ought to soak in pretty fast."

Florita stood up and headed toward the kitchen. "I'll tell cook that you need to eat early tonight."

Ray picked up the newspaper and resumed the article he had been reading. In contrast to the occupancy problems he had at Xtabay Lodge, the Foster Corporation's caye venture, the Villa Pedrano Hotel, was doing well. The newspaper carried the report that seventeen cabanas were being added.

Florita returned to the dining room. She started to sit beside him, but Ray pulled her onto his lap.

She traced his receding hairline with her finger tips. "It's getting a little thin here."

He nodded.

She gave him a reassuring peck on the lips.

"You don't mind my going into town tonight, do you?" he said, nuzzling his sunburned nose into the hollow of her brown neck.

"Of course not. I can manage here, particularly since we only have three guests."

Ray nodded ruefully. To break even, they needed at least six of their ten cabanas filled. "Thank God for Mrs. Christopher," he said. "If she hadn't seen the toucan yesterday, she and her sons wouldn't have extended their stay."

Florita smiled. "Imagine so much excitement over seeing a bird."

"Don't knock the birders. They're the only reason we're still in business."

"Ray," Florita said seriously, "how long can we keep going, the way things are?"

"I don't know. I called Chan Chich Lodge on the radio when I came in a while ago. They only have five of their twelve cabanas filled. Kendall knew ecological tourism would take a while to catch on, but he thought we'd be in the black by now. As it is, the only part of the Foster Corporation that's making a profit is the Villa Pedrano Hotel, and they can't be expected to support our operation out here indefinitely."

"It seems like it's so easy for them to attract tourists out to the cayes," she said wistfully.

"Well, I'm glad things are going well for Elijah. I remember the first year I came to Belize, Dad was concerned about his getting involved in the corporation because of his heart condition. But he's almost eighty now, and still going strong."

"I wish I had known your father, Ray. Whenever someone mentions him, it's with . . . respect."

"I wish I'd been able to spend more time with him myself. We only had a couple of months together . . . then he got killed." A silence followed. Finally Ray said, "I'm sure Dad would have had some ideas on how to get this eco-tourism thing off the ground."

"Ray, has Kendall said anything else about closing the lodge?"

"I haven't discussed it with him recently. He's been preoccupied with his own problems over at the farm. The coffee plants aren't taking the dry season well, and the four water buffaloes he brought over from Thailand still aren't reproducing."

"Is he having any luck at all?"

"Not with anything that's generating revenue. Last week, he told me about some experiments he's doing with chicle. I don't know why he's bothering with it. They stopped using it in chewing gum years ago."

Florita stared through the screened window and lapsed into silence.

Ray sensed her despair. Her passion since he had known her was to unearth the culture of her Mayan ancestors. For years, she had unsuccessfully tried to interest American universities in excavating the ruins that surrounded Xtabay Lodge.

She turned back to him. "Do you think Kendall will shut down the lodge?"

Ray sighed. "He may have to scrap the whole venture out here—the farm and the lodge. The Panamanian bank that's holding the note has asked for a year-to-date accounting."

The sound of clumping on the lodge stairs interrupted them. The door flew open, and Mrs. Christopher, clad in muddy boots and sweat-soaked khakis, strode into the dining room, followed by her two sons.

"Flo!" the matron said excitedly, "we saw a tinamou. It whistled every half-hour, just like you said it would!"

37. MORAYS

Clive ushered a middle-aged American couple into the lobby of the Villa Pedrano, then dropped into a chair behind the counter. Elijah welcomed the guests to the hotel and had them sign in. A hundred yards away, Tropic Air's sixteen-seat aircraft roared down the landing strip, heading to Belize City with a return load of tourists.

"If you are looking for something to do right now," Elijah told the couple, "Clive here is about to take some other guests on an all-day fishing excursion. They'll be leaving in a few minutes."

Clive attempted an ingratiating smile, but he was too tired and his effort fell short.

"Well . . ." the man said uncertainly, "we'd need a few minutes to get unpacked."

"We don't leave right on time," Clive said. "If you wish to go, I'll wait for you."

"We won't be inconveniencing the others?"

Clive shrugged.

"Well, thank you!" the man said, a little too loudly. "That's very nice of you."

"No big thing, mon," Clive said, stretching.

"What would we need to bring?" the woman said.

"Tanning lotion for sure," Elijah said. "And I would recommend wearing a hat, long pants, and maybe even a long-sleeved shirt. Don't let our cool breeze fool you. The Caribbean sun can burn you in no time at all. We have rest room and dressing facilities on board, so you can change into swim suits whenever you wish to go into the water."

Clive studied the pale couple. Most of their guests were divers or fishermen; his experience told him that these were neither. If they didn't heed Elijah's advice, they would look like boiled lobsters by evening.

"You say we'll be gone all day?" the man said.

"We'll return about five o'clock," Clive said. "This morning we go after bonefish, and this afternoon, tarpon. You'll also be able to skin-dive both places."

"I've . . . done very little fishing," the man said uncertainly.

"And neither of us knows how to dive," the woman said.

"We have all the equipment you need," Clive said. "And I'll be there to show you how to use it. Or, if you prefer to stay out of the water, you can watch from the boat. We have a glass window in the bottom that will give you a good look at our barrier reef."

The woman still looked uncertain, but the man said, "Let's do it, Margaret!"

She reluctantly nodded.

"We'll be leaving in about five or ten minutes," Clive said. "I'll wait for you here."

The couple hesitated.

"Do you need help with your luggage?" Elijah said.

"Oh, no," the man said quickly, and picked up both suitcases. "Get the key, Margaret."

Elijah handed the woman the key. "Yours is the cabana on the end," he said, pointing across the sandy courtyard. "Number fourteen."

"Right!" the man said. They left the office.

Elijah turned to Clive. "You look like shit, bwy."

Clive rubbed his sleep-deprived eyes. "I feel like shit." He downed the half-cup of coffee that had gotten cold while he was at the landing strip.

"Clive, you're over thirty now, bwy. You need to slow down."

Clive didn't reply.

"You should learn how to run things here in the office, instead of personally taking the charter boat out every day. I won't be around forever you know."

"It's too bloody dull here in the office. Besides, I think you *will* be around forever."

Elijah gave a resigned shake of his head. "Were you out last night with another . . . what you call them . . . 'spry stucky'?"

"This one was not so spry. By the time I got her home, she had too much shit pushed up her nose to be any damn good."

"Tourist?"

"No. One of the gyals that came over from mistah Pennington's yesterday and went diving with us."

Elijah gazed at him intently. "It's not my business, bwy, but I'm telling you again, you should stay away from mistah Pennington and his friends."

"You take his charters."

"I deal with him in the daytime. Nighttime is another matter." Clive rubbed his eyes again.

"That fat mon means trouble, bwy," Elijah said.

"Pound a belly, ounce a foot," Clive said nonchalantly.

"Those people he does business with? They ain't no 'pound a belly'."

"I knew people like them in Corozal Town."

"That was marijuana, bwy!" Elijah said impatiently. "These men ain't dealing 'Belize breeze'. They're filling those old conduits with cocaine. They destroy people."

Clive got up and walked over to the screen door. The Caribbean lay flat; it would be an easy day. He saw the door to cabana number fourteen opening. He gave Elijah a quick wave over his shoulder and stepped through the doorway.

An hour later, Clive stood beside the novice fisherman on a knee-deep, sandy shoal at the southern end of Ambergris Caye. The man's wife watched from the deck of the charter boat. Two more-experienced guests fished fifty yards away.

"I feel stupid wading around in long pants," the man said.

"You'll thank me tonight," Clive said, "when you don't come back with a bad burn."

"This isn't at all what we expected."

"No?" Clive reached over and pulled some line loose from the man's fly rod. A cruising school of bonefish had entered the flats.

"We were expecting something more like Barbados. We went there last year and enjoyed their discos and casinos."

"We don't have these things in Belize." Clive stepped back so the man would have room to cast.

"My wife and I were disappointed this morning when we arrived and realized how . . . primitive . . . things are here."

Clive ignored the criticism of his caye; he had heard it many times before by first-time tourists. He pointed to a spot on the shoal, midway between them and the mangroves. "Cast so the tip of your rod points to the fish you want. It should almost touch the water."

The man squinted where Clive was pointing. Suddenly he saw the school of bonefish, not twenty yards away. "Jesus! There must be fifty or more!"

"Cast into them," Clive said patiently.

The man whipped his fly rod back and forth.

"Cast," Clive said firmly, "or the fish will see your rod and swim away."

The man awkwardly cast toward the large school. His lure fell short of the main concentration, but the line immediately went taut.

"Set the hook gently," Clive cautioned.

The man pulled a bit too firmly, but the line stayed taut.

"Give him some line," Clive instructed.

The man released some slack. The fish made a dash toward the school and tried to hide among the other fish, who darted away from it. Suddenly it broke the surface.

"Jesus!" the man said. "Did you see the size of that son of a bitch!"

"Take up the slack when he gives it to you," Clive said, trying to keep the man from celebrating prematurely.

The tourist played the fish for nearly ten minutes, before bringing him across the sandy shoal. As the silvery bonefish gave a final fatigued thrash at their feet, the man started to raise it out of the water.

"Don't lift him!" Clive said, snatching the line so the fish remained beneath the surface. "The mouth of the bonefish is very soft. The hook will tear out if you lift him. Put your rod under your arm and pick him up with your hands."

The man did as instructed, and Clive eased the lure from the fish's mouth.

"How big do you think he is?" the man said excitedly.

"Five pounds I would think."

"Margaret!" the man shouted triumphantly, holding the fish over his head. The fish wriggled and almost slipped from his grasp, but the man smothered it against his chest and kept it from escaping.

Twenty yards away, his wife looked on disinterestedly.

The man turned to Clive and said enthusiastically, "Tarpons next?"

That night, Clive sat on a stool in the Tackle Box, a ramshackle bar out on the end of a wooden pier. There were few customers. On Saturday nights, Big Daddy's was the place to be. A half-dozen local fishermen and charter boat operators crowded around the other end of the bar, noisily following every pitch of a Chicago Cubs baseball game. With the arrival of satellite TV, the Cubs had developed a large following throughout Belize.

A handful of tourists sat at a table near the jukebox, mixing selections of Jamaican reggae with local punta. Several more tourists lounged on the rear veranda. They laughed and shouted as they fed the enormous bonefish imprisoned in the bar owner's homemade crawl. Sea gulls fluttered about the pier railings, wanting to be fed. Their squawks added to the general clamor.

Clive was exhausted. After returning from his fishing charter, he had stopped at his shack long enough to pull on a pair of basketball shoes. Then he had hurried over to the makeshift court near the tiny San Pedro police station. He and the other members of the San Pedro "Pelicans" had scrimmaged for three hours against pickup teams of American tourists. Now, he planned to finish his beer and head for home.

Kano, the Nigerian who played center for the Pelicans, returned from the men's room and sat down beside him. The seven-footer drew curious glances from the tourists. The locals had grown accustomed to his towering presence. Kano had arrived at the tiny village six months earlier and found the indolent lifestyle to his liking. Each month, his industrious family in Africa sent him money so he would stay away.

"We played damn good tonight, mon," Kano said. He signaled the bartender to bring him another bottle of Belikin.

Clive rubbed his eyes, tired from lack of sleep and the all-day glare off the Caribbean. "Yeah. We didn't play too bad."

"If we can beat Americans," Kano said, "we should be able to win next month's tournament in Belize City. Americans are the best basketball players in the world."

"Not *those* Americans, Kano. Some tonight weren't too bad, but the really good American players—the black ones—can't afford to come to Belize on holiday."

Kano shrugged and signaled the bartender to bring Clive another beer.

"No more for me, mon," Clive told the bartender. "I'm going home." He drained the last of his beer and stood up.

"Why you leaving, mon? It's not even ten o'clock."

"I'm tired, bwy. Do you want to come fishing with me in the morning?"

"I thought you had Sunday off?"

"I do. I'm going out and fish for myself for a change."

"Taking a gyal?"

"No, bwy," Clive said with a laugh. "Just fishing."

"What time?"

"Seven o'clock."

"Chuh, mon! Too early."

As Clive walked toward the door, he said over his shoulder, "I'll come by your room when I get back tomorrow. We'll get the others and play some ball."

Clive stepped through the doorway and bumped into the young blonde he had slept with the night before.

"I need to talk to you," she said, grasping his forearm and tugging him away from the door. Clive followed her over to the nearby pier railing. "I looked for you over at Big Daddy's," she said. "One of your friends told me you might be here."

"I'm too tired for messing around tonight, gyal. I call you tomorrow, uh?" He stepped around her.

"Mr. Pennington sent me," she said. "He wants to see you."

Clive paused and turned back to her. Enough light shone through the open bar window that he could see her pupils. She appeared to be straight. "I'll come by his place tomorrow."

"He wants to see you right away."

"I'm tired, gyal—" Clive stopped in mid-sentence. A large dark figure stepped from the shadows. The young woman pointed to Clive, then fled into the Tackle Box.

The swarthy stranger walked up to Clive. He was overdressed for the island—pleated slacks, a guayabera shirt, and patent leather shoes. "Are you Lightburn," he said in Spanish.

"*Sí.*"

"Mr. Pennington has a job for you tonight."

Clive shook his head. "I'm tired. I'm going home."

"You will come with me. Now."

The man's arrogance irritated Clive. He apparently was just an intermediary. "Are you Mr. Pennington's *coyote?*"

Suddenly the man was on him. Before Clive could react, the man pinned him against the pier railing and pressed a knife blade against his throat. Clive bent backward over the water. The man's breath blew across his face. Clive froze; to move was to have his throat slit.

After several agonizing seconds, the man slowly released the pressure and stepped back. A baleful expression crossed his face.

He folded the knife blade into the handle, but kept the weapon palmed. "Come!" he ordered.

Pennington opened the door of his third-floor condominium. The fat American appeared anxious. "Ah . . . yes . . . please come in, Clive. Thanks for coming on such short notice."

The swarthy stranger followed Clive into the living room and closed the door behind them. He walked over to a traveling bag that lay on the couch and withdrew a holstered pistol. He clipped the holster onto his belt.

"Permiso, uh," Pennington said deferentially to the stranger. "Come with me," he told Clive.

Clive followed Pennington through a sliding glass door and onto a concrete balcony.

Pennington slid the door shut behind them. "I don't think he speaks English, but I'm not sure."

Clive glanced inside. The stranger stood in the center of the living room, watching them. "Why did you send him after me?"

"He needs a boat. Right away."

"Is he one of your *coyotes?*"

Perspiration poured down the American's fat face. "Not mine. He works for . . . an associate . . . someone I have to accommodate."

"Why does he need a boat?"

"He flew in last night, to take delivery on some . . . merchandise . . . from the mainland."

Clive surmised the "merchandise" was drugs.

"A boat I contracted was supposed to make the delivery," Pennington said, "but it ran aground. The captain radioed me a couple of hours ago that he was stuck on Caye Negro. We need you to find the boat and unload the merchandise before dawn."

Clive glanced into the living room again. The coyote still watched them.

Pennington also glanced back, then licked his lips nervously. "His boss called about an hour ago to be ·sure I'd take care of things." Pennington reached into his wallet and peeled off ten Belizean twenties. "Here's your standard charter fee." Then he peeled off $200 more. "It's worth this to get that crazy bastard off the island."

Clive didn't take the money. "I don't want nothing to do with no drugs."

"You have no choice in the matter," Pennington hissed. "You not only have to do what he says, but you must please him when you do it."

Clive shook his head.

Pennington turned away from the living room and leaned against the railing, as if looking out at the night sea. "Damn it, man! Don't let him see you arguing with me! He needs to think you work for me, and that I'm just giving you instructions."

Clive also turned toward the sea.

"Listen to me," Pennington said through clenched teeth. "This man is dangerous! Take care of him, and we'll have no problems. Resist, or fuck up, and he'll probably kill you, and me."

Clive looked for a means of escape. The third-floor balcony was too high to jump, even to the soft sand below. He turned to Pennington. "Stop humbugging me, mon! Who the bloody hell is he?"

Pennington hesitated, then said, "He's the top *coyote* for a cartel in Matamoros, Mexico. The merchandise is cocaine. From here, he'll fly it up to Matamoros. Eventually, it'll wind up in Texas."

"Shit," Clive muttered.

"We've got to do what he says. His boss is more than a *patron*. His people regard him . . . like a religious prophet. Have you heard of *Magia Mala?*"

Clive nodded. "Evil Magic. It is the dark side of *Santería*—the worship of the saints. But in Magia Mala, sometimes there are human sacrifices."

The sliding glass door flew open. *"¡Vamanos!"* the coyote ordered.

The fat American thrust the $400 at Clive.

Clive took it.

Clive and the coyote stood side by side in the charter boat wheel-house. With the running lights off, they slowly navigated the lee-ward side of Ambergris Caye. Clive strained to see the spit of sand and mangroves known as Caye Negro.

"Do you know where you're going?" the coyote said impatiently in Spanish.

"We're close."

Several more minutes passed, then Clive said, "There it is." The silhouette of the mangroves was barely discernible against the night sky.

"Shut off the engines!" the coyote ordered.

They began to drift. The only sound was the waves lapping against the stern, pushing the boat toward the caye.

"Do you have a flashlight?" the coyote said.

Clive withdrew one from a drawer and handed it to him.

The coyote leaned out of the side window and flashed the light six times, then six more. After a long pause, the signal echoed from the mangroves, farther up the coast.

"Take me over there," the coyote told Clive.

Clive restarted the engine and eased along the coast of the caye, toward where they had seen the light. The keel grated against a sand bar. Clive backed up and moved farther offshore.

The signal flashed from the caye again, this time much closer. The coyote switched on his flashlight. The bow of a partially submerged launch protruded from the mangroves. A Mestizo stood on the deck, waving them forward. Clive brought his boat alongside, and the coyote and the Mestizo secured the boats together with a deck line.

"¿Sr. Torres?" the Mestizo said, as the coyote stepped onto his boat.

The coyote spun around and looked at Clive.

Clive pretended he hadn't heard the name spoken.

"How did you do this?" the coyote snarled in Spanish to the Mestizo.

"I'm sorry, sir," the Mestizo said respectfully. "I was monitoring the Belize Defense Force radio channel, and I heard they were coming this way. I came in here to hide, but I hit something."

"Is your cargo intact?"

"It's wet, sir. I fell asleep. I didn't know the boat was leaking."

"Bring me up a package!" the coyote ordered.

"Yes, sir." The Mestizo disappeared below deck. Clive heard him frantically sloshing about. Finally he reappeared, holding a water-soaked bundle. "I'm afraid this is all there is, sir," he said morosely. "The paper came loose on the others."

The coyote peeled back the wet paper and gazed at the white lumps inside. He angrily shook his head, then walked over to the side of the launch and dropped the sodden mess into the sea. When he turned back, his hand rested on the pistol clipped to his belt. "Pull his boat away from the island," he told Clive. "I want to sink it in deep water. Quickly!"

A few minutes later, they had moved a quarter-mile off the caye. Clive shut off the engine, and they all went aft. The Mestizo released the line and watched his launch slip beneath the surface.

"We can make it to San Pedro in twenty minutes," Clive told the coyote, hoping to bring an end to the incident.

"Go!" the coyote said.

Clive returned to the wheelhouse and quickly got underway. He checked aft, but the two men were out of his field of vision. He stared into the night, waiting for a shot to shatter the steady drone of the boat engine. He had both wheelhouse doors open, ready to make a dash for the side.

A few minutes later, he jerked at the sound of approaching footsteps. The coyote entered the wheelhouse with a satisfied smile, as if he had just been with a woman. He extended a blood-covered hand, and showed Clive a human heart.

The morning sun had risen from the Caribbean, when Clive arrived at his shack. He trudged across the sandy front yard and up the rickety stairs. He unlocked the door and stepped into the single room. The window shutters were locked. He closed the door behind him, plunging the room into total darkness. He felt his way over to his cot and lay down, not bothering to undress.

He closed his eyes. The horror of the night rushed back at him. He sat up quickly, eyes open, but unable to see. A rooster crowed from the shack next-door, triggering a recollection of San Ignacio. The memory of his peaceful mainland village momentarily allayed his fears. He again lay back, closed his eyes, and tried to imagine that he was safe amid the lush tropic mountains. He drifted into a disturbed sleep.

He stood on a vast expanse of white sand. Sea ferns appeared before him, suspended in midair, delicately undulating on unseen currents. A mountain of prickly black coral appeared to one side. Was he under water? No, he had no face mask, and he could breathe.

A man shambled toward him. He must be a fisherman. The delicate ferns transformed into ugly moray eels, mouths open, savage teeth covered with infectious slime. The luminescent sea serpents writhed in anticipation, awaiting the fisherman. Clive tried to cry out to warn him, but found he was mute.

As the man drew closer, Clive saw that he was quite old. Then to his horror, he saw that the fisherman was not a man at all. It was his foster mother, old as she had been in the final years of her life. "Mamacita!" he tried to shout, but no words came out. He frantically tried to move to her, but he was paralyzed. He now stood in a nest of morays. An enormous brown eel, six feet in length, headed for her. She didn't see it! Its knife-like teeth ripped into her frail chest. The eel withdrew. His mother's corpse remained standing, a gaping wound where her heart had been.

Clive's own heart began to pound. The eel would hear it! The hammering grew louder; he couldn't quiet it! The eel saw him. It was coming for him! It was on him!

Clive awoke with a start. Frantic pounding filled the dark room. Then it stopped. A man's voice shouted, "Clive! Are you in there?" The incessant pounding resumed.

Clive groggily got to his feet, staggered across the room, and threw open the door. Pennington stood on the veranda, looking furtively from side to side.

The fat American eased by him and closed the door. "Jesus Christ, man! It's like an oven in here!" He opened a shutter.

Clive sat down on the cot.

"Your trip must have gone okay last night," Pennington said, mopping his thick neck with a handkerchief. "Our visitor just left on the morning flight."

Clive didn't respond. He lay back on the cot and covered his eyes with his forearm. The cool sea breeze began to clear his head.

"Did you have any trouble finding the boat?"

Clive still didn't respond.

"God damn it, man, are you stoned? I said, did you have any trouble finding the boat?"

"What boat?" Clive said softly.

"What boat? Oh . . . yes . . . I see."

There was a long silence. Finally Pennington said, "I'll have more work for you, Clive. You'll be making a lot more money than you do on tourist charters. Come over to my place when you're rested. Debbie's still there. And next week, a young friend of hers is coming down from Miami."

After another long silence, Clive heard the door open and close, then the sound of the American lumbering down the outside stairway. Clive slowly sat up, then got to his feet. Awake, he could deal with his fear.

38. THE MINISTER

Ray sat across the desk from a Creole official who was talking on the telephone. The conversation apparently had something to do with missing cattle. A mahogany nameplate on the desk read: "Attorney General and Minister of Tourism and the Environment".

Ray waited impatiently; he had been summoned, not invited, to this meeting. He stood up, walked over to a window, and gazed down at the drab government plaza. The layout was supposed to resemble an ancient Mayan city. Inexplicably, the architects had arranged the cinder block buildings in a triangle, rather than a characteristic Mayan rectangle.

This inland capital had been built after Hurricane Hatti. The government's intent had been to provide Belizeans with a safe, modern city. Thirty years later, Belmopan still looked incomplete, although time and humidity had stained the gray cinder block an unsightly black.

Belmopan's population was only 5,000. People in Belize City had refused to move inland, preferring the excitement of their familiar slum to the bland, government-designed capital. Even the country's leading politicians preferred to make the fifty-mile commute.

The minister finally concluded his telephone conversation. Ray left the window and returned to his seat.

"Sorry to keep you waiting," the minister said. "That was the foreman out at the Landry farm. He has some cattle missing, and wants us to drop everything else and investigate it."

"You don't sound too concerned."

The minister shrugged. "When a thief thiefs a thief, God laughs."

Ray smiled, sharing the minister's low opinion of the Landry Corporation. "Your message said you wanted to see me right away." The minister reached into his top desk drawer and withdrew a manila folder. His expression turned somber. "Do you understand what we in government mean, when we say 'Belizeans First'?"

"Of course I do, Norman. And I agree with the PUP position that Belizeans should control economic development, not sell out to foreigners."

The minister handed him the folder. "This is a petition with almost 1,500 signatures, protesting the treatment of Belizean citizens at your lodge. They demand that I close it."

Ray's hand shook slightly as he read the petition. For the past two weeks, a debate over Xtabay Lodge had raged on the editorial page of the PUP organ, *Belize Times*. A letter to the editor, depicting the lodge as "a little South Africa", had been the catalyst.

"Norman," Ray said, handing the folder back to him, "do you really believe this nonsense about our discriminating against Belizeans?"

"A serious charge has been raised. If I find evidence that you have been discriminatory in your practices, as the attorney general, I must prosecute you. And if you are found guilty, as the minister of tourism, I will close down your lodge."

Ray hesitated, choosing his words carefully. The unusual distribution of governmental responsibilities in Belize put this bureaucrat in the position of judge and executioner in this matter. "Okay, let's clear this up. What do you need to know?"

The minister gazed at him intently. "Why are you turning away Belizeans?"

"We're not. This whole thing has been blown out of proportion. There was a single incident, where a man and his family—"

"Even one such incident is unacceptable!" the minister interrupted. "Why was this man embarrassed in front of his family and not allowed to stay at your lodge?"

"It was a simple communication problem."

"'Communication problem'?" the minister snapped. "I have

spoken with the gentleman myself. He speaks perfect English. He has no communication problem!"

Ray took a deep breath, trying to suppress his exasperation. "Norman, they weren't at Xtabay Lodge. They drove up to the outer gate of Kendall Foster's farm, and *thought* they were at Xtabay. They actually were two miles from the lodge."

"Who turned them away?"

"A guard."

"Whose guard?"

"Kendall's. He had to start posting guards on the farm access road to keep trespassers out."

"Is he hiding something?"

Ray took another deep breath. "There's nothing subversive going on, Norman. Kendall's doing scientific experimentation with crops and livestock. He can't have people wandering onto his property."

"Why didn't this guard direct the man and his family to the lodge?"

"The guards are new. Their instructions were simply to keep people away from the farm. Kendall spoke to them after the incident. They know how to handle visitors in the future."

"The problem is made worse by the fact that your lodge is operated by an American."

"Bullshit, Norman! Eighty percent of Xtabay is owned by Kendall Foster, a sixth-generation Belizean. Ten percent is owned by Elijah Ruiz, another Belizean. Yes, I run the place, but I only own 10 percent. And I've been a Belize citizen for seven years now."

The minister opened the folder again and thumbed through the pages of signatures. He looked up. "Something must be done."

"Like what?"

"I don't know," the minister said thoughtfully. "But you and your associates must do something to satisfy these people."

Ray sensed the minister was no longer concerned over the discrimination charge. Now he simply wanted to placate the 1,500 voters who had signed the petition. The last election had been too close for PUP to risk losing that many votes.

The phone rang, and the minister picked it up. He listened briefly, then put his hand over the mouthpiece. "You'll have to excuse me, Ray. This is about the body they found floating off Ambergris Caye. The one with the heart cut out."

Ray stood up, frowning. He hadn't heard about this latest gory murder on the coast.

As Ray turned to leave, the minister said, "You need to satisfy the people, Ray. And you must do it straight away."

Florita entered the lodge dining area. "The University of California group is flying down next week."

Ray looked up from the papers he had spread over a dining table. "Who? Oh, yeah . . . the California people. How many will there be?"

"Eight. We'll have plenty of room."

"Unfortunately," Ray said, "we always have plenty of room."

"A Professor Potter is in charge. He emphasized this will just be a cursory inspection of our site."

Ray smiled. Despite numerous rejections, Florita continued to doggedly pursue U.S. universities, looking for one that would unearth the secrets of her ancestors.

She sat down beside him. "How about you? Have you come up with anything?"

"I've got an idea that might work. The Interior Minister will probably accept any action I take, as long as it placates the locals."

"What's your idea?"

"Since we opened the lodge, we've concentrated on attracting foreigners. Now I think we should cater to Belizeans—people on holiday, school children on nature trips, the local Audubon Society, and so forth."

"But, Ray, most Belizeans can't afford our rates."

"How about if we offer them special rates, say 50 percent off?"

Florita thought for a moment. "It can't hurt. Better to be full at half rates, than empty at full rates."

That night, Ray sat on the bottom row of bleacher seats, cinching the laces on his basketball shoes. His San Ignacio "Saints" and the visiting Dangriga team warmed up at opposite ends of the court.

Ray straightened up and scanned the bleachers, surprised at the number of people already on hand. Although the Saints had been league champions the past five years, their games seldom filled the stands. And tonight was just a preseason game with the perennial last-place team.

His two sons ran over to him. "Daddy!" the older said, "I want a red Fanta."

"Ramón, I can't get you a soft drink now, Son. The game's about to start."

"I want a red Fanta too, Daddy!" chimed in his younger son.

"Gonzalo . . ." Ray said.

Mrs. Haylock, the coach's wife, sat nearby. "I'll see to them, Ray," she said.

"Thanks, Mrs. Haylock." Ray got to his feet and walked toward the court.

Coach Haylock intercepted him. "Oh, Ray," the elderly Creole said with a sly smile, "I don't believe I told you, I've invited one of my former players to play with Dangriga tonight."

"Is that right?" Ray said, adjusting his wrist bands.

The coach nodded. "Since Dangriga usually doesn't have much of a team, and since this is just a preseason game, I thought it would give us a better workout."

"Sounds good," Ray said. He and his Saints teammates dominated regional play each year. One player on the other team shouldn't make much difference.

There was a stir in the crowd, then a voice rang out, "Tall Bwy!" Spontaneous applause erupted. A familiar figure walked onto the Dangriga end of the court—a tall, light-skinned Creole, towering above his short, dark Carib teammates.

"Well, I'll be darned," Ray said. "Is he the reason so many people are here tonight?"

Coach Haylock nodded. "He visited me this afternoon, and I convinced him to play tonight. He seemed a little . . . lost. I thought it might do him some good. You know his brother, George. He manages Buckleys Dry Goods. George passed the word around town this afternoon."

Ray watched the former hometown hero warm up. "Looks like Clive's hair is getting thin in back."

"You know him?"

"We both work for the Foster Corporation. Every once in a while, we run into each other in the Belize City office. When we were kids, we played a couple of pickup games against each other. He was damned good."

"As you say, Ray, he was damned good."

The Dangriga team formed two lines for lay-ups. Ray walked down to their end of the court. "Hey, Clive!" he shouted.

The tall Creole turned at the sound of his name.

"Homecoming for you, uh?" Ray said as they shook hands.

Clive nodded. "You play for Coach Haylock now?"

"Yeah, the past few years. He's a good man. How about you? Been playing any ball?"

"A little."

Something was unusual in Clive's demeanor. In their past, brief exchanges, Ray had sensed an intense, smoldering resentment. But tonight, Clive seemed preoccupied.

The buzzer sounded, and they shook hands again. As Ray walked back to his coach, Clive slammed through a final warmup dunk.

Coach Haylock gazed down the court and said with a smile, "Tall Bwy has come home."

39. SISTER CLAUDIA

The Dangriga coach gathered his team around him for final instructions. "What position do you want to play, Tall Bwy?"

"It doesn't matter," Clive said disinterestedly.

"Okay, center then."

Clive nodded. He felt disoriented. This was the first time he had been home since his foster mother's funeral, six years earlier. The sight of the American huddling with Coach Haylock added to his sense of unreality. Clive scanned the sea of familiar faces in the stands. He had returned to San Ignacio to collect his thoughts privately. Instead, he was about to perform before hundreds of people.

The buzzer sounded. Clive and his teammates stacked hands, then jogged to mid-court. Except for the American, the San Ignacio players were all very young. But apparently they had heard of Tall Bwy Lightburn; they each respectfully shook his hand before the center jump.

Clive and the American slapped hands. The referee tossed the ball up between them, and the American stole the tip. The San Ignacio team raced down court and scored on an easy lay-up. The crowd applauded.

Clive trotted down the court and automatically flared out to a wing position. Then, remembering that Kano was far away on Ambergris Caye, he moved into his old center position. The American picked him up defensively. A stocky teammate threw the ball inside, but the American anticipated the pass and intercepted it.

"Run and shoot!" the American yelled, as the San Ignacio players raced down court for an uncontested lay-up. Another round of applause rippled through the crowd.

"Pick 'em up!" shouted the American. He and his teammates swarmed over the shorter Dangrigans, applying full-court pressure. A Dangriga guard panicked and threw a wild pass that soared over Clive's head and out of bounds.

Before Clive could get to his defensive position, the San Ignacio players pushed the ball up court and scored again.

As Clive trotted down to the offensive end of the court, he suddenly felt as if he had been hit in the chest with an ax. From his diving experience, he realized he was hyperventilating.

A Dangriga guard threw up an errant shot. The American grabbed the uncontested rebound and pushed his team down court again, yelling, "Run and shoot! Run and shoot!"

Clive stayed at the other end of the court, hands on knees, trying to catch his breath. After the San Ignacio basket, he signaled the referee for a time out. He glanced up at the scoreboard. One minute into the game, his team trailed 8 to 0.

"Are you all right, mon?" the coach said, as Clive walked unsteadily off the court.

Clive slumped onto the bench. He buried his face in a towel and tried to regulate his breathing.

The coach put a hand on his shoulder. "Are you sick?"

Clive raised his head from the towel, about to tell the Carib he was through. Then he caught sight of the San Ignacio bench. Coach Haylock watched him with a worried expression. Next to the coach, the American stood with hands on hips, looking perplexed. Clive forced himself to his feet.

The crowd chanted, "Tall Bwy! Tall Bwy! Tall Bwy!" The buzzer sounded, signaling that the timeout was over.

Clive stepped into the Dangriga huddle. "Make we go!" he said, then strode onto the court.

As the game clock ran off the final seconds, Clive and the American sat on their respective benches. Both teams had their substitutes on the court, finishing the contest. San Ignacio was winning handily, 85 to 68, but Clive had rewarded the partisan crowd with an array of power moves that had kept the game interesting through three quarters. Finally the home team, led by the American, had pulled away.

The buzzer sounded. An exhausted Clive got to his feet.

The young Carib coach shook his hand. "Can I convince you to move to Dangriga, bwy?"

Coach Hayman was next to shake his hand. "Fine game, Tall Bwy! You still got it, sah!"

The American walked up, holding two small Mestizo boys by their hands. The younger boy looked up with a wide smile and shouted, "Tall Bwy!"

The American freed one hand and extended it. "Good game, man."

"Thanks," Clive said. He held the grip long enough to add, "I got a team in San Pedro. Maybe we play a next time."

The American nodded.

Clive's brother, George, walked up, beaming with pride. Married, and the portly father of four, he looked every bit the prosperous merchant he had become. Clive shook hands with George, then waved to his sister-in-law, Ninette, and his nephews and nieces in the stands.

"Are you coming home with us, Clive?" George said, then added with a sly grin, "or have you made other plans for tonight?"

The scene seemed so familiar, but that was in the past. "No, George, I got no plans for tonight."

Clive stepped from his brother's blue stucco home. Mist still clung to the hillside, and roosters serenaded each other across the tree-covered valley. Below, the Macal River sparkled in the morning sun. Within the hour, washwomen would assemble at the shaded bend.

Clive strolled down the steep street toward town. He passed his late foster mother's shack, now occupied by another family. It was peaceful here in San Ignacio. Then the image of the coyote holding the human heart flashed into his mind. He tried to block it out by recalling the warm welcome he had received. But he didn't belong here anymore.

A bell pealed from the parochial school he had attended. He wondered if Sister Claudia was still there.

"I can't tell you how good it is to see you, Clive!" Sister Claudia said. "So often you are in my thoughts and prayers."

Clive stood in the middle of the familiar, austere office, feeling awkward and wondering why he had intruded on the old nun. "It's good to see you too, Sister."

"Please, sit down," she said.

Clive lowered himself into an uncomfortable straight-back chair. "I'm sorry if I've interrupted your morning, Sister."

"Not at all, Clive!" She sat down at her desk, piled high with papers. "I've been disappointed that you haven't stopped by before. I haven't seen you since your foster mother's funeral, but George keeps me apprised of your progress. Are you still living in San Pedro?"

Clive nodded. Again, he wondered what had brought him here.

"I was busy last night," Sister Claudia said, "and couldn't go to your game. But one of my novices went. She came back, chattering on and on about the reception they gave to Tall Boy Lightburn."

Clive smiled. "However, my team lost. It seems there is a next 'tall bwy' in San Ignacio now."

The old nun blinked. "Ah, yes . . . you must be referring to Ray Kelley."

"You know him?"

Sister Claudia fidgeted with the wide collar on her habit. "Ah, yes . . . his wife and sons come to church here when they're in town . . . and I knew your . . . *his* father." She abruptly stood up and walked over to a window that overlooked the school playground.

"Are you feeling all right, Sister?"

She took a deep breath, then turned to him. "Clive, often when my students return, they're troubled and hope to find answers here."

Clive gave a wry shake of his head. "Sister, when George and I were bwys, we didn't agree on much. But one thing we *did* agree on was that you could read minds."

The nun gave a tentative smile. "What answers are you looking for, Clive?"

The image of the coyote holding the human heart again flashed into his mind. This cloistered nun could never understand the life he led the past fifteen years. His hand went to the amulet that hung from his neck. He traced the etching of the slave with his finger tips as he groped for words. "I don't seem to know . . . where I belong . . . or who I am."

The old nun's eyes brimmed with tears. She turned away from him again. "Clive," she said, looking out the window, "your foster parents loved you very much. And your own mother would have too, had she known you." Her shoulders shook.

Clive suddenly realized she was crying. He rose from his chair, alarmed that somehow he had upset the old nun.

"And your father would have too," she continued with a sob.

Clive frowned. Sister Claudia had always been reluctant to talk about his father.

She turned to him, wiping tears from her weathered cheeks. "Your father was a *good* man, Clive."

Clive had a clear recollection of Ramón Kelley using those same words to describe Roland Lightburn. Clive crossed the room to the old nun and tried to comfort her. "Yes, Sister, I know that about my father. I talked to Ramón Kelley in Belize City, several years ago."

The nun's eyes opened wide. "You *know* that Ramón Kelley was your father?"

Clive stared at her; his mind raced. The conversation long ago in the fat man's office—his father! The basketball game last night— his half-brother! Clive turned and shifted his gaze out the window to the soccer field where he had played as a child. "Yes, Sister," he lied, "I've known that for a long time."

The next morning, Clive awoke in Belize City's Bellevue Hotel, his body soaked in perspiration. The sun had risen above the horizon and the stark room was already stifling. He gingerly climbed out of bed, head throbbing, and crossed the threadbare carpet to the window. He cranked open the dirty glass louvers and leaned against the window sill, letting the sea breeze blow across his sweat-covered skin. He had begun drinking beer on an empty stomach the previous afternoon and had continued long into the night.

A hundred yards away, the dredging machine that had awakened him pumped filthy gray silt from the mouth of Haulover Creek. Clive's stomach felt queasy, but he knew he needed to eat something. He glanced at his watch; it was 7:19. The hotel dining room should be open and serving breakfast by now.

A short while later, he descended the winding staircase into the cramped hotel lobby. Several guests crowded the counter, apparently checking out.

"Clive!" a woman's voice called out. "Over here!"

Clive suppressed a groan. The young Mestizo had left his room just a few hours earlier. Now she sat on a wooden bench against the lobby wall. Her pit bulldog drowsed on the dusty tile floor, his leash tied to a bench leg. Clive struggled to remember the woman's name. Finally it came to him: Elvia.

She smiled up at him.

"I need to eat," Clive said.

"Sit here. I'll get it for you."

Clive didn't want to eat in the lobby, but he was too weak to argue. He dropped down beside her on the bench.

"What do you want?"

"Some eggs . . . scrambled . . . and toast . . . and coffee."

She handed him a half-empty coffee mug. "Here, you can finish this." She stood up and headed for the dining room. The pit bull opened one eye, then went back to sleep.

Clive took a sip from her coffee; it was cold. He set it aside on the bench.

A prim pale woman, probably English, stood at the desk, drumming her fingers on the counter. A swarthy hotel clerk was on the phone, imploring someone, "But I have a very important person here!" An equally pale teenager stood beside the woman, apparently a daughter. As if to separate herself from the older generation, she wore layered garments suitable for an English winter, topped off with a pair of canvas basketball shoes.

Out front, a horn blew on Foreshore Lane. An old Ford sedan rumbled past, sending a cloud of dust across the lobby. On the other side of the street stood a low seawall. Past the seawall lay the Caribbean, turned a noxious gray by the dredging machine.

Elvia returned from the dining room and handed Clive another mug of coffee. "They'll bring your food out, directly."

Clive took a sip, then said, "Why are you here so early?"

She sat down on the bench. "I haven't been to bed yet. As soon as the police station opens, I have to file a report."

"What kind of report?"

"Bobby tried to kill me last night."

"Bobby?"

"I told you about him," she said petulantly. "He's my boyfriend."

Clive vaguely remembered her having mentioned an American boyfriend, somehow involved in drug trafficking. "Did he really try to kill you?"

She nodded.

"Because you were with me?"

She shrugged.

"What happened?"

"I thought Bobby was asleep when I got home, and I took Toro off his leash to feed him. When I went into the bedroom, Bobby jumped up and closed the door so Toro couldn't get in. We started to fight, and Bobby choked me with the leash." She pulled down the collar of her blouse and showed him an angry burn on the side of her neck.

"What happened?"

"I got to the door and let Toro in," she said, then laughed. "You should have seen Bobby! He jumped out the window, but Toro bit him before he got away!"

A busboy brought out Clive's food.

"Thanks, mon," Clive said. He took a bite of eggs, wondering if he would be able to keep his breakfast down.

Elvia stood up. "I'm going over to the police station. I'll be back, directly." She gave him a cheerful wave and hurried out the lobby door.

Clive finished his breakfast. He left his dirty dishes on the bench and headed for his room. As he passed the front desk he told the clerk, "Get my bill together. I'm catching the 8:30 boat to San Pedro."

40. THE ECO-TOURIST

The sounds of the Saturday morning tennis tournament drifted through the open windows of the Belize Pickwick Club. The waitress brought coffee over to Ray and Kendall's table, then returned to the kitchen, leaving them alone in the room.

"Sorry you had to fly in on such short notice, Ray," Kendall said, "but there are some matters I need to discuss with you right away."

The usually ebullient Belizean appeared drawn. Ray suspected the Foster Corporation's western venture was in jeopardy.

Kendall continued, "I've been working here in town the past few days, and I thought the club would be a good place to talk. I don't want our employees concerned about losing their jobs . . . before they have to be."

Ray nodded, waiting for the grim details.

Kendall took a sip of coffee. "My contact at the Bank of Panama phoned me last night. She says the directors have a meeting scheduled on Monday. The first thing on the agenda is our loan. Since we're seven weeks behind in our payments, they may be about to call it in."

"Damn," Ray said softly. Xtabay Lodge lay adjacent to the 17,000-acre tract that Kendall had put up for bank collateral. Despite 300 years of logging in Belize, the area remained virgin rain forest. Kendall had planned to leave it untouched, except for cutting nature trails for lodge visitors.

"Someone is undermining our project," Kendall continued. "The bank gets word of our problems as soon as they occur."

Ray frowned. "Do you know who's behind it?"

Kendall shook his head. "My contact hasn't been able to find out. It could be anybody, for any reason—political, economical, environmental. It might even be somebody whose girlfriend I've been in bed with. Whoever it is, they've got me by the bloody short hairs."

"Was that the reason you posted the security guard?"

Kendall nodded ruefully. "And all I accomplished was to touch off the movement to shut down your lodge."

"Incidentally," Ray said, "I talked to the minister of tourism yesterday. I think Norman understands the situation. At least I managed to buy us some time."

Kendall sighed. "Ray, I'm afraid we've 'come a cropper' on the whole western venture."

Ray sat in stunned silence. Everything he had worked for during the past ten years was tied up in the lodge, not to mention his wife's personal project of uncovering the ruins. "Any chance of your . . . selling off more property?"

"I'd have to find a buyer within the next week."

"How much would you have to sell?"

"The note balance is about $1,700,000 U.S., so it would probably take about 25,000 unforested acres . . . *if* I had a buyer."

"I hate to ask this," Ray said, "but what about Landry?"

Kendall frowned. "I haven't spoken to Landry in years. But yes, I'd consider selling to him again."

"How about offering him that large parcel to the east?"

Kendall thought for a moment. "He might be interested. It would be suitable for cattle. The trees were stripped forty years ago."

"Can you get hold of him before Monday?"

"I don't know," Kendall said thoughtfully. "I'll give it a try this afternoon, though. Tomorrow, I'm flying down to Panama."

"What can *I* do, Kendall?"

"Ray, if we get through this latest financial crisis, somehow we have to make your lodge self-supporting. Otherwise, we'll have to close it down. Elijah's Villa Pedrano can't continue to support both the farm and Xtabay."

Ray decided now was not the time to tell Kendall of his plan to cut Belizean rates to half-price.

Ray piloted his Cessna-172 in the direction of the setting sun. The compass on the forty-year-old aircraft was inoperative, but unnecessary. After ten years of flying across Belize, he was familiar with the landmarks, as seen from 2,000 feet. He passed over Ladyville, then the remote villages of Burrel Boom, Double Head Cabbage, and Bermudian Landing. Twice he crossed the Belize River, as it snaked through the jungle from the eastern coast to the western border.

The flight took twenty minutes. Ahead lay the Foster Corporation airstrip. He banked to the north and flew low over Xtabay, the signal for his wife to send a worker to pick him up. As he soared over the neatly landscaped lodge, he again appreciated how much he and Florita had accomplished in such a short time. Losing their jungle retreat seemed unthinkable.

He banked to the south. In the distance lay the Landry Corporation cattle farm. An ugly wide swath marked the latest area to have been cleared. As he began his descent, he noticed an unfamiliar twin-engine Piper Senecca-III, parked on the side of the landing strip.

A short while later, Ray entered the lodge dining area. Florita and two men he didn't recognize sat at a table. A map lay between them.

"Ray," Florita said excitedly, "these gentlemen are from *World Geographic*."

"What a pleasant surprise," Ray said.

The older man rose and extended his hand. "I'm Thomas Gardner, associate editor. This is Mark Richardson, my pilot." The younger man remained seated and responded with an uninterested nod.

"Glad to meet you," Ray said as he and the editor shook hands. Ray joined them at the table. "What brings you here?"

"We're going to do a feature article set in this region."

"Really?"

Gardner nodded. "I'm doing the preliminary site tour this weekend. My writers and photographers will be coming down later."

"This is the first we've heard of it," Ray said.

"Your lodge wasn't part of the itinerary. I just finished over at Chan Chich. They told me you people were setting up a similar operation over here. I had an extra hour before dark, so I decided to stop by on my way back to Belize City."

Ray's mind raced. He and Florita needed to take advantage of this opportunity. Being mentioned in *World Geographic* was publicity that money couldn't buy. "What's the theme of your article?" he said.

Gardner pulled a pipe and tobacco pouch from his starched safari-shirt pocket. "It'll focus on the ancient Mayan civilizations in Belize, Mexico, and Guatemala. We'll also acquaint our readers with the eco-tourism facilities down here."

"Well, Xtabay Lodge would certainly like to be included in your article," Ray said.

Gardner packed his pipe. "Actually, we've probably got all the information we need from the people over at Chan Chich."

"How long were you there?"

"I arrived yesterday morning."

"Can you stay overnight with us?"

"No, I need to get away from here before dark. Early tomorrow morning, I'm being driven from Belize City to the ruins at Altun Ha."

Damn it! Ray thought. A day for Chan Chich, an hour for us. "Well," he said, determined to make the most of the limited time, "we're delighted you stopped by, Mr. Wilson. I see my wife has been giving you an overview of the place."

"Your wife?" the editor said, registering mild surprise. "Oh, yes . . . she was explaining that you're not as far along as you'd like to be. It looks like your lodge is similar to Chan Chich."

"In many respects, yes," Ray said. "The people at Chan Chich helped us get started. However, there are some significant differences. As you noticed, they built their cabanas inside an old Mayan plaza. We chose to build ours some distance away."

"I rather like their approach," Gardner said. He finished filling his pipe. Tobacco shreds littered the table.

"They have a nice setup over there," Ray conceded easily. "However, our main pyramid is quite a bit larger than theirs. In fact, we think it'll prove to be the third largest in Belize."

"It just looks like a big hill," Gardner said. "I doubt you'll attract many tourists with that."

"We're negotiating with a major university to excavate it," Ray said. "That's the reason we didn't put our cabanas inside the plaza."

"Which university?" Gardner said.

"The University of California," Florita interjected. "I've been—"

"Your plan would seem to be contradictory to the definition of eco-tourism," Gardner said to Ray, cutting Florita short.

"What do you mean?"

"Eco-tourism is supposed to provide tourists with an environment that hasn't been disturbed."

"We won't disturb the environment," Ray said. "We'll simply restore the ruins."

Gardner shook his head. "The restorations I've seen have played havoc with the surroundings." He lighted his pipe and made no apology for the billow of smoke that drifted into Florita's face.

Ray suppressed his rising irritation and chose his words carefully. "The footprint of the old Mayan city is well defined. The location we've chosen for our cabanas will offer the tourists easy access to the pyramid, during and after restoration."

Gardner closed his eyes and took a deep drag from his pipe.

Ray realized he was blowing this opportunity. The editor obviously had been too impressed with Chan Chich to accept the different approach they were taking at Xtabay.

"Your lodge seems deserted," Gardner said.

"It's . . . a little slow today," Ray said.

The editor turned to Florita. "How many guests do you have?" Florita gave Ray an uncomfortable glance, then said, "One."

"And you have ten cabanas?" Gardner asked Ray.

Ray nodded, then tried to steer the discussion in a more positive direction. "Our structures are made from materials indigenous to the area, and the construction was done by Mayan workers."

"I saw something in the local newspaper about your not allowing Belizeans to use your facility," Gardner said.

Ray took a deep breath. "That was a misunderstanding, which I've discussed with the minister of tourism. A man and his family were turned away from a nearby farm. They mistakenly thought they were here at the lodge."

"Uh huh," Gardner said, obviously disregarding Ray's explanation. "As I recall, there also was concern that this place is operated by Americans."

"Xtabay is owned and operated by Belizeans," Ray said, his patience wearing thin.

"You're obviously an American," Gardner said.

"I'm a naturalized Belizean, married to a Belizean, in partnership with two other Belizeans."

"How long have you lived here?"

"Eleven years. But my father was a longtime resident. He tramped through this same region, thirty years ago."

"Doing what?"

"Cutting . . ." Ray began, then realized his mistake. ". . . mahogany," he finished lamely.

The editor looked triumphant. "So you're not the first generation Kelley to come in here and ravage the rain forest."

"That's enough!" Florita said.

The editor ignored her and continued with Ray, "Tell me more about your father's—"

"I said, that's enough!" Florita said. "I'm going to have to ask you to leave our lodge, mistah Gardner."

Gardner stood up and looked down at Florita. "I have all the information I need about your lodge for the article. I won't bother you again . . . *Mrs.* Kelley."

41. JOVITA

Clive stepped behind the Villa Pedrano check-in counter. Teresita, the desk clerk, was busy on the phone. Clive stopped in the open doorway of Elijah's private office.

Elijah looked up from behind his desk. "Come in bwy. I haven't seen you in days. How did your charter go today?"

Clive entered the office and slouched into a chair. "No trouble. The divers were all experienced and they had their own divemaster. I just drove the boat."

"What about mistah Pennington's guests?"

"I canceled them."

"Why?"

"The mon's too fucked up."

"Fucked up how, bwy?"

"Bush, cocaine, crack . . . all of it. You told me yourself, he's no bloody good."

"I know what I told you, bwy, but there is an old saying: sometimes we must kiss ass 'til we can kick ass."

"Chuh."

"Kendall Foster called me this morning, Clive. They're having serious financial problems at the farm and Xtabay. He asked if I knew of a possible investor. I suggested mistah Pennington. Kendall wants me to arrange a meeting as soon as possible. If you have been rude to him, your timing couldn't have been worse."

"We don't want nothing to do with that mon."

"I see," Elijah said. "Operating our charter boat has made you the Foster Corporation's financial expert."

Clive stood up to leave.

Elijah leaned forward. "What the bloody hell is the matter with you, bwy?"

Clive noticed Elijah take a labored breath. Remembering the old man's heart condition, he closed the office door and sat down again.

Elijah spoke first. "I'm sorry, bwy. I know something is troubling you. You haven't been yourself the past few weeks."

Clive started to speak, then lapsed into silence.

"Tell me what the problem is, bwy."

Clive sighed. "The reason I went to San Ignacio was that I . . . had some trouble here. I went back home to think it over. While I was there . . . a nun told me . . . about my father."

"About your father?"

Clive nodded.

"Told you what about your father?"

"That my father was . . . Ramón Kelley."

"She told you *what?*" Elijah barked.

"That Ramón Kelley was my father."

"You talking rot, bwy!"

"You telling me my skin isn't light?"

"Lots of light-skinned Creoles in Belize."

"Who sent the money for me and my brother all those years?"

"You telling me, Ramón Kelley was George's father too?"

"No. George is short and dark. He doesn't favor me."

"Lots of brothers don't look alike!" Elijah said exasperatedly.

"Do I favor my other brother?"

"What other brother?"

"Ray Kelley," Clive said. He watched closely for Elijah's response.

Elijah looked away for a moment, then turned back. "Chuh," he said unconvincingly. "Foolish notion."

The telephone on Elijah's desk rang, and continued to ring. Finally the caller gave up. "What kind of trouble did you get into?" Elijah said.

"What?"

"You said you got into some trouble here," Elijah said impatiently. "Why the bloody hell did you go to San Ignacio in the first place?"

Clive looked down at the floor and said in a monotone, "Mistah Pennington was involved in that killing a few of weeks ago—the one where the mon's heart was cut out."

"What you saying now, bwy?"

Clive looked up. "True word. I was there when the mon was killed."

Elijah jumped up from behind his desk. "What the bloody hell are you talking about?"

"Don't excite yourself," Clive said. "And stop shouting."

Elijah slowly sat back down. "Tell me what happened."

Clive took a deep breath. "There was supposed to be a big cocaine delivery here, but the drug boat broke down on Caye Negro."

"Pennington was involved?"

Clive nodded. "A coyote from Mexico came down to find the boat. Pennington pulled me into it. The coyote made me take him out to Caye Negro in the middle of the night. While we were out there, he killed the mon for losing the shipment."

Elijah frowned. "Who have you told about this?"

"Who would I tell?" Clive said with a snort. "The San Pedro police? The Belize Defense Force? Shit, Elijah, nobody in Belize can stop these people. You know that. Even the American DEA can't stop them. They're too powerful!"

"But you must to do something . . ." Elijah's voice trailed off uncertainly.

"Elijah . . . he cut out the mon's heart . . . and showed it to me!"

A knock on the door interrupted them.

"Yes?" Elijah called out.

The door opened and Teresita stuck her head in. "Mistah Ruiz, Tropic Air called. It is time for you to leave, sah."

"Tell them I'll be there directly."

Teresita nodded and left them.

Elijah got up and walked around his desk. "I haven't had a chance to tell you. My daughter is coming down from the States.

I'm flying into Belize City to meet her." He placed a hand on Clive's shoulder. "On the first thing you told me, bwy, lay it to rest. It makes no bloody difference. On the second thing, we need to talk again."

That afternoon, Clive closed the engine hatch of the Villa Pedrano charter boat. He looked up and saw Elijah and his daughter climb onto the pier. During Clive's fifteen years on Ambergris Caye, she had only made two brief visits.

"Clive!" Elijah called out as they approached.

Clive wiped the grease off his hands and stepped onto the pier.

"You remember my daughter," Elijah said with unmistakable pride.

"Hello, Jovita," Clive said, smiling at the lovely Carib. Her dark complexion contrasted sharply with her white shorts and tan halter.

"Call me Jo, Clive. My friends in the States shortened my name years ago."

"It's been some time since you were here, Jovita," Clive said.

"Almost two years. The last time was for Mother's funeral."

"Welcome home."

"Well, thank you, Clive."

Her manner made Clive feel as if he were being patronized by an American tourist.

"Actually," Jovita said, "since Daddy tore down the old caye house to build the hotel, this never feels like home to me. I grew up in Belize City, you know. Daddy moved out here after I left for the States."

"How long will you be staying?"

"I'll be here on the caye for five days, visiting Daddy. Then I fly over to Belmopan. I'm a nurse on a medical team out of L. A.— Los Angeles. We're donating two weeks of our time to staff a free medical clinic down here."

Clive frowned. She sounded like a bloody Peace Corps worker.

"What time's your next charter, Clive?" Elijah said.

"In about half an hour. I was just getting the boat ready. It's a short trip up the reef . . . the same divers I took out this morning." Clive turned to Jovita. "Would you like to come along?"

"I don't scuba dive."

"Have you ever snorkeled?"

Jovita nodded.

"We have equipment you can use. Or if you prefer, you can just come along for the ride."

Jovita looked inquiringly at her father.

"Go, child!" Elijah said. "Enjoy yourself. We'll have plenty of time to visit the next few days."

"Okay, if you're sure you don't mind, Daddy. If scuba diving looks like fun, maybe I'll take some lessons while I'm down here."

"Clive is a certified instructor," Elijah said.

"I'll get my swim suit and be back in a few minutes," she said.

Clive nodded. As he watched her walk to the hotel, his spirits rose for the first time in weeks.

Clive dropped anchor. The charter boat rode easily in the calm sea, protected by the nearby barrier reef. Jovita, clad in a bright orange bikini, sat next to him, watching the divemaster give his six American divers their final instructions for their afternoon exercise.

On the trip to the dive location, the divers had included Jovita in their excited chatter, but now she sat apart as they prepared to go over the side.

"It's more organized than I thought it would be," she said to Clive.

He nodded. "The divemaster knows his business. This is their third practice day. Tomorrow we come back for a night dive. Then the next day, we go out to Lighthouse Reef to dive the Blue Hole."

"What's the Blue Hole like?"

"It's very big—1,000 feet across and 400 feet deep. Caves begin at a hundred feet. Fifteen-foot stalactites hang from the ceiling."

"Do you dive there?"

Clive nodded. He didn't mention that diving the Blue Hole was difficult for him. The complex network of sea caves reminded him too much of a limestone cave in Guatemala.

The divers took their sitting positions on the gunwales. Then on the divemaster's command, they rolled backward into the water.

"How deep are they going?" Jovita said.

"Only about fifty feet, but it's a nice dive. There are some beautiful coral canyons down there, and thousands of fish."

Clive and Jovita went over to gunwale and watched the divers descend.

"I'd forgotten how clear the water is here," Jovita said. "It's beautiful."

"Beautiful," Clive agreed, admiring the heavy swells above her bikini top.

When the divers were out of sight, they moved into the shade of the wheelhouse.

"Have you lived on Ambergris Caye all your life?" Jovita said.

"No, I was born in San Ignacio. I came here with your father, fifteen years ago."

She raised her eyebrows. "Oh? You're so . . . efficient. I thought you were a 'caye bwy'."

She again sounded like a patronizing white tourist. "Jovita," Clive said, "do you ever think about returning to Belize?"

"Not really. I have a nice apartment in Los Angeles, and lots of friends. And please, call me Jo. All my friends do."

"Are your American friends white or black, Jovita?"

"Both," she said, obviously growing annoyed.

"And they accept you as if you were an American?"

"Yes," she said, almost too quickly.

"Your father is concerned that so many educated Belizeans leave our country. Like yourself—a nurse."

Before she could reply, a boat engine started nearby. A launch sped out of a secluded cut in the mangrove-lined coast, a quarter-mile away. The boat veered toward San Pedro.

Clive shook his head. "Government is trying to keep this part of the caye as a nature preserve," he said bitterly, "but all they're doing is giving the drug smugglers miles of hiding places."

"I'm embarrassed to tell my friends that I come from Belize," Jovita said.

"Embarrassed? Why?"

"Because drugs from Belize are responsible for so much misery in the States."

"Chuh! It is the Americans who buy that shit. No one holds a gun to their heads and makes them stick it up their noses!"

Jovita gave him a sharp look, then gazed out to sea. Finally she turned back. "Well, what do we do now?"

"Just sit and wait," Clive said, relieved she was still speaking to him. He wanted her to enjoy this excursion; he owed so much to her father. "With some groups," he said, "I'm the divemaster. But with this group, we sit and wait."

The slow rock of the boat lulled them into silence. The afternoon breeze carried the cries of soaring seagulls. Suddenly the divemaster and a diver broke the surface. "Cramp!" the divemaster shouted. The middle-aged diver's face was contorted in pain.

Clive helped the divemaster get the man on board. The diver yanked off a flipper and frantically massaged a toe that extended out unnaturally. Finally he stood up and walked about.

"Stay out of the water for the rest of the afternoon, Mr. Nelson," the divemaster said. "That's your second cramp today." He gave Clive a nod, then took a long stride off the stern deck and disappeared beneath the surface.

The diver gingerly hobbled over to the shade of the wheelhouse.

"Mistah Nelson," Clive said, "would you mind watching things here? I'd like to take my friend snorkeling."

"Sure, Clive. Are you going to catch some lobster for this evening?"

"Aren't you getting tired of lobster?"

"Hell no!" the man said with a grin. "You kids catch dinner. I'll keep an eye on things here."

A few minutes later, Clive and Jovita snorkel-cruised over a large coral patch. Clive pushed a diver-down float, with a lobster cage and a fish spear strapped to it.

Clive stopped, and Jovita swam up beside him. "This is a good place for you to dive," he said, then lowered the weighted line that would anchor the float. "It's like a coral jungle down there."

"I can see it!" Jovita said excitedly. "It's beautiful, Clive! Even from up here!"

"It's farther down than it looks. We need to take in plenty of air before we dive."

"How deep is it?"

"About fifteen feet to the bottom. Are you ready?"

She nodded eagerly.

"Okay. Take several deep breaths . . . now force all the air out . . . now one really deep breath and hold it . . . and dive!"

Jovita's surface dive was awkward, but once underwater, she propelled herself downward with strong strokes. Clive followed closely behind her. A dense school of brightly colored fish momentarily blocked his vision. He waved an arm and they darted away. He spotted Jovita near the sandy bottom, inspecting an array of sea fans and plumes. Clive swam over and tapped her on the shoulder. Jovita jumped at his touch. He gestured for her to watch him. He pointed to his feet in the sand, then to his knees as he flexed them. Raising his hands above his head, he pushed off and headed for the surface. Halfway up, he paused to be sure she was following. She was, and they continued up until they broke the surface.

"I wanted to be sure you knew how to recover," he said. "The first time you feel the need to breathe, immediately come up for air. And remember this technique: look up; reach up; go up."

Jovita nodded. "It's marvelous down there, Clive! Let's go back."

They dived for half an hour, before stopping to rest. They floated side by side, holding onto the empty lobster cage.

"You're doing very well," Clive said. "Are you sure you're not a 'caye gyal'?"

She gave a rueful shake of her head. "Clive, all afternoon . . . I've felt like I was saying the wrong thing . . . afraid I somehow was offending you. I want you to know, I'm having a wonderful time."

Clive was at a loss for words.

"Except for those eels," she said with a shudder. "I can't stand those eels!"

"They won't bother you, unless you frighten them."

"I know. That's what they told me when I was a little girl. But when you actually see them swimming toward you, opening and closing their jaws . . ."

"They're just pumping water through their gills."

"Uh huh," she said, sounding not quite convinced.

Clive looked toward the launch. "The divers are coming back," he said. "Time for me to get their dinner." He unhooked the fish spear from the float, then executed a backstroke and tuck, propelling himself downward. He stopped in front of a massive coral structure. With his spear at the ready, he reached into a crevasse and withdrew a large, struggling lobster.

Jovita had come down to watch. She gave him the "okay" signal.

Clive nodded and swam up to the surface. He put the snapping lobster into the cage, then loaded up on oxygen and dived again. When the bubbles cleared from his reentry, he looked about for Jovita. She was reaching into a coral crevasse!

Clive propelled himself forward with powerful strokes. He was still twenty feet away, when she withdrew a small lobster. She turned away from the coral and proudly waved the lobster for Clive to see. A disturbed moray eel emerged from the same crevasse.

Jovita saw Clive's alarm and turned toward the coral. She frantically flailed her arms, as the five-foot moray wriggled menacingly toward her. Clive grabbed Jovita's shoulder, pulled her back, and thrust his spear into the eel's open jaws. As the eel thrashed, Clive and Jovita fled for safety.

The instant they broke the surface, Jovita ripped off her mask and shrieked, "Clive!" She kicked frantically, terrified that the eel might have followed them.

Clive put his face beneath the surface and confirmed that it hadn't. His spear lay on the sandy bottom. The eel was nowhere in sight. He raised his head. "It's okay, Jovita! It's okay! He's gone back to the coral."

She grabbed him and held on tightly.

"It's okay," he said soothingly. "I'm sorry. I shouldn't have left you down there by yourself."

She released him and forced a smile.

"Wait up here for me this time," he said.

"You're not going down there again!"

"It's safe, if you know how. Sometimes the moray shares his home with a lobster. You always have to look before you put your hand inside. And I always take my spear, just in case."

Jovita shuddered.

Clive took her hand. "Come on. I'll take you to the boat first."

"No. I'll wait here for you."

That evening, as the sun set over the caye, Clive navigated the launch along the barrier reef. Jovita sat beside him in the wheelhouse. The divers had gathered on the aft deck, reliving their afternoon's scuba adventures. As darkness fell, the lights of nearby San Pedro became visible.

A diver called up, "Hey, Jo! Come on back and have a beer!"

Jovita acknowledged him with a wave, but stayed up front with Clive. "I don't know how they have room to drink! How many lobsters did we eat?"

"Eleven," Clive said with a chuckle. "Divers work up an appetite."

"Dinner was wonderful, Clive. Everything was wonderful."

"Everything?"

She gave a mock shudder. "Wait 'til I tell Daddy about the moray."

Clive nodded; however, he didn't think Elijah was going to be pleased with the story.

"Oh!" Jovita said. "What are those?" Several brightly colored luminescent lights, weaved eerily above the water.

"They're called 'glow sticks'," Clive said. "Windsurfers tie them to the masts of their boards when they go out for night sails." He slowed the boat to negotiate the reef channel in front of the Villa Pedrano pier. "That's strange," he said.

"What's strange?"

"That looks like Teresita there on the pier. She's our day clerk. I wonder why she hasn't been relieved."

Clive guided the launch close the pier. The divemaster jumped off and secured the mooring lines.

Teresita jumped on board and rushed into the wheelhouse. She tried to speak, but burst into tears.

"What is it, Teresita?" Clive said, taking her by the shoulders.

"Señor Ruiz . . ."

"¿Señor Ruiz que?" Clive said impatiently.

"Señor Ruiz tuvo un ataque del corazón."

"English!" Jovita shouted.

"Mistah Ruiz had a heart attack," Teresita sobbed. "They have flown him to Belize City."

42. NEXT GRANNY

Ray and Kendall walked down the main hallway of the venerable Dumaine Building in downtown New Orleans. They turned a corner and found the office they had been looking for. "The Landry Corporation" was emblazoned in gold leaf, on a solid mahogany door. Ray shook his head at the irony.

They entered the high-ceiling office foyer. A prim, middle-aged receptionist looked up as they entered. "Yes?"

"We're here to see Milburn Landry," Kendall said.

"And y'all are?"

"I'm Kendall Foster. This is Ray Kelley."

The receptionist turned to a computer and brought up her employer's calendar. "Oh, yes, Mr. Foster. You're scheduled from 10:00 to 11:00. Mr. Landry will be with you in a few minutes. Please be seated. If you'd like some coffee, we have two pots over there. You'll probably prefer the one on the right; the one on the left has chicory."

Kendall sat down on a leather couch.

Ray picked up a china cup and filled it from the pot on the left. He walked over to an old-fashioned, wood-frame window and gazed down at the heavy midmorning traffic. A block away, one of the city's few remaining streetcars rolled by. He smiled to himself. He was familiar with New Orleans, having grown up sixty miles away. However, after having been out of the States for six years, he felt like an outsider. He glanced down at his guayabera shirt and khaki trousers. He probably looked like one too. He took a sip from his coffee; it was undrinkable.

He looked up the street toward the Vieux Carré and felt a twinge of concern. He had left Florita and the boys at the

Monteleone Hotel, promising to take them sightseeing as soon as the business meeting was over. But knowing his wife, he suspected she and the boys were probably already touring the French Quarter on their own.

An office door opened, and Milburn Landry came out. "Kendall, good to see you." They shook hands. "And you must be Ray Kelley."

Ray nodded, as he grasped the portly man's moist hand. Landry appeared older than Ray had expected.

"I suppose you know that your father worked for me about thirty-five years ago," Landry said.

Ray nodded noncommittally, and followed the two men into Landry's office.

Landry walked around a polished mahogany desk and dropped into an oversized leather chair. "Have a seat," he said, gesturing to two hardback chairs across from him. "I heard Elijah Ruiz had a heart attack."

"Yes," Kendall said. "Day before yesterday. He's resting comfortably in Belize City."

Landry nodded. "Who's running the hotel on the caye?"

"A young man named Clive Lightburn," Kendall said. "He's been with Elijah for several years now."

"When did y'all get in?"

"We flew up last night," Kendall said.

"In your own plane?"

Kendall nodded.

"Any trouble clearing customs at this end?"

"A little. The DEA spent an hour going over our plane."

"There's been a lot of dope coming up from down there," Landry said. "When do y'all go back?"

"Probably the day after tomorrow," Kendall said. "I have some personal business to attend to while I'm here, and Ray plans to fly over to a town nearby to visit his family."

"Does your mother still live in Hammond, Ray?"

"Uh huh."

"Your grandfather teaches there at the local college, doesn't he?"

Ray nodded, surprised at Landry's knowledge of his family.

"Smart woman, your mother," Landry mused aloud, "leaving your father and getting out of that God-forsaken place." He turned to Kendall. "On the phone, you indicated you had an offer to make, concerning our western properties."

Kendall nodded. "As I said, we're doing some restructuring of our holdings and find we can offer up a 21,000-acre parcel on our eastern boundary, next to your property."

"And what did you say you were asking for it?" Landry said, as if the details of their recent telephone conversation had slipped his mind.

"Two million," Kendall said.

"And that was Belize dollars, right?"

"U.S. dollars," Kendall said patiently.

"I must have misunderstood you on the phone. My top offer would be half that—two million *Belize* dollars."

Ray glanced at Kendall, who shook his head. Landry obviously was toying with the Belizean. The week before, the Panamanian bank had grudgingly given Kendall a thirty-day extension. However, they had refused to accept any more land as collateral and had invoked a $100,000 late penalty. Payment of the total debt was now due in three weeks—$1,800,000 U.S. Landry's $1,000,000 offer was of no help.

"You brought us up here for nothing, mon," Kendall said bitterly.

Landry smiled enigmatically. "I have an alternative offer that will solve your financial problems once and for all."

Ray and Kendall exchanged glances. Landry obviously had his own agenda.

"I'm interested in acquiring your entire corporation. That would include Villa Pedrano, as well as the 47,000-acre farm and Xtabay Lodge. I'm prepared to offer . . . $4,500,000 U.S.."

Ray stared at Landry; a Belizean proverb echoed in his mind:

When a black man thiefs, he thiefs some; when a white man thiefs, he thiefs all.

"Our corporation isn't for sale," Kendall said.

"Perhaps not," Landry said coldly, "but some of your most valuable assets soon will be. You're overleveraged and behind in your payments. In three weeks, I'll be negotiating with the Bank of Panama for that prime property right next to your lodge."

Ray and Kendall exchanged glances again. Now they knew for certain who had undercut them with the Bank of Panama.

Kendall stood up. "We have nothing more to discuss!"

Ray remained seated; his mind raced. He hated the smug American across the desk from him, but he remembered his father's admonition against prematurely dismissing sources of financing. Somehow, he and Kendall needed to keep the Landry option open, while they sought funding elsewhere. "Rather than buying us out," Ray said, "would you consider coming in as an investor?"

Kendall and Landry both gazed at him intently.

"What do you have in mind?" Landry asked.

Ray paused; he was improvising. He looked over at Kendall.

Kendall nodded for Ray to continue, and sat down.

Ray rapidly estimated the value of their holdings. "Say . . . twenty percent of our corporation for . . . $2,000,000—US."

"Why do you think I'd settle for only a piece of the corporation?" Landry said.

Kendall reentered the discussion, taking Ray's lead. "If the bank forecloses on us, and you somehow get your hands on the collateral property, it would be of no value to you. Your only access to it would be by air, since my remaining 300,000 acres surrounds it."

"Property taxes would eat you up," Landry said. "You haven't been able to get your farm self-supporting. What do you plan to do with 300,000 acres of jungle?"

Ray spoke up again. "He's thinking about turning it into a nature preserve."

Kendall gave Ray an amused glance, and again took his lead.

"Which, of course, would exempt me from taxes. I can keep my land indefinitely."

Landry gazed at Ray for a moment, then said, "I'll need time to study this new proposal. Mind you, I think twenty percent is too low for a $2,000,000 investment." He turned to his computer. "Today is Wednesday. I'm scheduled in Houston this afternoon through next week. Then I'll be flying down to Belize City, the week after that. We can discuss this further then."

Kendall looked at Ray, then back to Landry and nodded.

Landry keyed the date into his computer. "Two weeks from today . . . nine o'clock . . . your office."

That afternoon, Ray piloted Kendall's Cessna-206 away from New Orleans. Florita sat in the co-pilot seat; their sons rode in back. Lake Ponchartrain passed beneath them. A few minutes later, Hammond came into view. Ray temporarily pushed aside his business concerns, looking forward to seeing his mother and grandfather. Arriving by air made it particularly enjoyable.

He put the airplane into a sweeping turn so he and his family could get a panoramic view of his hometown.

"Are we home, Mama?" Ramón shouted from the rear seat.

"Don't be silly, Ramón," Florita said. "You know we're not home. This was your father's home when he was a bwy."

"I want to go to *my* home!" Ramón said defiantly. His younger brother stared silently down at the tree-covered town.

Ray banked the airplane toward the east. As they approached the town airport, he shouted over the engine roar, "We're in luck! No car races today!"

"Car races?" Florita said.

"I'm joking. But when I was growing up, there weren't many people with planes around here. They used to hold sports car races on the runways. Sometimes, they had to stop the races to let planes land."

Florita smiled.

Ray concentrated on his landing approach. Kendall's new turbocharged 206 had more power than his older, smaller 172. He had to be cautious not to over control it.

They touched down smoothly and taxied over to an abandoned control tower. Nearby, a man in dirty white coveralls washed down an airplane. He pointed to where he wanted Ray to park.

As Ray shut down the aircraft, he looked through the windshield for his mother and grandfather. He had called them just before taking off from New Orleans International Airport, but now he didn't see them.

Florita leaned back and unfastened the boys' seat belts and wiped some chocolate from Ramón's face.

The worker came over to tether the airplane. He shouted up at Ray, "Hey, Gun! Is that you, man?"

For a moment, Ray couldn't place the black man grinning up at him. Then he remembered. "James Brodman!" Ray opened the door and jumped down. "How the hell you been, man?" he said, as they shook hands.

"Fine!" Brodman said. "You looking good. Where you been keeping yourself?"

"A little country in Central America called Belize. I've been down there about eleven years now."

Florita and the boys climbed out and joined them.

"James," Ray said proudly, "I'd like you to meet my family. This is my wife, Florita, and these are our two boys, Ramón and Gonzalo."

"No kidding!" Brodman said with obvious delight. "Well, I'm pleased to meet y'all. So Machine Gun Kelley's got him a family now, huh?"

"Machine Gun?" Ramón said quizzically.

"Boy, don't you know around here your daddy's known as Machine Gun Kelley?"

"Machine Gun?" Gonzalo said.

"It's just a nickname, boys," Ray said with a quick laugh. "It meant that when I played basketball here, I used to shoot too much."

"Didn't this outlaw ever tell you about the time he shot out the lights in Pearl River, Mississippi?"

"Outlaw?" Florita said, looking at her husband with an amused expression.

"Baddest white boy I ever saw," Brodman said.

"What's Tyrone up to these days?" Ray said.

Brodman's smile faded. "He's dead, man."

"Dead?" Ray said in disbelief. He had planned to look up his old high school teammate while he was in town.

"Yeah, man. Some dude across the river from New Orleans killed him."

A car horn blew, drawing their attention. A station wagon turned off the access road and sped across the tarmac.

"That must be Mom and Grandpa," Ray said. "I'm sorry to hear about Tyrone."

"Happened nearly three years ago," Brodman said with a shrug. "I'll check you later, man."

Ray nodded. The station wagon stopped nearby, and Ray's mother and grandfather got out. Ray hurried over to meet them.

"Oh, Ray," his mother cried as they hugged, "so good to see you!" Her eyes brimmed with tears.

"You're looking fine, lad," his grandfather said. They shook hands, then hugged.

"Mom, Grandpa, I want you to meet my family."

Florita brought the boys forward; they clutched her hands.

Ray's mother looked at her daughter-in-law and grandsons. There was unmistakable regret in her expression. She didn't speak.

Ray's grandfather said, "I'm so pleased to meet you at last, Florita." He stepped forward and hugged her. "And you too, boys," he said, dropping down to one knee. "I'm your great-grandfather."

Ramón glanced furtively back at the aircraft.

"This is your grandmother, boys," Ray said, attempting to close the gap that his mother was forming.

"No!" Ramón said.

"Yes," Ray said. "This is my mother, and she's your grandmother."

"Chuh!" Ramón said. "She not my granny. She just a white lady."

"Don't be silly, Ramón," Florita said. "You have two grandmothers. My mother is one; your father's mother is the other."

"We have a next granny?" Gonzalo said, frowning.

Ray laughed. "Yes, boys, you have a 'next granny'."

The younger boy went over to Ray's mother. "I am Gonzalo, Next Granny."

Ray's mother looked down at him. "Yes . . . well, let's be on our way then." As she returned to the station wagon, she furtively looked about, as if concerned someone she knew might see her with these brown visitors.

That evening, Ray sat on the familiar front porch of his grandfather's old frame house, a half-block away from Southeastern Louisiana University. For the past hour, he and Florita had told his grandfather about their life together and their hopes for Xtabay Lodge. The boys played happily in an ancient oak tree in the front yard. Ray's mother was conspicuously absent.

"Your lodge sounds wonderful, kids," the old man said. "I'd give *anything* to be down there when you uncover those ruins!" He reached over and patted Ray's hand. "I can't tell you how good it is to see you, lad, and to finally meet your wonderful family."

"Thanks, Grandpa. I wish I could have got everybody up here before Grandma passed away."

His grandfather nodded. "Even after all this time, I sometimes forget she's gone. A few minutes ago, it flashed through my mind to have you repeat that wonderful story for her, of how you first saw Florita standing on top of that pyramid and thought she was a Mayan goddess."

Ray smiled. "I still think she's a goddess, Grandpa."

Two coeds passed by, and one of them called out, "Hi, Professor Anderson!"

The old man waved, then turned back to Ray. "Lad, do you ever think of returning to the States?"

Ray shook his head. "I've 'drunk the water', Grandpa. That means—"

"I know what it means, lad. Your father explained it to me before you were born. 'Once you've drunk the water of Belize, you'll always return'." The old man's eyes crinkled and he added with a mischievous grin, "As I recall, your father suspected that it had something to do with buzzard droppings in the drinking water."

Florita laughed in full appreciation.

"You liked my dad, didn't you, Grandpa?"

The old man nodded, but before he could reply, the screen door opened and Ray's mother stepped onto the porch. "Why don't y'all come in now?"

"Come on out and join us, Kay," Ray's grandfather said.

"Next Granny! Next Granny!" the boys called out to her.

Ray's mother gave a barely perceptible nod in their direction, then reluctantly settled into a porch chair. "Are you sure your children aren't ready to come in?" she asked Florita. "Maybe they'd like to watch cartoons. Do they have television in British Honduras now?"

"Yes, Mrs. Kelley," Florita said with a smile, "we have television in Belize."

"Oh, yes," Ray's mother said, "Belize. I don't know why they had to change the name." Turning to her father she said, "Did you know that Belize was named after a pirate named Wallace? The people down there mispronounced his name so badly that it came out 'Belize'."

"'Belize' is a Mayan word, Mrs. Kelley," Florita said. "It means 'land of muddy water'. It refers to the many rivers that feed our lush rain forest."

Ray's mother glared at Florita, obviously irritated at having a pet anecdote challenged.

"Ray," his grandfather said, "you've obviously fallen in love with Belize. What does the future look like down there?"

"First I fell in love *in* Belize, Grandpa, then *with* it."

His grandfather smiled at Florita.

"Belize is a primitive, rugged land," Ray said, "on the verge of either turning into the success story of Central America, or failing miserably. The corporation I'm involved in is a microcosm of the whole country. We've worked for years to get where we are, but we're about to lose it all."

"What are you up against, lad?"

"Down there, we're . . . vulnerable. We're a poor country, and badly underpopulated. A single U.S. corporation can threaten our stability. For example, Coca Cola bought up hundreds of thousands of acres for its orange juice subsidiary. To appreciate our degree of vulnerability, just consider: Coke's annual budget is larger than Belize's."

"I see what you mean," his grandfather said.

"The dynamics are the same at our level. My partners and I are trying to compete with Dad's old company, the Landry Corporation. We're in a poker game, where we have limited resources, and Landry can raise the stakes indefinitely."

Ray's mother said, "Whenever I see anything in the newspapers about British Honduras . . . Belize, it has to do with the illegal drugs they're sending into this country."

Florita responded, "Because of the trade restrictions the United States placed on sugar imports, many farmers who once grew sugarcane now grow marijuana."

Ray's mother again glared at her daughter-in-law, then turned away and stared down the street, as if she had again been the victim of an uncalled-for rebuff.

"What about the political situation down there?" Ray's grandfather said.

"Belize has the most stable government in Central America," Ray said. "Since we got our independence in 1981, each of the two major political parties has spent time in power, and each did a fair job of running things. But in spite of their good intentions, economic progress hasn't got down to the people."

"Is there a need for U.S. aid?"

Ray shook his head. "The usual agencies are already down there—Peace Corps, USAID, DEA, and, some claim, the CIA. Belizeans consider the U.S. government to be as big a threat as the large American companies."

"Ray," His mother said sharply, "why on earth did you renounce your American citizenship?"

"Mom, you Americans—"

His mother jumped to her feet. "'You Americans'! Young man, just who do you think you're talking to? 'You Americans' indeed! Why don't you go back to that ghastly country of yours, and live like a . . . savage . . . with your Indians!" With that, she hurried into the house, slamming the screen door behind her.

Ray stood up and said tersely, "We'll be leaving, Grandpa."

"Oh, Ray, no!"

"We can't stay. I'm sorry."

"Lad, your mother just . . ."

"I know," Ray said, patting the old man's shoulder. "Give me a minute to get our bags, then take us to the airport."

Ray had loaded the luggage into the airplane. He and his family were hugging his grandfather, when a taxi pulled up beside the station wagon. His mother stepped out and called, "Ray!"

For a moment, there was only the sound of the breeze blowing through the wing struts.

"Get in the plane, boys," Ray said.

"Ray!" his mother cried. She stood alone on the edge of tarmac, her arms wrapped across her chest, clutching emptiness.

"Come on, boys," Ray said tersely, taking their hands and leading them toward the airplane door.

"Ramón!" his mother cried.

"Next Granny calling me, Daddy."

"Get in the plane, Son," Ray said firmly.

"Ramón!" his mother cried again.

"Next Granny calling me, Daddy!" the boy said defiantly. He pulled his hand away, turned, and ran toward his grandmother.

Ray grimaced at the sight of his mother dropping awkwardly to her knees on the tarmac. His son leaped into her outstretched arms, nearly knocking her over. His mother hugged her grandson tightly, and wept without shame.

Ramón looked over his shoulder and shouted to his younger brother, "Gonzalo! Come, bwy! Next Granny wants you no, sah!"

Gonzalo broke loose and ran full tilt toward his brother and his grandmother.

Florita smiled. "Unload the bags, Ray."

43. CACA TARRY

Clive strolled back to the Villa Pedrano after seeing off the morning charter. A week had passed since Elijah's heart attack; however, it still seemed strange to watch the dive boat pull away under the command of the new captain. For years, Elijah had encouraged Clive to get more involved in managing the hotel. It had taken the heart attack finally to bring it about.

As Clive crossed the hotel's sand courtyard, he contemplated the transition with mixed feelings. He missed the easygoing life of an island guide, but he enjoyed the challenge of having full responsibility for the hotel operation. The staff had responded to his leadership, and the guests hadn't registered any complaints.

Jovita had told him that she was going to insist that her father retire. Clive wanted to make the most of this opportunity to show Elijah that he could handle the job. Although he and Jovita had spent so little time together, he knew how he felt about her. He also knew that to maintain her respect, he would have to become more than just a "caye bwy".

Clive opened the screen door and stepped into the hotel lobby. Teresita looked up from the check-in counter. "Mistah Foster called for you just a short while ago, sah. He said for you to ring him back at the Belize office on his private line as soon as you return."

"*Gracias, Teresita,*" Clive said. It still seemed strange to be addressed as "sah". Teresita had switched to it the day Elijah was airlifted off the island. The other members of the hotel staff had immediately picked it up.

Clive went into Elijah's office and closed the door behind him. He sat down at the desk and glanced at an open composition book, where he had been jotting questions to ask the old Carib when he saw him next. He already had filled a page and a half.

Clive reached for the phone, but suddenly the office door flew open and Mr. Pennington barged in. "I need to talk to you, Lightburn," the fat American said, slamming the door behind him.

"I got no time for you," Clive said.

"I think you do, boy. I'm about to become an owner in this place."

"What?"

"The Foster Corporation needs money. My associates and I have decided to buy in."

Clive sat in stunned silence. Either Elijah hadn't had a chance to tell Kendall about Pennington, or Kendall knew and didn't care.

"You've made it a point to ignore me lately, boy," Pennington said. "That's a mistake. And you saw how we handle mistakes."

Clive didn't reply.

Pennington gave a satisfied nod. "I'm having a party at my place tonight. Got some new, young cunt coming down from Miami. Be there at 9:00." He turned and lumbered out of the office.

Clive's shoulders slumped. For several minutes, he stared at the desk top. Finally, still lost in thought, he picked up the telephone receiver and dialed Kendall's private number.

Kendall answered on the first ring.

"Clive here, mistah Foster."

"Oh, yes . . . Clive." There was a noticeable pause. "I'm afraid I have some bad news . . . Elijah passed away during the night."

"Passed away?" Clive said in disbelief. "But I spoke to Jovita on the phone, only yesterday. She told me he was recovering."

"He died in his sleep."

Clive gazed down at the composition book, trying to fathom that the old Carib would never return.

"The notices are being posted around the city," Kendall said. "The wake will be held this evening, and the funeral tomorrow. Do you have someone who can look after things there?"

"What?" Clive said numbly. "Oh, yes, Teresita can handle it."

"Good. Get her set up, then fly in. Be sure she has my number, so she can call me if she has any problems. I'm not sure what I'm going to do with that operation in the future. I'll decide that in the next few days. I've got a potential investor out there—a man named Pennington—who may want to run it himself."

Clive struggled to collect his thoughts. Elijah was dead. Pennington was taking over the Villa Pedrano. Jovita . . .

Kendall's voice came back. "Since Elijah didn't have a home here in the city, we're having the wake at the Bellevue Hotel. Plan on staying there. They only had a few guests. I've booked the rest of it."

"Yes, sah."

"I'll see you directly then, Clive."

"Yes, sah." The line went dead.

Clive rode in a battered taxi, transporting him from Belize City's municipal airport to the Bellevue Hotel. They passed the old clock tower. It was still stopped on 10:17, as it had been for the past fifteen years. Like my life, Clive thought.

The remains of the boarding house stood nearby, gutted and abandoned. He thought of Dorla and wondered what had finally become of her. A few years back, she had been the center of a flap between the British Army and local officials. A young British enlisted man, white and ten years her junior, had petitioned to marry her and had been denied permission by his commanding officer. Dorla had fought the decision through the local newspapers. The British Army eventually had surrendered.

The taxi rumbled passed the post office. Elijah's death notice would be posted there and on other public buildings, as was the local custom.

Clive momentarily close his eyes. Fifteen years on the caye, and he would have nothing to show for it. But he couldn't work for Pennington.

They bounced over the old swing bridge, and the driver impatiently leaned on his horn. The pedestrians walking in the street near Battlefield Park ignored him. The driver detoured around the side of the Court House, then sped down Southern Foreshore.

They pulled up in front of the Bellevue, and Clive heard music blare from the hotel's second floor. He stepped from the taxi and looked through the open windows. The bar was full; Elijah's wake had already begun.

Clive located Jovita's room at the rear of the hotel. The throb of punta rhythm echoed down the hallway. He knocked softly.

An elderly Carib woman inched open the door. "Yes?"

"Can I see Jovita?" Clive said.

"She's lying down."

"Would you please tell her Clive is here?"

"Who is it, Auntie?" Jovita said in a muffled voice.

The old woman looked back. "He says his name is Clive." Then she nodded and opened the door.

Jovita sat up as Clive entered the room. Her eyes were red and swollen. Clive walked over and she rose into his arms. The old woman quietly slipped out the door. The only sound was the faint throb of the music.

"Daddy's dead, Clive," Jovita said with a sob.

"I know, gyal," Clive said, caressing the back of her neck. "I can't believe it either. Back at the hotel, I have a list of questions . . ."

She drew back so she could face him. Her face contorted in anguish. "It's my fault."

He shook his head and smiled sadly, then held her close again.

"I shouldn't have listened to him!" she said with a sob. "I should have made him go back to the States for treatment."

"It was his time to pass, gyal. He would have wanted to be at home."

She drew back again, about to protest.

"Gyal," Clive said sternly, "don't question your daddy's judgment."

She gave him a sad smile of gratitude and rested her cheek against his chest. "Daddy and I had a lot of time to talk the past few days. I hadn't realized how disappointed he was that I stayed in the States, rather than coming back here after I finished school.

If I hadn't come home last week, I would have missed . . ." She broke off and sobbed again.

Clive patted her comfortingly. "He was a hell of a man, your daddy. 'He caca was tarry'."

Jovita drew back again and frowned up at him.

Clive laughed softly. Literally, the expression translated to 'his shit was sticky'. "In San Ignacio," Clive said, "that means he was like the jaguar—brave and smart."

"We talked about you too, Clive. Daddy liked you . . . even before . . ." She hesitated.

"Before what?"

"Before he learned that you were the son of his old friend."

Clive stiffened. "You know that Ramón Kelley was my father?"

"Daddy told me."

"Why?" Clive said, feeling betrayed.

Jovita put her cheek against his chest again and hugged him. "Bwy," she said softly, "you said it yourself: don't question my daddy's judgment."

Later, Clive escorted Jovita into the hotel bar. Friends filled the room, paying their final respects to Elijah Ruiz. Punta rhythm blared from the jukebox. A man standing near the door recognized Jovita and had the others make a path so she and Clive could enter.

As they weaved their way across the room, a familiar voice called out, "Jovita! Clive!" Kendall Foster waved from a table near a front window. Seated with him were Ray Kelley and a pretty Mestizo, probably Kelley's wife.

Clive followed Jovita over to the table. Everyone stood up as they approached. Kendall hugged Jovita. Clive reluctantly shook hands with Ray. This was their first encounter since Clive had learned they were half-brothers. Jovita took his hand. Clive cleared his throat. "Jovita, this is Ray Kelley . . . the son of a friend of your father's."

Jovita smiled up at Clive. "Ray and I have met. He came to visit Daddy in the hospital every day."

"Sorry about your dad, Jovita," Ray said. He gave her a hug, then said, "This is my wife, Florita."

"I think I've seen you before," Jovita said as they shook hands. "When we were girls perhaps?"

"You look familiar too," Florita said. "I am also very sorry about your loss."

"Is it all right if we sit here?" Jovita asked Clive. "I'd like to be where I can get the breeze."

Clive nodded.

"Honey," Ray said to Florita, "I've told you about Clive. He's the guy that shows up on a basketball court every few years, and kicks my ass."

Florita smiled at Clive. "Nice to meet you at last. You won't believe how often your name comes up at Xtabay Lodge."

Clive frowned.

"After that game in San Ignacio last month," Florita said, "our boys had Ray put up a basketball goal for them. Now they play out there all day long. One is always 'Tall Bwy', and the other is 'Machine Gun'".

"Machine Gun?"

"That's what they called Ray when he played in the States."

Clive looked over at his grinning half-brother—white and so sure of himself. Like Pennington, out on the caye.

Three elderly Carib women approached the table. They deferentially nodded to the whites, then each offered her condolences to Jovita in Garifuna.

When the women left, Jovita said, "I've been in the States too long. I couldn't understand what they said."

"Any chance you'll stay on here, Jovita?" Kendall said.

Jovita smiled at Clive. "A very good chance."

"Have y'all eaten?" Ray said. "The folks that came up from Dangriga brought a ton of food with them. I'm not sure what it is, but it looks good. I'd be glad to get you something."

"Thank you, Ray," Jovita said. "Maybe a little later."

Clive shook his head that he also wasn't hungry. He turned

away from the table and looked about the room. Off in one corner, two old men played checkers, and several others stood watching. At a table next to them, the three elderly women prayed with Jovita's aunt. In the center of the dance floor, a young couple rhythmically pursued each other, as called for in the punta. Jovita's comment that she planned to stay had been a commitment. Clive turned back to the table and settled back in his chair.

The following afternoon, Clive took a solitary walk down Southern Foreshore. The afternoon sea slapped against the low seawall, sending a fine spray onto the cobblestone street. Jovita had been exhausted from the funeral and had gone to her room as soon as they had returned to the hotel.

Clive had been pleased at the size of the turnout. Elijah obviously had touched many people during his eighty years. The Catholic church had been filled to capacity, and many more had stood outside, listening to the eulogy through the open windows. Then a horse-drawn carriage had transported Elijah's body from the church to the cemetery. As the procession of mourners, dressed in black and white, had wound through the center of the city, the shop owners had closed their doors and windows as a sign of respect.

Lost in his musing, Clive started when a filthy figure, clad in rags, stepped out from behind the corner of a fence. His aged features were distended. A deep scar extended from his forehead, through an empty eye socket, and across his broken nose. He fixed his bleary remaining eye on Clive. "Give me shilling, no?"

"Left me, mon!" Clive said, not breaking stride.

The old man slunk back to the fence and said with a sneer, "White mon's baby!"

Clive frowned; he had seen that man before. Something made Clive think of his father. Ramón Kelley's killer had never been apprehended, nor was the motive for his murder ever determined. Clive looked back over his shoulder. The man was gone.

Clive continued down the tranquil seaside lane. He frequently heard tourists in San Pedro complaining about the dangerous streets of Belize City. He couldn't disagree with them. Too many idle men wandered the city streets. And crack cocaine, not Belize breeze, was now the drug of the impoverished.

Southern Foreshore came to a dead end. Clive leaned against the tall chain-link fence, recently erected to protect Government House from intruders. He looked toward the cayes and thought about another murder, one whose killer and motive he knew.

A short while later, he stood in front of an open hotel room window, the telephone receiver pressed against his ear. Outside, a dredging machine pumped filth from the harbor floor.

The voice of a Belizean woman came on the line. "United States Embassy."

Clive fought the impulse to hang up. "I would like to speak to the American consul."

"Wait one moment. I'll connect you with his secretary." She placed Clive on hold.

Again, he considered hanging up, but took a deep breath and waited.

Finally the voice of an American woman came on the line, "This is Mrs. Franklin. May I help you?"

"I would like to speak to the American consul."

"The consul is not available."

"Then I would like to leave a message."

"And your name is?"

"The message concerns a mon named Torres."

"Are you Mr. Torres?"

"Mistah Torres comes to Belize from Matamoros, Mexico."

"Sir, I'll need *your* name."

"Do you understand? He comes from Matamoros, Mexico."

"Yes, sir, I understand, but I *must* have your name."

"Torres is a drug dealer, who receives shipments on Ambergris Caye from an American named Pennington."

"Sir!" the woman insisted, "You need to talk to—"

"Torres killed the mon they found last month with his heart cut out. The drug boat is sunk off Caye Negro. Tell the consul to inform the DEA." Clive hung up.

He gazed back out the window. Like the dredging machine, he was turning up decades of muck that had flowed from Belize. Now he would tell Kendall Foster.

44. JESUS CHRIST LIZARD

Ray walked up a shaded jungle trail that led away from the Xtabay ruins. A short while earlier, he had told his Mayan workers that he wouldn't need them today. They had been curious, but he couldn't bring himself to tell them that the lodge would soon close down.

He ruefully shook his head. Although the lodge cabanas had been empty all week, Florita still plunged ahead on blind faith. An archaeological team from the University of California was flying in from Belize City later in the morning.

A cloud momentarily blocked the sun. Ray paused and peered through the dense jungle canopy. It was still the dry season; it probably wouldn't rain today.

He left the trail and made his way to a secluded observation point that he particularly liked. He stopped beside a small lagoon and listened. His footfalls had silenced the jungle. The only sound was the breeze blowing through the tops of the trees. A cloud of white butterflies circled about his legs, then flew off. Colorless, they stood out against the rich jungle greens.

He stood motionless for several minutes, and the jungle slowly came back to life. Birds fluttered through the trees; an invisible creature snapped a twig behind him. He heard a faint rustling of leaves off to one side and turned to see if a genuine reptile was crawling among the serpentine roots that covered the jungle floor. He saw nothing; it must have been a swirl of wind.

Nearby, a jungle cat had delineated its territory by depositing its tarry feces in a claw mark, scraped into a bare patch of ground. From the length of the scrape, more than a foot, Ray knew that the cat was a jaguar.

Standing motionless, Ray was overwhelmed by the beauty of

the Xtabay forest. Tears of frustration welled in his eyes. Time was running out; they were going to lose it.

A sleek lizard raced across the surface of the lagoon. "Jesus Christ lizards" his workers called them, for their ability to run across the water. It leaped onto the near bank, veered a few feet from him, then raced up the trail. As Ray followed its flight, he saw his wife appear at the top of the knoll. The workers he had dismissed that morning must have spoken to her. She saw him and quickened her pace.

As he watched his Mayan goddess stride down the jungle trail, he smiled sadly. He remembered describing this life to his grandfather. The old man had sensed the adventure and had wanted to experience it. He had said . . . he had said . . . Ray's eyes widened. "Florita!" he shouted. He bolted from the jungle and raced up the trail to her.

"What is it?" she said, alarmed.

He grabbed her by the shoulders. "Grandpa!"

"What? Ray, what's the matter with—"

He put a forefinger across her lips. "I was standing over there, and something my grandfather said popped into my mind!"

"What are you talking about, Ray?"

"I remembered something Grandpa said!"

"And you ran up here to scare me half to death with it?"

"Florita, my grandfather said that he'd give *anything* to be part of our dig. Do you remember?"

She looked at him quizzically. "I remember he said something like that when we were in the States. What of it?"

"He meant it, Florita. He said it like he would actually be willing to *pay!*"

Florita frowned.

"*Pay*, Florita!"

"You want to charge your grandfather to . . ." Florita began. Suddenly she understood. "They'd pay!" she said. "People would *pay!* They'd pay to stay at our lodge and be part of the dig!"

Ray nodded eagerly. Then he frowned. "Do you think archae-ologists would accept the idea?"

"We can find out, this morning," she said, smiling.

"They should," Ray continued excitedly. "They use local laborers with no experience. Florita, some of these people would probably want to come back every year, just to see how it's progressing!" His mind raced with the possibilities. "Then once the restoration is complete, our setup could be better than Tikal. We'd have the only nearby accommodations!"

"First," she said, "we need to convince a university to dig. Let's get back to the lodge."

"I've got another idea," he said as they hurried up the trail. "If experience is a problem, we could train one of our own workers to oversee the guests."

His wife looked at him with delight. "Ray, I think I hear a plane."

They broke into a run.

Two hours later, the lodge dining area was full. The University of California contingent had arrived in two airplanes. The young Mayan waitress raced in and out of the kitchen. She had never before had to wait on more than three tables at a time.

Dr. Theodore Potter, the archaeology department head, folded the map in front of him so the waitress could serve him a freshly sliced mango. The tanned Californian ran a hand through his thick graying hair. "It'll take us a couple of months to make our preparations and fight the local red tape," he said, "but we should be ready to break ground here in early February."

Florita squeezed Ray's leg under the table.

"And I don't see any problem with your idea about using lodge guests on the dig. However, we'd need for them to sign a release, protecting us from any liability. Ray, your supervisor idea sounds good, but I don't think it will be necessary. Travelers who come out to a place like this are a special breed. I don't think they'll require much supervision."

"Dr. Potter," Ray said, "I'll be frank with you. I think this may save our lodge."

"Then by all means," the Californian said, "let's give it a try!" He dug into his mango.

"Dr. Potter," Florita said uncomfortably, "there's something else you need to know. An editor from *World Geographic* was out here last week. They're planning to do an article on the Maya of this region. The editor got some wrong ideas about what my husband and his corporation are trying to accomplish here. I believe the magazine article is going to be critical of our efforts . . . which could possibly reflect on your project."

Potter put down his fork. "I'm familiar with the piece they're planning. It's to be called 'Land of the Maya'. In fact, they've asked me to contribute to it. What were the editor's concerns?"

Florita looked to Ray.

Ray felt a sinking sensation in his stomach. He took a deep breath. "The man spent less than an hour out here. He formed the opinion that our lodge and our restoration plans presented a threat to the ecology. There was also an unfounded accusation—based on a single misunderstanding—that we here at the lodge discriminate against Belizeans."

The professor smoothed his mustache, then picked up his fork and took another bite of mango. As he chewed, his brow furrowed in thought. He finished the bite and put his fork down again. "Well, I tell you, Ray . . . I've seen your lodge; I understand your restoration plans; I've met your wife. Offhand . . . I'd have to say the man was full of shit." He turned to Florita. "Excuse the language, Mrs. Kelley. What was the editor's name?"

"Thomas Gardner."

"Oh, Christ!" Potter said. "I can't believe he's been allowed to run loose in the Tropics again! Gardner is about as representative of *World Geographic*, as I am . . . the Hell's Angels. Don't worry, I'll see to it that they get somebody competent down here. Now, what's this green fruit this young lady has just brought me?"

45. PROGENY

Clive and Jovita were the last to arrive at the attorney's office. Kendall met them in the foyer and ushered them into a conference room, where Florita and Ray were already seated. The women exchanged a friendly hug. Clive and Ray simply nodded.

"Clive," Kendall said, "I don't believe you've met Ernest Godfrey. Ernest was Elijah's attorney for nearly forty years, and has been mine for the past ten."

Clive shook hands with the elderly Creole.

"Please be seated, everyone," Kendall said. He took the chair at the head of the table. "We have two items to discuss this morning. Ernest will handle the legal aspects of both. First will be the reading of Elijah's will. Since ten percent of the Foster Corporation is included in Elijah's estate, Jovita has invited us all here for the reading. Second, while we're all together, I want to take this opportunity to discuss the future of the corporation." He nodded to the attorney.

"With everyone's concurrence," the attorney said, "I suggest we go right to the disposition of property. The articles prior to that deal with things such as identifying family members, establishing funeral arrangements, naming the executor, and so forth. Shall we proceed?"

Everyone nodded their agreement.

"Four days prior to Elijah's passing, he summoned me to the hospital to change the disposition of his property. The revised article reads:

I hereby give, devise, and bequeath all of my property—whether real, personal, and/or mixed—to the following persons in the following manner:

> *(a) To Jovita Maria Ruiz, my daughter, 50% of my shares in the Foster Corporation and 100% of the remainder of my estate."*

Everyone at the table turned to Jovita with interest. Her expression remained impassive.

The attorney continued:

> *"(b) To Clive Lightburn, the son of a friend, 50% of my shares in the Foster Corporation."*

Everyone now looked at Clive, who stared at the attorney in disbelief. He turned to Jovita, seated beside him.

She reached over and squeezed his hand. "Daddy told me of the changes he planned to make."

Kendall extended his hand to Clive. "Welcome, shareholder," he said with a bemused smile.

As Clive shook Kendall's hand, he glanced across the table. Florita gave him a congratulatory nod and smile. Ray frowned, apparently trying to understand the significance of Elijah's bequeathment.

The attorney took off his glasses. "As Kendall said, Elijah had a ten percent interest in the Foster Corporation; therefore, Jovita and Clive now have five percent each. I'll have copies of the entire will made for each of you before you leave. Now, unless someone has a question, I'm going to leave and let you get on with the second item on your agenda."

There were no questions, and the attorney left the room.

"The Foster Corporation was founded fifteen years ago . . ." Kendall began.

Clive was unable to concentrate on what Kendall was saying, struck by the sentiment of Elijah's gift, in Ramón Kelley's memory. He got to his feet and walked over to the open window. He stared down Regent Street, allowing his eyes to clear.

"You all right, Clive?" Kendall said.

Clive nodded. After a moment, he returned to his chair.

"As I was saying," Kendall continued, "The Foster Corporation was founded fifteen years ago by Elijah, Ramón, and myself." He paused. "Now I propose that . . . we dissolve it."

The others looked at him in surprise.

"My disbursement proposal calls for Jovita . . . make that Jovita and Clive . . . to receive the Villa Pedrano—outright. Ray will receive the 3,000-acre Xtabay tract, which includes the lodge and the ruins—outright. I will retain rights to the 47,000-acre farm, plus the 17,000 acres I put up as bank collateral." He paused.

Ray was the first to speak. "Kendall, what you're proposing is more than fair to us, but it's not fair to you. You're getting stuck with the corporation's biggest headache."

Kendall smiled. "A headache I have cured at last. The renewable crops I've experimented with over the years have come close to making the farm self-supporting, but not quite. Suddenly, I find that one of the least likely candidates is about to become the most profitable: chicle."

"Chicle?" Clive said. "Chewing gum companies stopped using chicle a long time ago."

"True enough," Kendall said. "However, a Japanese firm feels that the recent trend toward natural ingredients in U.S. products has reopened the market for a chicle-based gum. They've already begun constructing a processing plant in Japan and are willing to finance the purchase of cook-down equipment for my farm."

"That's great, Kendall," Ray said.

"It gets better," Kendall said with a grin. "They've signed a contract to purchase 200,000 pounds of dry chicle the first year. And based on that, the Bank of Panama has granted me a twelve-month extension on my loan . . . without penalty."

Ray said slowly, "That leaves Milburn Landry . . ."

"Sucking hind tit," Kendall said with obvious relish.

"Man!" Ray said. "I've got to be there when you tell him!"

Kendall smiled and nodded. Then he turned serious and said, "I have one other announcement. This doesn't have to do with the corporation, but I believe it will be of general interest. I plan to relinquish the remainder of my western property."

"Oh, no!" Florita said. "You don't plan to sell it to developers."

Kendall smiled. "No, not sell it. I'm donating it to Programme for Belize, the conservation consortium."

There was a long pause, then Ray said, "Kendall, that's a wonderful gesture . . . but are you sure? I mean, man, you'd be giving away almost 300,000 acres!"

"My motives are not entirely philanthropic. Ray, you in particular are going to find this difficult to believe, but I plan to enter politics—PUP politics."

"Do what? You got to be kidding! Christ, it's the PUP newspaper that's been on your back—accusing you of discriminating against Belizeans, ruining the ecology . . ."

Kendall grinned. "You haven't lived here long enough yet to understand Belizean politics, Ray. PUP will welcome me like the 'prodigal son'."

Jovita said, "Why have you decided to get into politics, Kendall?"

"I guess your father's passing gave me the final push. There are few strong men left—men like Elijah, Ramón, and even our illustrious prime minister, George Price. I've had my differences with George, but his willpower and accomplishments over the past fifty years are undeniable. But stubborn as George is, even he can't go on forever."

Ray nodded. "I remember when I first came down here, right after high school, a friend of my father's, Dawn Peterson, used the expression: 'larger than life'."

Kendall said, "I'm not sure our generation has such men, but at least there are those of us who can still remember them . . . and how they conducted themselves."

The door opened and the attorney came back into the room. "I've made the appropriate changes to your proposal," he said to Kendall, handing him several documents. "It now shows the dual ownership of the Villa Pedrano."

"Very good," Kendall replied. "Are we all in agreement on the disbursement?"

The four nodded.

"By the way," the attorney said, "Radio Belize just gave a couple of news items that may be of interest. A sunken drug boat was discovered off Caye Negro. The authorities have linked it to an American living in San Pedro—a mistah Pennington. Also, about five miles from your farm, Kendall, there reportedly was another incursion by Guatemalan troops."

Kendall shook his head. "Yanks on our coast and Guats on our border. What else is new?"

EPILOGUE:
TEAM BELIZE

Fans jammed the City Center for the Belize Games basketball finals. They buzzed excitedly, as Belize and Cuba completed their warm-ups for the gold medal contest.

Coach Haylock beckoned Ray to the sideline and handed him the official score sheet. "I forgot my glasses, Ray. Fill this out for me. Same starting five as last night."

Ray nodded and dropped onto the nearby bench. He penciled in the first three names, then entered his own. He looked over his shoulder. Three rows up, his grandfather was engaged in conversation with an elderly Carib. Ray's mother sat nearby, flanked by her two grandsons. His grandfather had been reluctant to leave the Xtabay dig, even to watch his grandson play in a championship game, but now he obviously was enjoying himself. Ray's mother clearly was not; however, she smiled bravely from the sea of dark faces, then pulled her grandsons closer, as if for protection.

Ray returned her smile, thinking, Mom drank the water too. His smile faded; he wished his father could have been here. He turned back to the score sheet, hesitated, then scratched through "Ray" and replaced it with "Ramón". Then he glanced up and saw Clive Lightburn, scowling as usual, drive hard for the goal and throw down a dunk. Ray smiled again as he made an entry for Clive, then rose and carried the sheet down to the scorekeeper's table.

The public address announcer began the introductions with the Cuban starting lineup. As one by one, the Cubans jogged out to the free-throw line in front of their bench, the old Creole coach from the hills of San Ignacio gave Team Belize final instructions.

Neither Ray nor Clive paid attention. Instead, they looked about the jammed field house. Their wives sat directly behind the team bench. Florita said something to Jovita that made her laugh.

The Cuban starting five jogged off the court, and the announcer said:

And now . . . at center for Belize . . . originally from Nigeria, Africa . . . now from San Pedro . . . Moses Kano!

The lithe seven-footer trotted out to the free-throw line amid enthusiastic applause.

And at small forward . . . from Belize City . . . Robert Staine!

Ray took a quick drink of water.

And at point guard . . . from Belize City . . . Philip Cabral!

Clive fiddled with the bone amulet that hung from around his neck.

And at the shooting guard . . . from the United States . . . now a citizen of Belize . . . Ramón . . . Machine Gun . . . Kelley!

Ray raced onto the court.

And finally . . . at power forward . . . from San Pedro

Clive jogged across the floor.

. . . Clive . . . Tall Bwy . . . Lightburn-Kelley!

Clive broke stride when he heard the name. With clenched fists, he swerved and ran directly to Ray. "Did you tell the announcer that shit?"

Ray nodded.

For several seconds, they held each other's gaze, mindless of the stir throughout the Center. Finally Ray said, "Make we go . . . bruddah."

The Cuban team stood waiting, hands on hips. Clive looked distractedly into the stands; Jovita waved to him. With a resigned shake of his head, he turned back to Ray. "Make we go . . . bruddah."

The sons of Ramón Kelley ran to mid court.

Printed in the United States
22795LVS00006B/67-69

9 780738 807171